Second Chances

Part 2 of Sophie's story.

She Chose another, but Darcy wouldn't give up hope for his own happy ever after.

S. Werboweckyj

Copyright © 2024 Shalleen Werboweckyj
All rights reserved.

No part of this book may be reproduced or transmitted in any form, or by any electronic or mechanical means, including photocopying, recording, or by any information storage and retrieval systems without written permission from the author, except for brief quotations in a book review.
For permissions contact, shallwobba@gmail.com.

This book is a work of fiction. Names, characters, businesses and places are all the product of the author's imagination and are used fictitiously. Any resemblance to actual persons, living or dead, is purely coincidental.
Of course, a trip to London and a show is a really fantastic idea. It's a great day or weekend break.

For updates on upcoming releases, including **Stolen,** please follow me on these social media platforms under - Shalleen Werboweckyj.
TikTok.
Instagram.
Facebook.

Please enjoy part 2 of Sophie's story.
Happy reading.
Shalleen

Important Note.

Mental health is absolutely crucial to me and to you, my readers, so, there are a few things I must bring to your attention before reading on.

This book is intended for adults from the age of eighteen and upwards only. This book should not end up in the hands of anyone **under** the above age.

There are a number of possible triggers within this story and I must make you aware before proceeding.

- Sexually explicit scenes between MMc's and MFc's.
- Swearing. A lot, including the use of the C word in exclusive excerpt of 'Stolen'
- Homophobic rhetoric. Queer phobia.
- Physical violence. Hate crime assault.
- Bullying, physical abuse from a parent.
- Death of a partner, car accident.
- Suggestions of sexual assault.
- Use of alcohol.
- Stalking.
- Grieving of a loved one.

And now that is out of the way, find out what is in store for Sophie, Darcy, and meet Mr Leo Trent, and find out what happens when he joins the cast of a new play.

Thanks for choosing my book, and I hope you enjoy the second part of Sophie's story.

Mental health matters.
Happy reading.
Shalleen.

Contents.

Chapter 1.

Sophie

"No, it can't be right. You're wrong. He's with his best friend." The tears escaped, rolling down my cheeks as I refused to believe what I was being told.

"I'm so sorry, Mrs Carter, but he was pronounced dead at the scene."

The nausea was swirling around my stomach, crawling up my throat and pain lanced through me as she took my hand and squeezed. This wasn't happening.

"Can we call someone to stay with you?" she asked.

I shook my head as my heart simply shattered into a million pieces. "It can't be Jake. Please say it isn't him. Take it back, god, please say you're wrong," I croaked.

My legs gave way and I sank to the floor, sobbing his name over and over. "Jake, no, please Jake, no."

"Is there someone we can call, Mrs Carter?" she asked again.

I nodded and croaked out Ella's name, then the anguished scream erupted out of me as my heart swiftly died.....

Arms engulfed me as the scream echoed around the room, the lights flickering on as Max crushed me into his body.

"I've got you, Sophe. We're right here," he whispered.

"I want him back, I need him back, here in my arms," I sobbed into his chest.

He gently stroked my hair, holding me tightly. "I know, I know. I wish he was here too," he replied softly.

"Why him? Why wasn't it the bastard that ran into them?"

"I feel the same way, Sophe."

"I can't.... It's just so fucking painful, I want Jake," and my voice broke.

Teagen was behind me with his hands on my shoulders, and the warmth of the two of them started to soothe me and slow the sobs. I didn't know a person could cry this much, but it had been two weeks since that son of a bitch rammed into Jake and Cameron's taxi. The driver was killed along with Jake, and Cameron had come out with some bad injuries. Fractured collar bone and a broken arm along with a couple of ribs. But this pain and loss was drowning me and I couldn't stand being here without my husband. Every second of every moment since the accident felt like tiny knives stabbing my heart over and over again, slowly slicing it into pieces until there was nothing left.

"Try to get a little more sleep," Teagen whispered. "It's going to be a long day."

I laid down, sandwiched between my brother and his boyfriend, squeezing my sore eyes closed. The funeral was finally upon me and I was dreading every fucking second of what was to come.

I managed a few more hours of sleep, but by six am I was walking into the bathroom to get a shower and try to wash the tiredness away. Max and Teagen were still sleeping, so I'd scooted out the bottom of the bed so as not to disturb them.

I stripped off Jake's old t-shirt and stood under the hot water allowing it to run over my tired body, head down as more tears escaped. I silently cried again because this entire house was filled with happy memories. Jake was everywhere I looked. Photographs of our life were dotted around every damned room, making this pain all the more horrific. How could I continue to fucking live here without him? I didn't want to. I really wanted to just disappear.

"Sophe?" called a sleepy Max.

"I'm okay," I called back.

"You need to eat."

"I'm almost done," I replied, ignoring the statement, because the last thing I wanted was food. The sheer idea of what I was going to endure today made me sick to the stomach.

"Kate's on her way over. Cam and Cora will be here in about an hour, along with Mum and Benson," he said.

"Okay," I simply replied.

I finished washing and turned off the water. As I stepped out and wrapped a towel around myself I caught my reflection in the mirror. Dark circles framed my tired, red eyes. I had lost weight in these last couple of weeks, and honestly? I looked like the walking dead. I ambled into the bedroom to find Teagen standing there with coffee and a toasted bagel, Max standing by the door I had just come out of. He took my hand and walked us both to the bed, then sat down and gave me the bagel.

"Eat all of it, Sophe," he ordered.

"You're going to watch?" I muttered.

"Yes. Because you've hardly eaten anything since," but he stopped.

The pain that coursed through me made a small sob fall from my lips, and he pulled me into his side. "He wouldn't want this, Sophe. Please eat it," he begged.

I dropped my eyes for a moment, trying not to cry again. Then I picked it up and bit down. Max didn't move until I finished the whole thing, then he kissed my forehead and left me to get dressed.

Max

Teagen was waiting for me in the kitchen and I was gathered into his arms and pressed against him.

"This is going to be fucking shitty," I whispered.

"Yes it is. I hope Sophie can handle this."

I sighed, the tension and exhaustion finally crashing into me all at once. Teagen seemed to notice and he squeezed me tighter.

"I just can't believe he's gone, T. Just like fucking that. And I hate seeing my sister suffering and in pain. I hate that I can't do anything to help her," I admitted, dropping my head onto his shoulder.

"Me too, baby. Seeing her hurting so much is fucking horrendous, but I've been thinking about her situation and I have a suggestion, baby."

"What's that?"

Teagen released me and touched my face, kissing me tenderly, his eyes full of nothing but love as he smiled at me.

"Let's take Sophie back to London with us. There's plenty of room. She can have the guest room, as it has an ensuite attached, and maybe she could start working back at the theatre? What do you think?"

I stared at him in surprise, and then a small smile crept onto my face. I pulled him closer, capturing his lips again, kissing him with much more passion.

"I fucking love you, babe."

"Love you right fucking back, sexy ass," he said with a wink. "So? Is it something you'd like? Having Sophie as our room mate?"

"I think it's a fucking amazing idea, babe." I reluctantly let him go and went to start making coffee for us too. "You think she'll go for it?" I asked.

"I think so. She's in so much pain being here, and there's no harm in asking her if she wants to live with us."

I smiled to myself. It would be amazing having my big sister back. As I poured the boiling water into mugs, Sophie appeared, and it made my heart lurch at the state of her. I had to hold onto her, so I strode over and I scooped her into my arms, squeezing her tightly.

"I don't want to say goodbye," she whispered.

"None of us do," I replied.

"I hate being here. Every fucking second of every damned day, without him," she stammered. "Everywhere I look he's there. It's killing me Max."

Teagen came up behind her and gently tugged her from my arms. "Sophe, we have a proposition for you," he said.

She turned around and fixed her sad eyes on my man. "What's that?" she asked.

"You hate being here now don't you?" he asked.

"Yes I do."

"Then come back to London with us? Stay with us at our apartment, and maybe work back at the theatre?" he suggested.

And that was the moment it flickered to life behind her eyes. Hope. She suddenly flung her arms around Teagen and hugged him tightly.

"You'd do that for me?" she asked in a whisper.

I smiled and touched her back. "You're my fucking big sister, crazy shithead. I'd love having you back with us."

"And you're my sister by default now," Teagen said.

She finally gave us a smile and tears pricked the corners of her eyes. "Not sure about the theatre, but yes please. I just can't be here anymore," she whispered.

She was suddenly crushed by both of us as we hugged the life out of her. I dropped a kiss on Teagen's lips and he winked at me with his sexy smile.

"Great. Then we'll have you packed up in no time," I said.

"Tomorrow. I want to leave tomorrow," she exclaimed.

Sophie

We were sat at the front of the church as Benson read out one of Jake's favourite songs. The words were very apt for what had happened but I didn't really hear it. Cameron was next, and he simply thanked people for coming and paused.

"I don't know why I survived. A part of me wishes I hadn't.... I just miss you man. It's always been the two of us.... I..... I'm sorry," and his voice cracked, and Cora quickly shot to her feet, hugging him as he broke down.

Max squeezed my hand and leaned in. "Are you sure?" he asked. "You don't have to say anything?"

I simply stood up and tried to walk on trembling legs towards the pulpit. As I reached my destination I turned and glanced up at the very full room. I put down the speech I'd written and took a deep breath with a tissue scrunched into my hand.

"Thank you all for coming. Jake would love to know how many of you cared," I started. "Jake is... was my world. He is, shit, was... He *was* my soulmate and my best friend.... He made me laugh, knew how to cheer me up. He is an amazing hugger. Oh, for fuck's sake, *was*."

I paused and glanced up at all of our friends and family gazing at me, and I tried to steady the pain coursing through me.

"Sorry for swearing Mum," I muttered.

Mum's eyes were filled with tears and she simply smiled up at me. I took a deep breath and looked down at the words on the paper, but they seemed cold, unfeeling, so I looked back at the friends and family gathered and let words simply tumble out of me.

"I miss him... like air. I feel as though I'm drowning with the pain of his loss. Jake knew how to make it go away with a simple hug and a smile. He had the patience of a saint when he tried to teach me how to play the piano. Safe to say I was bloody shit at it, but it never stopped him," and I heard a few chuckles at my words. "I thought we'd grow old together, watch our kids," and my voice finally cracked as the tears broke free. "Jesus, I just miss him, and I want him back."

Max was on his feet and tugging me into his arms as I broke down. He gently ushered me back to my seat and the rest of the service became a blur, only the pain and the loneliness slowly killing me where I sat. I eventually found myself standing at the grave side with Cameron as everyone else started to leave.

"God, Jake, I'm so fucking sorry," whispered Cameron.

"Don't do that, Cam," I said, my hand taking his own.

"I was in the same fucking car, Sophe. Why am I still here?"

I tugged him into a hug, his good arm wrapping around my waist. "Please don't say that. Jesus, if we'd lost you too? Just don't, please."

"I miss him so fucking much, Sophe. Every waking hour. I have nightmares of the accident, and seeing him just laying there, lifeless. Fuck," and his arm tightened as tears escaped.

Benson appeared and he touched Cameron's back. Jake's best friend stood up taller and turned. His head dropped as he wiped his eyes.

"Sorry Mr Carter," he whispered, then he hugged both me and Jake's dad before leaving the two of us.

"Why is he sorry?" Benson whispered, taking my hand in his.

"He feels guilty for surviving," I replied.

Benson's shoulders sagged and he pulled me into a hug. "Cameron has no need to feel guilty for living. Jake wouldn't want that."

"I'm leaving tomorrow with Max and Teagen," I whispered.

He looked down and gave me a tired smile. "I thought you might. I can look after the place while you're gone if you like?"

"Wouldn't that be?" and he nodded.

"Painful? Yes. Closer to him? Yes. Sophie, I know that you can't stay and I understand. Take some time and heal. I can send more of your things when you're ready, and don't look at me like that. I'm not hurt that you want to leave," he said.

I threw my arms around my father in law and held onto him tightly, and he wrapped me up in his own. In this silent moment I was saying goodbye and Benson understood that too.

Goodbye to the memories and my Jake, my love and soulmate.

"I'd like to say goodbye, if that's okay?" I asked.

"Go ahead, love. I'll wait with Max and Teagen at the car, and take as much time as you need," he replied, then kissed my forehead and walked away, leaving me alone with my Jake, my husband and the love of my life.

I stared at the dark earth piled up and I took a deep breath and walked to the bench beside it. This bench had memories too. The day I'd thought Jake didn't trust me. Where Darcy O'Sullivan had declared his love for me before kissing me.

"Shit, Jake. I thought we were endgame. Me and you, always and forever," I whispered.

"You're all fucking mine, Sophe. Always and forever."

"And now I have to try and live without you. How the fuck do I do that? Missing you hurts so damned much."

"... Hear me when I say this. You're mine. You belong to me. We belong together... we're endgame."

I was on my feet again and swiped the fresh tears gathering in my eyes. "I can't stay, Jake. I hope you don't hold it against me for running away, but I can't feel this way anymore. It's just too fucking painful."

I had to pause to take a shaky breath, then I looked up into the clouded sky and swallowed the lump in my throat.

"I love you. I always will, handsome. You will always have my heart, but I can't stay. I'll be with Max and Teagen, just know I'll miss you so much more than I can put into bloody words.... Goodbye Jake," then I took a few steps backwards, turned and walked from the graveyard, away from my love, my Jake and the pain threatening to drown me.

The following day, I had packed as much as the car would take, our wedding photograph hidden inside amongst my clothes. I rolled the last suitcase out of our bedroom and paused at the music room door. I placed my hand on the cool wood and swallowed the lump in my throat.

Then I strode out and locked up, climbed into my car and drove away.

Chapter 2.

Darcy

I stared out of the window of my childhood home, Christian chattering away into my ear about a new project. My mind, however, was on my little director, hoping she was coping after the loss of her music teacher. However much I had loathed him for winning her, I would never wish this on him, or the love of my life. Kathryn had informed me that rehearsals were on hold for a couple of weeks due to Jake Carter's death. A part of me wanted to drive up there and sweep her into my arms, but I hopped on a plane and came home instead.

"Ya always do this, Christian. I like to concentrate on the project I'm currently working on."

"Yes, but they are hankering for an answer. I know you'd be phenomenal in the role," he replied.

I sighed, rubbing my face, then glanced back at my big brother who had appeared. "Send it to me. I'll read through it."

"Great. And you need to be home tomorrow. Kate called and rehearsals start up tomorrow."

"Sure. Cheers fella. Catch ya when I get back."

"Bye Darcy," and he hung up.

Shay was watching me like a hawk as I pushed my phone back into my jacket pocket. My older brother was a similar height to me, dark brown hair and brown eyes like dad. He was an accountant, and a damned good one. Married for ten years and five children. Three boys, two girls. He came to stand beside me and noticed the photograph in my hand.

"Is this lass the reason for ya change in behaviour?" he drawled.

"Feck off, Shay."

"No. Ya haven't been in the gossip pages in years. Mam thinks ya turning into a bloody priest, but I find ya gazing at a picture of a very pretty brunette I recognise," he said.

I tucked it back into my jacket pocket and raked a hand through my hair. "Gotta go back to London tomorrow," I replied.

"Look, Darce, I'm not asking to fecking tease ya. I want to know me little brother is alright, because ya haven't been ya self for a long fecking time?" he said, patting my back.

I turned around and leaned against the chest of drawers, shoving my hands into my trouser pockets.

"I'm alright, Shay," I replied.

"Ya not. There's sadness in your eyes," and he frowned at me and smacked my shoulder, crossing his arms over his broad chest.

I walked to the drinks cabinet and poured us both a whiskey, then took a large sip. "I'm in love, Shay, but don't tell Mam. She married someone else and he's just been killed in an accident," I said with a sigh.

"And you want to swoop in and take care of her?"

"Yes. But I can't do that. She needs time to heal. But, well, I want her in me fecking life, Shay. I've thought of nothing else but her since that new year," I admitted.

Shay sipped his own drink and walked to the sofa, and I joined him. I loved my family and Shay had always been the one to bring the sensible to the table. He stepped in as a father figure once I'd left to pursue my acting career seriously as we'd done it together after dad died, helping Mam around the house with cooking and chores, getting our brother and sister to school, and helping with their homework. It had brought us all much closer as a family too. Now, he rested his ankle over his thigh and fixed his intense eyes on me.

"She doesn't need this right now. She'll be grieving. But, don't let her get away this time."

I smiled and nodded. "I don't intend to, fella. I want to be her forever, Shay. I've never felt this way before."

And at that moment, hope bloomed in my chest, my heart beating a little faster. Maybe, just maybe, I might finally get my happy ending too.

Twenty Months Later.

Sophie

Teagen was smirking at me as I smoothed down the burgundy dress. I turned around and Max appeared with a loud whistle.

"Christ, shithead, you look gorgeous," said my brother.

"I do?"

Teagen wrapped his arm around Max's shoulders and grinned at me. "Sophe, you look stunning," he said.

I rolled my eyes and picked up my bag, shoes and phone. I checked my hair and makeup in the long mirror and smoothed down the skirt of my dress. Deep red, capped sleeves with a sweetheart neckline, loose skirt which finished at my knees, and a low back. It was a treat to myself for tonight and I felt rather bloody sexy in it. I let out a sigh then walked to my two roomies.

"Thank you," I said, and Max chuckled.

"And now we have to sit through a fucking Shakespeare play," he groaned.

Teagen laughed and kissed my brother, then grabbed my hand and dragged us both into the kitchen. They were such a cute couple and I adored living with them. I didn't think I would have healed as much as I had without them. I finally felt happier again, and my heart had been put back together by my brother and his lovely man. Benson had indeed sent down pretty much all of my belongings after I'd told them I was staying. He had also informed me that there were a few things I might want once I was ready.

"You look nervous," Max whispered.

"I am. I'm about to start my first job there on Monday," I replied.

"It'll come back in a flash. Took you long enough to finally accept the full time position," he drawled.

I had been working for Sierra for a while, but the theatre was where I felt at home and Kathryn had finally worn me down. I accepted yesterday and she gave us tickets for '*A Midsummer Night's Dream*' as a thank you. Teagen came over and kissed my cheek, taking my hand.

"Come on sexy goddess. Taxi is here, and I'm looking forward to perving over actors in tights," and I snorted into a fit of laughter as Max glared at his boyfriend.

"They don't wear tights, T," I exclaimed.

"Yeah, and thanks babe," huffed Max.

Teagen swiftly tugged him in and kissed him. "Oh I love it when you get jealous, baby. You know I only have eyes for you."

Max smirked smugly and I grinned, wrapping my arms around their waists. "Come on. We'd better go, Kate will hate us if we turn up late," I said, and we left the apartment, my heart finally feeling whole again.

Darcy

The familiar sharp knock rang out as I finished buttoning up my tunic. I checked my makeup and strode to the door.

"Thirty minutes, Darcy."

"Grand, Kate," I replied. "And when was it ya job to do time calls?"

Kathryn leant against the frame of the door and smiled, but there was something wicked in her eyes.

"I know you prefer to be left alone before curtain up, but I wanted to let you know about some last minute VIP guests in the box," she said, and that got my attention and I fixed my eyes onto hers.

"And why are ya telling me this now?"

"Just so you're not surprised to see it occupied."

Her tone was way too sweet and innocent. Kathryn Reyner was up to something, so I stood up to my full height and crossed my arms.

"Fine. Whatever you're up to? It had better not distract me from me job?"

"You're a professional are you not?"

"Very fecking funny. Who is it?"

"You'll see. And here," and she handed me a folded piece of paper. "Don't open that until the interval."

"Ya know, that's like saying don't push the big red button, Kate?" I drawled, arching my brow at her.

She just smirked again and I groaned, placing it underneath my phone on the table.

"Promise you won't, Darcy."

"Fine. I promise."

"Have a great performance. Break a," but I growled at her.

"Don't fecking say that in here, Kate," I fired.

It was one saying I hated, and in my dressing room? I preferred good luck. She grimaced and nodded.

"Sorry. Forgot. Good luck, O'Sullivan," she said, then patted my back and disappeared.

I stared at the piece of paper and it was screaming at me to look, so I checked my tiny microphone and stalked out of the dressing room. Leo was at the side of the stage, and I smirked. The girls were constantly pestering him, but he wasn't interested. I had a sneaking suspicion that he was gay. But, one girl in particular wouldn't leave him alone. Eve Hemlock was a tad obsessed with this fella.

"Ya hiding?"

"Yeah. Fucking hell, they just don't get the damned message. Especially bloody Eve. How do you cope with it?"

This youngster was a dirty blonde with bright sapphire eyes. And he was a very handsome fecking guy. The female cast members had been trying to seduce him since day one, and I smirked at his annoyance.

"Tell them no. Simple, straight to the point."

"You make it sound so easy."

"It is. And *she* needs to fecking know ya not interested," I said and winked.

He leaned against the wall and sighed. "You're a well known woman magnet but you haven't looked at any of them?" he asked.

"Nope. One woman occupies me heart, fella."

"Well, didn't expect that, Darcy. Who is she?"

"Ah, that's mine to know, fein." and I smacked him on the shoulder. "And now it's time for me to get in the zone."

He nodded and I walked to a quiet spot so I could prepare for the final performance, and also find out who our mystery guests were in the VIP box.

Sophie

Kathryn met us by the side door and literally dragged us into the theatre and up to the VIP box without stopping.

"VIP?" questioned Teagen.

"Yes. Now get in there. Curtain is about to go up," she barked, shoving us inside.

"Fucking hell, bossy cow," grumbled Max, but I took his hand and squeezed.

"Yes, I am. And you are cutting it fine, turning up this late."

"Sorry, Kate," I said, nudging my brother.

"What?"

"Grumpy fuck face," I fired at him.

"Douche fucker," he retorted, getting us each a slap from Kathyrn.

"Get sat down, and enjoy the bloody show, children," she ordered, then winked at me before vanishing back down the corridor towards backstage.

We sat down and I had the one closest to the stage. The sight of the safety curtain made my heart race with excitement. I'd missed this and smiled to myself as Max threw a packet of skittles at me. I rolled my eyes at him as he smirked, lounging back in his seat.

"Thanks," I simply said, then the lights dimmed and my heart went giddy.

"Just made it," Teagen whispered, nudging my shoulder.

"Yes. And I can't bloody wait," I replied.

I happily leaned on the edge of the box and watched as the curtain lifted revealing the first scene, and I sighed as a joyous feeling blossomed from deep inside of me. The actors appeared and I relaxed, forgetting that my brother and his boyfriend were even here. As the show progressed *'Lysander'* and *'Hermia'* were left on stage. He was a talented guy and he had a cute face with dirty blonde hair and beautiful sapphire eyes. He was finishing the scene and his head whirled up towards the box where we were sat. His eyes seemed to lock onto mine as Teagen leaned forward too, staring at the handsome guy, and the jolt of excitement shot through me as I sat up a little.

He continued with the scene and disappeared offstage. Now, where we were seated, I could see into the wings of that side of the stage. He paused, turned around and back over at us, then he winked and grinned. We both grinned too, as it had been a long time since I had been looked at like that. My brother leaned forward too, touching his boyfriend's shoulder.

"That dude's flirting," whispered Teagen.

"With you, babe," whispered Max.

"Might be Sophe, baby," Teagen replied, and I had to smile.

He nudged my shoulder and he kissed my cheek. "That's what you need, Sophe," he whispered. "A sexy blonde."

I snorted into a stifled giggle, and Max slapped the back of my head. "Shut the fuck up you two, and remember you have a bloody boyfriend, T," he hissed.

Teagen moved and sat next to Max, kissing him before settling down to continue watching. I smirked to myself, but brought my eyes back to the stage. '*King Oberon*' and '*Titania*' appeared with stunning makeup and lavish costumes, hiding their real faces. '*Oberon*' started to speak and every nerve in my body exploded. His velvet tone floated up and wrapped around my entire body, ending right between my thighs.

"Shit," I whispered.

"Is that who I think it is?" Max's voice flew into my ear.

"Ill met by moonlight, proud Titania..."

And my heart slammed into my ribcage, pulse racing as I stared at the tall actor.

"Tarry, rash wanton. Am I not thy Lord?"

His head lifted and familiar emerald green eyes found mine and I couldn't breathe as my body set alight, as though a volcano was about to erupt. Feelings that I had long thought forgotten hit me like a tsunami. The final few weeks working together. How sweet he'd been, and the feeling of sadness as I'd watched him vanish from my life.

Jesus, holy fucking shit, lady.

His eyes widened for a fleeting moment, breaking character for a split second, then a flash of happiness seemed to wash over him. There was a pause, then he whipped his head back to the other actress and continued with the scene. I stared, watching every action and movement, heart racing at a thousand miles a second. The end of the scene was approaching and he started his monologue, then his eyes came back to mine.

"...Effect it with some care, that he may prove more fond on her than she upon her love. And look thou meet me ere the first cock crow..."

He paused, gazing right into my face, a spark of excitement in his emerald eyes. Then he turned and exited stage right.

Darcy O'Sullivan... *Jesus fucking Christ...*

Chapter 3.

Darcy

I marched to my dressing room, heart thundering like a jackhammer on speed. She was sitting right there, and I couldn't fucking breathe. Sophie, who was now Carter, in this theatre, staring right at me. And all I wanted to do was stride out there and scoop her into my arms, never to let go of her again. I swiped up the piece of paper and my eyes went wide as I gazed down at her name and number, then a fucking wink face from Kathryn.

"Fecking hell," I gasped.

I didn't hesitate and swiped up my phone, adding her to my contacts. Then I had to do it.

"Hello lass. I can't believe it's really you? You look beautiful. Dxx"

Holy mother of fucking god, the love of my life was in the same building as me. I stared into the mirror at my reflection. She was not getting away this time, that was for fucking certain. My phone buzzed and I grabbed it.

"Hi. Yes, Darcy. It's really Sophie and you did Shakespeare. S x"

Fuck, fuck fuck.

"I need to talk to you. Please stay for a drink? Dxx"

"I'd like that. Sxx"

"I have a lot to say to you. I've missed you, lass. Xx"

"Funnily enough, I've missed you too. xx"

I grinned at the extra kiss. My little director was in the same place as me, and she had fucking missed me.

"I'll see you in the bar afterwards. Thank you for coming. Dxx"

"Look forward to it. Sxx"

The knock told me it was almost time to start the second half, then I heard the voices outside my room.

"Jesus, Christ, Pedro," came Leo's voice.

"Gorgeous, right? And she grinned at me," said Owen.

"Never noticed," said Pedro.

"Dark beauty in the box? Do you not have eyes, dude?" Leo drawled.

I groaned, jealousy raging through me, and I flung open my door. "She's my little director, Leo. The one I was talking about," and his eyes widened in surprise as I stalked out of my dressing room. "

What?" he questioned.

"She's mine, Leo."

"The dark beauty in the VIP box?," he asked, an amused glint in his eye.

I whirled around and glared at him. "She's fecking mine, Leo. Don't even think about it," and I stalked towards the stage, possessiveness whirling through me like a tornado.

Kathryn was hovering backstage and I tapped her shoulder.

"Ya fecking sneaky cow," I whispered.

"So you saw her?"

"Of course I fecking saw her. She's in the VIP box, Kate," I scoffed.

Melissa appeared and grinned at the two of us. "Watch out, as I saw Leo winking at someone up there, and Sophie's the single one," she said.

"No. Not this time. Even if I have to fecking go at snail's pace. I have to be with her, she's me forever" tumbled out of me, and they each looked at me in shock. "She's fecking mine this time and I'm not giving her up."

Leo

It was a shitty predicament, but I liked him. He was a dark haired beauty with a stunning bloody smile. Darcy had warned me away, and sure, I got it. He was in love with *her*. My eyes were actually on the young guy sitting next to her. I walked down to the side of the stage and Darcy nodded at me. I returned the gesture and Melissa nudged my shoulder.

"They belong together Leo," she whispered.

"You're not wrong, Lissy. But it wasn't her I was winking at," I whispered into her ear.

"What?" she gasped.

I sighed and glanced over at the multi million earning sex god. "They had a relationship didn't they? That lady up there?"

"They did. And they have a strange connection. But, what did you just mean? Are you?" but she stopped as I hissed at her. "And no-one knows?"

"No. I haven't had the guts to yet. It's complicated."

There was a split second where she stared at me in surprise, then she wrapped me up in a hug. "Do it. Don't be ashamed of who you truly are."

I let out another sigh and shook off the nerves. There was a second half to do, then I'd think about the beautiful guy sitting in the VIP box above us. Maybe he was single? That was the moment Eve fucking Hemlock appeared and sidled up to me.

"Hey, fancy a drink after the show finishes?" she asked.

"No thanks. I'm not interested, Eve."

"The way you kiss me on stage says otherwise," she purred.

Jesus fucking Christ.

"No, thanks," I repeated. "And that's called acting."

"See you after the show in the bar."

She smiled and her hand actually brushed across my fucking ass as she sauntered to her starting position. I let out a frustrated groan, then Pedro appeared. He winked at me and smiled.

"She's seriously crushing on you," he whispered.

"And I'm seriously *not* fucking into her in the slightest."

"Well, she's staring at you as though she's about to fucking eat you," he said.

I dared to glance her way, and yes, she was and she waved and blew me a kiss. I simply turned away, ignoring her.

"Now she looks like she wants to kill you," Pedro said. "You need to watch her."

I smacked his arm and raked my hand through my hair. "She doesn't get it. I'm really not into her. All the girls have had a go. I just don't want to date them."

"Sure you're not gay?" he asked, and I arched my brows at him.

"What if I were?" I replied.

He leaned in and whispered into my ear and said, "It would make my day. You're bloody gorgeous," then he walked to his spot to start the show.

Melissa smirked at me and patted my shoulder. "See. There's plenty of guys out there that would love a piece of your cute ass," she whispered.

I had to smile and I raked my hand through my hair again. "Thanks, Lissy," and I winked at her.

I glanced over at Pedro, and the handsome Scottish actor with the stormy blue eyes winked at me with a very cheeky smirk, and I felt the blush rise up my cheeks.

"Shit," I muttered as Pedro had noticed, making him smile like a wicked devil.

The tannoy announced that the second half was about to start. But, I looked across at Blaine as though double checking that I was indeed gay. She was a stunning brunette, but nothing happened when I stared at her. My eyes landed on Pedro. Tall, dark hair with hazel eyes and a rugged mountain man look about him. The Scottish accent helped too. He'd look fucking hot in a kilt.

Yeah, no denying that I was one hundred percent gay.

"Your eyes just glazed over as you stared at him," Melissa said. "And you're blushing."

"Fuck's sake," I muttered.

My mind went into overdrive at her words, but I had to focus on the task at hand. Maybe my dark beauty could help me? And Pedro was now aware of my tastes in the dating market.

The lights went down and I took a breath, ready to finish the final performance. But Melissa's words stuck in my head, dancing around in there. I'd only slept with two girls as a teen before I realised that I preferred guys. But there was a lot of dislike for gay and Lesbians in my neck of the woods. Well, for all the LGBTQIA+ community, so I'd kept it a secret.

"Come on, Leo. I'll introduce you to Max and Teagen after. And another delicious treat is in the audience. He's called Henry, and he's joining us in the bar too," whispered Melissa.

Sophie

Max had vanished to grab a programme, Teagen disappeared to the loo and Darcy had sent me messages. Actual fucking messages, making my heart rate shoot through the roof. He wanted to meet me in the bar to talk and every single part of me was on fire. I really wanted to see him, talk to him. Hell, I wanted to just look at his fine, sexy, gorgeous fucking self.

"It's him," and a programme was thrown into my lap. "It's Darcy, Sophe."

I shuffled in my seat and smiled smugly. "I know. I recognised his voice."

"For fuck's sake," he grumbled.

I flicked through the programme and smiled as I saw Melissa, then the blonde. Leo Trent. Cute, but my eyes landed on him. The Irish handsome, sexy man I actually broke, and it was true. I missed him.

"Don't fucking go there, Sophe," Max growled, and I turned to look at my brother, Teagen, looking sheepish beside him.

"I will go wherever I fucking want to Max. I'm a bloody grown up," then I turned back around as the lights went down.....

The applause was immense as the play ended, and I grinned down at the Irishman. The blonde was now staring at Max and Teagen, which confused me a little. But Darcy fixed his eyes on me, blew me a kiss with a small bow and it made my body heat up and a giddy smile appeared on my face. The curtains closed and Teagen took my hand and Max's.

"Come on, we need drinks," he stated.

Max paused and looked at me. "You sure?" he asked. "Seeing him again?"

I smiled and wrapped my arms around him. "I'm going to talk to him, get to know him again. Then I'll see," I replied.

"He hurt you."

"I know."

"He might do it again?"

"If he does? You can smack him *after* me," I replied.

"Christ, Sophe. Please be careful."

"I promise you, Max."

Teagen grabbed both of our hands and dragged us downstairs to the bar. I didn't know what was going to happen, but I was suddenly itching to see him. As we entered the room my eyes darted around looking for the Irishman, but he was nowhere to be seen. Kathryn was waiting for us and had our drinks lined up as we entered the bar, then her arms wrapped around me.

"Sorry I didn't tell you, because I thought you wouldn't come," she said into my ear.

"I forgive you. And I'd still have come," I replied.

"He wants to talk."

"Okay," and she looked at me in surprise.

"Just okay?"

"He messaged me in the interval, and asked to talk."

"And?"

"I'm here aren't I?"

"So, you're going to talk?"

"Yes. I am."

"Oh god, that's amazing. Did you enjoy the show?"

"Yes. It was fantastic. I loved being back in the theatre," I answered.

Teagen took Max to the bar and picked up their drinks, Kathryn and myself following them. She smiled at me and picked up her wine.

"Are you okay? Looking forward to starting back here? You know both Darcy and Tara are in your first play?" Kathryn fired at me all in one go.

"What? They are?" I asked in surprise and Kathryn nodded and smiled like a wicked devil.

"That's why you need to talk to Darcy, so I wangled this for the two of you."

"He knew?"

"Only after I told him when the play ended. He threw rather a lot of curses at me," and she winked.

"Jesus, Kate. That's fucking devious of you, you bloody shady cow."

"And he looked like he'd won an Oscar," she added with a wink.

I stared at her in surprise, then she patted my arm and left me standing there with no words forming in my brain.

"Where are they? Where's my sexy little fucking director?" and I whirled around to see the face of a very familiar young man I'd worked with more than once.

He came striding in and he locked eyes on me first. My face lit up as he literally ran at me and hoisted me off my feet, hugging me tightly.

"Hello, sexy bitch," he exclaimed, and all that fell out of me was a fit of laughter as I was crushed in Henry's arms. And it really was a crush.

Henry was around five feet ten and built like a thoroughbred racehorse. He was sinfully handsome, with classic movie star features. The Italian in him was clear to see, and women would happily spread their legs for him. But, he was very much batting for the men's team.

"Jesus, H, put me the fuck down, you're going to break something," I laughed, and I was popped back onto my feet and he kissed my cheeks, a huge smile on his face.

"I know you're coming back under shitty circumstances darling, but fucking hell lady, I've missed you," he gushed.

"I've missed your crazy ass too, H."

"And you look bloody edible, darling."

"Thanks Henry."

He chuckled and noticed Max and Teagen. "Fuck, you two still going strong?" he fired.

"Yep, we live together too," replied my brother and Henry was over there in a flash, yanking them into hugs too.

"Shit, that's bloody amazing," he said. I'm so fucking happy for you."

Max and Teagen chuckled as he hugged them again. "Cheers Henry. You single? Or do you have a man now?" asked Teagen.

"Not found the one yet," Henry replied, and turned to smile at me again.

That was the moment the blonde actor with beautiful blue eyes appeared in the doorway, and Henry's eyes went wide.

"And who in the sinful heavens is that divine man?" Henry drawled.

Leo

My eyes landed on the most stunning looking man I'd ever seen, and my body burst into flames. He looked Mediterranean and he had the most beautiful dark brown eyes which were fixed on mine. Tall. Lean and muscular, and a face like a sinful devil. And fucking shit on a stick, I wanted him to do so many filthy things to me. Then he let out a cock hardening smile and I was a goner. I threw him a polite smile and swiftly walked to the bar, trying to still my beating heart. Shit, that guy was beautiful. Perfection in a tailored dark grey suit.

Pedro was beside me and he nudged my shoulder. "You going to step out of the closet, Leo?" he asked.

"Leave it alone, man." I muttered.

"Why? You know I'm gay, right?"

"Figured."

"And why can't you step into the light?"

"Please leave it, Pedro."

"Sure, but just know that you're being eyed up by a really fucking gorgeous guy," he whispered then ordered his drink.

I glanced behind me and he was coming this way. *Shit, shit, shit.* I ordered a large jack and coke, then took a huge swig.

"Shiraz, please, Tally," he asked the server.

"Well hello, Henry, honey."

"Oh, did you miss my fine ass?"

"Oh stop, gay boy. You have a fine ass, but it's certainly not for me," and she winked.

He was known by the staff, so that could mean he was an actor too? With those looks, he had to be, and probably not single. This man had to have been snapped up already with his stunning face, gorgeous eyes and, well, yes he had a sexy fucking...

"And I'd love to know *your* name, sexy ass?" and he turned his divine face to me.

I smiled, a little smugly I might add, then sat on the stool. "Leo Trent," I replied, and dared to look over at him.

"You are a very talented actor Mr Leo Trent. And I believe we will be working together as of next week?" he drawled.

Jesus, his voice was making my dick hard.

Then I registered what he'd just said. "Wait, what?" I questioned.

He arched his gorgeous brows and leaned on the bar, sipping his wine. "The new play? '*Porter*'," he answered.

My entire body felt as though I were inside a fucking volcano as this was a six week run. And I had to work with this damned sex god? *Jesus fucking help me.*

"Oh, right. Then I guess we will be," I replied and threw him a smile.

He smirked and glanced around the bar, but Eve was heading right for me and I silently cursed.

Shit, why wouldn't she leave me the fuck alone?

"Hey, Leo," she purred, her hand stroking my back. "You didn't wait for me. I wanted to walk down together, honey."

I gritted my teeth and tensed at her touch. The sex god beside me was studying my face intensely as I took another swig of my drink.

"What do you want, Eve?" I ground out.

"Aren't we having a drink after work?" she said sweetly.

I rolled my eyes and flinched away from her hand, now moving down to my fucking ass. "It's open to all the cast, *Eve*," I said, trying to remain calm.

She grinned at Henry standing next to me and her eyes narrowed as she spoke, and I couldn't quite believe what she said next.

"Who are you? This is my boyfriend, Leo."

"No, I'm not your bloody boyfriend," I snapped.

"We are. Dating since the show opened," she purred.

"We're not dating, Eve."

"We are. You're my man, Leo honey."

That was the last damned straw and I turned and glared at her. "Jesus fucking Christ, when will you get it through your thick skull, Eve. I'm not fucking interested. I'm not and never will be *your* fucking man," and I stood up, threw down my drink and stalked out of the bar.

Chapter 4.

I walked out into the lobby and towards the front doors, but his voice rang out and I turned to see Henry jogging after me.

"Leo Trent, stop," he called.

"I just want air," I muttered, slowing down.

It was a real fucking shock to see this sexy guy running towards me. He was decked out in a beautiful dark grey suit and white shirt. It hugged his exquisite body so sexily that I had to try and think about things like ironing, cleaning the fucking toilet, to stave off my boner.

"Let me walk with you?" he asked. "Everyone is heading to '*Starlights*' after, so we can meet them there?" he suggested.

I stopped and stared into those beautiful eyes, and I didn't want to look anywhere else for the rest of my damned life. This man had grabbed me the moment I'd walked into that bar.

"Why?" I asked.

"Because I think I know what's going on, and I want you to talk about it," he replied.

I frowned a little, then sighed loudly with frustration. "And what's going on, Henry?" I asked.

His lips crept up into that damned cock hardening smile and I felt my cheeks burn. "You have a secret and you're unsure how to tell them."

I turned away and started towards the doors, but he fell into step next to me. "What makes you think that?" I questioned.

"Because I've been in the same position. I came out ten years ago, and it was extremely hard for me. My family are Catholic, Mr Trent. My parents were very supportive, but I got a lot of hate from others, got beaten up a few times. That's why I started at the gym. Boxing and weights."

My feet came to a stop and I turned to look at this tall, sexy guy. He'd seen right through me in a matter of seconds, and I suddenly felt less alone.

"Shit, how did you fucking do that?" I muttered.

"That reaction to your girly back there," he said.

I glanced back at the theatre and grimaced. "Yeah, she's been chasing me since day fucking one. She doesn't get it. Even if I went for girls, she'd be at the bottom of the damned list," I said.

"Your words were very telling. So, come with me," and he took my hand in his and squeezed. "Let's go and get better acquainted."

Sophie

Henry had given me a knowing wink and then dashed after the actor, and now I was sitting with Melissa, Kathryn, Max and Teagen.

"It's so great to see you, Sophie," Melissa said.

"You were amazing as Titania. And it's really great to be back in the theatre."

"Did you enjoy the show?"

"You were all amazing," I said and grinned at her.

She lifted her glass and said, "A toast to Sophie coming back to work at the theatre where she belongs. I know it was because of a very sad event, but our theatre world missed you. And we are thrilled to get you back. Cheers."

"Fucking hell yes," Teagen exclaimed and they all lifted their glasses to me.

Everyone lifted their glasses to me and echoed her words making me feel as though I'd come home. I lifted my own glass and took a gulp too.

"Thank you," I replied.

"No need," said Melissa.

"Welcome home," Kathryn said and winked at me.

It was at that precise moment my eyes found him as he strode into the bar. His firm, powerful legs wrapped up in his signature charcoal grey suit. His sculpted chest snug inside a crisp white shirt, then his chiselled jaw, and finally those bright emerald green eyes, which were locked on me.

And my heart went fucking crazy.

The last time I'd seen him, he had waved from the back of the theatre as I hugged Jake. Then he had vanished from my life, until now. And the thing that surprised me the most? I had missed him.

He didn't hesitate and strode right for me and I was tugged to my feet and engulfed in his arms. My own wrapped around him too, and the all too familiar scent of stage makeup and nature washed over me. It felt weirdly lovely being held by the actor I knew intimately all those years ago, and I instinctively snuggled closer.

"I'm sorry about Jake, lass," he whispered.

"Thank you," I croaked.

I did it on instinct and buried my face into his chest, making him suck in a sharp breath, before looking down at me, eyes glistening with nothing but tenderness.

"Can we talk, lass?" he asked quietly. "Because I can't lose ya again."

His words flew right to both my heart and my lady parts, and I had to smile up at him. "Okay, Darcy," and he finally let me go.

"Max."

"Darcy. Fucking hurt her again? I'll bloody murder you."

"Heard ya loud and clear, Max."

I rolled my eyes but I understood my brother's warning. Also, I wouldn't take it this time. If Darcy fucked up? I'd smack him first then high tail it out the door.

The Irishman took my hand and led me to the bar. He ordered a whiskey and a glass of Shiraz for me. Then he led us over to an empty table, away from the rest of the cast. He gestured for me to sit and followed, taking the stool beside me.

"It really is grand to see ya lass," he said, keeping a tight hold on my hand.

"It's been a while," I replied.

"A while. It has. I enjoyed our last play. And it was a grand time."

"It was. You were a joy to be around the last few weeks before I left," I admitted.

He smiled as he squeezed my hand, and it caused my heart to stutter again. "That was down to ya, lass. Are ya alright? Ya look beautiful."

I returned the smile and nodded. "I moved back to London after Jake's funeral. I couldn't stay there."

"I get that. How are ya now?"

"Living with my brother and his boyfriend helped. They healed my heart, put me back together," I admitted.

Darcy's face softened and he took a swift sip of his whiskey, his gaze never wavering from mine.

"That's grand, lass. I couldn't quite believe ya were up there. Kate didn't tell me. God's I've fecking missed ya," he said quietly, so as not to be overheard.

"She didn't tell me either, the sly cow," I replied.

Darcy chuckled, then his entire face became extremely serious, leaning forward. "I need to say this, lass. And I need ya to hear me," he said.

"Okay," I replied. "I'm listening."

He traced circles over my skin and took a deep breath. "I'm not letting ya go this time, Sophie. The last few years have been fecking shite. Lonely. All I dreamed about was ya. I don't care how long it takes, but I'm never walking away from ya again. That was the most painful damned thing I'd done apart from the day I fecking broke ya heart."

I stared up into his emerald eyes, his words making my entire body hum with heat. But I had a few things to say too. I took a sip of wine and gazed back at him.

"I hear you, Darcy. But I need to go slowly. I need to know I can trust you again. I'm not going to stand for any kind of crap, including cheating. Do that? And I'm gone."

"Never gonna happen, lass. I want one woman for the rest of me life and she's right here, letting me hold her hand. Ya have me word that I'm yours for the rest of our lives," he replied.

The conviction in his words made my pulse spike, heart to fly up into my throat, and my breath to catch. I also couldn't quite believe that this famous, sexy as hell, actor wanted me?

"Jesus, Darcy. You're not messing around are you?" I said.

"No. Not this time. The last few years have been fecking shite. And I'm not gonna let ya go. I want us forever," he answered.

Every inch of me was on fire, heart going fucking nuts, and I couldn't quite believe what I was about to say, but it escaped my lips, making Darcy sit up taller.

"Shit, okay, Darcy," I whispered. "Slowly, promise?"

"Promise, lass."

I took a long gulp of my wine and watched him suddenly relax where he sat. Tension ebbed from his shoulders and he threw back his whiskey.

"I hear we are working together?" I said.

He ran a hand through his hair and smiled. The famous O'Sullivan grin, and he nodded. "Another reason why I wanted to talk to ya," he said.

At that moment, a female voice rang out through the bar. "Hey, everyone who's interested," yelled Melissa. "We're going to Starlights to finish the night off with a bang."

Darcy smiled at me, and it was tender and genuine. "Shall we?" he asked.

"Why not. Let's go, O'Sullivan."

He tugged me to my feet and we headed out into the busy London street.

Darcy

I had her by my side. I was holding her hand, and my heart was racing like a fucking crazy person. Sophie had agreed to be here and I couldn't be happier. I glanced down at my little director as she looked up at me, and she smirked.

"What's that for?" I asked.

"You look like a kid on Christmas morning," she said and snorted into a giggle.

Fucking hell. That sound. I'd missed that and her giggle. Jesus, I wanted to fucking kiss her.

I stopped, and she yelped as she stumbled backwards a little, hitting my chest. And that sound elicited a low groan from me.

"Lass?"

She looked up at me in shock and I smirked. "What the hell, Darcy?" she grumbled. "Warn me the next fucking time you want to just stop. I'm wearing bloody heels."

I smiled down at her annoyed face, and slowly turned her to face me. "Please can I kiss ya?" I asked.

She blinked up at me, her eyes widening, sparkling with a sudden mixture of panic and excitement. I watched her tongue dart out and lick her lips, and holy shit, it looked hot.

Please say yes, lass.

"Here?" she asked, eyes glancing at the rest of the cast and her brother.

"I don't intend to tongue feck ya in public just yet, lass," I teased, but my heart was racing, nerves on fire.

She glared at me for a second, then softened as she noticed the slight smirk. "Jesus, Darcy. Fuck's sake."

"Is that a yes?" I asked, desperate to taste her again.

Sophie didn't answer right away, then she slowly nodded. "Okay," she said.

I was swift and yanked her into me, wrapping one arm around her waist, the other behind her head, then I captured those soft lips I'd been dreaming about, and kissed her, slowly, confidently.

My entire body burned, skin erupting with goosebumps, then my heart soared as she gently touched my own waist, fingers digging in ever so slightly. I didn't push my luck and reluctantly pulled away, grinning sheepishly.

"Sorry, lass. Got a tad carried away," I admitted.

"Well," she gasped.

She seemed a little flushed with eyes a little glazed over, but the next words out of her mouth told me that this Sophie in front of me? She was *not* the same, and that got my juices flowing.

"If that was carried away, then you need some help. Because that was bloody tame for you," she stated.

"Excuse me?" fell out of me, and she lifted her brows, smirking at me.

"That was lame, O'Sullivan," and she started to walk away.

"That was bloody mean woman. Ya said slow, lass?" I called after her.

She turned and smiled with a very wicked look on her face. "When I said slow? I didn't mean snail speed," she drawled.

Well, that was a happy surprise. And I stood tall, raked a hand through my hair then set off after her. Not tongue fucking her? Well, I was about to do just that.

"Fighting talk, lass," I growled.

I grabbed her wrist and yanked her back into my arms, slammed my mouth onto hers, ravishing her, and the feeling when she moaned made my dick harden. Her hands flew to my chest as I rammed my tongue into her mouth, taking what I'd been craving for years. I eventually released her and winked.

"Better?" I whispered into her ear.

"Hell fucking yes," she replied.

I shook my head and chuckled. I took her hand again and we caught up with everyone at the VIP entrance. Murmurs filtered over to me, phones appearing, snapping my arrival, but I tuned them all out. I just glanced at the woman walking beside me, a huge smile on my lips, because she was all that mattered to me.

"You've gotten bold, lass," I said as we were shown up to the VIP area.

She smiled and walked to the huge window looking down onto the dance floor. "Over the years? Yes."

I noticed the sadness in her eyes and I pulled her closer. "Sophie, lass? You're allowed to talk about him. Miss him," I said gently.

She dropped her head and then looked up at me. "Thanks. That means a lot. Because you have a lot to live up to."

I nodded and turned her to face me. "I know, and I want to do that. What happened to you was fecking cruel. I didn't get on with him, but he deserved to have his happy ever after with such a beautiful, feisty woman."

The tears gathered at the corners of her eyes, but she smiled, swiping them away. I pulled her in for a hug, and allowed her a moment.

"Thanks Darcy. I do miss him everyday, but Max and Teagen have helped put me back together," she whispered.

"Glad to hear it. And I know you'll have ya moments, but ya have me too now," I replied.

I let her out of my arms and winked. "Now, let me get ya a drink."

Chapter 5.

Leo

Henry kept a tight hold of my hand and walked us towards '*Starlights*', and it felt so fucking good. "You *are* gay, right?" he asked.

I groaned and ruffled my hair, gritting my teeth before answering. "Yes."

"And you can't find it in you to tell people?" he asked.

I rolled my eyes and dropped my head. "Jesus, going right for the jugular aren't you?" I huffed.

"Yep. What's stopping you?"

I didn't answer right away as this guy was a stranger. I didn't know anything about him, yet I had never felt so comfortable as I did in this moment. It was as though I'd always known him, so I decided to be honest.

"My dad. He doesn't agree with it. Told me and my sister that he'd beat the crap out of us if we turned out '*that way*'," I admitted. "He fucking *hates* us with a viciousness that scares me."

Henry halted our tracks and frowned at me. I saw the anger there and I was suddenly pulled into a hug.

"I'm sorry, but you can't hide who you are, Leo. It's not healthy."

"You think I don't know that?"I said, my head dropping onto his shoulder. "My dad is a scary fucker, Henry."

"Have you told anyone at all?"

"My mum. And my sister knows," I replied.

His hands were roaming up and down my back, and my mind started to imagine all sorts of dirty fucking things that I wanted him to do to me. This guy was causing my entire body to fire on all god damned cylinders.

Oh shit, I was getting hard. I needed to let him go.

"Oh really?" he growled into my ear.

Fuck, too damned late. Shit.

He let me go and immediately looked down, and he grinned knowingly. "And same goes for you too," he said, and I couldn't help but look, and yes, there was a bulge, and this guy was packing.

"Leo Trent. Seems that we find each other attractive."

I rolled my eyes and started to walk on, adjusting my junk as I did, but Henry, sexy ass, caught me up again.

"Don't get all huffy, Leo. I took an instant liking to you when you walked into that bar," he said.

That took me by surprise and I had to smile. "You did?"

He nodded and took my hand again. "You've seen you, right?" he asked.

My hand rubbed my chin and I frowned in confusion. "Well, yeah. Every fucking morning in the mirror?"

Henry actually snorted into laughter and smacked my chest, making me frown at him in confusion.

"And no-one has ever told you that you look like a sinful angel? This dirty blonde hair and stunning innocent blue eyes? Then this tattoo peaking from beneath your shirt? With your beard and that fucking wicked smile, Jesus, you look like sin all wrapped up in pretty wrapping paper."

"What?"

"You heard me, Sin all wrapped up in angelic wrapping paper."

No-one had ever described me that way before. His expression was serious, honest and that literally floored me.

"Fucking hell, dude. You don't mess around do you?"

"No."

"I've never been described like that."

"Now you have. Come on. We're here," and I was dragged upstairs towards my fellow actors and a possible tongue fucking by the end of the night, because, so help me god, this man was like a bloody delicious temptation that I really couldn't see myself passing on.

And I was officially in deep fucking, divine trouble and I loved it.

Sophie

Standing with Darcy felt weirdly comforting, and his words just now made my heart beat a little faster. But, I had actually bloody flirted with him. Then he kissed me in such a way I almost came in my goddamned pants.

"Ya called me lame, lass," his voice floated from behind me.

"It was," fell out of me, and he chuckled. "Shit, I don't know what's fucking wrong with me," I groaned.

He handed me a glass of wine and stood beside me, his hand taking mine. I'd decided to stop overthinking anymore. After losing Jake so suddenly, life seemed so precious, so I'd decided to live every moment as though it were my last. And seeing Darcy on stage had caused a tsunami of emotions to slam into me. The one thing I needed him to do? Show me I could trust him again.

"Are ya alright?" he asked.

"Yes. I am, weirdly enough," I replied.

"Weirdly?"

"It's me and you, Darcy. We have a complicated history."

"Yes it is. And?"

"Doesn't it make it strange that it's comfortable? After all this time?"

"A little, but me happy heart overrides that."

At that I turned and looked at him, gazing up into those stunning eyes. He didn't break eye contact and smiled.

"So, what do I call you?" I asked after a few silently charged moments.

"Call me?" he asked, arching a brow with a smirk.

"Well, that kiss outside? You stuck your bloody tongue in my mouth, Darcy."

"Ya poked the bear, lass."

"Ha bloody ha, O'Sullivan."

"Boyfriend will work, lass."

The use of that word made my stomach flutter and my heart skipped a few beats. Darcy O'Sullivan calling himself my boyfriend sent a crazy wave of heat to fly straight to my pussy.

"Jesus Christ, fucking hell, really?" fell from me in shock.

Darcy smirked and stepped closer, the warmth from him wrapping around me in a delicious hug.

"I forgot how filthy ya mouth was," he growled.

"Yeah. That hasn't changed," I replied.

"And I don't want ya to change it, lass," he whispered into my ear.

I snorted into a giggle as his lips ghosted the skin beneath my ear. "Good job," I replied.

At that moment, as our eyes were fixed on each other, Henry appeared and he was pulling a rather flustered Leo with him. Darcy squeezed my hand and leaned in.

"I think Leo is gay. But he hasn't told anyone yet," he whispered.

"Shit. That means Henry *does* know. That man has the most accurate radar on the bloody planet," I replied.

Darcy wrapped his arm around me and kissed my temple. "Ya notice they are holding hands?"

I glanced down and sure enough Henry had the handsome actor's hand in his. They went straight to the bar and I watched as Henry leaned in and whispered into his ear.

"Ya know Henry and Leo are in the play with me too."

"Oh for fuck's sake," I groaned.

He grabbed my bag and winked. "Come on. Let's go and join the rest of them. Ya brother keeps glaring at me, so I think he needs to know that ya alright."

I had to smile and I allowed him to lead me to the gang of actors and my brother and Teagen.

Max

Teagen wrapped his arm around me and dropped his head on my shoulder as I watched the Irishman with my sister. He had a way of knowing when I was tense, and he always knew how to relax me. His lips ghosted my lips and then moved to that spot just below my ear which always caused my skin to heat up.

"She's a grown up, baby," he whispered.

I dropped my head and sighed as I leaned in and kissed him. His presence always soothed me even before we got together. In hindsight, I think it was a sign.

"I know. It's just worrying. Darcy has a fucking lot to prove to me before I trust him with our Sophe," I said.

Teagen's head flew up and he stared at me like I'd suddenly grown an extra bloody eye in the middle of my forehead.

"What?"

"You just said *our* Sophe, baby?" he purred into my ear.

I rolled my eyes and shuffled closer. "You said sister by default, T. She's our sister. Both of us slept in bed with her when Jake died. We both took care of her. We've gotten so fucking drunk together recently and fallen asleep in a heap on one bed."

My gorgeous man grinned and kissed me again. "Okay. And that was a fun night," he said, chuckling. "We need to do that again."

That was the moment Sophie and the Irishman strolled back over. And they were holding hands. Teagen pressed me closer and he whispered into my ear.

"Give him a chance for Sophe," and I nudged his thigh, but pecked his lips again.

Darcy gave me a smile and I nodded. Melissa was sitting with two other guys, and one kept eyeing up Teagen. Then Henry appeared with the ridiculously handsome blue eyes, and I instinctively pulled my man closer, holding onto him possessively.

"Here's to a great show," announced the Scottish guy.

"Yay. Well done everybody," Melissa yelled, and everyone lifted their drinks in a toast.

A tall brunette waltzed over from the bar with another woman with lighter brown hair. Her eyes were on the blonde and she looked fucking pissed off. Henry dropped his arm over blondie's shoulders and leaned back, making the woman suddenly seethe. Something was wrong there, so I looked right at him, caught his gaze and I held out my hand.

"I'm Sophie's brother. This is my boyfriend, Teagen. You're a pretty great actor."

The look in his blue eyes sparkled with some sort of relief. He held out a hand too and shook. "Leo. I hear that your sister is gonna be my boss?" he said.

I smirked at him, then noticed Sophe shuffle a little closer to Darcy. This was going to take some getting used to.

"Yes she is. Mine too," Henry piped up and smacked Leo on the back.

I noticed the way Henry was looking at the young guy, and it hit me. Leo was gay and that girl wasn't happy about it. She had a very jealous sparkle in her eyes as she glared at our friend. I heard the cough from her and I nudged Teagen with a slight nod of the head. He seemed to see exactly what I saw, so he stood up, pulling me with him.

"Well Leo, Henry. Let's have a fucking dance. Max is shit, but I bet you two are pretty good?" he said.

Henry stifled a laugh and smacked Leo again. "Come on, Sin. I know you can dance after the show. Let's show these two what we bring to the fucking table."

Teagen took my hand and we let Henry and Leo out before following them. "That girl seems to be a bit obsessed with Leo," he whispered.

"Yeah. I noticed that too. Creepy," I whispered back.

Leo broke free and walked on ahead, Henry behind with the two of us following. He didn't stop and walked towards the fancy balcony outside.

Henry winked at me as we all came to a stop in the cool evening air. Leo was stressed and on edge, and he turned and glared at Henry. "What's this for? She's not going to leave me alone just because I'm with you," he fired at him.

"Yes, brunette isn't giving up, I get that, but you need some space at least. So, hang out with us away from the rest of them."

Teagen leaned against the railing and winked at me. "Leo's gay right? And the creepy jealous girl in there won't leave you alone?"

Leo let out the most frustrated growl I'd ever heard, and he gripped the railing, staring out into the city below us. I was sure there was something else too, but I didn't push.

"She's fucking annoying. She constantly follows me around, stares at me, and she had the audacity to call me her fucking boyfriend at the theatre. She touches me without my permission and it drives me up the fucking wall," he exclaimed in frustration.

I glanced at my boyfriend and then looked into the club. This poor guy had a crazy girl chasing him and I really bloody felt for him. The stress, desperate frustration and rage was clear in both his face and body. Teagen patted his shoulder and Leo yanked the tie from his hair, allowing it to fall around his shoulders making Henry's eyes glaze over. Yes, our friend was seriously into the blonde actor.

"She can't change you and stop you from being gay, Leo," I said.

"They don't know," he muttered.

"That you're gay?"

"No. I haven't officially come out."

"Then tell them," I said.

He brought his eyes to mine and the fear surprised me. This guy was really afraid, so I pushed from my own leaning spot and walked over. I leaned on the railing beside him and smiled.

"I've been gay for just over four and a half years. It hit me like a fucking truck at high speed. I guess I was lucky to have such a fab circle of amazing mates. I'm thinking you might not have the same support?" I asked.

He looked over at Henry, then Teagen. His eyes then found me and he smiled a little. "Not really. Been alone most of the time. Then this guy waltzed in and called me out in bloody seconds," he replied.

Henry grinned and held out his hand to him. Leo took it and allowed him to pull him closer. "Yes, and we get to work together, and a really decent run to look forward to," Henry said.

"May I ask why you haven't told anyone?" I asked.

He flinched a little, staring out into the night sky, eyes dancing with that fear again. "Dad. He hates gays. Like, *really* fucking hates us."

"And that's the reason?"

"Yeah. He threatened me and my sister when we were kids."

Shit, this was bad. Leo was terrified of his own dad, and that wasn't fair in the slightest. No-one should be afraid of being who they truly were.

Teagen glanced at me as he noticed it as well, so I had to do it. "Look, take our numbers and come and hang out with us. You're alone in the city?"

"Yeah. This was my first decent role, so I've been by myself most of the time," he replied.

Henry grinned and said, "Not any more. You've got some guys to back you up and keep you company. Now, we just have to get rid of your stalker girl."

"Easier said than done, Henry," Leo muttered.

Teagen's spine suddenly locked up and he whipped his eyes to Henry and Leo. "And now is the bloody time, she's heading over looking for you."

"Jesus bloody Christ," Leo groaned.

I pulled Teagen to me, then Henry took Leo by surprise and tugged him into his body, lips slamming onto the young actor's.

"Guessing she'll get the message now," I whispered.

But we were very bloody wrong.

Leo

Henry was kissing me. Kissing me as though he wanted to steal every ounce of air from my body, and it was the hottest kiss in my entire fucking life. But, her shrill voice pierced the night sky and I wanted to scream.

"Put him down. Leo's mine and he's not bloody gay," she screeched.

Henry broke the kiss and held me close to him, his eyes landing on Eve. She looked ready to combust, and a part of me was fucking thrilled.

"Wow. You don't give up do you?" Henry drawled.

"Leo? Do I need to call security? He kissed you?" she whined.

"Go get her tiger," Henry whispered with a wink, and he smacked my ass.

Max and Teagen winked too and Sophie's brother gave me a slight encouraging nod. I leaned back against Henry's impressive chest and glared at her.

"Get fucking lost Eve. You have the wrong equipment and you are extremely fucking annoying," I said.

Henry's arms snaked around me, holding me close. And we all watched her as she tried to process what I had just said.

"You're not gay? You're with me," she gasped.

"Jesus, Eve. I've never been with you, you stupid cow. So get fucking lost," I growled in angry frustration.

"You are my boyfriend, Leo," she shrieked. "You're not gay," and she went to grab my arm. "Come and dance with me."

Henry gripped her wrist and threw it off me, his eyes narrowing at the sheer fucking cheek of her, and I groaned as I was moved behind his body protectively.

"Are you not listening, girly? He's not fucking interested in you. He's with me, so get fucking lost, crazy bitch," he hissed.

"He is not gay. He's with me you pervert," she squealed.

"Why can't he be gay?" asked Max.

"The way you kissed me every night. That's not a gay man kiss. You are *my* boyfriend and you are touching him inappropriately. I'm going to get security," she fired.

Henry laughed but it was cold, and he pressed me closer. "Do you hear yourself? Fuck off. Leo doesn't want you because you're an irritating, girl stalker with a vagina and tits."

I froze for a moment as her eyes widened. "You're not gay," she stammered. "This guy's putting crazy thoughts into your head honey."

That was the last straw. All shreds of self preservation flew out of the window. Henry seemed to sense it too and he kissed the crook of my neck and whispered into my ear.

"Tell her. Say it. We've got you."

I took a breath and glanced at the men around me, then glared at her. "I'm fucking gay Eve, not confused. I've been gay for fucking years. Get that through your bloody skull. I don't go for girls. I'm attracted to guys. Men. You don't have a fucking dick, Eve, so leave me the fuck alone."

She made an irritating squeak then shot back into the club. I relaxed back into Henry's body, his arm wrapped tightly around me, hoping this would be the last of it.

"Feel better?" he asked.

"Yeah. But I'm still not sure she believes me," I replied.

"Maybe not. But, you said it out loud to another person, Sin. That's fucking amazing."

The three of them grinned and the elation that I felt in that moment was the best feeling in the world. The feeling of not being isolated and alone, and I believed I'd made three new amazing friends.

Henry, however? Well, that was another whole bunch of emotions to contend with because he made my heart flutter and the feel of his arms around me felt so damned right. As though I was home for the first time in my life.

Chapter 6.

Sophie.

Max was hanging out with Teagen, Henry and blondie, Darcy had gone to the bathroom and Melissa was dancing with two of the actors. I finished my drink and wanted another, so I headed for the bar and the server smiled warmly as I approached.

"Hey, what can I get you?" he asked.

"Single malt whiskey please?" I said.

"Ice?"

"God no, don't ruin it," I replied with a wide smile.

As he chuckled and walked away my mind started to think about the night so far. I was here with Darcy O'Sullivan. The Irish actor who had both swept me off my feet, broken my heart, then waltzed back into my life like a bloody hurricane. Max hadn't smacked him yet, which I was thankful for, and I was about to work with Henry, Leo *and* Darcy. The most eventful night I'd had in a very long bloody time.

"Sorry. I need to go grab another bottle. Hang tight, I'll be right back," he said with a wink.

"No problem," I replied and gave him a warm smile.

Not long after the bartender vanished a slurred voice suddenly drawled into my ear, hands landing either side of me, caging me in.

"And what have we got here?"

"Shit, what the hell?" I gasped as beer breath wafted into my nose.

"Aren't you a pretty little snack?" and he pressed himself into me, panic clawing at my throat as I was crushed into the edge of the bar.

"Get off me. I'm not interested," I exclaimed, trying to wriggle free.

I was suddenly spun around and my eyes landed on dark brown, glazed eyes. A reasonably handsome guy who was dressed in a suit, dark hair and a dangerous look on his face. I was in trouble and there was no-one around to help. His hands were gripping my hips painfully hard, gaze roaming down to my cleavage.

"You're hot, little lady. I'd enjoy tasting you," he slurred.

"Get off, I'm not interested."

"Ah, you know you need kissing. Dressed like this? It screams fuck me."

"I said I'm not interested."

"Sexy and you would look amazing riding my cock."

The terror gripped a hold, causing a shiver to skitter down my spine. I was in serious trouble, and my eyes darted around for help, but I couldn't see anyone who I knew. I needed to get away from him. I rammed my hands onto his chest, trying to push him off me, but he was scarily powerful and didn't budge.

"Leave me the fuck alone, I have a boyfriend," I gasped.

"Then where is he? Or are you making him up? He shouldn't leave such a pretty thing alone. You've got a dirty mouth, and it would look fucking hot wrapped around my cock."

His hands were roaming around to my ass and I was absolutely terrified. This guy wasn't interested in anything I said, and he didn't seem to understand the word no.

"You and me? We'll make sweet music, gorgeous. I just want to taste you," and he leaned forward, mouth closing in, and I couldn't move.

"Stop it," I whispered. "Get off me," and I tried to lean back, the bar digging painfully into my spine.

"You know you are asking for a kiss," he drawled, and his hot breath hit my nose, making me gag. "Just a kiss, sexy," and his hands squeezed my ass as his body pressed against mine.

I couldn't help the panic rising up my throat, then I felt his hand on my breast, fondling and squeezing. His lips touched my neck then he licked upwards, and I couldn't breathe.

"You're so fucking beautiful," he drawled.

"Get off."

"After a taste, love," he growled.

His voice rang out and my entire body sang with relief as the drunken suit was yanked backwards and Darcy appeared in front of me like my knight in shining armour, and I wanted to cry with joy.

"Get ya dirty fecking hands off my woman."

Darcy shoved him backwards with enough force to make the guy stagger into some vacant stools. "Touch her again and I'll knock ya into the next century".

"And why do you think she's yours?" hissed the drunk guy.

"She's *my* fecking lady. *My* woman, ya gobshite."

"And you left her alone?" he snapped.

Darcy grabbed a hold of his shirt and growled right into his face. "Get the fuck out before I deck ya."

"Fine. She's a prick tease anyway," he had the audacity to say.

"She's nothing of the fecking sort. Bad mouth me future wife again and," then a huge mountain of a man appeared behind the drunk.

He reached out and grabbed the guy, yanking him to one side. "You, mate, have crossed a line. Get yourself out of this club, right now before I throw your sorry ass out myself."

The guy backed up, smoothing down his shirt, looking embarrassed, then he scurried out like a mouse being chased by a huge fucking cat. The mountain turned and touched my arm gently.

"Are you hurt at all Miss?"

"No. Darcy got here before," then I stopped, my voice trembling along with my hands.

"I'll report him. I'm here to keep an eye on you Mr O'Sullivan. Sorry I wasn't here faster."

"Thanks fella."

"Cass," and he smiled warmly.

Once Cass the mountain had disappeared into the background, Darcy took my hand and pulled me into his arms, crushing me against his body.

"Shite, lass. Are ya alright?" he asked.

"God, I thought he was going to force himself on me," I whispered, shaking in his arms.

He let out a low growl that vibrated through me. "Never lass. He's lucky I didn't fecking punch him for touching ya."

I just held onto him, thankful that he appeared when he did. The bartender came back with the whiskey and he frowned.

"What happened?" he asked.

I buried my face into Darcy's body, still trembling, and he squeezed me tighter. "A handsy son of a bitch touched me bare," he said.

"Jesus, really?"

"All sorted now, fella. He's been kicked out."

The shocked bartender gazed down at me and poured my drink. "Here. This is on the house, as your lady looks pretty shaken up."

Darcy stroked the length of my spine and winked at him. "Cheers fella. Much appreciated."

He handed me the glass and smiled lovingly. "Drink, and then, I want to talk," he whispered. "And not here."

I threw the whiskey down and gave the bartender a grateful smile, then Darcy walked us back to the table and scooped up my jacket and bag.

Melissa was sitting on one of the actor's laps and she frowned as she saw us. "You okay?" she asked.

"We're gonna go, lass. Will ya tell Max that Sophie's in good hands?"

"Sure. See you later," she replied.

"What are you doing?"

"Trust me? Please?" he asked.

That word rattled around my head and I paused. He gazed down at me and sighed with a little frustration.

"I'm not going to jump ya lass."

I was taken down the stairs and he walked us out of the club and into the crisp winter night. There was a town car parked and I suddenly resisted, so he stopped.

"I promise ya lass, I'm not going to take advantage of ya, kidnap ya or anything else untoward. Just trust me?" he said.

I glared up at him and crossed my arms. "That's a fucking car, O'Sullivan. And we've literally just met each other again?"

He rolled his eyes and hoisted me into his arms and started walking. "I'm going somewhere where we can sit, talk and then Carl can take ya home, unless ya want me to join ya? In the car, not, feck. What are you doing to me, lass?"

The snort fell out and I laughed. Loudly. I had just witnessed Darcy O'Sullivan get all flustered. "Me? Jesus, Darcy," I exclaimed. "Shouldn't it be the other way around?"

He groaned and put me down in front of the car, then the flashes started to go off. The press had found us and I noticed the panic in Darcy's eyes.

"Please, lass? Please trust me?"

I glanced over his shoulder and saw them. They were heading right for us, flashes already going off, so I slid into the back swiftly followed by Darcy. His entire face lit up as I fastened my seatbelt, and the driver moved the vehicle away from the curb.

"That was the bloody press wasn't it?" I asked.

He looked back and then over at me. "Yes. And they will have gotten something bloody nuts to report. That's why I need to talk to ya," he replied. "And after that fecker tried to," then he stopped.

I saw it in his eyes and I slumped back into the seat. "It wasn't your fault."

"It feels like I failed me first chance to protect," but I laughed, cutting him off.

"No, Darcy. You fucking saved me from the scumbag."

He groaned and gripped my hand tightly. "No lass, he had his hands on ya, and I wanted to smack him into the next fecking century."

I snuggled closer to him, allowing his scent to wash over me. "You can't protect me twenty four hours a day, Darcy. Stop beating yourself up. You got there in time. Now, where are we going?"

He relaxed back into the seat and ran a hand over his face, then turned to look at me. "Somewhere where I can talk to ya without being afraid to leave ya alone to be groped."

He kissed my hand and squeezed as I was whisked away to god knows where with my tall, dark and handsome Irish actor.

Darcy

I took a risk and had Carl take us home to my town house. I wasn't going to take advantage of my beautiful woman, but she was going to be very fucking pissed at me. After that guy in the bar, it hit me that Sophie was going to be a target now. Not only with the press, but with handsy fuckers that had no right to touch my woman.

We pulled up and Carl opened the door for us. I held out my hand and helped Sophie out. Her eyes narrowed instantly and she froze where she stood.

"What the actual fuck? I'm not going to someone's house party," she snapped.

"Not a house party, lass. Me home."

"What?"

"I'm going to repeat me self. I'm not going to jump ya, take advantage. I just want to talk," and I gently pulled her up the steps toward my front door.

I led a shell shocked Sophie inside and toward my kitchen, and a gasp fell from her. "Fucking hell. This is bloody stunning."

"Cheers lass. Drink?"

"Whiskey. Jesus Christ, it's the full length of the fucking building," and she wandered off, taking in her surroundings.

As I poured I glanced at my little director in *my* fucking house. Not one other woman had *ever* stepped foot in here except my Mam. Sophie was the only woman that I wanted in my private, personal space, and in my bed.

"Fuck, Darcy. You live here alone?" she asked.

"Yes I do."

"How many women have passed through here? Slept in your bed?" she questioned.

I smirked and she frowned at me, crossing her arms. "None. I never brought any other fecking woman into me home. You're the first and last."

Her spine locked as her cheeks turned a lovely deep pink. "Really? I mean, not one?"

"Nope. Me private space always stayed that way," I replied.

She walked back to where I was standing and took the glass offered. I could tell her mind was whirring, so I gestured for her to sit .

"Never?" she asked again.

"Never, lass."

"Why?"

"The only woman I want in me house is *you* lass. I kept this space for me and the future Mrs O'Sullivan," and I winked with a grin.

She blushed again as she dropped her gaze and sipped her drink. "So, you want to talk?"

I sat opposite her, showing her that I meant what I said. "I want us to start dating, lass. I know ya need to trust me and we've just met again after a long time, but I meant what I said. I can't let ya go this time. I can't watch ya walk away again. If ya say yes, the press are real. Ya had a taste of the worst kind of media snake, but I will do me best to keep ya protected from them. And that fecking slimy gobshite. Christian will too. Just let me try to show ya that I truly love ya Sophie lass."

She stared into my very soul for a long time, sipping her drink, and the waiting was fucking infuriating, making me grind my teeth in frustration.

"This is fucking crazy. I haven't seen you for years, but I remember that night I watched you leave. Shit, I can't believe I'm admitting this. But, I hated watching you disappear. And tonight? Seeing you brought feelings to life I thought I'd buried a long time ago."

Every emotion, nerve and specific body part blazed to life, and I grinned across at my lady.

"Give me a chance. Let me date ya Lass?" I asked.

She sipped her drink, eyes downcast, body clearly conflicted. "You would go slowly?" she finally asked.

"Yes, lass."

"Allow us to get to know each other again?"

"Yes."

"Not rush me to fuck you?"

As she asked that question, I was taking a sip of my whiskey, and I choked, spraying half of it across my kitchen island.

"Shit, you okay?" she exclaimed and giggled.

"Christ woman." I coughed.

She threw back her own and stood up, walking around to me. "Sorry. Didn't mean to choke you," and she stopped beside me.

I wiped my chin and looked at her, taking in her beautiful dark eyes. "Sure I want to feck ya, Sophie lass. But I won't rush ya. I just want ya to spend time with me. Get to know me again, be with me."

Sophie took my hand and smiled warmly. "Then I'll give you your chance, Darcy O'Sullivan, because, well, I *do* still care about you, very much."

Chapter 7.

Sophie

Darcy had kept his word and organised Carl to take me home after a soft kiss on the lips. And once I was back, I went straight to my bedroom and quickly jumped into bed, a huge smile adorning my lips. As soon as I had laid eyes on him, emotions came flooding back. Memories of the final days working on the play. He'd been so sweet, funny and a joy to be around. So much so that I'd felt a pang of sadness when he'd left the theatre that night.

Now we were about to work together again, so he'd laid it out on the line for me. He didn't want to let me go this time, and he wasn't going to take no for an answer. It didn't scare me in the slightest though, and that's what shocked me. He had taken me to his home and informed me that I was the *only* woman to be in his private space and the feeling of elation had taken me by surprise. I stared up at the ceiling, the glass of whiskey in my hand. The first play I was about to direct also starred Darcy, Tara, Henry and blondie Leo. This was going to be interesting. My phone suddenly pinged and I swiped it off the bedside table as I sat up. My mouth crept up into a small smile as I noticed the name.

"I miss ya already lass. Dxx"

"*You'll see me on Monday. Sxx*"

"*I want to see ya tomorrow. Let me take ya for lunch? Dxxx*"

Just as I was about to reply, the noise barrelled through the apartment as familiar voices rang out, and I groaned but smiled at the same time.

"*It might be a later lunch. Max and T have brought back company. S xx*"

"*Then that's a yes? Xx*"

My heart had gone crazy when he appeared in the bar tonight, and he'd saved me from Mr scary handsy fucker. But it had been his words as well as his actions that had caused my heart to skip and pulse to race. Yes, I was about to give the Irish actor a second chance.

"*It's a yes, Darcy. As long as you stick to your word. S xx*"

"*I want no-one else but you, Sophie lass. And I am going to prove it to you. Goodnight,*

beautiful. Dxxx."

"*Goodnight Darcy. Look forward to it. S xx.*"

At that moment my door flew open and a rather giddy Henry appeared. He turned his head and yelled over his shoulder.

"She's home all safe and sound Max. Hello sexy bitch."

He didn't hesitate and ran over, diving on the bed, making me snort into giggles.

"Jesus, H. Spill my fucking drink and I'll murder you."

My brother, Teagen, and an amused looking Leo Trent appeared and my bedroom was filled with gay men. Leo caught my eyes and he smiled sheepishly.

"Hey. I was forced here, just so you know," and he gave me a very beautiful smile.

Henry was shuffling to the bottom of the bed, Max and Teagen coming to each side of me.

"I had a feeling with these three. I guess you've been accepted," I replied.

Henry grinned over at the young guy. He reminded me of a sexy, naughty angel. "Come and sit with me, Sin," the actor stated.

Leo's eyes sparkled but looked at me, as though for permission. "It's fine, Leo. Come and join the reprobates," I said and smiled warmly.

"Cheeky cow," Max snorted.

"Truth," I replied.

"Leo is one of us now," Teagen said, winking at me.

"God help you, Leo," I said and smirked at him as he blushed a little.

He walked over and Henry yanked him onto the bed, making him sit in front of him, pressing him back against his chest.

"So, sexy director," started Henry. "Your Irishman?"

Max, who was huddled next to me, tensed a little. "He hurts you," he muttered.

I wrapped an arm around both my brother and Teagen and smiled. "He was a complete gentleman. So don't get your knickers in a twist shithead."

Leo gave me a small, warm smile and Henry jumped off the bed. "Drinks. T, Max, come on and help me," and they shuffled off the bed.

"Keep our new boss company. We'll be back asap," said Henry, and he kissed Leo's forehead and winked at him.

As they vanished I looked at the actor. Dirty blonde hair, bright sapphire eyes and a smile that could possibly melt every female heart around the world. Men too to be fair. He looked a little uncomfortable, so I climbed out of my bed and grabbed my bluetooth speaker. I linked my phone and picked my '*favourites'* playlist.

"You have friends here?" I asked as the music floated around the room.

"No. So, your brother and those two have been amazing tonight," he replied.

I had to smile as I climbed back into bed. He watched with inquisitive eyes and I chuckled. "Do you realise how gorgeous you are?" I asked.

The blush was instant and he ruffled the top of his head. "Never thought about it. H said I look like a fucking sinful angel. Never been called that before."

"You do. And you know he's sweet on you?" I said.

He grinned and he pulled the tie from his hair, letting it fall around his shoulders, and holy hell, if I didn't know he was gay? I would have melted into a hot mess. The way it framed that angelic face was bloody stunning. A dusting of stubble covering his chin and upper lip, and those very tempting lips. Henry and Leo would make an extremely hot and sexy couple.

"Please don't tell anyone?" he asked.

"That you're gay?" I questioned.

"Yes. I have family... issues. Don't want to stoke the fire."

I nodded and reached out to touch his arm. "It's not my place, Leo. Just know, Henry likes you rather a lot."

Leo glanced at the door then back at me, and that beautiful smile appeared again. "He's pretty cool. I kinda like him too. And that scares me."

"Because of your family issues?" I asked.

"Yeah, pretty much."

"Henry's very understanding and trustworthy. So, don't worry about him saying or doing anything to make problems for you," I replied.

"Thanks, Sophie."

My brother, Teagen and Henry reappeared, drinks in hand and I knew I wasn't going to get much sleep tonight. Leo smiled at the three men and took the glass offered.

"Thanks Henry," he said.

"Oh no problem, Sin. Now, I think Sophie should tell us where her Irishman took her."

I rolled my eyes, shook my head and sipped my drink. "Not happening, fuck face. What about you and Leo? You two would make an adorable couple."

Leo smirked as Henry grinned like a wicked devil. "Oh, this young man is going to get to know me so much better during this play."

"Presumptuous of you, Henry," Leo teased.

"Nope, Leo Trent. Facts," Henry replied and pulled Leo into a very heated kiss.

Max and Teagen whistled and cheered, and I simply soaked in the laughter, the company, and I finally felt wholly happy after losing Jake.

"To getting Sophe back where she belongs," Henry announced, and we all clinked glasses together as laughter echoed around my bedroom.

I awoke to an empty room and voices coming from the kitchen. I glanced at the clock and it read nine fifteen. My head hurt as we had drunk rather a lot more once the guys had camped out in my room. Leo seemed like a really sweet guy, and I was looking forward to seeing him grow as an actor. Henry was clearly smitten so I knew it was only a matter of time before they would have to come clean about their relationship.

But it saddened me when Leo had asked me to keep it a secret. I just hoped that three of my favourite people would help him finally come out and tell everyone. I knew Henry. When you became his friend? He would never shy away from showing that to everyone. I could only imagine how he would act when in a romantic relationship. But, along with the three guys, me and Darcy, we'd have his back no matter what.

After relieving my bladder, washing my face and cleaning the god awful taste from my mouth, I scooped up my phone ready to hunt down a vat of caffeine. My eyes dropped and I smiled as Darcy had left me a message.

"*Good morning lass. Hope you're not too tired. Is one too early to pick you up?*

Your D xxx."

Last night was the most eventful in a long time. Darcy O'Sullivan had whirled in like a tornado and declared that he was never letting go of me ever again. He'd taken me to his home, called himself my boyfriend, and I had also found out that I was about to work with him again.

Along with Henry, Tara and Leo. The decision to let him back into my life had surprised both Darcy and myself. But, I was done hiding away from life. After losing Jake the way I had? I was about to take life by the horns and live.

"Morning to you too, Darcy. Tired. A little hungover. But it was a fun night. You

were right about Leo, and One is fine, and where are we going? Sxx."

I walked in to find two half naked men lounging on the sofa kissing each other's faces off. Their hair was messy and their body language told me they were post bloody fucking.

"Jesus, you two. Glad I didn't hear anything," I groaned, heading for the coffee jar.

"Sorry, not sorry, Sophe," drawled Max.

Teagen huddled into him, kissing his stomach and chest, and I had to smile. They were just as loved up as the day they'd found each other, and I adored them both. It felt as though I'd gained another brother in a weird way.

"So, what are you up to today bitch face?" my brother lovingly asked.

"Lunch with Darcy, douche fucker," I replied.

He shuffled a little and I saw the flash of worry in his eyes. Teagen simply dropped his lips to Max's and kissed him.

"She's a grown up, remember, baby," I heard him whisper.

"Yep. I'm capable of smacking him if he fucks up, Max. Just trust me."

He kissed Teagen and climbed off the sofa, heading right for me, and I was yanked into his arms and hugged within an inch of my life.

"I love you, Sophe," he whispered.

"Love you right back, Max."

I heard another set of footsteps and I was crushed from behind as Teagen wrapped his own around us too.

"Okay, half naked gay boys, enough squishing of your sister. I'm in desperate need of coffee," I stated, and Max snorted while Teagen chuckled as I was released.

"Are we still boys?" Teagen questioned. "And can you make your brother from another mother one too? Your brother is insatiable and kept me up half the fucking night."

Max smacked his ass and grinned, and I let out a groan. "Fuck's sake. Too much bloody information," I groaned.

"Again, sorry, not sorry. Can't help that I've got the sexiest boyfriend on the fucking planet," he drawled.

I saw the slight blush appear on Teagen's face and it was adorable. Max grabbed his hand and tugged him closer, kissing him tenderly.

"Go put some bloody clothes on and get me a sick bucket," I exclaimed.

They laughed into each other's mouths and Max shot me a wink. "Fuck off shit head," he replied, then they disappeared into their bedroom.

I walked back to my own with coffee in hand after delivering Teagen's and my phone pinged as I sat on the bed.

"*It's a surprise lass. I want to treat ya. See you at one. And I can't fucking wait. Dxxx.*"

"*Well now I'm intrigued. See you in a while. Sxx.*"

I smirked and dropped my phone onto the bed and swigged my welcome hot drink, excitement and nerves starting to crackle to life. I was about to go out in public with a very sexy, world famous movie star.

Jesus bloody hell fire. This was crazy.

Darcy

Workout done, showered and dressed, and now I was sitting eating my Irish breakfast and checking the media pages. And low and behold there I was, looking as though I were kidnapping my Sophie and I ran my hand over my face and read the brief article below.

> "*Who is the mystery woman? Darcy O'Sullivan has been unattached for almost five years, but last night he was caught bundling a petite female into his car before disappearing into the night...*"

Bundling her into a fucking car? Jesus Christ, that sounded almost criminal. I picked up my phone and called my agent.

"Hello sweet man," and Effie's light voice floated into my ear.

"Hello, lass. What a great sound to hear on a Sunday. Ya old man around?" I asked.

Christian's wife giggled and it made me grin like an idiot. She was such a sweet woman. "He's here. Not sure about the old, Darcy. You sound lighter?"

"I got me girl, Effie lass," I said.

"Oh, Darcy, that's amazing. He's here now. Bring her over for dinner," then she handed the phone to her husband.

"Less of the damned old, Darcy. Now, why are you calling? Nothing wrong?" he fired.

I had to smirk, then I glanced back at the photograph on my laptop. "Ya seen the latest? Apparently I'm a fecking kidnapper now."

He let out a groan and went quiet for a few seconds. I knew Effie was helping him to find the article.

"Who is that, Darcy?" he asked. "And don't spin me a damned story. Is that a certain someone from your past?"

I sat up taller, my heart rate spiking and said, "Yes. And I want to ask her to the premiere in three weeks."

Chapter 8.

My agent was very rarely stuck for words, and he didn't say anything for what felt like a fucking eternity.

"Didn't expect that, Darcy."

"She came to the final performance. Kate gave me her number after sitting her in the VIP box, dangling her right in front a me nose."

"Sneaky. And?"

"She also informed me that Sophie is directing '*Porter*'. I asked Sophie to talk to me. She fecking agreed, Christian. I told her that I wouldn't let her go this time, and she's said yes to dating me."

"And?"

"Feck, I brought her home, chatted and I'm taking her to lunch today," I blurted, excitement coursing through me like a tsunami.

Christian laughed loudly and I had to chuckle. Then I glanced down at the ridiculous story and groaned.

"You need to be seen today. Then it will make this idiotic story make sense. And I'm happy for you. Just don't ruin it this time," he stated.

I wasn't going to. This time I was keeping my little director. She was the love of my bloody life and I intended to marry her and grow old with Sophie Carter. I was never going to let her get away. She was mine. Forever.

"Never. She's me future, fella."

He let out another chuckle and said, "I'm truly happy for you. Now, don't worry too much about this story. It'll soon make sense when you take her for lunch today. Enjoy yourself. I have to go as my in-laws are here."

I said goodbye and cleared away my plate and mug. Then I jogged upstairs to prepare for my first real date with my future wife.

The car pulled up outside a large ground floor apartment and Carl smiled as I stared at the front door.

"You'll be fine Sir," said my driver.

I grinned at him and arched my brow. "Sir?" I questioned.

"Practising for your date."

I chuckled and patted his shoulder. "No need, Carl. You've been me driver for too long now. Darcy's grand. And ya've met Sophie, right?" and I winked.

"I have, but I can see you're nervous, Darcy."

"I am. Sophie is me forever. But, it's been a long fecking time since I've done the dating thing," I replied.

Carl smirked and I rolled my eyes. "Just be you, Darcy. That's who she's expecting, right?"

I had to smile back at my driver and I nodded. "Very true, Carl. Cheers fella."

"No problem. Now go. She's waiting."

I opened the door and climbed out into the bright afternoon and smoothed down my suit. Carl was right, I was a fucking bag of bloody nerves. I hadn't dated since my ex broke me. And that was a long fucking time ago. I took a deep breath and strode to the door and knocked, but I wasn't expecting the sight that greeted me.

Sophie smiled, her dark eyes warm as she did. My heart went crazy and my stomach started to go nuts, but I simply threw her my smile and said, "Hi lass. Ya look beautiful."

"Thanks Darcy," she replied.

I noticed her brother lounging on the sofa with his boyfriend. He shot me a glare and I understood. Max didn't like me at all because of my previous actions. Actions that I regretted every single waking hour. But, I would show him that I was a very different man now, and I would look after and protect her for the rest of my life.

"Max, Teagen," I said with a polite smile.

The boyfriend gave me a wide smile, but Max simply nodded and said, "Darcy."

"Knock it off Max," Sophie fired at him.

I looked down at my little director and she was wrapped up in a stunning blue dress with a lace over layer. Short sleeves and the loose skirt stopped by her knees. Her dark hair was scooped up into a messy bun, showcasing her gorgeous neck, and she stood a little taller in a pair of matching heels.

"Am I too dressed up?" she asked as I gawked and drooled at my gorgeous woman.

"No lass. Ya look perfect," I replied and I heard a derisive snort from her brother.

Teagen nudged him and he literally rolled his fucking eyes. "She is, right Darcy?" he called.

"Fucking behave yourself, O'Sullivan," Max shot at me.

Sophie groaned and walked back to him, kissing his forehead. Then she waltzed her sexy ass back to me and took my hand.

"I'm hungry so where are you taking me? Later douche fuckers," she called over her shoulder and tugged me back towards the car.

I chuckled as I allowed this feisty and beautiful woman to drag me along the pavement. "Douche feckers?" I asked.

"Yes, douche fuckers," she replied.

"Is that how ya always talk to them?" I asked.

"Yep, now where are we going on our first date?" she questioned.

The ease at which she said it made my dick twitch and heart to hammer against my chest. I couldn't believe she'd said that out loud. Carl opened the door for us and Sophie slipped inside. My driver winked at me and I patted his shoulder.

"Savoy please," I whispered, then climbed in to join Sophie.

Sophie

Darcy was wearing his signature charcoal grey suit and his dark hair looked slightly messy, as though he had run his fingers through it numerous times. Was he nervous too?

Jesus, I fucking hoped so, because I was shitting myself.

I'd been worried about wearing this dress, wondering if I was overdressed, but he'd told me I was perfect and that caused a whole range of bloody emotions to fly through me. My body also enjoyed his emerald eyes roaming down it too. So much so I had to squeeze my thighs together. Darcy O'Sullivan was very well endowed downstairs, and he also knew how to use it. I felt my cheeks burn as memories came rushing back, so I squirmed a little in my seat.

"Are ya alright lass?" he asked, that smooth velvety tone making my pussy scream for attention.

"I'm fine," I squeaked, then cringed at the sound of my voice.

His hand found mine and he laced our fingers together, turning in his seat. "I'm nervous too, lass," he said gently.

I sighed and gave him a grateful smile. "Where are we going?" I asked.

"I want ya to know that ya getting nothing but the best, so we're going to afternoon tea," he replied.

I bit down on my bottom lip, chewing furiously. His finger landed under my chin and he tilted my head up, making me look at him. He leaned in and pressed his mouth to mine, kissing me slowly, confidently, and I couldn't help but sigh happily.

"Are ya hungry?" he whispered.

"Fucking starving," fell out of me, making him chuckle.

He squeezed my hand and sat back, and I relaxed a little. "Ya always had a way with words, lass," he said.

"Yes. Still swear like a bloody trouper," I admitted. "But I know when to behave."

The car pulled up and I finally dragged my eyes from the beautiful Irishman and gasped. He winked as the car door was opened by a smartly dressed man in uniform. Darcy stepped out and reached out for me. I took it and emerged from the car, staring up at the famous hotel.

"Fucking hell, Darcy. The Savoy?" I hissed.

"Yes. And they do the best afternoon teas. I've also ordered some champagne," and we were led inside the stunning building.

He didn't let go of my hand and strode confidently through the lobby. He stopped outside the Thames foyer and the Maitre'D smiled warmly.

"Mr O'Sullivan. How lovely to see you again," he gushed.

"Hello fella. Me usual table, please."

The man nodded then noticed me tucked into Darcy's side. "And this lovely lady is joining you?" he asked.

"This is me girlfriend, and yes she is joining me. From now on," and he winked at him.

"Oh how wonderful. Pleased to meet you, Miss."

"Hi. And god, it's Sophie, not Miss," I said with a smile.

"Very well, Sophie," he replied with a warm, amused smile. "Please, follow me," and we were taken to a table by the far window.

Once seated, I noticed eyes on us and I sighed. It was something I would have to get used to now I'd agreed to this. I took a deep steadying breath and tried to ignore the stares.

"We were seen last night," he said as he started to open the champagne.

I sat up taller and glanced around the large room. "What? The press at the nightclub?" I asked, nerves spiking.

He ruffled his hair, his eyes locked onto mine. "I was accused of bundling a mysterious woman into the back of a car, lass."

I snorted and let out a loud laugh, covering my mouth as we were suddenly stared at. "What? Like a fucking kidnapper?" I whispered, and Darcy rolled his eyes, but his mouth crept up into his sexy smile.

"Happy ya find it funny, lass."

"Oh come on. It is," I replied.

He popped the cork from the bottle and poured mine first. As the bubbles settled I arched my brows.

"That's not full, O'Sullivan," and I gestured for him to top it up.

He chuckled and did as I asked. He then moved seats and sat right beside me, taking my hand again.

"To us, beautiful," he said and we clinked our glasses together.

Now, I was still suffering from a hangover due to my cheeky shit of a brother and his boyfriend who invited Henry and Leo over last night, so I took my glass and swigged half of it down. Darcy watched me with an amused sparkle in his eyes, and I groaned and put down my glass.

"I did mention the hangover right?" I questioned.

"Ya did, Lass."

"Henry and Leo didn't leave until nearly four in the bloody morning," I said.

He smirked and took a sip of his own drink. "Ya look stunning to say ya didn't get much sleep, lass."

"I'm bloody knackered, Darcy. They know how to bloody party."

"And we are all working together as of tomorrow," he replied.

Before I could answer the food arrived, and this was a very fancy looking afternoon tea. I frowned at all the types of foods on offer, then glared at Darcy.

"All this is for us?" I gasped.

"I don't know what ya prefer. Any leftovers? I take it to the waiting staff. That's why they like me," and he winked with a grin.

The waiter smirked and I had to giggle. "Is that true?" I asked him. "Darcy gives you the leftovers?"

"Yes Miss. We usually get fed pretty well when Mr O'Sullivan dines with us," he answered.

"He's a kind guy then?"

"Yep. He even tips each of us," he whispered.

Darcy smirked as he started on the sandwiches and he patted the young man on the arm. "Because ya work fecking hard, fein."

The waiter disappeared and I stared down at the array of food in front of me. It was all extremely fancy.

"What the bloody hell is all this?" I hissed, clearly feeling out of my league.

He shuffled closer and wrapped his arm around the back of my chair. "Coronation chicken, egg and cress, salmon gravlax and dill, cucumber," he said as he pointed out the various selection of sandwiches.

I let out a puff of air and pointed to the other stuff on the trays. "What about these? And I only bloody recognise the fucking scones," I muttered.

"Savoury bites. Duck, squash. And apart from the scones. Sapphire tart, Autumn choux, blossom cake, lavender chocolate cube," then he picked up an egg and cress triangle and held it in front of my lips. "Take a bite, lass."

I glanced around the room, and yes, we were being photographed and filmed. Shit, this was all suddenly very real. I was having lunch with an extremely famous, sexy guy, and we were getting rather a lot of attention. *Shitting hell.*

"We're being filmed, Darcy," I whispered.

"I don't fecking care, beautiful. Now eat," and he wiggled the sandwich.

Rolling my eyes, I took a hold of his wrist and did as he asked. I bit into the small triangle and it tasted delicious. He winked and started to pile food onto his plate. I did the same and it wasn't until the first sandwich was finished that I realised how hungry I truly was. I relaxed over the course of the meal, trying some of the fancy bites and treats. He topped up my glass whilst we ate and his hand kept grazing my thigh under the table, which felt bloody amazing, causing my body to tingle with heat, making me squeeze my legs together as my pussy was getting extremely bloody excited.

"I know we have a brand new play to put on lass, but I have another public engagement coming up in three weeks," he said.

A part of me tensed, not knowing what he was about to say. "And what's that?" I asked, grimacing on the duck bites. "*And* I don't like duck."

He smirked and leaned in, his breath ghosting my neck. "It's a film premiere, lass," he whispered, and my eyes whipped up to meet those delicious emerald pools which were gazing right back.

"What film is that?" I asked, our focus now solely on each other.

"It's a tale of love and loss. A pirate. Tortured soul who wishes to avenge the death of his one true love," he whispered. "Lost Love's Revenge."

His eyes dropped to my lips as I bit down on my own and chewed. My entire body was on fire just from the closeness of him. The way he was gazing at me made me squeeze my thighs shut as my lady parts started to flutter even harder.

"Oh?" I breathed. "Does he get his happy ending?"

"I can't tell ya that lass, because I want ya to come with me as me date."

Back the fuck up, what? He wanted me to go to a fucking film premiere? As his bloody date? Fuck, fuckity fucking bollocks.

Chapter 9.

"What?" I squeaked.

"As me girlfriend, lass. I want the fecking world to know that ya mine," and my brain literally imploded. "And I'm yours."

"What?" I repeated.

He chuckled and picked up a lavender chocolate bloody cube and eased it between my parted lips.

"Eat," he ordered.

I glared at him for a moment, making him smirk wickedly. I rolled my eyes and opened my mouth, and he popped it inside. It simply melted on my tongue, and it was delicious.

"I want ya to accompany me to the premiere. And to all the future ones too?" and he did it.

He leaned in and closed the gap, kissing my lips, tasting the remnants of the treat in my mouth.

A small moan fell from me, then he backed away, grinning like a damned devil. He picked up the second bottle of champagne and started to pour as I processed what he'd just said. As I took a huge gulp of the fizz, I fixed my eyes onto my hands now resting on the table. My heart was going fucking nuts at the thought of attending a premiere. The world's media would be there, and my life would never be the same again.

Darcy sat back, sipping his own drink, watching every damned emotion fly across my face. I squeezed my eyes shut, pinching the bridge of my nose then I felt the warmth of his hand on my thigh and my eyes flew open again.

"Please come with me, lass?" he whispered.

"I don't have anything to wear," I blurted.

"Not a problem."

"I'm not red carpet worthy."

"Yes ya are."

"Everyone would," but he interrupted me.

"Would know. That's the fecking point, beautiful."

"All the press."

"And reporters asking questions."

"Fuck, Darcy."

He chuckled and kissed my temple. "I *will* beg if I have to, lass. I want to make sure everyone knows ya mine."

My cheeks burned, body setting on fire with a desperate need for him to bloody grab me, throw me over the table and fuck me into next year, but I took a breath and threw back the champagne.

"I'll go with you. As long as you," but he slammed his mouth onto mine, kissing the bloody life out of me.

Once he allowed me to suck in air, I glanced around the room, and yes, we were now blatantly being filmed, photographed and whispered about.

"Too late, Sophie. Everyone is going to know by tonight," he drawled. "Because we'll be all over social media in the next few hours."

"What?"

"Diners have been taking pictures since we arrived, lass."

"Shit," I muttered.

"Indeed, Sophie. Ya gonna have to get used to it," he whispered, then started to kiss my neck. I let out a quiet moan at the sensations of his lips on my skin, and for a few seconds I lost myself in my Irishman's touches.

"Oh god, Darcy," I sighed, hands now gripping his shoulders as he pulled me flush against his body.

"Ignore them, Lass," he whispered.

My eyes scanned the room, and he was right, as I noticed phones pointing in our direction, eyes subtly watching us and some were blatantly gawking.

And this just got scarily bloody real.

Leo

I was laid on my sofa, cramming lines for tomorrow when my phone started singing. I looked down and saw Henry's name, and my whole body went crazy.

"*Hey Sin. Are you busy? Hx*"

I smiled and typed out a reply. "*Just going over lines. Why? Leo X*"

The thought of his lips on mine last night, hands on my hips? It made my dick hard. He was swift to reply and I had to grin.

"*Let's get coffee in the morning, Sin? Xx*"

The fact that he called me Sin made me chuckle. I took a gulp of my tea and sat up. "*Sure thing. Where? X*"

"*There's a great place I want to try. Hxx*"

I smirked at the cryptic message, but looked forward to seeing him. Henry had literally swept me off my feet, and he had informed me that he was playing my boyfriend in the play, which had come as a bit of a scary surprise. It would mean that I couldn't invite my family to see it. Dad would go fucking ballistic. Sophie and her brother and boyfriend were great fun too, and I was looking forward to both working with her, and hanging out with them. I finally felt like I wasn't alone anymore. And I could be myself with the guys.

The knock rang out and I frowned as it was late afternoon on a Sunday. I jumped from the sofa and headed for my front door. I swung it open and Henry was standing there grinning at me. "Want to play around, Sin?" and he held up a bag and winked.

I groaned, running my hand over my face as I let him inside. "Play around how?" I asked as my body started to heat up.

The images flying through my brain were dirty as fuck, but I moved away from him as he walked into my kitchen. He pulled out two bottles of wine and leant against the counter. He then reached into his jacket and a toothbrush appeared.

"I want to play around with you, Sin. And go to work together." he replied. "If not, just say, and I'll leave and jerk off in the shower thinking about you."

I arched my brows at him, at this stunningly beautiful man in my home, and grinned. "We've just met, Henry." I said.

"So? We both feel it."

I ran my hand over my face again and sighed. "Jesus, you don't hold back do you?" and he winked.

"Not when I meet the man of my fucking dreams, no."

At that I didn't know what to say, so I reached into the cupboard and grabbed a couple of glasses.

"That's a yes?" Henry asked, moving closer.

"Yes to a drink if you help me with lines first?" I fired back.

The way his eyes lit up caused a volcano to erupt in my boxers. Jesus, I wanted him to fucking wreck me in the best way. I turned away and poured us each a drink, then I felt him standing right behind me.

"You sure, Sin? Because I saw that twinkle in your eyes, Leo Trent," he whispered, and his hands touched my hips and roamed up to my shoulders.

I shivered at his touch, and it was not because I was bloody cold. As he pressed himself against me I felt his huge boner digging into my ass and a small groan left my lips.

"Jesus Christ, Henry," I breathed as he left a seering trail of kisses up my neck.

"We can have a drink afterwards and run lines fucking naked as the day we were born, Sin. What do you say?" he growled into my ear.

All sensibility flew out of the window and I whizzed around, slamming my mouth onto his, hands gripping his hips and grinding myself against him. His mouth was divine and his hand landed at the back of my head as he literally plundered mine like a demon possessed.

We weren't soft and fluffy either. Clothes were discarded as though they were on fire, and Henry's hand went straight to my cock, fisting it with his own.

"Fuck, H," I moaned, bucking into each movement, slowly edging us to the wall.

"I need to be inside this sexy ass, Sin," he whispered into my ear, his own voice nothing but gasps.

I grinned at his gorgeous face and reached for the drawer to the cabinet filled with books. I reluctantly backed away from this Adonis of a guy and retrieved my lube and started backing out of the kitchen.

"And where are you going, Sin?" he asked with a wicked smirk, still stroking his dick.

"Come and take this ass then, H," I called and I turned and strode, butt naked, to my bedroom, Henry's laughter echoing from the kitchen.

Darcy

The flicker of realisation in her eyes made me take her hand and squeeze it tightly. Sophie had agreed to date me, slowly, but she hadn't really understood the true meaning of being my girlfriend.

"Ya get used to it, lass. And that guy over there? Sitting on his own? He's been taking sly pictures since we got here."

She whipped her head around and the reporter dropped his arm under the table. Real fecking subtle fella, I thought.

"Is he as bad as that guy, the nasty one?" she asked.

"Ah, no. He works for one of the celebrity gossip magazines. The photos will hit its online pages within the fecking hour. His magazine is pretty harmless," I replied.

She narrowed her eyes at him then did something I really hadn't been expecting. She waved at him with a smile then spoke loudly across the room.

"I think you've gotten enough to be getting on with, so scurry along and leave us the.... Hell alone,"

I stared at her in both shock and wonder as the reporter actually blushed and shot to his feet, then practically sprinted from the building. As she brought her gaze back to me she frowned a little.

"Why are you bloody gawking like I've sprouted horns or something?" she questioned, sipping her drink.

I shuffled my chair closer then yanked her from hers, making her yelp in surprise. "What the fuck, Darcy?" she hissed.

I chuckled as I steadied her on my lap, arms around her waist and her own came to rest on my shoulders.

"Let me get this straight, lass. You're absolutely alright telling a reporter to, well, pretty much feck off, but you're terrified of a film premiere?" I asked, my brows arched in happy amusement, and a wide smile on my face.

She literally rolled her eyes and snorted at me. "That's bloody different," she replied. "He's on his own."

I had to do it, and I slipped my hand around the back of her head, easing her face closer. I captured her filthy lips with mine and kissed her lovingly, possessively, silently telling her that she was mine.

"Ya coming with me, Lass. I'm gonna show the world that I've got ya, and I'm not ever letting ya fecking go," I whispered. "Ya're all fecking mine, lass. And I'm all yours too."

She blinked up at me, clearly nervous, but I stroked up her spine, pulling her into a hug. "What about an outfit?" she whispered.

I took a deep breath in and inhaled her scent. She smelled divine, like delicious exotic fruits.

"Not a problem," I whispered back.

"Jesus, Darcy," she muttered. "Okay. Deal."

I tensed and crushed her tighter for a second, and her warmth washed over me. "Thanks lass. You've made me the happiest man alive."

She suddenly giggled as her head rested on my shoulder, her nose brushing against my neck. "Jesus, what have I let myself in for?" she groaned.

I just held onto her, not quite believing she was here. "A future with me, lass," I simply replied.

Once we'd eaten until we were bursting, I took Sophie's hand and held on tightly. She had no idea how hard this was about to get, but I would protect her with my fucking life now. I also made what could be called a very idiotic decision for someone who hadn't had sex for a very long fucking time.

"Three weeks to go, Lass. Then you are going to be naked in my bed," I whispered as I led her outside.

"What?" she gasped.

"Ya heard me, beautiful. After the premiere, I'm taking ya home and I'm going to feck ya all damned night," I growled into her ear.

Her cheeks burned that adorable deep pink, but she yanked at my hand, stopping me in my tracks.

"That's a very bold fucking statement, O'Sullivan. What happened to slow?" she fired at me.

"It'll be a month. What's the problem?"

"Still fucking presumptuous."

"Alright. I'll make ya a deal. If ya *don't* want to be naked in me bed with me three weeks down the line, so be it. I'll have to continue using me hand while imagining ya riding me until I filled ya with me come, beautiful."

She glared at me, but I saw the fire behind those eyes sparkle to life. I'd hooked her in, forcing her to imagine that. Her on top of me, my cock buried deep inside her pussy, watching as she came all over me.

"What the fuck, Darcy?" she squeaked, then her gaze dropped to my crotch, making me smirk.

Yes, Sophie, lass. You remember what I can do with it too.

"What, lass?"

"I didn't need that much information," she huffed, but I could tell she was a little flustered.

I paused our steps and tugged her into my arms. "Just so ya know, lass. It will be very different this time. And that's because I fecking love ya."

She sighed, wrapping her own around me, bringing her eyes to mine. "Alright, Darcy. Challenge accepted. And good luck."

I leaned down and kissed her, slowly, confidently, and gave her my winning smile. "I'm going to seduce the feck out of ya," and I winked.

Sophie rolled her eyes, but I noticed the smirk on her sexy mouth. I grinned and started walking again, knowing that I'd have my true love naked in three weeks time. I smiled at Carl as we approached the car, and he opened the door for us.

"Where to, Darcy?" he asked.

"That's up to me girlfriend. Where to, beautiful?" I questioned.

She frowned as I took her hand and gestured for her to get in. "It's my choice?" she asked.

"Yes, lass."

"And if I wanted to go home?"

"I'd be sad, but I'd take ya."

She chewed on her bottom lip and I moved on instinct, running my thumb over it, eyes watching the action as I imagined sucking it into my mouth.

And now I was getting fucking hard.

"Can we go to your house?" she asked, and my heart stuttered in surprise.

"Sure lass. Carl, take us home please."

My driver arched his brow with a small amused smirk. "Will I be needed to take Sophie home?" he asked.

The cheeky fucker winked at me and I inwardly groaned. But Sophie piped up and took my breath away.

"If we go via my house I can grab a few things and we can go to work together tomorrow?"

I almost gave myself whiplash as my head whirled around to stare at her. Had she just said that? *Jesus fucking Christ.*

"You have a problem, O'Sullivan?" she asked with a wicked smile. "All about trust right?"

Carl stifled a laugh as I stared at Sophie in happy surprise and she smiled up at me then climbed into the car. I smacked my driver's arm and he smirked as I followed her into the back seat.

"Ya sure, lass?" I asked.

"You set a challenge, Darcy and I want to see how serious you are about that statement," she replied.

And there she was. The feisty little firecracker I adored. And I had to keep my dick in my pants until after the bloody premiere. Fuck.

Chapter 10.

Leo

My heart was racing, cock bobbing in anticipation as I reached my bedroom. Henry was right on my tail and I let out a curse as he rugby tackled me onto the bed.

"Fucking hell," I exclaimed, and he laughed, turning me over and kissing down my chest.

"I need to taste you first, Sin. And running from me? You'll pay for that," he drawled, and his words caused my skin to burn and goosebumps to ghost over it.

"You did say fun, H. Thought I'd get you to work for it.... fuck," and his mouth descended over my cock.

My hands flew to his dark hair, moaning loudly like a fucking porn star, and I gripped fistfuls of it. "Oh my... fuck yes, god, yeah," I gasped.

His dark eyes lifted and he winked, swirling his tongue around my tip as he cupped my balls and my hips moved without warning, bucking up into him. He gagged but grinned around me, taking me right to the back of his throat. And Jesus, he was the most heavenly fucking sight. I bit down on my lip, watching him. Watching my cock slide in and out of his mouth, grunts and sighs escaping my lips. I didn't think it could get any hotter, but the lube was thrown at me and he wiggled his fingers.

"Fuck, really?" but I swiftly covered them with the cold liquid.

As I felt my climax spark to life deep in my belly Henry pushed a finger inside my ass, and holy fucking hell, my entire body went nuts.

"Fuck, shit, H," I cried out, bucking into him again. He pushed another finger in and I moaned loudly. "Fuck, yes, yes, ohfuckjesusyes," and I started to fuck his mouth.

Henry pushed in another, stretching me and hitting the perfect spot over and over, and every inch of me was burning with pleasure, my climax swiftly racing to the surface. My body started to tremble, hands fisting Henry's hair, then it slammed into me, and I exploded into his mouth. He didn't let up until I sagged back into the mattress, sucking me dry, then he brought his face up to mine with a huge grin and licked his lips.

"Fucking hell, Henry. That was amazing," I gasped, squeezing my eyes closed for a moment, gathering my senses together after they'd been shredded into delicious pieces.

"I haven't finished with you yet, Sin," he growled, pushing my knees towards my chest.

My eyes flew open and he rammed his mouth onto mine, kissing me as he added another finger. I moaned into his lips and reached for Henry's massive cock bobbing above me.

"Fuck, Sin, that's so good," he breathed into my lips.

"God, I just need you to fuck me now," I gasped, his speed ramping up as I fisted him faster.

He stopped and growled at me. "Stop. I want to come inside you. Knees to your fucking chest," he ordered.

I smirked but did what he asked. He lubed up his impressive cock and leaned over me. "Are you ready, Sin?" he whispered into my lips as he kissed me.

"Oh you have no fucking idea, sexy ass," I fired back.

He grinned and lined himself up, teasing me first. "Jesus, you are god damned divine," he moaned, then he slowly thrust his hips forward.

Our sighs were synchronised as he kept moving deeper, and I hissed at the feeling of him. He let out a loud moan as he bottomed out and our eyes locked onto each other.

"Jesus Christ Leo Trent. I don't want to fuck another man ever again," he whispered.

My heart stuttered at his words, but he suddenly slid almost all the way out, paused for a second then slammed back in.

"Fuck, yes," fell out of me as Henry cried out.

And he didn't hold back. He leaned over me and literally fucked me hard and fast, slowly shoving us up the bed until I had to stop myself from hitting the headboard. The room was filled with our grunts, gasps and moans as I was railed by the most divine damned guy I'd ever met.

"Shit, Sin, I'm almost there, Fist your cock for me, Let me watch you come," he stammered, his strokes becoming erratic.

I took my cock and started pumping with gusto, wanting to fall with him, and in moments he slammed into me with a loud roar, my own exploding over my stomach almost at the same time.

He didn't pull out straight away, and ran his tongue through my cum and grinned.

"Christ, Henry, that was fucking amazing," I breathed.

He slowly pulled out and I dropped my trembling legs onto the bed. Henry laid beside me and propped up his head with his hand.

"Yes it was. Glad you gave in now?" he drawled.

I laughed and looked down at the mess I'd made. "How the fuck could I have resisted, H. And I need to clean up."

He quickly jumped from the bed and walked to the bathroom. I heard him turn on the tap and then he came back with a warm wet towel. He winked as he wiped my stomach and I gazed at him as he took care of me.

"Roll over, Sin," he said.

I smirked and did as he asked, and he gently cleaned my ass as he left a trail of kisses down my spine. "Your tattoos are fucking sexy, Leo. I knew you were a gorgeous devil wrapped up in angelic packaging."

I rolled back over and smiled warmly. "I really like the way you describe me, Henry. And I never said I was innocent when it came to sex."

"I was hoping you weren't," he replied.

I sat up and ruffled my hair, then I tugged him closer and kissed him. "Drinks and lines, remember," I reminded him. "And thanks for taking care of me."

He winked as he climbed off the bed. "The one who gives takes care of their man. That's my own personal rule. Let's go get the drinks," and he held out his hand and yanked me into his arms.

The feel of his body against mine was the most heavenly thing I'd ever experienced and I kissed his shoulder, our hands roaming over each other's hot, naked bodies.

"You don't want to fuck another man again?" I questioned.

He arched a brow and his lips curved up into that knee trembling, cock hardening smile. "And I meant it, Leo Trent. I want to keep you, my sinful angel," and my brain shut down, heart stuttering like crazy as Henry led me back to the kitchen.

Had I just met and fucked my soulmate? Jesus, I fucking hoped so, as I wanted to keep him too.

Sophie

I didn't know what had come over me, but I wanted to stay with Darcy. I wanted to stay close, hold his hand, and cuddle. And I had to admit that his words had set off a crazy stream of dirty thoughts about riding his talented bloody cock.

Dirty, filthy, sexually frustrated cow.

Now? I was packing up my things for tomorrow and glanced at the framed photograph of Jake and myself on our wedding day. I sat on the bed and picked it up. Stroking his face, I sighed and spoke quietly.

"I know you hated him, Jake. So, for that I'm sorry. You know I'll always love you, but I want to live. Taking a risk on Darcy is crazy, I know. I can see you rolling your eyes where you are. And I'm just giving you a huge hug, wrapping you up in my arms. I miss you every fucking day. Every hour and every minute. I just needed to tell you."

I kissed his face and put him back where he lived, on my bedside table. There was a familiar knock and I turned to see the worried face of my little brother.

"What happened to bloody slow, shithead?"

"I'm not jumping straight into bed with him, fuck face. I want to know that he will do what he's promised," I replied.

He leaned against the frame of my door and smiled. "Okay. I hear you, but *please* don't rush into it. He lives his fucking life with the shitty press watching his every move."

I finished gathering my stuff and walked to him. I rose up on my tiptoes and pecked him on the cheek.

"I get that too. I'll be back later tomorrow. Love you little douche fucker."

"Funny, crazy cow. Love you too."

Teagen gave me a tight squeeze and kissed my forehead. "Get you off to a sleepover at a famous movie star's house," he drawled.

I literally grinned and turned to the door. "And I get to work with him too."

"Will you ask Leo and Henry if they want to go out again?" asked Max.

"I can do that. Now, enjoy some alone time," and I hugged them both again.

I noticed the flash of concern in my brother's eyes as I started toward the front door. So, I walked back to him, taking his hands.

"I'll be fine, Max."

"Check in, okay?"

"I promise."

"Go, fuck off to your famous man's pad," and he winked at me, kissing my forehead.

I nodded with a wave and blew them both a kiss as I walked back to the door. I stepped outside and strode nervously back to the black town car where Darcy was leaning seductively against, looking like a sinful dessert.

"Ya got everything, Lass?" he asked.

"Yep. And remember that you said three weeks time, O'Sullivan," I replied, and winked cheekily as I slipped back inside the car.

He raked a hand through his hair and groaned as he followed me. I buckled my belt and looked up at the Irish hunk sitting beside me. This was a risky move on my part too, as I wasn't blind to the exquisite man who's home I was about to stay overnight in. The attraction was very real, and I hadn't had sex for a very long time. Sure, I had a vibrator and my fingers. But it was *not* the same. I had carnal knowledge of Darcy O'Sullivan, and he was very talented in the bedroom department.

"So," he started. "What are we doing when we get there?" he asked.

"I want to know about you. Your family, and what little Darcy was like," I said, watching him squirm in his seat.

"Really, lass?" he groaned.

I giggled and took his hand in mine. "I'm kidding, but I'd love to know at some point. We need to do lines for you. Are you up to date?"

He shot me a glare then smirked. "Well, there's the boss. I'm getting there, lass. It's a pretty great play."

"Brand new playwright, and very talented," I said. "Can't wait to get back into that bloody theatre and get my hands on it. Tasha is so bloody talented. The story, characters and that ending, Jesus, it'll blow everyone's socks off."

He chuckled and turned around to face me. "The theatre world has missed ya too, lass. Especially me."

I smiled down at my hands and glanced up at him. "I never realised how much until I walked back inside there yesterday."

That's when it hit me like a fucking truck. Shit. It had only been yesterday that Darcy had come crashing back into my world. And here I was about to stay the night at *his place*. He seemed to see the panic and fear which graced my face and he leaned in and kissed my cheek.

"As soon as I knew ya were up there? I swore I wasn't going to fecking lose ya again. Letting ya go was one of the most painful things I've ever fecking done. I'm holding on tight this time, lass," he said.

I nodded and lifted my eyes to him. "This is *so* fucking strange, Darcy. You only just came back into my life last night, for god's sake. Now I'm in your car and about to stay the night with you," and he smiled smugly, earning him a slap to the chest.

"Your idea, Sophie lass."

"Ha fucking ha, O'Sullvan," I retorted.

"I'm not going to complain, lass. I was surprised, but ya made me very happy," he replied.

I turned in my seat and faced him, my heart racing and body starting to burn up as I looked up into his handsome face. If I were to be honest with myself? I wanted to spend time with him, be near him and I'd made a snap decision earlier.

"I want to be honest, Darcy."

"Sure, lass," he said softly, our gazes fixed on each other now.

"I didn't want to go home because, well, I'm enjoying being here with you," I whispered.

He sat up a little taller and his hand shot through his hair, and I noticed the sparkle in his eyes. I never thought I could get the sexy actor flustered, but here he was as he fidgeted in his chair.

"Ya don't know what that means to me lass," he said, then he leaned in and captured my lips with his in a very tender, delicious kiss.

The car came to a stop and Carl the driver announced that we'd arrived. And that was the moment that my stomach lurched as the nerves slammed me. Darcy gave me a wink then opened the door and turned to his driver.

"Go home, fella. And say hello to ya lovely wife."

"Cheers Darcy. Nine thirty tomorrow morning?"

"Yes, that'll be grand. Goodnight fella."

"Goodnight Miss."

"Goodnight, Carl. And it's Sophie."

The lovely man winked with a grin and a wave, then Darcy stepped out and helped me to climb out too, taking my bag from my hands, slinging it over his shoulder.

"Let me get ya a drink and settled in me guest room," he whispered.

I arched a brow at him in surprise and he winked, taking my hand and leading me up to his front door.

"Guest room?"

"Yes, lass. Ya said slow," he replied as he led us inside.

I smiled up at him, and nudged his shoulder as he started to climb the stairs. I glanced around at the beautiful home of this sexy movie star, and held tightly to his hand. I saw a glimpse of a living room, and then another flight of stairs, wondering if he were truly going to take me to his guest room. He had a tight hold of my hand as he pushed open the door to a very beautiful room, and my eyes went wide as I took in the huge wardrobe, giant double bed and I glanced up at a very tense and nervous Irishman. He was being true to his word, but I had to ask myself a very important question. Was I going to sleep in this lovely room? Or stay with Darcy?

Darcy

I dropped her bag in the guest bedroom and it felt wrong, so fucking wrong. She walked up behind me and nudged my shoulder.

"This is a very lovely room, Darcy."

"Thanks lass. The only people that have slept in here are me family."

This was going to be *so* damned hard, knowing she was down the hall from me. I pretty much knew that I wasn't going to sleep much knowing she was so close yet still out of reach. I watched as she wandered around the room, taking in her surroundings, including opening the door and taking a peek into the small ensuite bathroom.

My eyes soaked in her curves in that sexy fucking dress, her shapely legs in those bloody heels, and then she turned to look at me, a small smirk on her face. Sophie was watching me intently, then strode back to me, bent down and picked up her bag. She turned and stepped closer.

"You were really going to let me sleep in here?" she asked.

I frowned in confusion, then she took my hand and pulled me from the room. "You said we're dating right?" she questioned.

"Yes lass. Where are we going?"

"And I can trust you?" she asked.

"Yes."

She stopped outside my bedroom door and grinned up at me. "Is this your room?" she asked, and I stared at her in surprise.

"Yes, lass."

"Then people who have a history, who've seen each other naked, and are now dating, sleep in the same room," and I died and went to fucking heaven.

She kicked open the door and tugged me inside, then stopped short, dropping her bag onto the floor.

"Fucking hell, Darcy. This is a beautiful room. Is that a bloody walk in wardrobe? Jesus, that bed could fit four people in it," and she waltzed around, looking over her surroundings.

All I could do was chuckle as my heart soared at the sight of my woman wandering around my fucking bedroom. Happiness, joy and a wide grin on my face.

"I can sleep on the floor, lass. I have a camp bed I can use," I said.

She whirled around and her hands covered her mouth, fingers laced together, and her brows shot up in surprise.

"What?" she fired at me.

"Ya can have the bed, Sophie," I replied.

Sophie strode over, halting directly in front of me and she smacked my arm, hard. Her beautiful lips crept up into a smirk and I had to frown at her, confusion dancing across my face.

"Why the fuck would I want you to sleep on the bloody floor?" she questioned.

"Going slow, lass," I answered.

"Oh for fuck's sake, Darcy. No. We are sharing that fucking huge bed. No arguments."

My brain was empty of any words as I stared at my little director, in my fucking bedroom, telling me we were going to sleep in my bed? Together?

Jesus, holy Mary, mother of god. Died and gone to fucking heaven.

"Are ya sure, lass?" I had to ask once the shock wore off.

Her eyes found mine and she smirked. "Yep. And it's going to be fun watching you squirm when I huddle up next to you."

The cheeky little bare was teasing me, so I stalked towards her and yanked her into my arms, and she yelped as I crushed her against me.

"Ya bad girl, lass. And I'm looking forward to watching ya try to resist me," and I kissed her.

She relaxed in my arms, but I needed to let her go otherwise I'd throw her onto the bed and *show* her how much I'd missed her. And that stupid fucking decision to wait until the premiere? *Dumb ass fucking move O'Sullivan.*

"I need to leave this room, lass. Otherwise I won't be responsible for me actions."

She giggled and stepped away from me. "Okay. Which side do I take?" she asked and looked up at me with her beautiful big brown eyes.

"Any. I don't care as long as you're here," I admitted.

She shook her head and looked at each side. My alarm clock was sitting on my bedside table, along with my diary, glass of water and my other watch. She glanced at me then walked around to the other side.

"I'll take this side then, as you sleep on that side," she said and dropped her bag.

Chapter 11.

My little director was causing all manner of bodily malfunctions as she continued to surprise me. The one woman I had fallen madly in love with was right here. In front of me, about to sleep in my bed. And I was finding it hard to believe, expecting to wake up from a great yet torturous dream.

Life without her had been fucking horrific, and I'd chosen to stay away from any other women, as all I craved was Sophie. And here I was watching her pick a side in my bloody bed. I ran my hand over my face and into my hair, and finally found my words.

"I'm surprised ya want to sleep in here," I said, and she smiled that beautiful smile that caused my body to go into fecking heat like a randy dog.

Sophie left her bag there and walked back to me, taking my hand. "You bloody swanned back into my life like a tornado and told me that you won't let me go again, called yourself my fucking boyfriend and kissed the bloody life out of me. You bundled me into your car, took me to your house, and all in one night. How is any of this normal?"

I snorted into a fit of laughter and engulfed her in my arms. "Jesus, woman. I've missed ya like fecking air."

She wrapped her own arms around me and hugged me too, and it felt as though I'd come home. I didn't want to move, but I needed a drink after everything that had happened today.

"Let me get ya that drink, then we can run lines before tomorrow," and I led my beautiful director towards the door.

"Okay, O'Sullivan," and she dragged me from the room towards the stairs and down to the kitchen.

I gestured for her to sit and she strode to the far end of the room and dropped onto the sofa which looked out onto a small patio and neatly kept garden. I couldn't help the smile that crept onto my face as I watched her getting comfortable. I grabbed two tumblers and swiftly poured two fingers of whiskey in each.

"Lass," I said as I passed one to her.

"Thank you," she replied. "Now what?"

"What would ya like to do, Sophie?"

I noticed the smirk and the flash of wickedness in her eyes as she stared at me, sipping her drink. "Well, you could tell me about your film?" she suggested.

I sat beside her and put down my glass, but I wasn't prepared for what my sexy little director did next. She jumped to her feet, flinging her heels off onto the rug by the door. The next moment? Sophie fucking Carter was sitting on my lap, arms around my neck, and I had no words.

"Is it an action film? Or a romance?" she asked.

Nothing formed in my brain as I stared into her dark and hypnotic eyes. Sophie was finally mine. My lady, girlfriend and future. She was here, sitting on my fucking lap like a dream. All bloody mine.

I smirked to myself then placed my hand at the back of her head, easing her towards me. I kissed her swiftly and wrapped my own arms around her waist.

"Well, lass. I can't tell ya all of the plot, but it's a tragic love story, pirates, sword fights and an evil enemy trying to kill me too," and she listened intently as I explained the basic story to Sophie Carter.

My woman, my true love, who had chosen to sleep in the same fecking bed.

The alarm pierced my brain and I groaned as I rolled to turn it off. I rubbed my face then froze as I heard a small female moan.

"Crap," she muttered, and my entire soul beamed. "It's too fucking early."

I had Sophie Carter in my fucking bed. Her arms came around me and she kissed my shoulder. "Well, you were a very good boy last night," she purred into my ear.

I sucked in a breath as my dick stood to attention, begging for some action. "I promised ya lass," I croaked, then cleared my throat.

"Thank you," she whispered.

I turned and found a gorgeous messy haired girlfriend rubbing her eyes. She was wearing a t-shirt I'd given her and, fucking hell, waking up to see her in it was delicious torture.

"Ya want to shower?" I asked.

She sat up and smiled at me, and I inwardly groaned, adjusting my junk as she started to climb out of bed.

"Oh," she exclaimed, then scooted back and dropped a gentle kiss on my lips. "As long as there's enough time for both of us."

I smiled happily, touching my mouth as I watched her rummage through her bag. "I'm going down to work out, lass. Routine, and there's a shower down there. So go for it."

She stood up and turned, holding onto her wash bag. "This was lovely, Darcy. Last night. Dinner and TV. Spending time just chilling."

I swung my legs over the side and ruffled my hair, heart hammering wildly as I looked up at her.

"It was. And I wish you'd stay here with me."

"Stay?"

"Yes lass. I've woken up with ya. Don't want to wake up without ya now, beautiful," I admitted.

She didn't move, just locked her eyes onto mine. I knew that her mind was whirring, thinking things through, but I really didn't want to be without her one more fucking second.

"Is that going fast rather than slow?" she asked, then bit down on her lip.

"Maybe. But ya feel this, right?" I said. "This feeling of... ease with each other?" I asked.

She sighed and walked to where I was sitting, and I tried to hide the huge boner I was sporting. The wash bag was dropped onto the bed and she sat next to me.

"Can I be really honest?" she asked.

"Sure, Lass."

"When I lost Jake? I almost lost myself too. I let grief begin to drown me, the pain and hurt. Most of all, after that passed, loneliness took over, and it was fucking horrific."

I touched her hand and she took it and squeezed. "He was gone. Just like that and, after a few months, I realised that I needed to live my life. Stop fucking hiding away and just, well go with the flow. Take the opportunities that came my way. Jake wouldn't agree with you at all, shit, he bloody hated you," and she smiled wistfully. "Our past is messy, Darcy, that can't be changed. But *you* changed, so, when you appeared in the bar, I decided to take that chance."

I touched her cheek and cupped her face before planting a swift kiss on her soft lips. "And I'm over the fecking moon that ya did, lass," I whispered into her ear.

"I enjoyed waking up to you too, so why don't we try the 'I stay here and you stay with me'?"

"And Max?" I asked, heart rate speeding at a million miles an hour.

She snorted into giggles and leaned against me. "He'll have to bloody deal with it," she replied. "Then we can see what it's like, you know, doing the living together kind of thing?"

I gazed down at Sophie and I couldn't quite believe that I'd been given this second chance to love her, be with her, so I nodded with a smile.

"Alright lass. But I want ya here tonight, deal?"

She shook her head and nudged my shoulder. "Okay. Deal, but I'll need some more clothes."

Leo

The alarm was loud and Henry's arm shot out and smacked the snooze button. He pulled me into his body and I sighed, completely relaxed. The sex had continued after we'd had a few drinks, some pizza as we ran lines, then I had been dragged back to my bed. He kissed my shoulder and neck, arms wrapping around me, and I smiled as this felt so damned good.

"And now the new job starts," he drawled sleepily.

I turned in his arms and kissed his lips, the nerves suddenly slamming every part of me. He must have felt it as he pressed me closer.

"I'm not going to out you, Sin. Just think about it. I won't let any fucking homophobic bastard hurt you," he whispered, his fingers languidly moving through my hair.

I snuggled into him, feeling safe and wanted. It was so fucking insane as we'd only just met, but this man? I wanted to keep him with me forever. His eyes were studying my face as he smiled and then captured my lips in another searing kiss.

"Thanks H." I whispered.

"I've been there to an extent. Coming out is fucking terrifying. And you have an extra complication. You're safe in my hands, sexy ass," and he kissed me again. "Now, we'd better get ready, as we both need a fucking shower because we reek of sex," he announced.

I laughed and climbed out, morning wood happily on show. Henry followed, his own cock standing to attention. I turned on the shower and Henry swiftly yanked me under the hot water, his hand wrapping around both of us.

"Relax and let me get us both off," and he kissed me.

I held onto him as the water cascaded over our naked bodies, Henry's hand swiftly fisting us, and I moaned into the crook of his neck, thrusting into his hand.

"Fuck, yes," I gasped.

"Fuck, Sin, I love your cock," he croaked.

He worked us both swiftly, our moans, sighs and grunts mingling with the running water. He crushed my mouth with his and devoured my lips, his movements picking up speed.

"Fuck, H, god, Oh... oh yes," I moaned into the crook of his neck.

"You close?" he croaked.

My hands gripped his shoulders and I groaned into his ear. "Yes, fuck, yes, so fucking... shit."

"Oh god, fuck," Henry moaned, his hand now working us both hard, desperately. "Shit, fuck," and we both exploded together.

"Jesus, H." I stammered.

He kissed me, languidly, his hand still working us until we were both empty. I held onto him, kissing his shoulder, neck and back to his mouth.

"Feel more relaxed now?"

"Yes, H. *Way* more relaxed," I purred into his ear.

He kissed me again, and I pressed myself into him, enjoying every single touch from Henry. "We'd better get ready. Don't want to be late on our first day," I whispered.

Henry smiled widely and ran his fingers through my wet hair. "No worries, Sin. Let me wash your hair?" he asked.

I grinned at this gorgeous naked guy and he winked, turning me around. His hands roamed up my spine and I sighed happily. "Okay," I replied.

Henry trailed kisses across the back of my shoulders as he explored my body sensually, and my head lolled back for a moment, loving his hands on me.

"And after this, I'm making us breakfast as I'm fucking starving," he announced.

As we walked into the quiet theatre, he nudged my shoulder and winked. "Stop looking so fucking terrified," he said. "I'm not going to out you. You have to do it yourself when you're ready."

He took my hand, gave it a squeeze and pecked my cheek. He then winked and smacked my ass, and walked in first. I started towards the door but a very familiar brunette flew out of the doors and slammed right into my chest.

"Shit, fucking hell," she gasped.

"Bloody hell, boss," I exclaimed, and her eyes lifted as she rubbed her nose.

She groaned and patted my arm. "Sorry, Leo. Need the bathroom," and she started to walk away, but stopped. "You and Henry?"

I dropped my eyes for a moment, then lifted them to find a boss who knew exactly what was going on.

"That's great and I'm happy for you," she said as she blatantly saw it in my face.

"We just clicked," I whispered.

"I saw that on Saturday night," and she started to walk away, but paused. "Please know that you can trust us. Because it must be extremely hard to hide your true self away all the time," and she winked before sprinting to the ladies.

I raked my hand over my face as I watched Sophie disappear, then I took a deep breath and pushed the door to the auditorium and stepped inside. Henry turned and winked at me as I strode down the aisle, and as I approached him, I knew I would have to make a difficult decision eventually. As there wasn't a chance in hell that we would be able to hide our feelings for each other for long.

"Sit with me?" he asked with that damned hot grin.

"Put him down," one of the female actors called.

She sauntered over and held out her hand. "Tara Madden," she said with a warm smile. "I see you've met this wicked devil?"

"Leo Trent," I replied. "And yes. Closing night of Midsummer. Ended up hanging out with Henry and Sophie's brother and boyfriend."

"Well, you've made the right choices in friends. They're a great bunch," she said. "Sophie and Max are great friends of mine too, along with Henry."

My nerves prickled as she sat down in front of us, but I felt the soft brush of Henry's fingers against my hand, and I turned to find his dark eyes trained on mine.

"Tara is a really great friend, Leo. Very trustworthy," and he winked.

I groaned, sinking into my seat as he took my hand in his. Tara just smiled knowingly, and in that moment, I understood what he meant.

"Are you as intuitive as Henry?" I questioned, skating around the real question I wanted to ask.

"Pretty much. I think that's why we get along so well. Can't hide a thing from each other," she replied.

Henry squeezed my hand and the warmth from that simple action calmed my nerves. "Tara has a strange sixth sense. Can't hide a fucking thing from this bitch face," Henry drawled.

"Oh really?" I said.

"Thanks for that, you queen," Tara fired at him, making him snort into laughter. "So don't worry, Leo. You can trust me," and she smiled warmly and winked, then turned to read through her script.

Henry leaned closer and whispered into my ear. "Relax, and don't worry. Let's just get on with our work," and he grinned, handing me my script.

I had to smile back as I took the manuscript, settling back in my chair and looking down to where Sophie had reappeared, chatting quietly to Darcy. Surely I could trust them? But, the terror that engulfed me won out, for now at least. So I opened up the play in my hands and got down to the job of going over lines.

Sophie

Darcy kissed me and gave me a swift hug before slapping my ass lightly. "Go get em, feisty pants," he whispered.

I snorted but stifled the giggle, and shot him a half hearted glare. He simply smirked which turned into a tender smile. I took a deep breath and turned to look over the new and familiar faces I was about to work with. It was a mixture of ages and talent ranges, so this was going to be interesting.

"Good morning," I started, and all eyes found mine. "Some of you I know," and I glanced at the trio sitting together, Henry grinning wickedly and Tara throwing me a little wave.

I rolled my eyes at the cheeky, yet very talented actors and carried on. "The rest of you don't know me, but you soon will. Three important things you need to know about me. I don't tolerate laziness, attitude and tardiness. That gets you a one way ticket to the job centre. Finally, my name is Sophie. Not Mrs or Miss Carter. Are we ready to get started?" and they all began to stand up, scripts in hands.

As I watched the cast climb the steps onto the stage the adrenalin kicked in as I walked down the aisle and stopped and gazed up at them all. Excitement coursed through me and I smiled to myself as I opened the script to '*Act 1*'.

Leo's voice suddenly appeared in my ear as he gave me a brief hug from behind. "Thanks for Saturday night. It was great," he said quietly.

"No problem, Trent. It was a lot of fun, and I had a right bloody headache the next day."

"I was okay. Henry walked me home. But, I was knackered the next day," he replied.

"Walked you home?" I asked, smiling at the slight blush on his face.

"Just that, filthy woman," he whispered.

I had to chuckle and I squeezed his hand with a cheeky wink. "And Max wants to do it again, so send him a message," I replied. "Because you can be yourself with the three of us and Darcy, and you need that until you decide," and he dropped his gaze for a moment.

"Thanks, Sophie. Means a lot," he said.

He dropped a light kiss on my cheek, then strolled up onto the stage, dropping onto the floor beside Henry.

We worked until lunchtime, and I was very satisfied with the talent coming through already. Henry and Tara I already knew, and they were amazingly talented. Darcy? Well, that man was gifted. He was like a chameleon in roles. The rest? There were some very new actors to professional work, including Leo. But, Mr Trent was *extremely* talented. He seemed to have the gift too. When he began acting in his scenes? Amazing.

I had even noticed Darcy watching him work with intense interest, and that was unusual, speaking volumes. Henry and Leo in their scenes? Simply stunning. They were going to be a hit, and in more ways than one. The chemistry sizzled between them in every single scene they were in.

"Can we run out for food, Sophie?" asked Asia Beckett.

I nodded and smiled. "Don't be long, as we're on a tight rehearsal schedule, okay?" I replied.

"Sure. It's literally minutes away. We'll be there and back in a flash," and she returned my smile.

Tara, Henry and Leo disappeared and I had to smile to myself as they had hit it off instantly. Darcy wrapped his arms around my waist and pressed me against him.

"Let me buy ya lunch, beautiful?" he whispered. "We'll be there and back in a flash?" and I rolled my eyes with a smirk.

I leaned back into him, and he dropped a kiss into the crook of my neck. "Fine, but we'd better go now. Celia?" and I glanced around to find my assistant director munching on a very healthy looking pasta salad.

"Yes, boss?" she replied with a cheeky grin.

"Clock anyone who's late will you? We're just heading out to get lunch."

"No problem. And Sophie?"

"Yes?"

"It's great to have you back where you belong," and she winked with a knowing smile.

"Thank you, Celia. It's great to *be* back," I replied.

"And I always knew Darcy was crushing on you," she said, a very wicked grin on her face.

I groaned and glanced up at my Irishman who was sporting a rather smug smirk on his sexy lips. I smacked his arm and threw Celia a glare.

"Ha bloody ha, Celia," I fired, but smirked at her.

Darcy waved at my assistant director as he chuckled, tugging me up the aisle as Celia's giggles echoed through the auditorium.

Chapter 12.

Darcy took my hand and dragged me up the aisle, through the lobby and out into the busy crowded London street.

"Hold ya horses Mr O'Sullivan," and we both whirled around to see a huge ruggedly handsome guy in a black suit and shirt.

Darcy grinned and walked back to the burly man. "Stefan, How are ya, fella?"

"Your agent sent me. I'm security."

I heard the Scottish accent and he winked at me as he caught me staring at the very distinct butt of a gun under his jacket. Darcy smacked the man mountain with a chuckle.

"She's off limits ya fecking flirt," he drawled.

"Apologies. Now where are you heading? And don't mind me, Miss?"

"Sophie, and please don't call me Miss."

I held out my hand and he shook it with a polite nod. "Noted, Sophie. After the two of you," and Darcy patted his arm, then set off down the street.

He didn't seem to care about the stares from passersby or the phones snapping away. He simply ignored the attention and held onto me tightly until we stopped in front of a cute cafe.

"This makes the best food, lass. Ya gonna love it."

Stefan remained outside as Darcy led me inside, and the woman behind the counter lit up like a Christmas tree.

"Darcy O'Sullivan," she beamed, and the Irish accent washed over me as he stopped at the counter.

"Hello lass," he said warmly.

"And this pretty bare?" she asked.

The word '*bare*' piqued my interest and I frowned a little in confusion, but Darcy simply tucked me into his side and grinned like a Cheshire cat.

"Me girlfriend, Stella. Me oul' doll from now on," he replied, then touched my lips with his.

"Well, that's lovely news, Darcy. I'm happy for ya. Ya want *two* of ya usual?" she asked.

"Please, lass. That'd be grand."

Once she disappeared I nudged him and said, "What does '*bare*' mean? And what the hell are we eating?"

"One of the best sanger's you'll ever taste," he replied. "And bare means woman."

"Oh, right," I said. "Oul' doll?"

"Me woman. Girlfriend, lass."

I snorted into giggles and smacked his shoulder. "Sounded like fucking old, O'Sullivan," I fired at him.

He smirked and tilted my chin before capturing my lips in a tender kiss. "Ya not old, love. Ya sexy and fecking gorgeous," and he smiled, pulling me in for a hug. "What are ya thinking about?" he asked, his eyes studying my face intently.

"Just how strange it still is. You know? Being called your girlfriend in public, well anywhere if I'm honest," I replied, smiling back.

"Ya'd better get used to it, beautiful," he said, and kissed me again. "Because ya mine forever now, lass."

I heard the whispers around us and I nudged his shoulder. He simply winked and pulled me closer. I huddled into him, trying to ignore them too.

"Here ya go, Darcy, love. And don't you two make an adorable pair."

"Thanks, lass. And we do, don't we," and he winked at her and chuckled as he paid.

He grabbed the paper bag and started for the door, but as we were about to leave, a young woman let out a loud squeal.

"Oh my god," she gasped.

We both turned to see two young women practically drooling where they stood. Darcy let loose his famous heart stopping smile and they giggled, blushing furiously.

"Oh god, please can we have a selfie with you?" one of them asked.

"Sure lass," he drawled, his famous persona locked in place.

He stood between them and took a couple, then handed the phone back. "God, thank you Mr O'Sullivan."

"Ya welcome, lass." he replied.

As we were about to leave, the other shyer girl spoke. "Are you his girlfriend?"

I turned and smiled up at him first, then over to the two fans. "Yes I am. And I feel very lucky."

Darcy chuckled and shook his head, pulling me closer. "*I'm* the lucky one. Have a grand day ladies," and he winked as I was ushered from the cafe.

Stefan was waiting and he smiled with a wink as we appeared. "Ready to go?"

"Sure thing, fella," and we swiftly made our way back to the theatre.

I glanced up at the sexy actor. "How are you lucky, Darcy?" I asked as we walked hand in hand.

He simply chuckled and squeezed a little. "Because, beautiful, I fecked this up all those years ago and I thought I'd lost ya, but I got a second chance to be with the only bare I've ever really loved," and he winked at me with his cheeky, pussy fluttering smile.

And shit, he had been bloody right, three weeks was going to feel like a lifetime. Fucking hell.

Leo

Tara and Henry had pulled me into the backstage area, as Tara had been out and bought us all lunch. We sat in one of the empty dressing rooms and Tara closed the door. Then she handed out our sandwiches, salad bowls and drinks. Henry didn't hesitate and pulled me into his body, munching happily on his food and I smiled at him, then glanced at Tara.

"Thanks for the food, Tara."

"You're very welcome. Henry's turn tomorrow," and she chuckled.

"We'll be making a pack up from mine then," Henry drawled.

"Cheap skate," she replied, making Henry chuckle.

Tara didn't say much as we started eating, but I felt her eyes on the two of us. Henry was very relaxed in her presence as his hand gently caressed my thigh.

"Are you going to spill? As it's obvious that the two of you are way more than friends?" she finally said.

"I'm keeping this one," Henry simply said with a mouthful of food.

She arched her brows and smirked as she chewed. I dropped my gaze and focused on my food, nerves firing on all cylinders.

"Keeping him?" she pressed.

"Yep. Man of my dreams right here," and my eyes snapped up to stare at him in surprise as Tara almost choked.

I turned around and locked eyes, but he just winked with that fucking beautiful smile. "You're not fucking joking are you?" I fired at him.

"Nope. And I wasn't joking yesterday when I said it," Henry threw back.

My head whipped around to Tara and she was watching us intently. "You've already had sex havent you?" she asked.

I groaned and took a huge bite out of the delicious turkey sub, my cheeks flushing furiously. Henry simply sat up and dropped a kiss at the base of my neck.

"Yes. And it was off the fucking charts sensational. All night, and this morning? I gave my sinful angel a little release before today," he answered.

"Fuck, H. Don't hold back," I groaned again.

Tara sat forward and smiled at me. "Henry has no filter when he's with people he's comfortable with. But, I feel like you're afraid of something? Because you are hiding this aren't you?" and I stared at her with a creased brow.

"You don't hold back either do you?" I muttered, hand rubbing my face.

"Nope. Why can't you be open?" she asked.

I felt Henry tense behind me, his arm suddenly wrapping around my waist protectively. I finished the sub and wiped my face, then took a deep breath.

"My dad and a few of his friends are extremely homophobic," I said, my voice wavering as I remembered discussions I'd overheard.

"That makes my blood boil," Henry growled.

"Mine too. But, it has to be bad to hide this?" said Tara.

I took a swig of the water and sighed, leaning back into Henry's embrace. "I overheard him a few times. They talked about beating sense into the '*sick bastards*'. I'd just started noticing things about myself around the time, and that statement terrified me. One of his friends said he'd happily castrate every last one of them then string them all up."

No-one spoke for a few charged moments, so I continued. "I heard dad saying that he'd enjoy watching that. I remember the day he sat me and my sister down and told us, in no uncertain terms, that he'd beat us senseless if we turned out '*that way*', so I hid it. I was sixteen when I truly knew that I was gay. But dad had put the fear of God into us, especially me."

"So, I've been living a lie ever since. I had a boyfriend for a while, but he dumped me when I told him I couldn't tell my parents yet. He didn't understand. It wasn't until I went to University when I had my first real gay experiences, but I didn't dare have an actual relationship, because I didn't want dad to find out about me. So I never went home for holidays, except Christmas and summer."

Henry pulled me into a hug, kissing me, holding me tightly. "Would he still do that now? You know, beat you?" asked Tara.

"I honestly don't know," I replied.

Tara stood up and came over, crouching down in front of the two of us. "Look, Leo, I get it so your secret is safe. And I know this one won't say a word either. And, well, you two are cute together, but you *will* have to tell everyone eventually, because it'll become obvious that you two are a couple."

I nodded, smiling gratefully, and Henry crushed me closer. "That's a point, Sin, because you're all mine now."

"Sin?" Tara questioned.

"Yes. He's a sinful devil all wrapped up in heavenly packaging don't you think?" he drawled.

I chuckled as my cheeks warmed again, and Tara laughed, patting my shoulder. "He's kind of right, Leo. If I were a guy and a few years younger," and she winked.

I laughed, hand raking through my hair, tugging out the hair tie holding it in its messy bun. "Thanks Tara."

"No need."

I snuggled back into Henry's body as I finished the last of my salad bowl, and at this moment I'd never felt so happy and relaxed.

"We'd better get back," Tara said.

I glanced down at Henry's watch and sat up. "Yes. Don't want to be late."

We walked towards the auditorium, but Henry stopped me before we entered. Tara winked and left us alone, then I was tugged into Henry's body, his lips landing on mine, kissing me greedily.

It was swift, then he smiled. "Stay at mine tonight?" he asked.

"I'd need some stuff, H. You sure?"

"Fuck, Sin. You know how I feel. So, we'll call at your place and pick up some stuff. Then you're coming home with me."

"Okay. Deal," I replied.

Henry nudged me towards the stage, smacking my ass . "Go Sin. I'll be there in a minute, and his hand went to his crotch.

I grinned and nudged his shoulder lightly before I stepped out of the wings. Minutes later Henry sauntered out and straight over to Tara and me. As we started to get ready to start again, my phone pinged and it was an unknown number. I frowned, but opened it.

"*Hey Leo. It's your Eve. Just hope you're okay after that guy attacked you?*

Let's grab a drink this week because I miss you honey. What day works best for you?

Yours forever. Eve Xxx."

I froze as I read it again, then swore. "Jesus fucking Christ. How the hell did she get my number?"

Henry turned and frowned in confusion, so I showed him the message. His eyes darkened and he let out a very bloody sexy growl.

"She doesn't know when to quit," he hissed. "Attacking you? Jesus fucking hell, the bitch."

I raked my hand through my hair again, then glanced around the theatre. “I want to know how she got my fucking number. I didn’t give it to her.”

Henry looked ready to explode, but we were in the theatre. A part of me wanted to fight the urge, but I gave in, not happy with the look in his eyes. I moved on instinct and pulled him in for a hug. His whole body was tense but he suddenly relaxed as I held him.

“This isn’t fair,” he whispered. “She’s fucking nuts.”

I felt the stares, and suddenly stepped away from him, glancing around the room. Not one person looked surprised, they looked as though they already knew. I groaned and stood up tall.

“What? I’m just giving him a hug?” I exclaimed.

“No issue here, Leo,” Zane stated.

“Not a one, dude,” Asia said.

“It was just a fucking hug,” I fired, panic gripping my heart.

The murmurs echoed around the room, then I was yanked back into Henry’s arms as the all too familiar terror erupted in my chest.

Sophie

Something was wrong and Leo looked like a deer in headlights as the rest of the cast were staring at them. Darcy noticed too, but I was already striding towards him.

“What’s wrong?” I asked.

Leo didn’t say anything as Henry released him. His eyes were on everyone else, and their attention was focused on him.

“They all know? Oh god, he’ll find out,” and he started to back up.

Tara was behind him and stopped him in his tracks, but he looked as though he was about to throw up. I needed to speak to him in private, because something had clearly happened to both upset Leo and cause the rage in Henry's eyes.

"Start running lines. Now, and I don't want to tell you all twice," I ordered the cast.

They jumped into action but I could feel their sly glances, so I shot them all a glare, and they knew. I grabbed Leo's hand and gestured with my head to Henry.

"With me. Now. Celia, take over until I get back," and I marched them from the auditorium and into the empty bar.

"Sit down," I ordered.

Henry dropped into a chair and he tugged Leo into the one next to him, holding tightly to his hand.

"I want to know what the fuck is going on, Leo. Please tell me? The colour left your face way too bloody fast," I said.

"I can't, shit, he'll find out," he stammered.

"Find out?" I asked.

"He'll hurt me," Leo whispered, and I didn't like the look of sheer terror on his face.

He was engulfed in Henry's arms as the tears formed in the corners of his eyes. "If they all know? It's going to get back to dad," he whispered.

I frowned but I saw the rage in Henry's face. "He's not going to fucking touch you," he hissed, crushing Leo into his body.

"Tell me, please?" I asked. "Why are you so terrified?"

Darcy appeared, hovering by the door, a frown adorning his face. "I'm sorry, but why are ya worried about ya dad finding out?" he asked.

Leo's head snapped up and he glared at him with such intensity I thought he might punch him. "Did *your* dad think it was fine to castrate all gay men? Did your dad and friends laugh about beating gay men into a fucking pulp?" he snapped.

Darcy's eyes widened in surprise and he shoved his hands into his pockets. "No, Leo. He really said that?" he asked.

The young actor sat up and looked down at his hand in Henry's and nodded. "Yeah. Him and his mental friends talked about stringing up all gay men and beating them with fucking bats. He called us sick and twisted, and that's why I'm terrified of him finding out."

"Why?" I questioned. "What would he do to you?"

Leo let out a sigh, his hand flying through his hair. "When we were thirteen he sat us down and literally said he'd beat it out of us if we turned out that way," he answered.

"Shit," I groaned.

Darcy took a few steps closer and touched his shoulder. "Ya know, talk like that gets people arrested these days. Sorry, fella."

"Sorry for snapping at you. Dad's a scary bastard. He put the fear of God into us when we were kids," he said quietly.

I gazed at the two loved up actors and sighed. This was turning out to be another drama filled play. Leo looked over at me, then up at Darcy.

"You guessed it, didn't you?" he asked my Irishman.

He smiled and gave him a nod. "Yes. Ya know me reputation with the fairer sex. And the old Darcy would have definitely gone for Blaine. Ya never batted an eye at her, Eve or Melissa."

"Lissy's gay too. Found that out when she introduced me to her wife during rehearsals," Leo replied. "That's why we got on so well. That pressure wasn't there."

Henry pressed Leo closer and I let out a long sigh. "So what got you so spooked in there, to threaten outing yourself," I asked.

Leo suddenly groaned and pulled out his phone. He opened up his messages and handed it over to me. "I think I have a problem, Sophie."

I read the message and frowned, looking back up at them. "When were you attacked?" I asked in confusion.

Henry pulled Leo onto his lap, holding him close, then gritted his teeth, jaw muscles clenching as Leo took his hand.

"No-one did. Eve wouldn't fucking leave me alone. I never gave her any signs that I was interested in her. Then she called me her bloody boyfriend so I stormed out of the bar. Henry followed me out and saw right bloody through me," and he paused.

"I noticed and I think Pedro figured it out," said Darcy. "Ya never gave the girls a second glance."

Henry smirked and Leo rolled his eyes. "Yeah. He called me out on it in the interval of the final show, then pointed out that this one was eyeing up my ass," and the dark haired devil grinned, and snuggled his head into Leo's neck.

"You have a very fucking sexy ass, Sin," he drawled.

"So, why did Eve say ya were attacked?" asked Darcy, getting them back onto the issue.

Leo ran a hand down his face and rolled his shoulder as he flinched at the mention of her name. "We were on the balcony with Max and Teagen. She bloody found me, so H kissed me as she got to us. I told her I was fucking gay, but I had a weird sinking feeling that she didn't believe me."

As I looked down at the message it pinged again. "Shit," I muttered.

"What lass?" asked Darcy.

"She's a borderline stalker," Leo muttered. "And she sent me that, saying Henry was attacking me."

I raked my hand through my hair, releasing it from its ponytail. Darcy walked over and sat behind me, pulling my stool backwards towards him.

"She's sent another," I said.

Leo's face fell as Henry looked ready to commit murder. "Read it out loud, lass," Darcy said.

I looked at the young blonde and his eyes held a mixture of rage and frustration and he simply nodded with a sigh.

"Okay. '*How about we go for a drink this weekend and catch up. I've missed you, and I can kiss that guy off you. Your Eve xxx*'. Well, she definitely didn't get the message," I stated.

It pinged again and I frowned as I read the next message. "Shit, Leo. She *really* didn't get the message. This says '*I love you, honey. See you soon*'," and he swore under his breath.

"Fuck."

"Jesus fucking Christ, she's bloody nuts," Henry growled.

"Tell Sophie her last name, Leo," Darcy said.

"Hemlock. Eve Hemlock," Leo said.

My eyes darted from Darcy to Henry, and it was clear we all had the same thought. "Fitting. As she seems poisonous. Block her. Now," I said, passing him the phone back. "Do not reply."

Leo was swift and put the phone back onto the table.

Darcy kissed me and stood up. "Alright, fella. Don't worry ya self. Ya safe in this theatre," and he patted Leo's shoulder. "I'd better get back into the auditorium, lass," and he disappeared.

I sat quietly for a few moments, not quite believing that I had to deal with a potential stalker on top of everything else. Henry looked livid and Leo looked both terrified and angry at the situation he had found himself in.

"Okay. You two are just adorable and I'm thrilled for you. But, I am concerned about this Eve, and your dad. Is either of them likely to show up here to cause trouble?" I asked.

Leo sighed, looked at Henry and then back at me. "I don't know. I wouldn't put it past Eve to show up because she knows about this job. She was there when I was telling Lissy about it."

I glanced at the door where Darcy had disappeared through, a thought forming in my head. "And your dad? You know, if he found out, would he show up here too?" I questioned.

Leo's face flashed with a deep seated fear of a man that had instilled the terror in him from a young age. The anger I felt was immense, and I wanted to hug the young actor.

"I don't know. I mean, he's always been a tough son of a bitch, and he was always built like a truck. Spent loads of time in the garage where he'd set up his own gym, but I haven't seen him in a fair few years. He was very vocal about his hatred of gay people though, that's why I've kept it a secret, Sophie."

I took his hand and squeezed. "Look, here in this theatre? You are my priority, so don't worry," and I stood up. "I've got an idea, okay? Be back in the theatre in five minutes. No later," then I strode out of the bar and back to the auditorium.

Darcy was waiting for me and I was pulled into a hug. "Well, that was a revelation, right?" he whispered.

"Yep. And it's day bloody one," I muttered.

"If we get ahead of it, it can be nipped in the bud, lass."

I sighed in frustration as we walked back towards the auditorium. "Can you organise some extra security? You know? Being the great and sexy, famous Irishman that you are? As I'm not happy with only having your Scottish man mountain as our only security."

He smirked as his brows shot up. "I get ya, lass. I'll call Christian. And Stefan will enjoy being called a mountain," and he pulled me in for a very swift yet heated kiss.

"Thanks, as I need to protect my actors too. And that's because he is."

He chuckled and kissed my forehead, then he pressed me into his body, holding me for a few minutes. He laced our fingers together as we approached the doors.

"Come on, beautiful. Let's get back to work," and he led me back inside to get back to the amazing play we were working on.

Chapter 13.

Two days later

Leo

I waltzed into the auditorium, Henry not far behind and we found Tara, Zane and Asia. There were no signs of our director and Darcy yet, or the other members of the cast. We had organised a night out tonight with Max and Teagen, and I was really looking forward to being able to drop the pretence.

"Morning," said Tara.

"Morning, gorgeous," drawled Henry, and he winked with a cheeky smile.

"Hey Tara," I said, and smiled at the others.

Zane seemed to be studying me intensely, a look of curiosity in his eyes. I turned away and sat next to my man. Henry subtly stroked my thigh as he stared down at his script. We'd spent every night together since we'd met, and there were already various clothes and possessions appearing in each other's places. The sex was off the charts amazing too. Being with him felt as though I'd finally found home.

"Zane's staring at us," I whispered.

"So? He probably fancies you."

"What?" and I turned and looked at the man I was addicted to like a fucking drug.

Henry chuckled, his hand roaming higher up my leg. "He's gay. Haven't you noticed that he's made friends with all the girls, but hasn't approached us yet?"

I relaxed back in my seat, enjoying Henry's touches and smiled. "And that makes sense," I said quietly, and he chuckled again, making me smile as I stared at my lines.

The voice rang out through the auditorium and my spine locked up as I tensed in my chair. Henry whizzed around and the hatred in his eyes blazed like wildfire.

"Leo? Hey honey, I thought we could get some food together?" she called out.

"What the actual fuck?" Henry growled.

My heart lurched and hands balled into fists, as this could go horribly wrong for me. Zane, however, suddenly locked eyes on me, throwing me a very knowing smile, then grabbed Asia and suggested they go grab some bottles of water, and that told me one thing. He'd guessed that Henry and I were a couple.

Shit, shit, shit.... And this fucking bitch.

"Oh, hey you. Guessing you haven't got my messages yet?" Eve said in that irritatingly silky tone. "I've missed you, honey. Let's go and grab some breakfast. Away from *him*."

Henry was on his feet, stalking towards her, but I moved like lightning and grabbed his wrist. He would throttle her if he got the chance.

"Jesus, woman. What the fuck is wrong with you?" he snapped. "He's not fucking interested."

"You should be arrested for what you did to Leo," she hissed. "He's not gay at all. We were getting on fine before you appeared and spoiled it. He's mine, not yours."

I groaned and shot to my feet, turning to glare at the crazy cow I seemed to have acquired. I fixed my eyes on hers and she actually beamed at me, seemingly thinking she'd won something.

"Come on honey. Let's go and get breakfast and then we can get on with our life together," she purred.

I glared at her as Henry almost combusted where he stood. "Jesus Christ, Eve, there was never anything between us, for fuck's sake. How many different ways can I say it. You're the wrong fucking sex." I growled at her.

"No, I'm not. We are a couple, Leo. So, leave *him* here and come and get some food with your girlfriend," she whined.

Henry made to step closer, but I tugged on his wrist again. "Don't, H. She's just a bloody nut job. Fuck off, Eve. Leave me alone," I said quietly.

"Why? Because *he* told you to say that? Let's go get a coffee and get on with our life, honey. You and me forever," and she took a step closer.

"Are you fucking stupid?" Henry fired.

"Leo, come on?" she said, her gaze locked on me.

I pulled Henry into me and hugged him tightly. "I've got this, babe. Just try to stay calm, okay?" I whispered into his ear.

He simply crushed me into his body, the anger coursing through him like a hurricane.

"Leo? What are you doing? Let's go," she whined. "Stop hugging him."

I released him and Tara had sauntered our way. She took Henry's hand and held it while I glared at the crazy person in front of me.

"Everything okay here?" she asked.

"That perve is trying to steal my Leo," whined Eve.

Tara's eyes narrowed a little as she studied the brunette. "Henry isn't a pervert, young lady. He's a very beautiful soul. And my friend, so watch what you're saying."

Eve glared at Tara and reached out for my hand, which I swiftly yanked from her reach. "Leo is *my* boyfriend. And *he* is poisoning him against me," she snapped.

There was a dangerous rage behind Eve's eyes that I really didn't like. Henry took a step towards her, but I stopped him, touching his shoulder. "H, babe, look at me," I whispered. "Look at me, Henry."

His eyes flickered up and met mine, and he relaxed as I gave him a tender smile. I turned to the crazy girl and took a deep breath. I gripped her shoulders roughly and glared at her.

"I want you to fucking hear me, you stupid girl. I. Am. Gay. I am attracted to men. I sleep with men. I fuck men. You are the wrong fucking sex. Get it through your thick skull. I was never into you. I was acting, you know? What we do for a living? So leave me and my boyfriend the fuck alone, or I'll call the damned police and have you physically removed."

Her eyes flickered with some sort of recognition, then the damned shutters went down and she scrunched up her face, anger and frustration seeping into her expression. She whipped her eyes from my face and glared at Henry, and I knew this wasn't going to be good.

"This is your doing. You've brainwashed him. Trying to steal my boyfriend," she seethed. "This isn't over."

She reached for my face and rose up on her tip toes, trying to kiss me, but I backed away from her, making her let out a high pitched squeal. "Leo, honey. Kiss me," she whined.

I rolled my eyes and rubbed my face. How the fuck did I end up with a psycho woman who was obsessed with me?

Jesus Christ, this was messed up.

"No, Eve. I'm not your fucking boyfriend. Never have been. That's in your fucked up head, for god's sake. Just leave me the fuck alone," I yelled, and I turned and grabbed Henry's beautiful face and slammed my lips onto his, kissing him like a starving man.

I heard her shriek echo through the auditorium, her hands suddenly grabbing my t-shirt, yanking at it, trying to pull me away from my man.

"Stop it. That's disgusting. I'm your girlfriend Leo. I can't let this sick man get his claws into you," she screeched. "I'll help you, honey."

Henry broke the kiss and stalked around me, and even though I tried to stop him, he kept going. She backed up as he ended up in front of her. His hand flew out and he dug his finger into her shoulder with practically every word.

"You are a fucking psychotic little cow, Eve. Leo is not fucking interested in you. Now turn your crazy little ass around and get the fuck away from him before he slaps a restraining order on you for fucking stalking," he growled.

She let out a high pitched squeak, then hissed at him. Taking a few steps back, Eve fixed her eyes on me and then Henry.

"I'll get you help Leo honey. This guy's abusing you," then her hand flew out and she slapped Henry's cheek. "You're a disgusting pervert," she fired at him, then she spun around and sprinted up the aisle just as Darcy and Sophie appeared, and she shoved past them before disappearing through the doors.

"What the hell?" gasped our director.

Darcy stared after the bitch as she vanished then his eyes narrowed as he looked over at the three of us.

"Was that who I think it was?" he asked.

"The fucking bitch slapped me," Henry growled.

I grabbed a hold of his hand and pulled him to me, my arms flying around him, holding onto him tightly.

They walked down to us and surveyed the state of both me and Henry. I was engulfed with Henry's strong arms as he crushed me into him. I could feel him trembling in my arms, and the tears pricked the corners of my eyes as I tried to climb inside of him.

"Why me?" I stammered.

"What the hell just happened?" asked Sophie.

"Eve fucking Hemlock," growled Henry. "And Leo has a serious problem."

Max

Leo and Henry were sitting on our sofa, drinks in hand and they had filled us in on the crazy girl, Eve. Now, we were looking at her social media and it was at that moment we realised Leo did indeed have a serious problem.

"She's got photo's of you at the coffee shop, the pub and coming in and out of your fucking house. She's following you," I said, showing him her pages.

"Fucking hell," he muttered. "She really is stalking me."

Henry let out a groan and pulled Leo closer as I scrolled through more of her posts. Teagen was checking her other pages and he let out a whistle.

"She's set her relationship status to '*In a relationship with Leo Trent*'. There's pictures of you on here from your last job. She's making it out as though she's taken them. Is this your front door?" my boyfriend said.

"Fuck, yes it is," Leo croaked.

"She's dangerous," I said, watching the rage dance behind his blue eyes.

I looked at Leo's page and she had indeed saved them or screenshot them and added them to her own page. I raked my hands over my face and through my hair.

"You should get in touch with the police, Leo. This is dangerous," I said.

Leo threw his jack and coke back and stood up. "I can't, Max. If I do that it's more likely that my dad will find out that I'm gay," he said.

I frowned and looked at Teagen then Henry. I kissed my man and followed Leo to the kitchen. He was pouring a very strong measure and I leaned against the counter as he filled his glass with cola.

"What's the deal with your dad?" I asked.

He didn't answer right away, his shoulders slumping as he stared down at his glass. "He's really homophobic, Max. He once sat me and my sister down and threatened to beat the shit out of us if we ended up gay. We were thirteen, for fucks sake. He's been in prison for almost beating a guy to death after he put his hands on mum's ass," and he finally turned and gazed over at me. "I'm so scared that he'll find out because he might turn up on my doorstep and hurt us," and his eyes moved to Henry.

The way he was looking at the actor made me smile a little, but I gave his arm a light touch. He smiled back and picked up his glass.

"You think he'll do that?" I asked. "You're a grown up now, and you should be allowed to live your life any way you want. And fall for anyone you want to."

There was a flicker of what I could only describe as fear. Pure unadulterated terror. His dad had seriously scared the crap out of him.

"You were really lucky. You have a bunch of friends and family that love and support you. Mum and my sister have to pretend they don't fucking know about me, and it kills me. It's the main reason why I never go home these days," he replied. "Why me, Max? Why did I have to get a fucking crazy stalker? She doesn't realise what she's fucking doing. Dad could turn up and," but he stopped, his voice cracking.

I grabbed his hand and yanked him in for a swift hug. "You're not alone anymore. You've got Teagen and me. And Henry is hooked on you. I think you really bloody like him too?" I said with a grin.

"Thanks Max."

"For?"

"Being a great friend. I'm so happy when we come over to yours."

"But, you should feel like that *all* the time," I said.

He gave me a sad smile and leaned against the counter. "Dad is a scary bastard. His friends are too. I want to be myself, but I can't yet. I'm really scared."

I hated the terror in Leo's face. It wasn't fucking right to make your own child hide who they truly were. I nudged his shoulder and smiled.

"Okay. Well, let's make sure your crazy stalker doesn't do anything else fucking nuts," and gestured for him to follow me back to our boyfriends.

Two and a half weeks later...

Darcy

Rehearsals were going grand after the first few day's events. Sophie stayed at my place, and I'd stayed at hers. Safe to say it had been tense the first time. Max was cold and closed off, and I understood why. I'd hurt his sister in the worst fucking way, but he seemed to warm to me as we figured out a way to help Leo.

His stalker girl had caused a scene on day three, so security now joined us at the theatre everyday since. Radio silence had ensued, but it didn't stop Leo being on edge. Henry never left his side and the rumours were flying around the cast. It was obvious that they were together and the cast had been caught whispering a few times. Sophie and I just needed him to trust us with his secret, as we all wanted to help.

I awoke to find a half naked Sophie draped over me, and I didn't want to move. Since that Sunday night? I'd woken up to this delectable beauty, and each time? I wanted to just revel in the feeling of her body flush against my own. But, my bladder won out each fucking time.

Well, that and the huge morning wood. It was taking every last shred of willpower I had to stop from pinning her down and fucking her all day, all night. Shite, all damned week. After relieving myself I slipped back into bed and pulled her into my arms, and she let out a little moan, then shuffled to get comfortable.

"What time is it?" she asked sleepily.

"Just after eight, love," I whispered.

"You're itching to work out aren't you?"

"Ya know me too well, and I'm desperate to feck ya," I replied.

She snorted into giggles and buried her face into my chest. "And who's fault is that?" she teased, gently stroking her hand over my abs.

"Very funny," I growled.

Sophie suddenly started to kiss down my chest, and my cock pulsed as she got lower. "What are ya doing, love?" I hissed.

"Relieving the tension," she simply replied.

I stared down as she freed my cock, then her hand wrapped around the base of my shaft, and I couldn't fucking breathe. My gaze dropped to watch her as her tongue darted out and licked the precum from my tip, and I groaned, the divine feeling making my toes fucking curl.

"Feck, lass," I gasped, gripping the sheets in my fists.

But, I was not prepared when she covered my entire shaft, right to the back of her throat. My entire body burst into flame as I watched, unable to take my eyes from my gorgeous woman taking my cock deep, saliva dripping onto my dark curls nestled around the base, then her hand cupped my balls and I rammed the pillow over my face, stifling the moan coming out of me.

"Jesus, holy mary mother of god," I cried, then moved the pillow because I needed to watch her.

Sophie had seriously taken me by surprise.

I had given her orgasms with my fingers since we'd gotten together again, but this was the first time my sexy woman had taken me in her mouth, and fucking hell, she had become skilled as she relaxed her throat around me, and my hips bucked up into her.

"Feck, yes, lass, yes, Sophiemefeckinggod, yes," spilled out of my lips as my climax came racing towards me.

I gripped her hair, fisting tightly, then fucked her talented mouth. My entire body was on fire, my orgasm building, balls drawing up as I stared at my little director taking my cock like a damned champion. All control suddenly flew out of the window as I thrust roughly, chasing my release, grunts and moans falling from me as the need to come in her mouth overwhelmed me.

"Yes, lass, feck, I'm gonna ... Jesus, God," and I exploded right at the back of her throat, and she didn't stop until she'd sucked me dry, then popped off and grinned up at me.

"Better?" she asked, her eyes dancing with wickedness.

"Jesus, love. Didn't expect that."

"I didn't make any deals to keep *my* hands or mouth to myself," and she kissed her way back upwards, over my stomach, chest, finishing at my mouth.

"Ya didn't. That was me own dumb fecking decision," I admitted.

She giggled as she nuzzled her face into my neck then she gazed down at me with her dark brown eyes.

"Still sticking to it?" she asked.

"I'm a man a me word, lass," I replied.

But, after Sophie's fucking amazing surprise? I had to have a taste of her too, so I flipped her over, making her giggle. She looked so fucking stunning with her messy bed hair, sexy curves, flushed cheeks and that stunning smile, and Jesus, I wanted to make her cry out my name too, so I grinned at her with a wink.

"Cheeky aren't ya, Sophie love?" I growled. "I only said that I wouldn't feck ya with me cock."

I grabbed the t-shirt and yanked it over her head, groaning as she was naked underneath.

"True," she purred, and I kissed down between her gorgeous breasts, caressing them as I did. "Oh shit," she moaned as I took her hardened nipple into my mouth and rolled my tongue around it, pinching the other between my fingers.

"Do ya want me to taste ya, lass?" I asked, slowly making my way down over her stomach, hip and inwards towards her stunning pussy.

"Fucking hell, yes," she gasped as I eased her legs open.

I grinned as Sophie was glistening and my eyes gazed hungrily at the sight. "Yes ya do, don't ya," I breathed.

"Yes, god please, Darcy," she moaned.

"Then, allow me, beautiful." and I licked the full length of her making her yelp and arch off the bed.

"Oh my god," she gasped again.

The sweet taste of her hit my tongue and it sent a jolt of electricity flying through me and straight to my fucking cock. The groan was loud as I descended on her clit, hands hooked around her thighs, keeping her open for me.

"Jesus Christ, yes," she cried out, then grabbed the same pillow I had used, to muffle her moans.

And holy hell, I was home, and I never wanted to fucking leave.

Chapter 14.

Sophie

The groan that fell from him made my heart race, desperate for his talented lips and tongue. He didn't hold back and he licked and nipped enthusiastically, making my whole body writhe under his ravenous onslaught.

I gasped, cursed and moaned into the pillow as my climax sparked to life deep down inside my belly.

"Fuck," I croaked as his finger slipped inside, his thumb replacing his mouth for a moment, and I removed the pillow to look down.

"I've missed ya lass," he croaked.

I smiled as he winked and pushed a second finger in, and my head flew back against the pillows.

"Oh my god, Darcy, shit," I yelped, trying to stay quiet, but his tongue went back to my clit, and I couldn't breathe.

It started in the pit of my stomach and blazed outwards, my hands flying to Darcy's luscious onyx hair, fingers gripping hold as I started to ride his face.

"Darcy.... Shit... I'm gonna... Yesgodyes," and my entire body locked up as I came undone, my orgasm ripping through me like a tsunami.

My body arched off the bed as the pleasure rocked through every muscle, a long moan falling from my lips as his tongue continued to swirl and lick, teasing my clit as I shook with each delicious wave.

He didn't let up until I slowly stopped shaking, slumping back into the bed, then he kissed upwards, back over my hip, stomach, pausing at my breasts. Then he looked up and smiled lazily.

"That was fecking divine love," he drawled.

I chuckled and relaxed back, very happy and satisfied. "Get up here and kiss me, sexy ass," I ordered.

He laughed and joined me, his handsome face appearing above me. "How can I say no to the bare I'm madly in fecking love with," he whispered, then did as I'd asked, kissing me deeply, lovingly and I sighed happily into his mouth, tasting myself on his lips.

He stroked his finger down my cheek, eyes gazing down into mine, and I smiled. "You okay there, handsome?" I asked.

"I love ya lass," he simply whispered. "And today we get ya a gown for the premiere," then he jumped out of bed and disappeared into the bathroom.

I loved that he never waited for me to return those three words, and I smiled as I watched his naked self in my bathroom. During the last two and a half weeks Darcy had been a saint.

He had only acted when I prompted him, and it wasn't until the end of the first week that we moved forward and Darcy's fingers had given me the first amazing orgasm since my Jake.

And now? I was desperate for him to fuck me, just as he'd bloody predicted.

I chuckled quietly and climbed out of the bed too. Darcy was now in the shower and I couldn't help but stare at his muscular frame, how the water rolled over the defined lines of his chest, abs and that divine shapely ass of his.

"Ya want to join me?" he suddenly called out, and I grinned.

"Just enjoying the show."

"Afraid ya can't resist me, love?"

"Is that a challenge?"

"Yep."

I got to my feet and strolled towards the door, and his eyes darkened, watching each step. I noticed his dick slowly stand to attention, and I smirked.

"Shall we see, O'Sullivan?" and I opened the door, steam escaping into the bathroom, then I stepped inside.

Max

Teagen was acting weird today. Shady as fuck, and I didn't like it one damned bit. We'd had sex last night, then he'd disappeared into the shower before I woke up, which was very unusual. We normally cuddled before going to get breakfast together then shower.

Shady as fuck.

I was also beginning to get used to Darcy O' Sullivan being here. It had been so fucking weird bumping into him that first morning in our kitchen. Awkward too as we were both wearing boxers and nothing else. He did seem to be a changed man these days, and he made Sophie glow again, so I'd bitten the bullet and decided to give him a chance. I was now sitting watching the TV as Teagen came into the living room, and he walked to the kitchen and started to make coffee.

"T?" I said, worry gripping my heart.

"Yeah, baby?" he asked.

I sat up and turned to look at my soulmate, the love of my life, and watched him, his back to me. That was the moment I noticed the tension in his shoulders.

"Have I done something wrong?" I questioned.

He whirled around and the look of surprise in his eyes gave me a jolt of hope. "What? No? Jesus, shit, no baby."

I got to my feet and walked to him, his eyes seemingly on high alert, as though he were hiding something.

"Then why are you acting so fucking weirdly, babe?" I asked.

He let out a groan and ran his hand over his face, then yanked me into his arms, hugging me tightly. "Sorry baby, I just, well, I wanted to take you for lunch, make it special, but I'm so fucking wired that I can't wait," came tumbling from him.

I frowned, totally confused, so I stroked his spine tenderly, as I knew it soothed and relaxed him. He buried his face into the crook of my neck, his own hands holding tightly onto my shoulders.

"Can't wait for what?" I asked softly, the relief washing through me.

He suddenly cupped my face with his unusually very hot hands and kissed me. He caressed my lips confidently, lovingly and I moaned into him, my body craving him all over again.

"Come here," and he tugged me into the living room, sitting me onto the sofa.

He crouched down in front of me, his cheeks slightly flushed. "I've never loved anyone like I do you, Max. You mean fucking everything to me, and I don't ever want to be without you," he said, his voice filled with emotion.

"I love you the same way, T," I whispered.

He reached into his jeans pocket and my heart slammed into my ribcage, pulse spiking and my stomach churning with nervous energy. In his fingers was a white gold band with a row of small diamonds around the top.

"Fuck," I gasped.

"Max Ashforth. Will you marry me?" he croaked.

I blinked in utter shock, heart racing as I stared into Teagen's gorgeous dark eyes. I reached up and touched his cheeks softly, fingers running across his kissable lips, and my own slowly crept up into a wide grin. He looked absolutely terrified until he saw me smiling at him.

"Teagen Samuel Laurier, yes I'll fucking marry you," I announced.

He let out a breath and said, "Thank fuck," and slipped the ring on to my wedding finger. "Crap, you've just agreed to marry me, baby."

I slammed my mouth onto his and kissed the fucking life out of him, making him laugh against my lips. I'd never felt as happy as I did in this moment and I laughed too as I devoured his mouth, our tongues dancing together hungrily.

Once I'd released him, he reached back into his pocket and pulled out another, handing it to me.

"You got two?" I asked, running my hands through his dark hair.

"Yeah," he replied sheepishly.

I took his left hand and slipped the ring onto his own wedding finger, then I yanked him back to me, making him straddle me where I sat.

"I thought I'd done something wrong," I groaned.

"Shit, no. I was so nervous, baby. I wanted to do it at lunch, make it special, but," and he dropped his head onto my chest.

"Babe," and he groaned. "This was fucking perfect, fiancè, and I love you, you fucking sexy gorgeous man."

"I love you more, baby."

Our mouths locked onto each other and I crushed him against me, then the polite cough startled us apart and Sophie was smirking at us, Darcy behind her, doing the same.

"Don't mind us, shitheads," she drawled.

"We won't, because your fucking brother just agreed to marry me," Teagen announced.

Her eyes grew as wide as saucers, then she literally launched herself on top of us, squealing like a banshee.

"Oh my god, Congratulations fuck face, shithead," she cried.

We pulled her in for a hug but she slipped off onto the floor. "Shit," she gasped, then Teagen climbed off me, laughing at her in a heap on the floor.

Darcy hovered by the hallway, not interrupting our family moment, and I was secretly grateful, so I threw him a small smile.

"Congratulations fella's," he said with a genuine smile of his own.

"Thanks," I replied.

He was irritating me, and it wasn't because he was doing anything bad. He was the perfect boyfriend to Sophie. He hadn't pushed her at all. He wasn't flirting with *any* other women, and he was treating her like a goddess.

And that pissed me off, as I'd enjoyed hating him, and now I couldn't, damn it. Bloody perfect douche fucker.

I stood up and walked to the fridge, then Teagen yelled at me before I opened it. "Wait, let me, baby."

I turned and arched my brows at him, an amused smile on my face. He looked flustered and literally sprinted to where I was standing, then he ushered Sophie and Darcy into the living room.

"I've got some bubbly, but I got Max a special present," he exclaimed.

Sophie grinned and took Darcy's hand leading him to the sofa. I leant against the counter and gazed at the man I had just agreed to spend the rest of my life with.

"What the hell did you get?" I drawled.

He opened the fridge and pulled out a box, then showed it to me. I snorted into laughter as my eyes landed on a dick shaped cake, and the words '*Max & T forever*'.

"Fucking hell, I love you," I said, chuckling, and cupped his face, kissing him lovingly.

Sophie

I sat with Darcy beside me, a glass of fizz and a small slice of dick cake in my hands. Max had Teagen on his lap, feeding him the sweet treat, both of them so loved up. I couldn't have been happier for them, and I was hoping to be here when they facetimed mum and Benson.

"I've sent messages to Ella," said Max.

"I've told Cam."

Then my brother's phone started ringing. "It's mum," and he answered. "Hey mum."

Max put her on speaker and she was shrieking into the phone. "Oh my days, munchkin. Congratulations. Is Sophie there?"

"Yes. With Darcy O'Sullivan," he replied.

"What? Sophie Carter?"

"Hi mum."

"Hello Mrs Carter," Darcy said.

"You had better be on your best behaviour, young man."

"Ya have me word, Mrs Carter."

"Right, well, that's a surprise, but I'll have to deal with that later. Now, Max, Teagen, you need to set a date."

"We'll let you know, mum."

"And Sophie's going to a film premiere with the Irishman."

"What? Really? Why did you fail to tell me the other day, young lady?"

I rolled my eyes and stood up. I smacked my brother's shoulder and he smirked smugly. "Douche fucker. Sorry mum. I *was* going to tell you, but I *am* going as his date."

"Oh my god, lady. You and him? You're dating a film star? And my son is getting married. Anything else you've failed to mention?"

"Sophe's been serviced by the film star," Max announced.

"What?"

"Max is eating cock cake."

"Excuse me?"

Darcy picked up a small piece of the cake and popped it in his mouth with a smirk. "Never thought I'd see Darcy O'Sullivan with cock in his mouth either," drawled Max.

Darcy suddenly coughed in surprise and almost choked.

"Shit," I gasped.

"Language you two. If I were there I'd bang your heads together. And I didn't need to know what type of cake. My children have become even more foul-mouthed living down there."

My man took a swig of his own fizz and shot my brother a glare, then snorted into laughter. I groaned and smacked Max again, but he was hiding his own laughter, Teagen's face buried in his neck, shoulders shaking.

"There's a first for everything, Max," he said and coughed again.

"I'm still here, so knock off the filthy talk."

"Sorry Mrs Carter," Darcy said.

"Thank you, Darcy, love."

That was my moment to smirk as I saw the slight irritation in my brother's eyes. It was killing him that Darcy was treating me well, and Mum actually liked him too.

"When are you both coming home to visit? I can cook a lovely meal for Darcy and Teagen. You could all stay at the farm?"

After a few more questions and a quick catch up from Mum and Benson giving out congratulations, Benson asked to speak to me before ending the call.

I took the phone off speaker and walked towards my bedroom. "Hi, dad," I said.

"I just wanted you to know that I'm happy for you. Jake would want that too. Not sure he'd like the fact that it's Darcy though."

I sighed, sitting on the bed. "I know. He'd have a bloody fit, right? But I am happy, dad," and he chuckled.

"Good. After losing Jake so suddenly, your mum and I had a long chat. We put your old place up for sale."

"Okay."

"There's some personal things here at home, photographs, his music collection and some other things. But only when you're ready, love," he said gently.

I glanced over at the door and Darcy was gazing at me, eyes filled with nothing but love. "Thanks dad."

My heart lurched a little as I looked down at the wedding picture. "Bring him up for the weekend," Benson said.

"I will. We have a play to work on for now. When the run finishes we'll come for a visit. And I'll get you both tickets for the closing night," I replied.

"Sounds lovely. Look forward to it. Now take care of yourself, and put Max back on," he said.

My brother appeared as if by magic, so I waved at him. "Here. Dad wants a word," and I handed it over, kissing his cheek.

"Hey, Pops...Not sure. Want to spend the day with my fiancè, alone," he replied.

Teagen appeared too and grinned as he wrapped his arms around Max, and I knew exactly what they were planning.

"Alright lass, Carl will be picking us up in a few minutes," he said, gesturing for me to go to him.

I didn't hesitate and walked into his outstretched arms and kissed him. "I'll get the bags," but he shook his head, squeezing me tighter.

"Nope, I'll get them," he whispered.

He patted my brother and Teagen on the shoulder as they were leaning against the wall, then paused. "And that'll be the only time I'll ever have dick in me mouth, Max. I know what ya doing, but I'm not the same man you knew in the past. Ya sister changed me for the better," and I stared at my brother with a rather smug smirk as Darcy sauntered towards our bags.

I grabbed my brother's arm and dragged him into the kitchen, Teagen going to grab their drinks.

"Well?" I asked.

"Well what?"

"You know what, shithead," I said.

"Oh fine. It's pissing me off that I'm starting to fucking like him. Happy now, fuck face?" he muttered.

I grinned, rose up and kissed his cheek, followed by Teagen's. "I love both of you. And I'm over the fucking moon that you two are engaged."

Teagen smacked my ass and winked with a very naughty look in his eyes. "And we heard how well your Irishman is taking care of you."

I groaned and smacked the back of his head, but I felt my cheeks burn as the blush appeared.

"Oh, god, yes Darcy," Max teased in a high pitched moan.

I smacked his shoulder as they burst into laughter. "You think I never heard the two of you moaning and grunting, little brother," I fired at him.

"Oh for fuck's sake, bitch face."

"And sorry, not bloody sorry," I answered.

My brother tugged me into a tight hug, Teagen joining in, squashing me between them. He released me and kissed my forehead before punching my shoulder and running to the sofa.

"I'll get you back for that," I exclaimed. "Love you douche fucker."

"Love you too, shithead."

I threw back the remnants of my fizz and left my glass on the counter by the sink. Darcy reappeared and headed right for me.

"Ready to go, love?"

"Yes I am handsome."

"Then I'm taking ya to get a gown as gorgeous as me sexy bare is," and he smacked my ass before striding to the door.

"Bare?" questioned Teagen.

"It means woman," I replied.

"Okay, well bare, go fuck off to your Irishman's pad so we can get naked and celebrate getting engaged, fuck face," Max drawled with a very wicked wink at his boyfriend.

Darcy slipped into the car next to me and he took my hand in his. I leaned closer and his arm wrapped around my shoulders. The car set off and we sat in silence for a few minutes then his phone started singing in his pocket and he kissed my temple before answering it.

"Alright Christian," and he winked at me.

I sat up and allowed him to take the call, but he tugged me back to him, turning to smile at me. "Stay, please love," he mouthed.

I shook my head and smirked. "Okay, handsome," I mouthed back.

I settled into his body, his arm draped around my shoulders as Darcy chatted about some new project that his agent wanted him to consider, then he mentioned the premiere.

"Yes. She's me plus one from now on, and that's for all future events. Yes. Look, got to go. We're here. I will, see ya," and he hung up.

I stayed quiet as I processed what he'd said. His plus one from now on. Shit, that sounded both exciting and terrifying in equal parts. The car slowed and pulled up outside a huge white building. Darcy grinned and took my hand, helping me from the car.

'Raphael's' read the sign above the large front window.

"This is a dress shop?" I asked, and Darcy chuckled. "What? Apart from the sign? It looks like a fancy house."

"Come on, Cinderella, and I'll show ya."

"Does that make you my knight in shining armour?" I asked, smirking.

"If ya want to be? Then ya wish is my command, love," and he winked with that pussy fluttering smile, tugging me to the very subtle entrance.

He opened the door into a stunning boutique. A light grey sofa sat in front of the window, a fancy matching chair next to it with a little coffee table in between them.

A counter ran along the left hand wall, a black curtain hiding an archway in the centre. Various racks ran along the right side of the room, and a deep red curtain was pulled across the back wall.

"Bloody hell, Darcy. Look at those dresses," I gasped as my eyes landed on the various stunning gowns on show.

"Darcy?" and the curtain was flung aside.

Chapter 15.

A tall, very well groomed guy appeared wrapped up in grey suit trousers, bright white shirt and matching grey waistcoat. There was a tape measure hanging around his neck and he froze as he fixed his eyes on my actor.

"Fuck me on a biscuit, hello stranger," he stated, hands landing on his lean hips.

He had a beautiful dark complexion, big brown eyes and hair cropped extremely short. But, his grin widened as he clocked me standing beside him.

"Where the bloody hell have you been hiding, and *who* is this deletable lady?" he drawled.

"Ya alright Raphi?" Darcy said with a warm smile, and he shook the man's hand.

"Andrew," Raphi shouted. "The prodigal ladies man has returned. And he has a sexy, gorgeous young lady with him."

I had to smile at the word '*young*' and I dropped my gaze as I felt the blush on my cheeks rise. Darcy held me tightly to the side of him and kissed my lips tenderly.

"Ladies man. Figures," I teased.

"Very funny, lass," he replied.

A smaller olive skinned man appeared looking a little flustered, then froze as he saw us standing there.

"Merda. Darcy O'Sullivan has returned. Oh, ciao bella," he said and winked at me.

"Off limits Andrew," Darcy fired at him.

"Yeah, hi, but I'm with this guy," I said, huddling into Darcy's body.

He held up his hands but threw me a wink, and I had a funny feeling I knew why he was flirting. Darcy the ladies man was in front of him.

"Where the devil have you been hiding?" Raphi asked.

"I've been pining over this lady for a long time. And now I've got her for the rest of me fecking life. This is Sophie Carter." and he captured my lips again, kissing me lovingly.

Neither men said anything for what seemed like an eternity, then Raphi was in front of me, yanking me into a very tight hug.

"You're the little director?" he asked.

"Erm, yes?" I answered.

"The one he was bundling into a car a few weeks ago?" questioned Andrew.

Darcy

I groaned at Andrew's comment and he chuckled as he winked at Sophie again. "I was protecting her from the feckers." I said. "And stop fecking winking at her."

Sophie giggled as Raphi let her go. "I know, right? Sounds like he was bloody kidnapping me. But, he's right. I got in willingly," she replied.

Raphi smiled gently, then looked over at me. "This lovely lady is why you stopped frequenting my store. You fell in love?"

I raked my hand through my hair and tugged her back to me. "Yes, fella, I fell in love. And I'm the happiest man on the planet." I admitted.

Andrew chuckled and patted my back, Raphi simply grinning at me. "And now I will stop winking. Congratulations, Darcy," Andrew replied.

"Cheers, Andrew," and I patted his shoulder with a grateful smile.

Raphi disappeared for a few moments and Andrew went back to the counter, picking up some material, but his eyes were glancing over at the two of us.

"Never thought I'd see the day, Darcy," he finally said as he expertly ran a needle through the fabric.

Sophie touched my arm and she smiled at me. "Neither did I, but I can safely say that Darcy O'Sullivan is a changed man."

"Oh really?"

"Cheeky fecker," I muttered.

The boutique owner reappeared with his usual flourish and he had a bottle of fucking champagne in his hands.

"Open this, Andrew darling. We need to celebrate, immediately," he drawled. "Because this is a delicious miracle and you make such a yummy pair."

I rolled my eyes but pressed a very amused Sophie into my side protectively. Andrew started on the cork as Raphi grabbed champagne flutes. "And I am presuming you need a gown for this stunning petite lady. For what?" he questioned.

"Film premiere."

"Oh," he said, his eyes lighting up. "What kind of film is it?"

"Pirates. Tragedy. Lost love's revenge. Why Raphi?" I questioned.

He arched a brow and glanced back at the curtain. He reached out for Sophie's hand and she grinned as she reached out. Raphi had that look in his eyes. That creative sparkle and he raked his gaze over her frame. A jolt of jealousy whirled through me, but he winked with a grin.

"And I have the perfect outfit. Andrew, find me Scarlett."

I saw his assistant's eyes sparkle with what looked like fucking glee. He vanished behind the curtain and Raphi smacked me on the shoulder. He took over opening the bottle and swiftly poured us each a glass.

"To the two of you," he announced, clinking his glass against ours. "Now sit Darcy. Help yourself to the fizz, or there's a bottle of whiskey behind the counter, as I need to fit this beautiful lady into the perfect gown."

I rolled my eyes but smiled, kissed Sophie and went in search of the good stuff. Sophie was taken to the red curtain and they disappeared behind it.

I smirked and sat down on the sofa. Andrew appeared with a clothing bag and froze as he saw me sitting there, waiting.

"You're staying?" he asked.

"Yes. Why?"

"You usually just tell us to put it on your tab?" and that statement hit the mark as memories of my previous visits slammed into me.

"Sophie's me future," I replied, then Raphi shouted the assistant's name and he nodded and disappeared too.

He was right. I'd offered to buy outfits, but never hung around. I hadn't cared, as long as they looked respectful. I just fucked them afterwards then left. I heard muffled voices, then Andrew reappeared with a knowing smirk on his face. He winked and walked behind the counter. I sipped on my drink and waited with baited breath. Andrew was sewing and I felt his side glances. My ankle was resting on my thigh, foot shaking with nerves.

"I hope you're prepared, Darcy. She's going to look stunning in that dress."

"She looks stunning in anything, fella."

"Raphi's been hoping someone petite with the right shape came in. He had a weird premonition when he started making it," and he winked at me.

My entire body was firing with nervous energy. It was true that I didn't care what she was wearing, but I wanted my beautiful woman to steal the fucking show.

"Darcy, prepare to be wowed," called Raphi, and I sat up, heart racing.

The curtain was pulled back and my breath caught in my throat. She was still staring at her reflection in the mirror. The dress was backless, and it stopped just above her sexy ass. I slowly got to my feet, eyes locked on Sophie.

"This way, darling lady," Raphi said, turning her to come face to face with me.

And fuck me, I was staring at my goddess. The front was one of those sweetheart necklines, hugging her breasts snugly, thin straps over her shoulders. There was a slither of naked leg, all the way up to mid thigh, and I wanted to scoop her up and take her home to my bed. Her eyes found mine and she smiled widely, her hands smoothing down the dress.

"Does she pass for the red carpet, Darcy?" Raphi asked.

"Fecking hell," fell out of me.

"Is that it?" fired Raphi.

"You are a genius, Raphi," Andrew said.

"I knew I hired you for a reason, darling."

I found myself standing in front of the platform, gazing up at the woman I loved, and she looked breathtaking.

"Ya look stunning, Sophie love." I whispered.

"Do I pass for a film star's date?" she asked.

"Goddess. And girlfriend, love. Sophie, you're me girlfriend, not just me date," and I reached up and lifted her from the platform.

"I do actually feel a bit like Cinderella," she whispered.

I had to grin and I pulled her into me, kissing her soft lips. I couldn't resist and my hands moved up over the naked skin of her spine. I hoisted her from the floor and her arms wrapped around my neck, a sigh leaving her lips. Her legs wrapped around my waist and I was in seventh heaven.

"Well, it's official. Darcy O'Sullivan is really in love," Raphi's voice echoed in my ears.

I didn't care, as my hands were under Sophie's ass, and I was tongue fucking her in front of two men in an exclusive boutique.

"Fucking hell, handsome," she gasped.

"I love ya, lass," I replied.

I didn't care that she hadn't said it yet, and I wouldn't push her either. I just needed her to know that *I* did.

The glasses appeared over my shoulder and Sophie blushed as she stared down into my eyes.

"Congratulations, Darcy," Raphi drawled. "We just witnessed the forever bachelor fall in love."

Leo

Henry stretched out in my bed and tugged me on top of him, making me laugh. "I just need to say this, Sin. I want to spend the summer with you. I know it's only the end of January, but I need you to know that."

I relaxed into him and sighed happily. "Fine with me. I've spent the last few alone," I replied.

He tipped me off and climbed on top of me, his eyes suddenly serious. "Seriously? You spent your summers alone?"

"Didn't want to go home. For obvious reasons."

He kissed my lips, jaw and down my neck, then looked into my eyes again. "Come home with me, you know, if we're not working. They will fucking love you."

I rolled him off me, and he chuckled, snuggling next to me. "Where are you from, you know, your family?"

"Italy. Mama and Papa moved here when we were all between seven and thirteen."

"Shit. Do you speak Italian?"

He smirked like a fucking devil and stroked his fingers over my skin, causing my body to shiver with heat. "Si, bello."

"Oh dear fucking god."

Before Henry could say more the alarm started screaming at us. He sat up and ruffled his hair.

"H?" I said, and he gave that beautiful smile.

"Si, my sexy man?"

"What's your name in Italian?"

He climbed back onto the bed and pulled me into his arms. "Enrico, Sin. Mama told me I could use Henry for a stage name."

I snuggled into him and just enjoyed being in his arms. "Maybe I might call you Rico," I said.

"I wouldn't mind, but know my sisters call me that."

"How many brothers and sisters do you have?" I asked, and he grinned, pulling me closer.

"My family are catholic, Sin. I have two brothers and three sisters. Mama and papa have these huge family holidays in Italy, and I know you'd love it. Food to eat until you popped, drinks and a lot of fun," and he kissed me.

"Isn't being gay frowned upon in the Catholic church?" I questioned.

"Si. But Mama and Papa said that God loves all of his children, so they gave me their blessing to be happy."

The sheer thought of having a family that accepted you for who you were caused a painful ache in my heart, and my eyes dropped as I gritted my teeth. Henry seemed to have noticed the tension in my body, so he wrapped me up in his arms.

"Talk to me, tesoro," he whispered into my ear.

"Just a little jealous. Your family accepted you just like that. I wish I had the same," I admitted.

"Your Mama and sister love you as you are, right?" he asked.

"Yes. But, dad will never accept a gay son, Henry. Never. He'd prefer to beat the crap out of me instead," I replied.

Henry didn't say anything. He simply tightened his arms around me and kissed me tenderly. We stayed huddled together for a while, just enjoying the closeness, then the phone pierced the silence and I lazily reached out for it, not wanting to move.

"Hello," I answered without checking who it was.

"Leo?"

"Shit, mum?"

"Oh god, are you alright?"

I sat up, Henry frowning at me. "Why would you think I'm not?" I asked, my heart starting to race. "Mum?"

"Some girl posted on social media saying you were attacked in a nightclub?"

"What? I haven't been attacked," then it hit me. "What girl?"

Henry was frowning, anger dancing in his eyes."A young woman. She said you'd been attacked by a gay man. Your dad's going crazy. He wants to know who it is?"

My entire being shuddered, heart stuttering, and I couldn't breathe. "Mum, listen to me. I wasn't attacked. No-one touched me."

Henry was out of bed, grabbing boxers and his jeans, but mum sounded scared. "Mum, seriously, I was never attacked by anyone. I'm totally fine."

"Dad's threatening to come and find them."

Every nerve ending shivered and I froze at her words. The terror slammed me, nausea churning like a tornado. This was Eve and she had no idea what damage she was potentially unleashing.

"Mum, listen to me, please. No-one attacked me. I'm fine, happy and unscathed. I'm working and the play is going to be amazing. Just tell me, what was her name?"

"She's on as Eve and Leo. One word. She said she was your girlfriend?"

"Fuck. What the bloody hell?" I exclaimed. "She's not my girlfriend, Mum. She's just bloody obsessed with me. Won't leave me alone. Where's Dad now?"

Every part of me was fucking terrified. I needed to report her to the bloody police because this was turning into real fucking stalking.

"He went to Pauls to vent. Are you sure you're alright, Leo?" she asked.

"I'm fine mum. The guy kissing me is my boyfriend," I replied.

She let out a sigh, and I relaxed a little. "Oh that's lovely. I'm so happy for you, just don't eat too much pizza. And stay hydrated. I love you," then she hung up.

Chapter 16.

The rage crashed into every pore and the fear was deafening. Henry was studying every tiny emotion flying over my face, then he let out a low growl.

"What the fuck has she done?" he said, and I saw the anger in him too.

But, I was equally as worried. Mum had told me not to eat too much pizza and stay hydrated. That was our secret code. Dad wasn't in a good place.

"Sin, babe? What happened?"

"What?" I stammered.

He sat beside me, his hands cupping my face tenderly. "Leo, babe. Look at me," he said gently. "Talk to me. What happened?"

My eyes finally focused on Henry's beautiful face and I managed to find my words as the terror began to subside with my boyfriend's touch.

"I don't like this, H. Mum used our code words. The ones that told us he was seriously pissed. Eve actually put a post on social media and said she was my fucking girlfriend. Said I was attacked by a gay man," I ground out. "And Dad's seen it."

Henry's eyes narrowed, but he leaned in and swiftly kissed me. He jumped from the bed and picked up his phone. "You have to report her to the police, Sin. She's put both of us in fucking danger. He knows where this place is?" he asked.

"He'd be able to find out easy enough, because Mum has the address," I replied.

"Then we can't stay here, Sin."

"And where do we go?"

"Pack plenty of things, because you're staying with me for a while," he said. "I'll empty the fridge and freezer too," and I watched him go into the bathroom as I looked down at my phone.

That bitch had called me her boyfriend. She had announced that I'd been attacked by a young guy and he'd kissed me without my permission. I wanted to both cry and smack her. She had no idea what she was fucking messing with, making me hate her all the more. My man reappeared and picked up my phone, and called the one person who could help.

"Hey Max, me and Leo need a favour."

We got to their place around an hour later and Max was fuming. Teagen looked equally pissed, but I noticed the rings on their fingers and I groaned.

"Shit, you got engaged and I'm ruining it."

"Fuck off. It's totally fine. We've had some fun already," Max replied.

I groaned and gave them both a swift hug. "Congratulations," I said.

"Thanks. Now explain what happened?" asked Max.

I pulled out my phone and pulled up Eve's social media pages to show them. Both Max and Teagen stared down at the post and then back up at me. "She said I'd been attacked for fuck's sake," I said.

"That's fucking ridiculous. We were there," Teagen said.

"Stay here and we'll bring some more fizz back for later," Max drawled.

He yanked on the underside of the sofa and it turned into a bed and he winked. I walked over and threw my arms around him. Max chuckled and wrapped his own around me.

"Shit, man. What's this for?" he asked.

"Just thank you," I whispered. "I'm not used to having people in my corner."

Max frowned as Teagen draped his arm over his fiancè and raked a hand through his hair. "You do now. Me, Teagen and Henry. *And* you've got Sophe."

I had to smile as I glanced around the room at the three men. "Shit, thanks, really."

"No need. But that girl needs reigning in because she might cause real damage if your dad turns up," he replied. "We're off shopping for a few bits, so stay and chill out."

Henry patted each of them on the shoulder then they waltzed from the apartment, leaving us alone.

"And we're here, why?" I asked.

"I thought we could stay here tonight, then go to my place. Throws whichever one is going to bloody turn up," Henry replied.

I threw my arms around him and hugged him hard. This man had waltzed into my life and swept me off my feet, and I *really* wanted to keep him too. My feelings for him were straying into very intense waters.

"I'm in serious danger of falling for you, H," I whispered.

He tightened his grip on me and kissed my neck. "You have no idea what that fucking sentence means to me, Sin."

I was yanked onto the bed and Henry's mouth descended on mine. And I was kissed within an inch of my life. I didn't know what was in store for the two of us, but I wanted to see where this relationship would take us. I was fucking terrified about dad turning up, but together? I hoped that we could keep each other safe against him.

I also had to deal with the crazy cow that had caused this fucked up situation. She had no idea what she'd set into motion. But, for now? I just wanted to enjoy being with this divine man. A man who was possibly my soulmate.

Darcy

That dress had caused my entire bloody brain to shut down. The way it had skimmed her curves, the sight of her sexy spine, the split showing off her thigh. Jesus fucking Christ, I was ready to fuck her right there in the store. Instead, I treated her to matching shoes and a bag, then organised a make-up artist and hairdresser to come to *our* place on the day of the premiere.

"You've spoiled me too much, Darcy."

"No, I haven't. Not nearly enough love."

"I don't need things, Darcy. I just want you," she replied.

I tugged her close, wrapping my arms around her. "Ya have me, love. Ya've had me for years, me beautiful little director. I love ya, and I'm happy to spoil ya whenever I can. And I won't take no for an answer."

She slapped my arm but let out a delicious giggle, hugging me tighter. "Just know that's not what I expect," she replied.

Carl appeared with the car and he opened the door for us, throwing Sophie a warm smile. She paused and looked up at my driver of ten years.

"Thanks Carl," she said, patting his arm.

"You're very welcome Miss."

"Shit, again, call me Sophie."

He chuckled and nodded with another smile. "Sure, no problem. And you make my boss very happy."

I smirked as Sophie brought her eyes to me, and I leaned in and kissed her. "Ya do, love," I said, taking her hand. "Now, I believe we're staying at your place tonight?"

"Yep," she replied .

Carl nodded and we climbed into the car, before setting off to my lady's apartment.

As we entered, Henry and Leo were half naked on the sofa bed, scrambling to cover themselves.

"Shit," Leo exclaimed.

"Fuck," Henry groaned, and I averted my eyes as Sophie cursed out loud.

"Fucking hell, why are you two about to have fucking sex in the living room?" Sophie exclaimed, smacking the back of Henry's head.

"Didn't know you were coming, sexy bitch," Henry replied, grinning at the two of us.

I stayed by the door for a few moments while they sat up, wrapping the sheet around their waists. Leo threw us an embarrassed smile as he tied up his hair.

"Max said it was fine for tonight," Henry stated.

She groaned and said, "One of you should've warned me. Fuck's sake."

Leo looked extremely uncomfortable, but there was something in his eyes I didn't like. "Leo? What's going on?" I asked.

My instincts were right as he let out a low moan. "Eve," he simply said, and Sophie stopped in her tracks as I walked towards her.

"What?" she asked.

"I'm going to stay with Henry because of Eve fucking Hemlock," Leo replied.

Neither of us said anything as we stared between both Henry and Leo.

I wrapped an arm around Sophie's waist, pressing her backwards into my body protectively. "Explain," I asked.

"She's got no fucking idea what damage she's causing," said Leo.

I kissed her lips gently and took the clothing bag. "Get us some drinks, love?" I suggested. "I'll take these into our room."

She nodded and started pulling down mugs while I swiftly took our bags to my lady's bedroom. I dropped them onto the floor by the wardrobe and pulled out my phone. I fired off a message to Christian, then raked my hand through my hair.

It seemed as though drama followed us around. Sophie, me and more fucking shite to deal with. I took a deep breath and shoved my phone back into my pocket, knowing that I had to help Leo. He didn't deserve any of this.

When I returned they were all sitting on the sofa bed. I dropped into the chair and Sophie jumped up and settled herself on my lap.

"Okay, so tell us what's happened?" I asked.

Leo raked a hand through his hair and huddled into Henry. "Eve has no idea what she's doing. Mum called me this morning, and dad is threatening to come down here to hurt Henry, and possibly me too."

I sat up taller and gritted my teeth as Sophie let out an annoyed sigh. "What the feck did she do?" I asked.

Henry was holding onto Leo as though he might disappear, his eyes sparkling with a rage I recognised. Leo sat up and yanked his t-shirt over his head and looked down at his hands.

"She posted this on her social media," and he handed me his phone. "Said that she was my girlfriend, and I'd been attacked by a gay man. Dad's fucking furious."

We both stared at them in shock, then I cursed as I looked down at the post. There were two photographs of Leo and Henry in the club that first night.

Another was at a cafe down the road from the theatre. That lass was following him. She had announced that Henry had attacked him, and Leo was her boyfriend?

"Feck. Is ya dad going to show up?" I questioned.

"Mum said maybe. She used our code words," Leo replied.

I kissed Sophie and set her on her feet. "Love? Will ya let me take this?" and she smiled tenderly, cupping my face and kissing me again.

"Okay, handsome. I'll get the whiskey as I think Leo and Henry need one."

She patted Leo and Henry's shoulders, pecking them on their cheeks, then left the three of us. I sat forward and fixed my eyes on the young blonde.

"Code words?" I asked.

"Yeah. When dad was in a shitty mood, we told each other not to eat too much pizza and stay hydrated. He liked to throw shit, haphazardly."

I arched a brow at his words, then he let out a frustrated sigh. "Throw shite?" I questioned.

He nodded and absently rubbed his right temple where a small scar was visible.

"It was usually after a few beers, then something would piss him off, and he'd throw the remote for the TV, or his coffee mug. Got one of them to the head once," Leo muttered. "My sister usually managed to get us out of the line of fire, but I wasn't fast enough. Had a decent cut over my eye."

Henry wrapped his arms around him protectively. "And I apparently fucking attacked him. Kissed him without permission. I mean, shit, that makes me out to be," but he stopped.

"The security I have at the theatre need a photograph. Of ya dad. I want to help. It's not right to feel like ya can't be who ya really are. Trust me fein, it's fecking shite."

Leo was swift and found a family photograph in his phone gallery. He sent it via message and I opened it up to see a very familiar face. I stared down at Leo's dad and noticed the jawline, blonde hair, and I looked back at the young actor.

"Ya look alot like him, fella. Ya mam's eyes though," I said.

"Yeah. Thank god I'm nothing like him in any other fucking way," he replied. "He does love us. He just doesn't show it in the same way as everyone else."

Henry pulled him closer as he spoke, but I could see the conflict in Leo's eyes. I stood up and patted his shoulder. "I'll use her photograph from the Midsummer program. I have to make a call," and I started towards the kitchen.

"Darcy?" Leo called.

"Yeah, fein?"

"Thank you," he said.

"Don't worry, Leo," I replied, and I smiled and threw him a wink, then went to Sophie.

I pulled her in for a hug, and kissed her lovingly. "Need to make a couple of calls, love," I whispered.

She nodded and pressed herself against me. "Thank you. I don't think you realise how grateful that guy is over there."

I glanced over at the loved up couple and sighed. I'd hidden my true self away for decades, trying to protect myself, but all it did was make me even more bloody miserable. I didn't want a young guy like Leo to go through that.

"No-one should have to hide who they really are, love. Ya taught me that."

She buried her face into my chest and sighed too. "I just hope his dad doesn't show up, Darcy. And Eve needs to be dealt with."

"That's what I'm gonna try to fix first. I love ya, lass," and I kissed her soft lips once more.

Leo

Darcy had promised to help and it felt amazing having people in my corner for the first time in my life. Apart from Mum and Mia? I'd been alone. My phone was sat on the coffee table as we waited for him to come back, the picture of my Mum and Dad staring back at me.

Sophie took the chair and allowed Henry and myself to huddle up on the sofa.

A tumbler was handed to each of us with a very generous measure of whiskey in each. I didn't normally drink it, but I took a large gulp, stifling a cough as it burned down my throat.

"Would he really try to attack Henry?" she asked. "And you?"

I sat forward, sipping the whiskey again, head whirring with past memories. My twin sister, Mia, had always been protective of me, especially as she called me little brother due to the fact that she had been born eight minutes before me.

"I've got a twin sister. She's pretty much a female version of me. When dad used to fly off into one of his temper tantrums, she always made sure I was out of the firing line," I said quietly. "Didn't always make it," and I touched the scar over my right eye.

I showed them the photograph on my phone and my man whistled as he stared down at my sister. We did look very much alike.

"She literally is a female version of you, Sin," Henry said, staring down at the two of us standing at each side of mum and dad. "And your dad is looking at your mum with such love?" questioned Henry.

"Oh, he never purposely hurt us. He tended to throw things without worrying where it would land. And he never laid a finger on any of us purposely. But he once went after a guy who tried to feel up mum. Beat the crap out of him and he spent time in jail for that," I admitted. "He almost killed him with his fists."

My childhood had been very explosive at times, and dad was usually the cause. I remembered the day he sat us both down for the '*If you turn out gay, I'll beat some sense into you*' chat.

He'd scared the fucking shit out of both of us.

"Why does he hate gay people so much?" Sophie asked.

"I don't know. He came back from prison, different. More angry at the world, especially the gay community," I replied. "He didn't like them before, but after he came out of prison? He fucking despised all of them."

Henry pulled me close again, and I snuggled into his embrace. Dad had definitely changed when he came home. Harder, colder, and even more protective of us all. The hatred for gay men was scary, so I had no choice but to hide it.

"Mum and Mia knew something was wrong when I was a teenager. Dad was still in jail. Mum took me and Mia out for tea. That's when she asked me if I was gay."

Sophie was listening intently and Henry's fingers were making lazy trails up and down my arm. "I was fucking terrified of Dad finding out, but they promised to look after me. Hiding who I was? Shit, I hated it. Still fucking hate it."

That was the moment Darcy strode back in and he had a wicked smile on his face, putting me on edge with anticipation.

"What?" I asked.

"Christian has contacts that can find out everything about Miss Hemlock, and ya need to keep everything that she sends. Don't delete a thing. And an extra security guy will be at the theatre tomorrow," and Darcy pulled Sophie to her feet.

I let out a relieved sigh and smiled. "Thanks Darcy."

He returned the smile and looked at Henry sitting next to me. "I've called Carl. We're going to stay at my place tonight, love. It'll give ya both some privacy that ya need."

Sophie looked a little shocked, but smiled at the famous actor.

"That's a good idea," then she walked over and shuffled in between us. "Enjoy some time together and we'll see you both at work," and she hugged both of us before standing and joining Darcy.

"I'll get our bags, lass," he said.

He disappeared and Henry tucked me into his side, holding me protectively. "Thanks Sophie. For what you are all doing for me," I said gratefully.

"You're not just a cast member anymore, Leo. You're a friend. And we try to help our friends as best as we can," she replied.

"Still, I'm really not used to it, Sophie."

"Well try, Sin. Because we're not going anywhere. Especially me," Henry purred into my ear.

Sophie snorted and let out a light laugh. "Seems you've gained four new friends and a very sexy boyfriend. And we're all in your corner," she said with a warm smile.

Darcy reappeared and they left around five minutes later, Henry not keeping his eyes from my face. Once alone, Henry picked up our glasses and went to refill them.

I stretched out and tried to relax, but thoughts were flying through my mind. Dad loved us, that much was true, but something had to have happened to him in prison. He'd always had a temper, and always disliked the LGBTQ+ community, but the level of his rage became so much more potent when his jail time had ended.

Henry appeared and sat beside me, pulling me into his arms once he'd set down our glasses.

"Sin?" he whispered.

"Yeah?"

"Are you okay?"

"Been better, but I've been thinking."

He tugged me onto his lap, making me straddle him. His lips caught mine and he kissed me greedily. We had almost been caught with my dick in Henry's ass, and that would've been fucking embarrassing, but now we were alone and I needed to be close to my man.

"I'm here for you, Sin," he whispered into my ear, hands roaming up my spine.

"I know. And I'm glad you are."

He cupped my cheeks with his hands and gazed into my eyes. This man? I was falling hard for and I'd only known him for a couple of weeks.

"I have a theory," I said quietly.

"Oh?"

"About my dad."

Henry leaned forward and picked up his glass, then passed me my own without allowing me to move.

"How old are you, Leo?" he asked, removing my hair tie and running his hand through it.

"Twenty six. Why?" I questioned.

"Then I have a fucking toy boy. Because I'm thirty two," he drawled, caressing my ass.

I had to grin at him, taking in the stunningly handsome guy underneath me. I wanted to tell the fucking world that he was mine, but I needed to figure out what to do about my dad.

"Your theory, Sin?" he said, leaving a trail of kisses down my neck.

I took a breath, trying to focus, as the sheer closeness of this guy made me horny for him, and caused all rational thoughts to fuck off on holiday. Henry paused his exploration of my body as he noticed the serious expression on my face.

"What if he was attacked by a gay prisoner?" I said.

"Well, that would make sense. The hatred he has for us?"

"It's the only thing that does. If he knew that we weren't all like that, maybe," but I stopped.

Henry smiled and nodded. "It would make sense. But, let's forget all that right now. I want to make you come hard. Let me," and he took the glasses and set them down on the coffee table.

I was suddenly tipped onto the sofa and stripped of my jogging pants before Henry's talented mouth descended onto my excited cock, and all other thoughts were forgotten.

For the moment at least....

Chapter 17.

Sophie

The rest of the week had been pretty quiet. Leo and Henry swanned in this morning and Zane waltzed straight over to them with Asia, Fiona and Carlton. I walked closer to them as Leo looked panicked all of a sudden.

"Hey, Leo?" Zane said.

"Hi. What's up?" Leo asked.

I noticed Henry was standing very close and I understood what was possibly about to happen. I put down my script and watched in case of fireworks. Asia reached for Leo's hand and she smiled warmly at him.

"We know about you two. You make a beautiful couple," she said gently.

"What?" Leo stammered.

"We know Leo. It's been obvious since the first day," she replied.

Zane was next and he smiled too. "Look, I know what it's like. Hiding who you are. I did it for three years because I was petrified of what my parents would think."

Henry stepped closer and he smiled. "What did they say, Zane?" he asked, and Zane gave them both a warm smile too.

"Dad took it a bit hard, but they came around. When I take my boyfriend round, we just keep the touching and kissing down to the bare minimum."

Leo's eyes seemed to glisten with emotion, causing Asia to hug him. "Why do you look so upset?" she asked.

"I wish I had that, that's all." "

Just know we won't say anything if you don't want us to," Zane said.

Henry's arms snaked around Leo and he kissed Leo's neck then grinned like a wicked devil. "Thanks. And please don't say anything."

"Yes. Please don't say anything. I've got some... issues to work out first," Leo said.

Asia suddenly hugged him and I had to smile. "You've got our word. Your secret is safe with us."

Leo seemed to relax and I moved back a little. I'd let them decide how to go ahead. Carlton was beside the pair and he smacked Leo's back.

"Whatever is going on? Be yourselves around us. Life's too short, so bloody enjoy your lives. Just know that you can trust your fellow cast mates," and he winked at the two stunned men.

"Thanks," croaked Leo.

"No need," Carlton replied then walked back to his seat, rifling around for his script.

I smiled to myself as Darcy strolled in with coffees and a bag of treats. He noticed the look on my face and frowned a little.

"Have I missed something, love?" he asked.

I nodded and gestured towards Leo and Henry who were now hugging and kissing each other.

"They were outed by the cast and told that their secret is safe," I replied quietly.

My man grinned and looked over at the loved up pair. He handed me a coffee and kissed me, hand wrapping around my waist.

"I'm glad. At least they can relax here. And it's Friday. Ya know what that means, love?"

I froze for a moment, then it hit me. Film premiere.

Shit, shitty fucking crap.

He noticed the look in my eyes and yanked me into a hug. "Ya don't need to worry, love. We're already trending on social media," and he winked.

"It's true," piped up Tara. "Everyone's chattering about confirmed bachelor swanning about with our petite brunette director."

Henry smirked as he glanced over at us, Leo hiding his face with his script. "Yeah sexy bitch. They were talking about you on the celebrity news channel last night."

I rolled my eyes and slapped Darcy's ass. "Bloody brilliant. But tomorrow I'll be walking down a fucking red carpet with you in front of a mass of bloody press."

He chuckled and kissed my lips. "Ya know, Henry's right that they are questioning our relationship on the various news channels here in the UK and in the States?"

"Really? Henry isn't just winding me up?"

"Really, love. And I can't wait to announce to the *entire* fecking world that ya mine," he whispered.

I sucked in a breath as he released me and scooped up his script. I watched his sexy ass walk to the stage and join the rest of the cast, and Darcy's words floated into my mind. The part about being naked in his bed...

And my filthy mind went flying straight to the bloody gutter. Dirty woman.

As they all started to chat together, Leo and Henry joined them and they were hugged by everyone, including Tara. At that moment I felt extremely proud of them all. I took a sip of coffee and took a deep breath. I had to try and forget the terrifying event coming up tomorrow, and also try to empty my mind of the gorgeous man who would be wrecking me in the most delicious way later, as I had a job to do, so I strode over and started the day's rehearsal.

The day had been a great success, and we were flying through this amazing play at an impressive rate of knots. I was smiling very smugly as we had a bloody talented bunch of actors when a familiar voice appeared from behind.

"Sophie?" and I turned to see Leo standing grinning at me. "I just, well, thanks," he said, and I was yanked into his arms.

He hugged me tightly and I had to chuckle. "For what?" I asked.

"Everything. You're an amazing director, but you're also a fucking beautiful human," he whispered.

Once he let me go, Darcy and Henry sauntered over, along with the others, Carlton calling a goodbye as he left for the weekend.

"We're getting drinks in the bar. You and Darcy coming?" asked Zane.

I was hugged from behind as Darcy's arms wrapped around me, his lips brushing the spot just below my ear.

"We can't stay long. We have an important engagement tomorrow," my Irishman stated.

They all stared at him and I groaned as Leo and Henry smirked. "Something you want to tell us boss?" Henry questioned.

"Not what you're thinking," I muttered.

"Then what?" asked Leo.

Darcy had moved away from me, gathering up our things. "Sophie is coming with me to me film premiere," he said.

Tara whistled as Henry and Leo laughed, hands clapping with glee. "Oh, Sophie's going to be announced as Darcy O'Sullivan's sexy bitch of a woman," Henry drawled.

"Yes she is. And I can't fecking wait, Henry."

"Sexy bare right Darcy?" Tara piped up.

"Knock it off, fuckers," I groaned.

Tara laughed as she pulled on her jacket. She nudged my shoulder as Fiona, Zane and Asia started for the doors. "I'm happy for the two of you."

"Thanks Tara."

"Ready lass?" Darcy asked.

"Yep," and he took my hand and squeezed, then we all made our way to the theatre bar, Darcy holding onto me, Leo and Henry snuggled up as they walked on ahead.

Tara fell into step with us and nudged my shoulder. "Weirdly familiar, yet really bloody different," she said.

"True. But it's really great to be back," I replied.

"Leo and Eve?" she asked. "And his dad?"

I glanced at the two guys, happy, holding hands, and I sighed. "I don't know. Eve needs to be reigned in. If she spouts any more fucking crap? Leo's dad is going to bloody end up after Henry, and Leo."

"Hence the extra security at the front doors?" she questioned.

Darcy chuckled and nodded. "Yes, lass. I hid me self away for decades. He doesn't deserve that fate as well."

Both Tara and myself stared up at him in amused surprise, but my mind started to wander to the upcoming event. A moment in my life where everything would change. I was about to attend a film premiere where the world's press would capture the two of us together, announcing to all and sundry that I was Darcy's girlfriend.

Jesus, fucking hell.

Darcy seemed to notice me zoning out and tugged me into his arms. "What do ya want to drink, love?" he asked.

"Just a gin and tonic please."

He captured my lips in a swift kiss and left me with Tara as he went to the bar. I grabbed her hand and literally dragged her to a table.

"Shit, Sophie. What's wrong?" she exclaimed in a whisper.

We sat down where Leo, Henry, Zane, Fiona and Asia were huddled beside us. I didn't really mind them overhearing as they all knew anyway after Darcy's announcement in the theatre.

"I'm going to a fucking film premiere, Tara," I hissed.

"And you're shitting yourself?"

"Wouldn't you be?"

"Guess so, but I'd also really bloody enjoy it, Sophie. Just think of all the hot actors that'll be there too."

I groaned and slapped her arm with a glare. "My life is about to get majorly complicated, Tara."

"And you have *the* super famous, hot actor boyfriend to help you navigate. Don't forget that he's been through all of this for years," she replied.

Asia touched my arm as she leaned over from the other table, a wicked glint in her eyes. "Sophie, just enjoy it. Darcy won't let anything happen to you. The way he looks at you? Jesus, I wish he'd look like that at me. I'm crazy jealous," she said and grinned at me.

"Me too," Zane piped up with a cheeky wink. "I wish he'd look at me like that too."

I had to chuckle and smile at their faces as they glanced at my Irishman. At that moment Darcy sauntered over and sat beside me, kissing my cheek.

"Am I being talked about? Feel me ears burning," he said then kissed my lips tenderly.

Tara smirked along with the others as Darcy literally lifted me from my stool and dropped me onto his lap, arms wrapping around my waist. "What are ya gossiping about?"

"The premiere," Tara said. "And the fact that Sophie is shitting herself."

Henry snorted into his wine and Leo chuckled. The others started to join in and I groaned as I smacked Tara's arm.

"Very fucking funny you bunch of shit heads," I muttered.

Darcy looked into my eyes and he fucking smirked like a devil. "I want the world to know I'm taken. And I can't wait until after, love."

"What's after?" Henry piped up.

"Nothing to bloody do with you," I stated, my cheeks flushing.

"Oh, I get it. You're on a bloody promise," drawled the cheeky devil. "You're going to get right royally railed by the one and only Darcy O'Sullivan."

I hid my head in the crook of said Irishman's neck and groaned as my cheeks burned hot, Darcy chuckling as I did.

"She is that, Henry, ya cheeky gobshite," Darcy drawled.

I lifted my head, glaring at my famous actor and smacked his chest, causing a deep chuckle to vibrate out of him.

Leo nudged Henry's shoulder. "Leave them alone, H. Their issues are nothing compared to ours."

Asia and Zane stared at the pair in confusion, so I stayed quiet, letting Leo decide how much he wanted to tell them.

"What issues? Can we help?" asked Asia.

Henry groaned and Leo let out a long frustrated sigh. "Remember Eve Hemlock from my last show?" he said.

"Wait, Eve crazy cow Hemlock?" Fiona suddenly exclaimed.

All eyes were on the actor as she sipped her wine, and Henry and Leo sat to attention.

"How do you know her?" I asked.

"She got attached to one of the guys in the show we were in together. Like really really attached. You know, wouldn't take no for an answer attached," she replied.

We were all listening intently, Leo and Henry even more so.

"What happened?" Leo asked.

"She was slapped with a restraining order and her dad came to take her home. Didn't realise she would be allowed to come back to work after the stress she caused Ben," Fiona said. "She's got issues."

"What exactly did she do?" asked Henry.

Fiona put down her glass and sighed. "She started following him around everywhere, like a shadow. Kept touching his arm, then his back. Even his butt a few times. He told her to knock it off, but she never listened. She followed him outside of the theatre too, took a bunch of pictures and posted them to her own socials. She even changed her status to '*being in a relationship*' and mentioned him by name as her boyfriend."

The four of us shared knowing looks, and the other cast members gawked at her in shock.

Darcy was on his feet, phone in hand. He kissed me swiftly then strode from the room. I glanced at the loved up pair and they were staring at Fiona, surprise and annoyance in their expressions. I had a funny feeling that Darcy was relaying the information to his agent.

"Jesus fucking Christ, Sin. It's practically the same," Henry growled.

"Yeah. This is all I fucking needed. She stalks me and spreads shit online, poking the damn bear, then I get a fucking beating because of her," Leo stated, making all eyes focus on him.

"Beating?" gasped Asia.

Leo's hand ran over his face with a very frustrated groan, as Henry leaned in and kissed his cheek.

"My issues? Dad is extremely fucking homophobic. Eve's spouting utter shit online and it's making him absolutely bloody furious," Leo admitted.

Zane was already scrolling through the social media pages, and Henry and Leo were showing him her crazy posts.

Darcy sauntered back in and sat down taking my hand in his. "Christian is tracking down her dad," he whispered.

"And that's how we get rid of her," I asked quietly.

He glanced at the two actors as he took a sip of his drink. "Yes, love. And Leo needs a restraining order on her too. There'll be two security here at the theatre and two to chaperone if needed."

"Mountain man?" I asked, grinning at him.

"Ya cheeky bare. But yes. Don't let Stefan flirt with ya."

I rolled my eyes but smirked as the Scottish security guy appeared in the doorway, throwing me one of said flirty winks.

Asia and Fiona were also gawking at the body guard as he leaned very seductively against the doorframe.

"Jesus, holy mary, mother of god," Darcy groaned as he clocked us all gazing at him. "Really lass?"

I just snorted into a fit of giggles as I was yanked onto his lap. I buried my face into his neck, taking in his delicious scent of nature.

"Are you jealous, sexy hot movie star?" I whispered into his ear.

His hands snaked tightly around my waist and a deep, almost feral growl vibrated through him, causing my entire body to go into heat.

"Ya mine, lass. Fecking mine, and I'm all bloody yours," he whispered, then kissed me possessively.

Film Premiere

Darcy woke me and whispered into my ear. "Stay in bed love. I'm going down to the gym. Love ya," and he kissed my lips softly.

I smiled and cracked open my eyes to see that it was indeed six thirty in the morning. I watched his sexy self disappear out of the bedroom and snuggled further into the bed.

Then it hit me. It was Saturday and I covered my head with the duvet. Nerves were instantly on edge, and going back to sleep?

Nope. Not going to happen now.

I rubbed the sleep from my eyes and sat up, climbed from the bed and made my way to the bathroom.

Once I had finished relieving my bladder, washing and cleaning face and teeth, a naughty thought popped into my head. I decided to give my Irish hottie a sexy surprise, so I picked up his discarded shirt and slipped my arms into the sleeves. I fastened only a few of the buttons and headed downstairs, a wicked smile on my face.

Darcy had a gorgeous home. He'd given me the tour and it had taken my breath away. The top floor had two large bedrooms, both ensuite, and a smaller one with its own little bathroom too. Middle floor housed a living room and a cinema room, storage cupboard and an extra loo.

The ground floor was made up of the most beautiful kitchen, dining, and sitting area. Darcy's gym was also down there, with a shower attached.

I got to the hallway and made my way to the door and froze as my eyes found him. He was doing bicep curls with a barbell. The way his muscles flexed as he lifted and lowered was mesmerising.

Sweat slowly rolled down his skin, over the defined muscles of his shoulders and arms. I bit my lip as my body started to heat up. I took another couple of steps as he dropped the barbell with a thud, reaching for a towel and wiping his face and the back of his neck.

"Knock knock, handsome," I finally said.

His head whipped around and he grinned wickedly as he noticed my attire. "Well, aren't I a lucky fella," he drawled.

I smirked, staying by the door and leaning against the frame, fiddling with one of the fastened buttons. He stood up and dropped the towel onto the bench, then strolled over.

"I thought ya would still be asleep, sexy lady?" he said.

"The fact that it's Saturday and the upcoming bloody scary event stopped that from happening," I replied.

Darcy took another couple of steps closing the gap. "And I'm all sweaty, love. But ya look like a delicious fecking treat in me shirt."

I smiled at him and rose up on my tiptoes, hands on his sweaty shoulders. "Just bloody kiss me, O'Sullivan," I ordered.

His arm came around my waist and I was yanked into his body, his lips crashing into mine, ravishing my mouth, and holy fucking hell, I felt his huge dick now digging into my hip. His hands were at the back of my head, holding me tightly.

I didn't care that he was sweaty at all, and my own snaked around him too, enjoying his kisses, the closeness of him. But, he pulled away and squeezed my hands, equally as turned on as I was.

"Ya naughty bare," he growled into my hair. "I'm very tempted to drag ya into the shower and have me way with ya."

"Still waiting till tonight?" I purred.

"I am ya sexy little devil."

I giggled and he pecked my lips once more. "I'll go and make us coffee and some breakfast."

Darcy's eyes were sparkling with nothing but love. "I love ya lass."

It fell out of me without thinking. "Love you back, handsome."

"What?" he croaked.

I blinked and bit down on my lip, heart racing all of a sudden. I stared up into his beautiful eyes, his handsome face, and it hit me like a train. I did. I loved him.

"I love you Darcy O'Sullivan," I repeated.

He ran his hand over his face, eyes glistening with actual tears. "Feck, lass. Say it again."

I pressed myself into him, smiling warmly. "Darcy O'Sullivan, I love you, you handsome, sexy man."

"Again," he asked.

I smiled and wrapped myself around his sexy sweaty body. "I love you, I love you, I love you," I said, and it felt good, so, so good saying it out loud, and I truly meant it.

"Jesus, holy hell, Sophie. Ya just made me the happiest fecking man on the planet," and I was engulfed in his arms, and kissed within an inch of my life.

Chapter 18.

Darcy

My heart was thundering in my chest, pulse racing after Sophie had said those three fucking words. I had dreamt about her saying it to me for years and I thought I'd missed out on having a second chance with her, but she fucking loved me back. Sophie Carter had finally said '*I love you*'.

Jesus fucking holy Mary mother of god.

As she disappeared to the kitchen, I got myself moving, workout forgotten. I showered in a happy daze, then headed towards the love of my life. She was making food, coffee mugs sitting on the counter, and the sight of Sophie cooking in my fucking kitchen was the most amazing feeling in the damned world.

I gazed at her for a few moments before walking into the room, taking in her curves, those sexy legs, the line of her neck, then her beautiful face and I grinned smugly.

"Hey," she said as I waltzed over to her.

"Hello, love."

She reached up and cupped my cheek, tugging me down to her. I grinned then kissed her lovingly.

"Ya love me, lass," I whispered into her lips.

"I do, O'Sullivan," she replied.

I hoisted her into my arms, deepening the kiss, and she wrapped her legs around my waist, her own arms coming around my neck. I never wanted to put her down, but I needed to because I was so fucking turned on, cock standing to attention, desperate for some action.

"Shite, love. I need to put ya down," I growled, kissing down her neck.

She giggled and wriggled in my arms. "Then put me down, handsome," she replied.

"Don't fecking want to, but I'm starving, so," and I dropped her back onto her feet. "And ya cooked for me."

"It's not your famous Irish breakfast, but I hope you like it," she said.

"Smells grand, lass."

I took the mugs and filled them with coffee and watched her. I would never tire of looking at my little director. As she plated up scrambled eggs, toast and bacon, I noticed the look in her eyes.

"What is it, Sophie love?"

"What happens today?"

I sat on the stool and sipped my coffee. "The hair stylist and make-up artist will arrive at two thirty this afternoon. We set off from here at five."

Sophie nodded and I noticed the slight panic in her eyes. I reached out and took her hand, squeezing it with a wink.

Her gaze lifted from the plates and I smiled lovingly at her. "I can't wait for the world to know about us, love."

"It's scary, Darcy."

"Yes, lass. But ya not alone. I'll be right there with ya, holding on tight."

"Still fucking terrifying."

I chuckled and winked at my beautiful woman as she slid the plate over to me, and she had given me one hell of a decent portion. I arched a brow at the size of her own.

"What?"

"That gonna fill ya?"

"Yes. Have you got enough?" she asked, sitting next to me.

"Got everything I will ever need, love," and I planted a swift kiss on her lips before piling some eggs into my mouth.

Secretly, I couldn't bloody wait to walk down that fucking red carpet with Sophie on my arm, showing the whole world that I was finally head over heels in fucking love. And this sexy, filthy mouthed, gorgeous woman was now *all fucking mine for the rest of our lives.*

Max

Teagen stretched out then snuggled back into my arms, but I groaned as I noticed the bloody time. It was only seven in the morning.

"Fuck's sake."

"What's up, baby?"

"Why are we awake?"

He propped himself up on his elbow and kissed me. "I don't fucking know, fiancè. But, I need to piss."

I snorted and smacked his bare ass. "Shit, babe. We've got to plan a bloody wedding."

"And I can't wait, baby."

He climbed out of bed and disappeared into the bathroom, my eyes looking down at the ring on my finger and I'd never felt so happy.

"Hey, baby? Sophe left us an envelope. Did you pick it up last night?" he called.

I sat up and scooped said envelope off the bedside table. The handwriting was very flamboyant and I frowned. This was *not* my sister's, so it had to be Darcy's. Teagen strolled back and climbed into bed.

"That's the one. Kiss me."

I looked up and smiled. My hand cupped his cheek and I captured his sexy lips, kissing him deeply. I loved this guy with every ounce of my being, and I couldn't wait to marry him.

"Love you," I whispered.

"Love you, baby. Now open this," and he tapped the envelope.

"This isn't Sophe's handwriting," I said as I opened it.

Inside sat two VIP passes to the after party of Darcy's film. A note was in there too and I unfolded it to read my sister's message.

'*Hey shithead. A little engagement present for you both from Darcy and me. After party access. Love you both. Sophe Xx*'

"Shit. Perks of having a sister dating a film star." he said.

I noticed the bottom of the note and I groaned as I read the rest of it.

'*Hope you can join your sister and me at the party. Congratulations on your engagement. Darcy*'

"Seems we have a fucking fancy party to go to, baby."

"Full of famous people, T. Fucking hell," and my man chuckled as I stared at the note.

I ruffled my hair and the smile crept onto my face. Even though I wanted to hate Darcy, he was wearing me down, and this was one hell of a gift. A thoughtful gift too.

"Hey, look. We each get a plus one," Teagen said.

I looked down at the pass and I smirked as an idea bloomed to life. "And I've got an idea, babe," I replied. "Pass me my phone."

Sophie

The stylist arrived at exactly two thirty pm along with a make-up artist, and the nerves were churning as they strolled into the kitchen. Darcy was on the phone to his agent while my hair was slowly fastened into a classy updo, decorated by small red flowers.

"I know, fella.... Drama? Me? Oh ye of little faith... We'll be on time.... One hour," and he glanced over at me, the flash of annoyance sparkling in his eyes.

I simply smiled sweetly and blew him a kiss, making him glare at me before catching the kiss and winking with a devilishly sexy smile.

"No... Only an hour, Christian. I have a very important place to be tonight. Alright... I'll let ya go," and he hung up, turning to me and watching as the final strands of hair were fastened into place.

"Hair finished Miss Carter," said the young guy.

"Thank you," I replied with a warm smile.

"My turn," and the other young man stepped up, laying out an array of make-up. "I'm going to turn you into an even sexier goddess," and he started to contour, blend and turn me into a red carpet worthy girlfriend.

After having my make-up done, nails shaped and painted to match my gown, the young man, Dane, finally grinned at me and said, "There you go. All finished."

"Jesus, how did you do that?" I gasped as he showed me what I looked like.

"Make-up magic," he replied with a wink.

"You're a bloody genius," I said, staring at myself.

A covering of smokey eyeshadow and black mascara, and eyeliner that flicked up at the corners. A deep red on my lips to finish the look and I was stunned. I couldn't quite believe that it was me in the mirror.

"Thank you," I said.

"You are very welcome," he replied.

Darcy appeared and stopped short as he caught sight of me. I smiled and his eyes darkened.

"Do I pass?" I asked.

"Thanks, Aiden, Dane. Feck, ya look stunning love." he said.

The stylist packed up as the make-up genius did the same, and Darcy let them out, then I was ordered upstairs to get changed. Darcy soon followed and the look in his face made me feel so special.

He didn't say anything as he walked into the wardrobe and re-emerged with a black suit and white shirt and the classy bow tie in a clear clothing bag.

"Darcy? Are you okay?" I asked.

His eyes locked onto mine and his expression softened. "All I want to do is stay here and strip ya naked, and bury me self inside ya *all* fecking night, love."

I smirked and walked over to him. I finished fastening the last two buttons of his shirt and helped him into his jacket.

"I'm looking forward to tonight too, Darcy. You're not alone. But, I'm also looking forward to seeing your film. Not looking forward to the press crap though," and I ran my hands through his soft dark hair.

"God, I love ya, Sophie."

"And I love you, O'Sullivan. Now scram while I get myself dressed," and I kissed his lips lightly, trying not to smudge my lipstick.

He grinned and pulled me in for a hug. "Don't take too long. And there's a gift on the dresser for ya," and he kissed my forehead and strode from the room.

I turned and there was a dark blue rectangular box sitting by my make-up, brush, hair ties and my heart stuttered in happy surprise. But, I didn't go and investigate as I needed to get my fancy gown on.

Heart racing, I strode to the clothing bag and pulled out the most beautiful item of clothing I'd ever owned. I stepped into it and pulled up the zipper. I slipped on the matching heels and took a deep breath. I didn't look like me in the full length mirror as I stared at my reflection. I felt like fucking Cinderella.

"Shit," I muttered.

My stomach was beginning to churn now, and I walked back into the bedroom. I picked up the box and pulled up the top.

"Fucking hell," I gasped.

Sat inside was a silver chain with an infinity symbol hanging from it. A ruby sat inside each loop, diamonds surrounding them. A pair of ruby teardrop earrings sat next to it, and I smiled happily.

"Shit, Darcy," I whispered as I ran my fingers over the jewellery.

Grabbing my bag, phone and the jewellery box, I headed down to my sexy, handsome Irishman, and he was waiting in the kitchen, glass of whiskey in his hands.

"Feck, love," he exclaimed as I entered, but I marched over and glared at him.

"This is for me?" and I thrust the box towards him.

"Yes. To complete the look, and feck lass, ya look stunning."

I ended up in front of him and took the glass from his hand. I took a swig and let out a nervous sigh.

"This is too much, handsome," I said, handing him his glass back.

He simply chuckled and shook his head. "Nothing is too much for ya, love," and he winked, smacking my ass as he stared down at me.

I rolled my eyes and slapped his chest. "I'm not with you for what you can buy me. I love you for bloody you," I stated.

He grabbed my waist and yanked me into him, his eyes darkening with what I could only describe as pure fucking lust, and it made my own body heat up, wanting his hands on me, mouth on my skin, and his dick inside my bloody pussy.

"Say it again, beautiful," he growled.

"Say what, O'Sullivan?"

"Ya know what. Don't fecking tease me."

I smirked and pressed myself closer, my fingers tracing lines up over his biceps to his shoulders. "I love you," I whispered.

"Fecking hell," he groaned, then he kissed my neck. "Again."

I rose up on my tiptoes and put my mouth against his ear, wickedness pulsing through me. "I love you. I love your hands on me, your lips kissing mine, and I remember how fucking good your dick felt in my pussy, O'Sullivan. And I can't bloody wait for you to wreck me in the best fucking way tonight," and his hands were gripping my hips tighter with each word I uttered.

"Ya bad fecking girl," he growled, then bit down on my neck, sucking hard.

"Shit, yes," I moaned.

He suddenly released me and slapped my butt with a frustrated groan, and he tipped the last of his whiskey down while adjusting himself.

"Jesus Christ, love," he said, making me grin up at his flustered face.

"Put this on for me?" I asked, handing him the jewellery box.

"Turn around love," he asked, and he placed the necklace around my neck, fastened it then dropped a kiss on my shoulder. "I love ya too, lass. And I can't wait until tonight either ya cheeky bare."

I quickly put in the earrings and looked back at him. "I try my best, and thank you," I said.

"For?"

"The necklace, dress, shit, Darcy, just thank you," and I flung my arms around him once more.

He simply chuckled and pulled me close. "Ya deserve the moon and the stars, love. And I'm going to give ya all of it, including the wrecking ya want."

I giggled and ran my hands through his hair again. "Good to know, handsome," I replied.

I didn't need the gifts, clothes, or jewellery. I just wanted the man in front of me, but he wouldn't take no for an answer, so I just enjoyed being held in his embrace.

The knock rang out, startling me and my stomach went nuts. My hand flew up and pressed over it and Darcy noticed the sudden panic.

"Oh shit," I squeaked.

"Ya look bloody heavenly, love, but know that I'm looking forward to this dress being on the floor tonight," he whispered, kissing my forehead. "And ya naked self under me."

I smirked as excitement coursed through me at the thought, and I watched him pick up my bag and the wrap for my shoulders, heart beating at a million miles an hour. This was it as I noticed the time.

Five pm.

I was about to attend my first public event with Mr Darcy O'Sullivan. The famous Movie star, and I would be photographed by the world's press by his side.

Shitting fucking hell, Sophie. Crap.

Chapter 19.

"Ready, Sophie love?" and I flicked my gaze up to the deliciously handsome face of my very, very famous boyfriend.

"No. Not one little bit," I admitted.

He chuckled again, taking my hand and giving it a squeeze. "It'll be grand, lass. Just stay close to me, and smile," and he winked.

He led me to the front door and Carl was waiting, but there, sitting outside, was a huge black limousine.

"Bloody hell," I stammered.

"Evening Sophie," Carl said with a wink. "You look very beautiful."

"Yeah, hi, thanks," was all I could manage as I was led down the steps and towards the mammoth car.

As we set off my stomach began to tie into knots, pulse racing, and the realisation of what I was about to do caused my heart to stutter. My nerves were on fire as the thought of all those cameras flashing at us replayed on a loop. The memories of my experience with them in the past was *not* pleasant.

Darcy's hand took mine and he laced our fingers together, and I looked over at the actor. He looked very much the film star in his black suit, and I bit down on my lip, knowing he actually loved me, and I loved him.

Who would have bloody thought I'd be back with my Irishman.

"Breathe love," he said as he turned and caught me gawking at him.

"Easy for you to say, O'Sullivan," I fired at him.

"No, love. I hate these things. Ya *do* remember that, lass?"

I frowned and a memory floated back to mind from our steamy fling all those years ago, and that phone call he'd made where he'd complained about having to attend one of these came crashing back into the forefront of my memory.

"Yes. I do," I replied.

He squeezed my hand tighter and lifted it to his lips, kissing the back and he winked. "I love ya," he whispered.

"You're lucky I love you too," I said and smirked. "And you looking fucking hot, Darcy."

His eyes darkened as he leaned forward and whispered into my ear. "I can't wait to feck ya so hard ya won't be able to remember ya name, love."

"Jesus Christ," I gasped as my body burst into flame, my pussy suddenly throbbing with anticipation.

It also made my brain malfunction and words came tumbling out of me. "Yes fucking please, O'Sullivan. All bloody night."

His eyes sparkled as he let out a frustrated groan and his hand flew through his hair. "Damn it, lass. And ya forcing me to the fecking after party."

I snorted into giggles as he glared at me. "For one hour. And to see Max and Teagen."

"This is going to be fecking torture lass. Because I want to rip this off ya right now," and he ran his fingers up my thigh.

I had to bite my lip as my skin burned from his touch, and we stared into each other's eyes with pure unadulterated lust. As his fingers reached the top of my thigh, they started to move inwards, and I gasped as his other hand brushed across the front of my chest, his lips trailing kisses down my neck.

"Fuck," I croaked.

"Here Darcy," called Carl, suddenly breaking the sexual frustration between us, causing the two of us to fly apart from each other in surprise.

He touched my cheek and winked. "Take a deep breath lass, and prepare for a lot of flashing lights."

The door opened and he stepped out first, smiling and waving, camera flashes going crazy. His hand appeared just inside the door, so I took that deep breath and reached out to take it. I swung my legs out first and I stood up to a barrage of shouts, flashing lights and absolutely shit loads of people.

And holy fucking shit. This just got very bloody real.

The noise was deafening and I had to look down at the floor to stop the flashing from bloody blinding me. Darcy held on tightly to my hand and he gazed down at me, smiling warmly. He gave me a little wink and leaned into my ear.

"Smile, love. And give a few waves."

I blinked and nodded. "Sure. Easy right," I muttered.

He waved and started to walk us along the red carpet. My stomach was churning as I finally looked up and saw all the fans screaming at him, waving and wafting various things for him to sign. He didn't let go of my hand as he chatted to fans, had selfies and only when he signed autographs did he reluctantly let go. It was so surreal to be here standing next to this exquisite man, seeing the drooling fans ogling Darcy's fine frame and handsome face. He was moved on by the security team and he grabbed my hand once more and started towards the spot I was terrified of. The fucking mass of press.

"Sorry lass, have to do this," he whispered.

He walked us over to the TV presenters and I recognised one of the women waving at us. Darcy aimed straight for her.

"Hello lass," he drawled, his famous persona on show.

"Hello Darcy. How are you feeling about tonight?"

"Excited for everyone to finally see it, lass."

"You've been attending these alone for a fair few years. What's changed? As you've been snapped with this new lady over the last few weeks?" and her eyes came to me as I was trying to hide behind his body, and he glanced down at me, winking.

I noticed the wicked glint in his eyes and I sucked in a deep breath, panic slamming into me like a train. Darcy leaned forwards and dropped his voice into a stage whisper.

"I'll let ya in on a secret, lass. This beautiful woman is going to be me future wife."

I watched his words sink into her brain then her eyes went wide and stared at me in surprise. He simply stood back and carried on walking. It took a few moments for the statement to filter through them all and then the questions came thick and fast.

"Have you proposed?"

"When are you getting married?"

"Is it true love, Darcy?"

"How long have you been back together?" but Darcy simply ignored them all and continued along the carpet towards the entrance to the theatre.

Darcy

I couldn't help the smug smile appear on my face as I walked on, shaking the hands of my fans, holding tightly to my little director. I gazed down at her and she was smiling and looking so god damned beautiful, causing my heart to go bloody crazy, and I felt so fucking happy.

I had one last trick up my sleeve for the mass of press gathered, so I walked up the steps towards the front of the theatre, but paused at the top. I turned Sophie to face me, holding her close to my body.

"Ready, love?" I whispered.

"For what?" she asked, her eyes fixed onto mine.

"To show them all who I belong to now?" I said.

I crushed her against me and slammed my mouth over hers, kissing her ravenously, my arm around her waist, my other hand at the back of her head, and the flashes went fucking wild. She moaned as I claimed her for the whole fucking world to see, and when I released her? She was all flustered with lipstick smeared over her delectable mouth. She was staring up at me then snorted into laughter as she reached up and wiped my own lips.

"You've got a bit of something," she giggled.

"Ya do too, love," I drawled then a firm hand smacked my back.

Tom was grinning at me and gestured for us to head inside. "That's one way to make a statement, Darce," he said.

I tucked Sophie tightly into my side as we entered, and my agent was striding towards us. A young woman was scurrying behind him, make-up kit in her hands.

"Sort out their faces," he ordered. "Hello lovely lady," he said to Sophie, taking her hand and kissing the back.

"Hi Christian. Long time no see."

"Indeed. You had to bring the drama didn't you, Darcy."

"Couldn't help me self. Sophie looked too fecking tempting," I replied as I watched her lips being fixed, mind drifting into dirty territory.

She snorted and tried not to laugh, making me grin at her. Sophie was perfect for me. She truly understood me, made me feel good about myself, and she never took any of my bullshit. I could be open, vulnerable and *myself* for the first time in my bloody adult life.

Once her lipstick had been reapplied and my own mouth cleaned up, we were ushered into the huge theatre. Eyes followed us as I led my woman to the front of the room. Tom and Violet were already seated, and I gave them a huge smile as I ushered Sophie into her seat.

"Hello, Sophie. Great to finally meet you," said Tom.

She bit down on her lip and I saw the flash of awe as she sat next to the famous actor. "Hello," she replied. "I love your work."

"Thank you. We'll probably see a lot more of each other, as this guy is a great friend of ours. This is my wife, Violet."

I sat too as they shook hands and Tom side eyed me and winked. I understood the simple gesture and nodded, returning the wink. Sophie chatted comfortably with the famous pair, and I just relaxed and enjoyed watching how easily she adapted.

I placed my hand in hers and squeezed. She turned and gave me her beautiful smile and I returned it, smugly, as I had the most stunning woman by my side. That's when the lights dimmed and I saw the excitement in her eyes and body language, and I had to lean over and kiss her cheek.

As the applause rang out and the lights came back up I yanked Sophie to her feet and started for the doors.

"Shit, Darcy. After party remember," she exclaimed.

"How can I fecking forget, love," I replied and she giggled.

"You made a very sexy pirate, and slow the fuck down," she fired at me.

I stopped and she bumped into me with the momentum from tugging her along behind me. "Bloody hell, man," she yelped.

I smirked and scooped her into my arms and continued towards the exit. She groaned and slapped my shoulder, but I saw the fun in her gaze.

"I'm capable of walking, O'Sullivan. And what's the bloody rush?" she asked.

The way Sophie looked and the fact that I'd had to sit through my film, her naked thigh tempting me as the dress fell open, the way the fucking dress hugged her curves? I was literally rabid for her now.

"The sooner we get there, the sooner we leave," I replied.

As we hit the outside of the building, the flashes almost blinded Sophie and she buried her face into my chest.

"Feck," I huffed, but I didn't stop, heading for the car.

The press yelled questions at us but I ignored all of them. Ridiculous ones at that because I was carrying my woman like a bride.

"Kidnapping your date again, Darcy?"

"Did your date pass out, Darcy?"

"Where are you taking your date?"

"Is your date injured?"

Sophie lifted her head, looked at me and grinned like a devil, then she lifted her head and waved at them.

"Nope to all, Just in a hurry you bunch of nosey fecking beggars," she yelled and giggled, dropping her head onto my shoulder.

I snorted into a chuckle and shook my head in amusement at her cheeky words. "Ya naughty lass, teasing them like that," I whispered into her ear.

"Don't bloody care," she said and kissed my lips lovingly.

Jesus, this woman was my perfect soulmate. She was just her, never caring about rules and conformity. Christian was about to have double trouble, and it made me love her all the fucking more. Carl had the door open ready for us and I plopped Sophie back onto her feet.

"In sexy woman," I ordered.

"Bossy," she replied but climbed inside.

My driver arched a brow with a smirk on his face. "Home?"

"Unfortunately, I agreed to an hour at the after fecking party," I muttered. "At this address."

I handed him the card with the directions on it and he laughed. "She's already got you wrapped around her finger. And I think it's great."

"Hilarious, Carl. But fecking true and I love it," and I climbed into the car too.

Leo

Henry stalked back and forth completely naked, script in hand, trying to run lines between our two characters. I was laid out on the bed half covered in the sheet.

"Talk to me Wentworth?"

"I can't. Because I, well, you won't like what I have to say."

"What? That you have a child with a fucking woman? I know that Wentworth, but we can't keep doing this."

Henry paused and groaned, hand running down his face. He turned and glared at me. "Don't tell me," he stated.

I smiled at him and sipped my coffee. "You sure?"

He paused his pacing and ruffled his hair. "Fuck, what does it start with?"

"Give me..." and his eyes lit up.

"Give me time Sawyer, because that is a lot for me to lose."

"You had to fuck her at least once or twice to make a god damned baby."

"And I hated it. I'm alive only with you, Wentworth."

"I hate this. I just want you," and he dropped the script onto the bed.

There were a lot of our scenes that seemed fitting for our predicament. And it was very strange how we'd been cast, especially how we'd ended up as a couple, unable to go out in public.

Our characters were having a clandestine affair, and his brother, Porter, played by Darcy, didn't know that Henry's character was cheating on Porter's wife's sister, and drama was to erupt later in the play. He came to me and climbed into bed and I grinned and pulled him into my arms, relishing the feel of him.

"This is a bloody great play, Sin."

"It is, and I'm loving the fact that you're in it with me," and I kissed him.

I ran my fingers through Henry's hair and gazed into his eyes. "Have you played a gay role before?" I asked.

"No. The ones I was offered were way too stereotypical. This is the first that really spoke to me," he replied.

"I never dared before this year. I took a chance on this because it was such a great story," I replied.

"I had the same feeling. Seems fate stepped in for us, Sin."

He kissed me as his hands caressed my stomach and down over my hips, and I sighed into his lips. But, my phone suddenly started to sing and we both groaned. I scooped it up and I smiled.

"It's Max. Hey, what's up?"

"You have any plans tonight?"

"Except for running lines and, well, you know," and Henry smirked.

"Got a surprise."

"What surprise?"

Henry shuffled close and frowned a little. "Sophe and Darcy gave us an engagement present. Two VIP passes to the premiere after party tonight. We each get to bring a plus one. So, we decided to bring you two," said Max.

I sat up, heart racing and excitement flooding my system. "What? Really?"

"Yep. Be ready for ten thirty. We have a car coming to pick us up."

Chapter 20.

Now, we were dressed up in our best suits and waiting patiently in the kitchen. Henry looked stunning all decked out in a navy blue suit, white shirt and slim black tie. I had gone for my royal blue suit and white shirt, but I didn't want a tie, so the top two buttons were unfastened.

"This is amazing, Sin."

"Yeah," was all I said.

I was fucking nervous as I'd had time to think about it, and press were usually at these events. Henry came to me and cupped my face, kissing me lovingly. We'd had a day of running lines, having sex, eating and then showered for tonight. Now I was feeling apprehensive.

"It will be fine. Max and Teagen are going to be there too. Don't worry, Sin."

"It's the press, H. What if," but he silenced me with a kiss.

"No. I can't have you worrying so much that you can't go out and enjoy yourself."

Before I could answer, the knock startled us and Henry kissed my lips swiftly. He strode to the door and Max grinned at the two of us.

"Ready?" asked Max.

"Yes we are," Henry replied and walked back to me, tugging me towards the front door.

Teagen was standing by the black car and waved. "Come on love birds. Let's go and schmooze with famous people."

Henry ushered me from the apartment and locked the door. He took my hand and we walked to the waiting car. Nerves bristled and I huddled into Henry for a moment.

"I'm nervous, H. What if we get photographed? It'll get back to dad?"

"Stop. Life doesn't come to a halt. You, my sexy, sinful angel are not allowed to hide away in fear. You have friends and a boyfriend in your corner now."

He gave me his gorgeous smile and kissed me, then we climbed into the car with Max and Teagen, heading for a party full of famous people.... and press.

Sophie

Once we got inside we were met with more photographers, making us pose in front of the film's small billboard. Darcy held me tightly against his side and only allowed one or two, then he waved and tugged me into the huge party room.

My eyes swept the place and I didn't know where to look. There were famous actors everywhere, singers, TV stars and I groaned as Darcy walked us to the bar.

"You *are* going to have to speak to people," I stated as he ordered our drinks.

"I know, love. I just want ya home in our bed, naked," he whispered into my ear.

"You keep saying that, wait, *our* bed?"

"Yes lass. Ours. I sleep in it with ya."

"I like the sound of that," and I clamped my mouth shut.

He turned and tilted my face up to his. "Ya know I want ya to stay with me. But I won't push ya, beautiful."

"Thank you. But, I kind of enjoy staying with you," I admitted.

Darcy's face lit up and I had to grin at him, then a very familiar voice called out from behind us.

"Hey shithead," and I turned to see my brother, Teagen, Leo and Henry.

Darcy chuckled and, to my surprise, Max strode straight to him and held out his hand.

"Thanks, Darcy. You'll be happy to know you're growing on me."

My Irishman beamed with a genuine grin and snaked his arm around my waist, holding me close to his side.

"Cheers fein. Glad ya could make it," and he took Max's outstretched hand, shaking it.

My eyes landed on Leo and Henry and I had to go and hug the two of them. One arm around each of their waists and I said, "Glad you're here. And I think you both look hot as sin."

"What?" Leo whispered.

I looked at the two of them and smiled. I kissed Leo's cheek, then Henry's. "In here? You are safe to be yourself. Press isn't allowed."

"Really?" asked Leo.

"Yep. They are only allowed outside. The Party is a closed event," I replied.

Watching Leo relax was priceless. Henry hugged me and he whispered into my ear. "Thanks sexy bitch. You look fucking stunning."

"Thank you, shithead," I answered. "You look pretty hot too."

"Oh, I know. And I have the hottest boyfriend in here," he drawled.

Darcy rolled his eyes but smirked wickedly, kissing my lips again. "I think ya might have competition, fella."

Max smacked Henry and pulled Teagen into his side. " Yes, because my man is the sexiest in this room," and I had to chuckle at them all laughing and enjoying themselves.

Darcy's whole demeanour changed once my brother, Teagen and his fellow cast mates appeared and I beamed with pride as Max had spoken to him and shook his hand. Tom and Violet came sauntering over and he had a very wicked glint in his eyes.

"Jesus fucking Christ," fell from Henry, and the others just stared at the famous actor.

Tom smacked Darcy on the shoulder and gave polite nods to the rest of us, and a wink for me.

"Well, isn't this a rare sight to behold," Tom drawled.

"Not me choice fella. This one made a fecking deal with me," Darcy huffed, sipping his whiskey.

I had to hide my smirk as Darcy resembled a moody teenager as he leaned against the bar, his arm firmly around my waist.

Tom arched his brows in amusement, and Violet giggled. "What did you do, Sophie?" she asked.

Darcy looked down at me and I grinned at him. "I told him I'd sleep in the guest room tonight," I purred.

"Fecking mean, love," he muttered.

I reached up and touched his cheek, and he captured my lips in a swift and tender kiss. I heard quiet laughter coming from the boys and Henry simply snorted and grinned.

"Ha, Darce. So, if you didn't show your face here, our naughty director was going to keep you bloody hanging?" he questioned.

"Feck off, Henry," Darcy fired at him.

"Oh, it would've been hand job only," Henry teased.

I smacked him, but couldn't help the smirk as I looked up at my famous boyfriend. Darcy rolled his eyes as he pulled me into his body.

"Yes, and that would do it," Violet stated.

"And this merry band of four are with you two?" asked Tom, noticing the starstruck stares.

I smiled at the actor and nodded. "Yes. This is my brother Max and his fiancè. That filthy loud mouth is Henry, and the sexy man at his side is Leo. These two are in my latest play that I'm directing," I said.

"A director?" asked Tom. "Ah, theatre, right?"

"And she's very talented fella," Darcy replied, winking down at me, a warm smile on his face.

Tom did a dramatic bow and winked too. "Theatre is much more exciting than making films. That adrenalin you get when the lights come up, and the curtain opens. Can't beat that can you?" he said.

Henry was the next to speak, drawing their attention away from the two of us, so Darcy pulled me in for a hug, and whispered into my ear.

"Do we really have to stay for the full hour, love?"

I snaked my arms around his waist and leaned into him. "Maybe not, O'Sullivan. Because you're not the only one looking forward to going home," I replied.

Darcy

I froze as I gazed down at my little director, and my entire brain shut down. Sophie fucking Carter had just called my house '*home*'.

"Home?" I croaked, the rest of the room seemingly fading into the background.

"What?" she asked, frowning a little in confusion.

"Ya called me house home, love?"

"Did I?"

"Yes, lass."

She lowered her gaze for a few moments, relaxing into my body. My hands roamed up her spine as I watched her contemplating what to say.

Those dark brown eyes eventually lifted back up and locked onto my own, and the next words out of my woman's mouth simply took the oxygen from my body.

"Well, home is, erm, it's wherever you are," she finally answered.

Jesus, holy Mary, mother of God.

I glanced over to see a very happy quartet of guys chatting to Tom and his wife, and I didn't fucking care any longer. I needed to get her home.

"Sorry fellas, Violet. But we're leaving. It's been grand," I announced.

Tom simply smiled into his glass of wine, and Violet grinned. The guys started to laugh, and I was patted on the shoulder by Henry.

"We get you. Go have lots of sexy time, Darce," he drawled.

"I'm gonna, fella. Later," I simply replied with a grin.

I took a hold of Sophie's hand and literally marched through the crowds towards the exit. I was aiming for the door I usually escaped from as I had asked Carl to park around the side of the building.

"Darcy," gasped Sophie, as she tried to keep up in her heels.

"Sorry lass, but ya can't say something like that and expect me to stay for, what?" and I looked down at my watch.

"Twenty fucking minutes, Darcy. That's how long we've been here."

"I'm not staying for another fecking second love."

I shoved open the exit door and started through the lobby of the hotel, guests, photographers and staff bustling around.

"Slow down Darcy. I can't, I'm wearing bloody heels," Sophie yelped at me.

I stopped and grinned at her, then I hoisted her over my shoulder and marched towards the car.

Flashes were going off around us, but I didn't give one fucking care. I'd waited a long time to finally have Sophie naked with me again. Nothing else was going to get in the way of me finally having this little firecracker as I'd been waiting not just the month we'd been back together. I had been waiting years.

"Bloody hell, Darcy," she exclaimed, and she smacked my ass as we hit the cool evening air. "Put me down."

"Nope. Not until I get to the fecking car, love."

"Oh for God's sake," she complained.

I smacked her own ass and she let out the most delicious squeal, making a feral growl fall out of me. I wanted to be inside her so damned badly. Carl chuckled as I arrived with my woman over my shoulder.

"Take us home, Carl," I said, plopping her back onto her feet.

"Bloody hell, Darcy," she fired at me, and smacked my chest. "Hi Carl."

I yanked open the car door and raked a desperate hand through my hair. "Get in, lass," I ordered.

She arched her brows and her sexy lips curled up into a very wicked smirk.

"Bossy," she purred.

"Get in the fecking car, sexy woman," I fired back.

Carl disappeared around to the drivers side as Sophie sidled closer. She smiled like a devil and she literally smacked my ass, hard.

"Hot and bothered are you, O'Sullivan?" she asked.

Jesus, this woman would be the death of me.

She winked and climbed into the car, but I had to take a couple of deep breaths. I ruffled my hair, painfully turned on, and Carl sniggered as I caught his gaze.

"She's perfect for you, Darcy," said my driver, then slipped inside too.

I climbed in after my little sexy minx and the split in the dress had fallen open, giving me a stunning view of her divine thigh.

"Feck," I muttered as she turned to face me. "Get us home, Carl."

The car came to a stop outside my townhouse, and I practically launched myself out of it. "Catch ya Monday, Carl. Cheers fella," I said, then held out my hand for Sophie.

As soon as she took it I yanked her from inside and she let out a little yelp. "Shit, Darcy," and she giggled. "Night Carl. Thanks."

"Come on lass," I ordered, striding to my front door.

As it clicked shut and the lock was turned Sophie started towards the kitchen. "Shall I get us a drink, Oh fuck."

I grabbed her wrist and pulled her backwards and my mouth descended on hers as I crushed my body against her, pinning her to the wall. Her hands came to my waist and swiftly upwards, knocking off my jacket. My own were hoisting up her dress, looking for her pussy. I needed to be inside her, and Sophie was equally as eager, her fingers working to free my cock as I plunged a finger inside her.

"Feck, lass," I groaned against her lips.

"Shit," she gasped, bucking her hips into my movements.

It was desperate, hungry and fuelled with such a powerful need for each other. She moaned as I pushed two more fingers inside, and I grinned as she finally freed my cock.

"I have to feck ya, love. Legs," I demanded.

She allowed me to lift her, then, without hesitation, lining myself with her slick entrance, I rammed my painfully hard cock into my one true love.

"Jesus, fuck, Darcy," fell from her as my hips slammed into hers.

"Jesus, ya feel fecking stunning," I croaked, holding still for a few seconds, as I didn't want to come like a fucking inexperienced teenage lad.

"And I forgot how fucking big you are," she stammered and giggled.

"Are ya alright, love?"

"Course I am. Just fuck me, O'Sullivan."

I grinned at Sophie pinned to the hall wall, then I winked, took a deep breath then slid almost all the way out, locking eyes with hers.

"Jesus, lass. I fecking love ya," I whispered, then I thrust back in and started to pound into her, roughly, greedily, and the gasps and cries coming from her were heavenly.

"Yes, god, fucking hell, oh my god, don't... fucking... stop," she moaned, her fingers digging into my shoulders.

I didn't. I just rocked back and forth at a punishing pace, chasing that climax, crushing her into the wall. But, I wanted her to come with me.

"Fuck, Darcy," she cried. "You're gonna... make... me, Ohmyfuckyes."

And her body went rigid, her pussy clamping down onto my cock, and I groaned loudly as she triggered my own, and I exploded.

"Feck," I growled, grinding into her as she milked me for every fucking drop.

I held her tightly as I waited for her to come back down, our pants and gasps echoing through the silent hallway.

"Fucking hell, Darcy," she finally croaked.

"I couldn't fecking wait, love," I replied breathlessly.

She dropped her head onto my shoulder and giggled. "I noticed, O'Sullivan, and it was fucking amazing," she whispered into my ear.

That was music to my heart, so I looked up and grinned at her, our faces flushed, eyes sparkling. "Now, we can get that drink, lass."

"Just so you know, I love you right fucking back, Darcy," she said as I pushed us from the wall.

I was still inside her, reluctant to pull out, so I carried her as her legs were wrapped around my waist, arms around my neck, and her sexy dress all bunched up around her hips. I massaged her ass as I entered the kitchen.

"I don't want to put ya down, love," I admitted.

She lifted her head and ran her hands through my hair, kissing my neck, and I was in fucking heaven.

"You're going to have to, even though I'm rather happy here, O'Sullivan," she replied.

I sat her on the stool and a small moan left my lips as I pulled my cock out of her divine pussy.

"What would ya like, love?" I asked, tucking myself back into my boxers.

I headed for the sink and washed my hands, then turned to smile at her. She was unclipping her hair as she sat there, and I felt my dick twitch back to life.

"Whiskey please, handsome," she replied.

I smirked and walked to my drinks cabinet. "Handsome am I?" I said.

"You angling for a compliment, Darcy?" she asked.

"Maybe," I said, and winked as I poured us a large measure.

Sophie

That had been so fucking hot and Darcy had made me come like a bloody champion with only his dick. He'd literally slammed me into the wall and ravished me with such fire, I was instantly soaking wet for him. I was sure there might be a bloody Sophie shaped dent in the hall wall after that. My body was still humming, but I noticed the bulge reappearing and I smirked.

"Here ya go, love," and he handed me the tumbler.

"Thanks. What now?" I asked, trying to sound as innocent as possible.

The look in his eyes told me exactly what he had in mind, and I smiled into my glass as I took a sip. Darcy had just gotten started. So, I allowed my heels to fall to the floor, and gathered my gown's skirt up into my hand.

"What are ya doing lass?" he asked, but his voice had turned into liquid gold.

I simply smiled as sweetly as I could, jumped from the stool and set off for the stairs. I ran as fast as I could in the dress I was wearing, and I heard his laughter as he started after me. My legs were burning as I reached the top floor and shoved open the bedroom door. Darcy wasn't far behind me and I squealed as I was yanked from the floor and thrown onto the bed.

"Ya cheeky devil," he growled as he climbed on top of me.

"Need to make you work for it, right?" I giggled.

He left a trail of kisses down my neck, and his fingers were working the zipper down on my dress.

"Oh really," he whispered, suddenly yanking the gown downwards.

"Crap," I gasped, as I was shunted down the bed with it.

He simply lifted my ass, then tossed it onto the floor. Next came his shirt, which he started to unfasten, then lost patience and yanked it over his head. My eyes soaked in his sinfully hot body as he climbed off and swiftly removed his trousers. He came back to me and hooked his fingers under the band of my pants.

"Lift," he ordered, and I raised my butt in the air as he pulled them down my legs.

The last remnants were shed and he was crushing me into the mattress, kissing me like a starving man. It was swift and he suddenly rolled us over so I was laying on top of him.

"And now, lass, for that little stunt at the car? Ya gonna ride me so I can watch ya come all over me."

His words caused a hot shiver to skitter down my spine, and my cheeks burned as he stared into my eyes. His hand was slowly fisting his impressive dick and it looked so damned hot.

"Now sit down, love. Sit and make ya self come for me," he ordered.

I smirked and kissed his sexy lips as I straddled him, his eyes dropping as I lined myself up over him.

"Jesus, love. Fecking sit down," he groaned as I trailed more kisses down and across his shoulder.

I didn't move right away, taking my time, then I yelped as his hands gripped my hips and yanked me downwards, sending his cock so deeply that I cried out with both shock and pure pleasure, and he fucked me, roughly rocking me swiftly back and forth, our gasps, moans and grunts filling the room.

All bets were off. We had finally unleashed the desperate need to be as close to each other as we possibly could, and we didn't stop until we literally collapsed from exhaustion.

Chapter 21.

Leo

I groaned as I cracked open my eyes, Henry's beautiful face beside me. His hair was all ruffled and I couldn't help but stare. My head was pounding, mouth as dry as a fucking desert, and I really needed to piss. But, I had to kiss his soft lips.

"Morning, Sin," he muttered.

"Morning sexy ass," I replied.

I sat up and crawled out of bed, but Henry's hand grabbed my wrist. "Get back here, Sin."

"Need the bathroom, bossy, H."

He chuckled and let me go. "Hurry up. I need to snuggle," he drawled.

I had to smile and went to relieve myself.

Once finished, hands washed and a swift drink from the cold tap, I walked back to my man. It had been an amazing party, and we'd managed to get quite a few selfies with loads of famous actors.

"Get here, sexy man," Henry ordered and I smirked and crawled into his waiting arms, kissing his lips slowly.

This man had already climbed inside my heart and set up camp there, and he made me finally feel wanted for who I really was. We were ridiculously happy in our little bubble and I never wanted to leave.

"What are you thinking about, Sin?" he asked.

"How comfortable this is," I answered, making him finally open his eyes and look into mine.

"It is. Because you're my fucking soulmate. I knew as soon as you walked into the bloody theatre bar, Sin. Why do you think I went after you?" he whispered into my hair.

"Really?" I asked, my heart starting to race as he buried his face in my neck, hands gently exploring my body.

"Really, Sin. Tara was telling the truth when she said I had no filter with people I care about. I fucking adore you, Leo Trent."

My heart skipped several beats as his lips caressed my skin, fingers running through my hair.

There was a sudden loud crash coming from Henry's living room and we both shot out of bed.

"What the hell?" I exclaimed.

Scooping up our boxers and slipping them on, we ran down the hall and stopped at the doorway. Max and Teagen were sitting up on the sofa bed staring at the broken window. Their eyes found us as we started to come in.

"What the actual fuck?" Henry growled.

There was a brick on the floor and two words on a piece of paper attached to it. '*Sick bastards*' it simply read.

"It just came flying through the fucking window," Teagen stated, staring down at the projectile.

"Are either of you hurt?" asked my boyfriend.

"Luckily, no," replied Max.

I ran my hand through my hair in frustration and looked at Henry. "This is the final fucking straw, H."

He stopped me from going any further and pulled me in for a hug. "It is, but this could be your dad," he whispered.

The fear that coursed through me made my heart jolt. I fixed my eyes on his and gripped his shoulders tightly.

"Why do you think that?" I croaked.

"Brick through a window is old school. Eve is younger, so maybe this isn't her style?"

Max jumped over the back of the sofa and strode towards us. "Your dad is a fucking bully, and we won't let him hurt you. But it could be Eve," he said.

Teagen did the same and he ushered us away from the glass. "We need clothes on and shoes before we try to clear this up," he said.

"You sure you two are okay?" asked Henry.

"We're fine. Don't worry, H," Max replied

I backed away and turned towards Henry's bedroom. The fear was threatening to choke me as I thought about dad showing up. I felt physically sick as I grabbed my phone and looked down at the screen.

"Shit," I muttered.

There were numerous messages from mum and Mia. I opened them up and the blood drained from my face as I read their words.

"*Hey Honey. There's been some pictures posted online and Dad saw them. He's already left for London. Call me Leo. Mum xxx*"

"*Leo, someone posted some pictures of you dancing with a guy. You were kissing. Dad got tagged in them by that girl called Eve. Please be careful. Give me a call. Mia xxxxx*"

I dropped the phone and my knees threatened to give out. The room started to shrink around me as it felt as though something was crushing my chest. I couldn't fucking breathe. My fucking bully of a dad was on his way here. Henry was right there, arms coming around me as I crumpled into a heap on the floor.

"Dad knows," I gasped. "He's coming here."

"What? Sin, how do you know?" he asked, holding me as I trembled in his arms.

I buried my face into his chest and took a deep breath of him, his scent, and it helped to calm me a little, but the tears gathered as he tightened his hold on me.

"My phone. Mum, Mia, they sent messages to warn me. Social media, there's photo's of us, and that stupid little bitch tagged my dad in them. We were kissing. Jesus, he's going to hurt me," and I held on tightly to him, stomach churning with sheer terror and nausea.

"No, he fucking won't. I'm right here for you, beautiful," he whispered into my ear. "No-one will lay a fucking finger on you."

Darcy

I had Sophie snuggled next to me sleeping soundly. For the first time in a very fucking long time, I didn't want to move. I stayed here, holding her. The workout would be squeezed in at a later time today.

I was in some sort of blissed out state after last night. We didn't put each other down until around three in the morning, and every fucking second had been breathtaking. I looked down at my sleeping woman and smiled. Messy post sex hair, soft lips and all fucking mine.

The phone vibrating startled me, and Sophie groaned as I reached out and swiped it off the bedside table.

"Shit, what time is it?" she muttered, snuggling closer into my chest.

"Sorry, love. Go back to sleep," I whispered.

"Tell them to fuck off. I need more sleep because you kept sticking your talented cock in me."

"And I'm not sorry that I did either, love. Go back to sleep."

I leaned in and kissed her, then opened my phone as best as I could without disturbing her, but frowned as I read the message.

"Leo's dad is on his way. Eve tagged him in photographs from social media. Brick came through my window this morning. God knows how she got Leo's dad's name. But he's a mess. Can you help? H x"

"Shite," I whispered.

"Darcy?" and Sophie looked up at me, those dark eyes warming my very soul. "What's wrong?"

"Trouble, love."

I eased her from my arms and kissed her again, then sat up and tried to rub the tiredness from my eyes.

She did the same and frowned at my serious expression. I just handed her my phone with the message from Henry.

"Oh, for fuck's sake. Really?" she groaned.

"Really. Let me call Christian, love. He knows people," and I reluctantly climbed out of bed and found my boxers.

Sophie laid back and let out a loud sigh. I picked up my shirt and slipped my arms inside as she bit down on her lip and ran her hand through her hair.

"Why does drama seem to follow us around?" she asked.

"I can't answer that, love."

I grabbed a pair of jogging pants from the drawer and pulled them on, then walked back to her. I took her face in my hands and kissed those divine lips.

"God, Sophie. I love ya."

"Love you too, Darcy," she whispered back.

"Stay here. I'll call Christian then make coffee."

"No. I'll make coffee, you call your lovely agent," and she sat up and jumped from the bed.

I watched for a few moments, as she was completely, deliciously naked. Then I caught myself and started for the door.

"Grand. Meet ya in the kitchen?"

"Yep. Kitchen. Go, sexy ass."

I strode out and called Christian as I jogged down the stairs. It was only just seven in the morning, but he had contacts that would help and hopefully keep it on the down low. We also didn't need that piece of shite Casey getting wind of this.

"For the love of god, Darcy. Do you know what time it is? On a bloody Sunday?"

"Sorry, fella, but it's important."

"What is it?"

"Henry had a brick thrown through his window not long ago. There were some pictures put on social media, and Leo's stalker? She informed his fecking homophobic dad."

"What?"

"Leo's dad is on his way to find Henry. Potentially to bloody harm him and Leo."

"Okay. I'm on it. Also, check out the pages for your premiere. I don't want any drama from you either."

"Grand. Thanks, fella."

"Send me Henry's number, and Leo's. I'll need to speak to them. Also, tell them not to worry."

"And the press?"

"I will try to contain, but that's a big ask, Darcy."

"I understand. We had better brace ourselves for any fallout then."

"I'm afraid so."

I walked into the living room and stopped by the back window, staring out at my little garden. "Just make sure they're safe, Christian. Leo's a mess. He's terrified of his fecking dad."

"It will be handled. Now send me those numbers and enjoy the rest of your day," and he was gone.

I ruffled my hair and let out an annoyed sigh. Leo didn't deserve this. He was a great guy and very bloody talented, and he shouldn't have had to hide such a huge part of himself for so fucking long. I knew that all too well.

I walked downstairs and Sophie was making coffee as I wrapped her up from behind. "What the hell happened?" she asked.

"Seems Eve tagged Leo's crazy dad in some photographs from last night. Want to check in on them?" I asked, kissing the crook of her neck.

"Yes. Can we go and see them?" she questioned.

"Of course, love. She needs fecking stopping before someone gets bloody hurt," and I kissed Sophie's shoulder, head pounding and a sense of dread building in my gut.

"I hope Leo is alright."

"Henry said he's in a mess."

"I'm going to let Max know. He needs friends in his corner."

"Grand idea, love," and I turned her around so that I could kiss her.

Max

Teagen and myself cleaned up the glass and covered the hole in the window while Henry looked after a very terrified Leo. His dad had scared his own son beyond repair as far as I could tell. Our friend had turned whiter than white as he was led away by Henry.

"This is fucked up," my fiancè muttered.

"Yeah. You'd think this kind of thing wouldn't happen any fucking more," I answered.

I raked my hand through my hair and tugged Teagen into my arms, pressing him tightly to me. He dropped his head onto my shoulder and buried his face into my neck. I wouldn't ever let any fucker hurt this man. He was my world.

"We have to help him. We can't let his dad hurt either of them," I whispered.

"Yeah. I was thinking the same," he replied.

Henry and Leo reappeared and I didn't hesitate. I walked over and hugged him. "You have us too, Leo. You're not walking into this alone."

He sighed, his own arms wrapping around me. "Thanks, Max. And I've decided to come out. Dad might want to fucking hurt me and Henry, but I'm sick of this, this bloody all consuming fear of him," he said quietly. "I'm terrified, but I'm doing this."

Henry took over and held onto him, sitting down on the sofa. "I'm very adept at protecting myself, Sin. And I'm tempted to smack ten bells out of that stupid bitch."

Leo's phone suddenly started ringing and he frowned as it was a private number. "Answer it, Leo," I said.

He pressed the green icon and took a deep breath. "Hello? It is.... Oh," and he sat up taller. "Sure. Really?... Okay..... That's amazing.... Thank you..... Yeah, okay. We'll be here.... I will and tell Darcy thanks too," and he hung up.

We were all staring at him as he visibly relaxed where he sat, hands running through his hair, but he didn't say anything, a look of shock in his eyes. I groaned and waltzed over, smacking his shoulder.

"Jesus, what was that all about?" I questioned.

"Yeah, Sin. Spill," Henry asked.

Leo suddenly beamed at the three of us, his hand grabbing Henry's. "Seems Darcy got his agent to get me and Henry a security detail, plus he's going to pick up Eve," he said.

"What?" Henry asked. "Pick up Eve? What does that mean?"

Leo turned to his man and kissed him. "I'm not sure about Eve, but the security will be outside in the morning to drive us to work, and he's sending someone to come and fix your window. They'll be here in about an hour."

"Fuck, that's amazing," Henry exclaimed.

Teagen took my hand and squeezed. "Again, perks of your sister dating a famous movie star, baby."

I rolled my eyes but smiled, and pulled out my phone. "Find the pics online, babe. Let's see what that bitch set in fucking motion."

"And let's find the pictures from the premiere. I want to see our sexy director strutting her gorgeous stuff on the red carpet," Henry drawled.

Teagen kissed me and started to head to the kitchen. "I'll make us all coffee. Grab your laptop, Henry."

Henry kissed Leo on the forehead and patted my arm as he passed. "Thanks for clearing up the glass, Max," he whispered as he did.

"No worries. We stick together," I replied.

Leo came up behind me and touched my shoulder. I gave him a warm smile and winked. "Thanks Max. I'm fucking terrified, but you and Teagen sorta gave me the courage."

"And we're not leaving you to deal with it alone either. Come on, let's see what those photos have in them," and I led him to the kitchen where we all sat at the dining table.

Chapter 22.

Sophie

Darcy was standing at the kitchen counter, laptop open, his sexy, muscular chest on show as he hadn't fastened the buttons of his shirt. His hair was all messy on top and I wanted to run my hands all over him.

"What did Christian say?" I asked, finishing my coffee.

"He's sending someone to fix the window, and a security detail for Leo and Henry."

He moved swiftly and reached out, then I was engulfed in his arms and hugged tightly.

"I'd better make more coffee, as I'm bloody exhausted, O'Sullivan."

"And make it strong. We didn't get much sleep last night, did we, lass?" he growled.

His hands were on my butt, lips kissing up my neck, and I sighed as his touches had the desired bloody effect. Darcy's hands were running up my spine and his mouth found mine, kissing me confidently, the lingering taste of coffee on our tongues. My skin tingled as my fingers languidly raked through his hair, pussy fluttering with excited anticipation again, and I moaned into his lips.

"Feck, I need to put ya down. I'm knackered," he whispered into my hair. "Love ya, lass."

"Love you too, handsome. I messaged my brother and they were there last night. They stayed over, so they were fucking lucky they didn't get hurt."

"True, love. Eve has no idea what she's fecking done."

I walked over to the coffee machine and started to prepare the fancy contraption for more caffeine, and turned to stare at my man.

"Have you spoken to them? Henry and Leo?" I asked.

He nodded as he scrolled the social media sites for Eve's pages. "And they are severely fecking pissed. Got her. Shite, she got into the damned after party. Here, take a look. Little Miss Hemlock is dangerous. She's been following him," and he gestured for me to join him.

I filled our mugs and walked to the island, his arm snaking around my waist, dropping a kiss on my lips.

"Ya seeing what I am, love," he said.

"Oh shit," I exclaimed as I looked down.

My eyes landed on three rather clear photographs of Henry and Leo slow dancing in each other's arms. The first was of the pair on the dance floor. Leo's head was resting on Henry's shoulder, arms around each other, and fucking hell, they looked so beautiful and very much a couple. The second had them gazing into each other's eyes, and shit, it was obvious that these two were falling for each other. But, it was the third that told everyone in the world what they were to each other. Henry had his hands on Leo's cheeks and their lips were locked in a very intimate kiss, and I groaned as I read her words underneath.

"This man stole my boyfriend. Leo was the love of my life until Henry Rossi corrupted him. Poisoned his mind. And they are in the same play together with Darcy O'Sullivan. My heart is broken."

"Christ, she's crazy. How the hell did she get the gig after her dad came for her the first time?" I muttered.

Darcy pulled me in and kissed my lips. "Don't know yet. Christian is dealing with it. But, it's clear that she's been following them. To get into a private exclusive party just to follow Leo? That's very worrying behaviour, lass," he replied. "It's tantamount to stalking."

"Yes. Fuck, I hope Leo is okay."

He smiled and stroked a finger down my spine. "He will be, love. Christian will see to it. He knows a lot of people, lass."

"Oh? Like who?" I asked.

He just smirked and winked like a fucking devil. "He's got connections all over the place, lass," was all he said.

He started to search for the coverage of the premiere so I went to top up our mugs for our third coffee of the morning. After a few more moments Darcy let out a long whistle.

"Well, love. We made the headlines, lass. And ya look like a fecking goddess."

I finished filling Darcy's and walked over to pass him his mug. I looked down and froze as I saw the photographs and the headline.

'*Head over heels in Love*'

The pictures were of that epic kiss, Darcy carrying me from the theatre, another of me wiping his lips as I giggled, then the last made me snort into a laugh. Darcy was striding through the hotel, me over his shoulder, smacking his butt.

"Great view of ya sexy ass, ya gorgeous little minx," he said, then smacked it, making me squeal and giggle.

He'd kissed every bloody inch of my body last night in between the amazing orgasms both with his talented fingers, mouth, and his very impressive dick.

"What are ya thinking about, love?" he whispered into my hair.

"Last night, and, well, the reason why we're both exhausted," I replied.

Darcy smirked, but I saw the wicked sparkle in his beautiful eyes just a fraction too late, as I was hoisted over his shoulder again, making me yelp and giggle as he marched us from the kitchen island towards the stairs.

Leo

Henry held onto my hand tightly as we climbed into the black car waiting for us. My nerves were a mess after yesterday, and my boyfriend had taken great care of me.

Max and Teagen were amazing too, and I was so fucking thankful that they hadn't been hurt. I'd thought about it all damned day and Henry had eventually agreed with me. My Dad was a fucking bully, and he wouldn't have shied away from confrontation. He would have knocked the fucking door down and charged in, fists at the ready. So, we agreed it had to have been Eve.

"You okay, Sin?"

"Yeah. Just having a fucking breakdown," I groaned.

"Everything will be alright, my sexy angel," Henry purred, and leaned in, turned my face to his and kissed me, making me instantly relax into the moment.

"I fucking love you, H" came flying out of my mouth, and Henry froze.

He pulled back and he stared at me in shock, and the panic slammed into my gut as I stared right back.

"What?" he whispered, his hands grabbing my head, forcing me to stare right back. "What did you just say?"

"I, well, shit, I'm sorry," I stammered, terror seeping into every pore.

"What the fuck? Why are you sorry? Because I love you, Sin, so fucking say it again," he ordered.

I blinked in surprise, my heart skipping more than a beat. "Wait, you do?" I gasped. "You love me?"

"Say it, Sin, so fucking help me God, repeat it. I want to hear you say it again," he growled.

I took a deep breath and looked right into those gorgeous dark eyes. "Henry. Enrico Rossi, I fucking love you," and his mouth descended on mine.

I gripped his head with my own hands, kissing the bloody life from him, and in this moment, I had never felt so fucking happy.

"Shit, I need to put you down, Sin."

I chuckled, slightly out of breath. "Yeah. And now I've got a huge fucking hard on."

Henry grinned and raked his hand through my hair, pulling out the tie. "Wish you'd wear this down more," he whispered.

"Maybe I will, if you ask nicely," I replied, winking wickedly.

The car pulled up outside the theatre, and our eyes glanced out of the window. "Jesus fucking Christ," Henry gasped.

The entrance to the theatre was flooded with press photographers and reporters. I ran my hands over my face, and slumped into the seat as my nerves shot through the roof. As soon as we stepped out of the car? It would be very clear that we were a couple. I had agreed to finally come out as gay, but it didn't help the nausea and fear churning in my stomach.

"Crap, that's a lot of reporters," I huffed.

Henry unclipped our seatbelts, took my hand and squeezed. "What did we talk about? You need this, sexy ass. Now, take a deep breath and let's go."

The car door was opened by the huge sandy haired security guy and he winked. "Stay between the two of us, and you'll be fine," he ordered.

"Yeah. Sounds simple," I muttered.

We stepped out and the flashes went crazy, practically blinding us. Questions were coming thick and fast from every damned angle, microphones being shoved into our faces. The two security guards simply surrounded us as best as they could, but the voices rang out all around us.

"What about your girlfriend? Are you going to break up with her?"

"Are you going to tell her?"

"Do you know that she's heartbroken?"

"How long have you been sleeping together?"

"Did you hide the fact you're gay from her?"

"Do you usually go around stealing boyfriends Mr Rossi?" and that voice made Henry's eyes snap up and glare at the blonde guy.

The two burly security guys hustled us inside and I wanted to scream and punch something. This was all because of that fucking stupid crazy cow, and she had no damned idea what she'd fucking done. No idea that she'd poked a very violent and vicious bear, and we were in the firing line.

"Fucking hell, I don't know how Darcy does it," Henry groaned.

"They knew your last name, Henry," I said, and the rage started to simmer.

Henry didn't say anything and turned to the two men. "Thank you. Do you hang around now?"

"Yes, Mr Rossi. Mr Trent."

"What do we call you?" I asked.

"That's Ben, and I'm Stefan."

Henry stepped a little closer and spoke to Stefan. The guard was built like a fucking train with giant arms and thighs. He had dark brown hair, cut extremely short. Tattoos, dark blue hypnotic and serious eyes, and I noticed the gun under his jacket.

"There's a reporter out there. Blonde, looks like a fucking weasel. He's one of the scumbag reporters, and he's a snake. If Casey's here? Trouble is on the bloody cards," Henry said.

Stefan glanced into the street and I followed his gaze as he zeroed in on the man in question. He turned back to the two of us and nodded.

"I see. We keep an eye out for that one, and your dad." he replied, his Scottish accent echoing around the quiet lobby.

I let out a sigh and gave the mountain of a man a smile. "My dad is pretty much an older version of me. And look out for that bitch too. This is all her fucking fault," I said.

Ben walked to me and patted my arm. He was fair haired, not as bulky as Stefan, and he had hazel eyes, and a rather cute smile. "You might be surprised when you go in there. Now go do the acting thing," he replied.

I smiled genuinely and the dark haired Stefan threw me a wink. "May I say something?" he asked.

"Sure," Henry replied, taking my hand.

"That woman? Eve? She's blatantly not your girlfriend, right?"

"Never has been, Stefan," I replied.

Henry tugged me into his side and kissed my lips. I smiled at both of the men standing in front of us, and they knew what I was getting at.

"She's done a shitty thing then," said Ben.

"Yes. She's fucking crazy," Henry replied. "And thanks. We know Darcy sorted this."

They each smiled and Henry pulled me closer. "If you need to go out of the theatre come and get us. We're here for your protection. Use us Mr Trent, that's our job," said Ben, and they each gave us a nod then walked back towards the front doors.

Henry grinned at me and took my hand. "Let's go rehearse, and be our loved up selves," he whispered, and we walked into the auditorium, hand in hand, and sauntered down to the front of the stage, not realising that there was a tall, exquisitely dressed man waiting for us.

"Mr Rossi. Mr Trent," he said.

The man in front of us was a very gorgeous, blonde, blue eyed Adonis. He exuded confidence and power.

"That might be us?" Henry replied, pulling me closer.

"Christian West. Darcy's agent," and he held out his hand.

I grinned and strode over, taking the offered hand. "Oh shit, you're the reason we have Ben and Stefan. Thanks so much."

"Very welcome. Now, Eve has been found. She has been telling us some rather interesting things," said the agent.

Henry frowned as I rubbed my face with frustration. "Like what, exactly?" he asked.

Christian looked a little worried as he stepped closer. His blue eyes landed on me first before speaking.

"You two were soulmates. You were going to get married and have three children. And that is for starters," he finally replied.

I leaned into Henry as I heard a low growl emanate from deep inside him. "There was also some rather vicious things about Henry here, and her father wanted to speak to you about it," and he stepped to the side.

A tall slender, white haired man walked onto the stage and down the steps towards us. He had grey blue eyes and a look of both shame and embarrassment.

"I believe my daughter managed to upend your life, Mr Trent. And for that I'm so very sorry," he said.

I stared at the tired and very sad guy in front of us and sighed. "She did. I never, not once, gave her any sign that I was interested in her," I said.

"She is accusing this fine man of attacking you, forcing himself on you, and a lot of other rather nasty things," Eve's dad said.

My boyfriend let out an annoyed groan and walked towards the older gentleman. "I need you to know this, because lies like that can ruin lives Mr Hemlock," and her dad nodded. "Accusing me of attacking my boyfriend is the furthest from the truth. I love this guy, and I could never hurt him."

He sighed, running a frustrated hand through his hair and he came to me and took my hand squeezing it tightly.

"I'm so sorry. She will be escorted home and we are getting her some help. She won't bother you any longer. You have my word," he said, his voice laced with pain and sadness, and I nodded, but he had no idea what his daughter had set in motion.

"She threw a brick through my window," Henry exclaimed. "Two of our friends were sleeping in there. They could've been seriously hurt."

Eve's dad stepped closer and the frustration was clear to see in his expression. "The police have been informed by me. She will be charged for that as she told me she'd done it. I can't change what she did, but know that you are safe now."

"Thank you, but, well, the thing is," and I stopped, not sure how to word it.

Henry squeezed my hand and moved closer. "Tell him, Sin because he needs to know."

I looked at Eve's dad and let out a sigh. "My dad is extremely homophobic. He's seen the photographs she posted. He's heading here to... find Henry, and to beat some sense into me, well, both of us if I'm honest," I said, and his eyes closed.

"God, son, I'm sorry. I'm taking her home again. The place where she was staying dropped the damned ball, let her leave. She's a great actor, but she can't, well, it's happened before. She is unwell and we didn't realise until the first young man complained and got a restraining order. That was when I was contacted and informed what had been happening. She was staying in a private complex with instructions to not allow her to leave."

I let out a long breath and nodded. "Thanks for coming here. It does mean a lot, but my Dad could potentially try and hurt me and my boyfriend. All because of your daughter."

He seemed to visibly age in front of us, and I felt for him. "I presume that's why this gentleman got in touch with me?" and I nodded, Henry wrapping me up in his arms.

I nodded. "Yes it is, Mr Hemlock. And I hope you can make sure that she stays far away from these young men and get her the help she needs?" said Christian.

"You have my word," he replied. "And I am so very sorry Mr Trent."

Chapter 23.

Sophie

The car approached and we both saw the masses of reporters. Darcy cursed. "Shite. This is down to that little crackpot mentioning me bloody name."

I took his hand and squeezed. "You, Mr O'Sullivan, are used to this. So, you just need to keep your woman safe."

He smirked and yanked me into him for a kiss. "Always, love. And hearing ya call ya self me woman makes me want to go straight home and strip ya naked all over again."

I snorted into a laugh, smacking his chest. "Behave, sexy ass."

The car came to a stop in front of the hordes of reporters and Carl turned to look at us. "Sorry boss. No other entrance is available today."

"Come on, Mr. Famous movie star. Do your stuff, handsome, gorgeous, randy fucker," I purred into his ear.

I heard Carl stifle a laugh, and Darcy's eyes sparkled with wickedness. "Ya gonna pay for that later, love. And ya just as bad, naughty bare."

"And you bloody love it, O'Sullivan," I whispered sweetly.

He chuckled, yanking me into his arms and slamming his mouth on mine. It was a passionate kiss, but swift. We each took a deep breath, calming our racing hearts, and Darcy opened the door, climbing out to a barrage of flashes all over again. He held out his hand and I joined him, the two of us fighting through the crowds. Two huge men in black suits appeared like two knights in burley, intimidating armour.

"Ben, Stefan? Is Christian here?" Darcy asked as they surrounded us and helped into the theatre.

"Yes, Sir."

"Cheers, fein. This is Sophie. The love of me life," he said.

They each threw me a polite smile. "Great to meet you, Miss," said the fair haired saviour.

"Sophie, please," I replied. "And thanks for the save. Those fuckers are bloody scumbags."

The dark haired one smirked as he dropped his gaze. "You need to go out today? Come and find us. That's what we're here for," and he winked.

I was swiftly tugged into the auditorium and we stopped short at the sight of Darcy's agent, Henry and Leo, and a very sad looking older gentleman.

"Christian," Darcy said as we made our way down to the quartet.

The familiar blonde smiled warmly at me, and he gave me a swift hug. "You are very good for him," he whispered.

"Thanks, Christian."

"He's been a very lonely and sad guy for a long time. You've given him his spark back."

His words caused me to turn and look at my Irishman. He was talking to Henry, Leo and the older guy.

"Yes, lady. He's waited for you. Not one female has touched him since that new year. You seem to complete him, and allow him to let his real personality shine through. You brought him back to life, Sophie."

I had to smile, but my eyes went to the stranger among us. "Thanks Christian. He's done the same for me too. But I have to ask, who is that?"

"Eve's dad. They picked her up last night. She was spouting a lot of nonsense. They were going to get married. Henry was forcing himself on Leo, and she admitted to tagging Leo's dad in the pictures and throwing a brick through Henry's window. She also had a box full of creepy items."

"Creepy items?" I questioned.

"Used tissues with stage makeup on them. A used coffee cup. She even had a pair of his socks and a t-shirt," he replied.

I arched my brows in surprise and glanced over at Leo then back at Christian. "Jesus, that's bloody scary," I muttered.

"She is going to be charged with criminal damage and her hate speech was flagged. The names she called Henry were disgusting. But, her mental issues will also be taken into consideration," he said.

I dropped my bag into a chair and let out a loud sigh. Something about me, Darcy, Tara and henry working together seemed to attract nothing but bloody drama. And there was still the issue of Leo's dad.

As though he was reading my thoughts, Darcy's agent said, "No sightings of Leo's father yet, and that is a worry."

I sighed and looked back at the loved up pair. The last thing we needed with all the press outside? A crazy dad storming in here and causing a scene, but also causing harm to two of my cast members, and great friends too.

"Thank you for your help, Christian," I said.

"Not a problem, now your other actors are appearing," and he patted my shoulder.

"Why don't you stick around? Henry is very talented, and so is Asia, and I think you'd be rather surprised with the gifted Leo Trent," I whispered.

Christian arched his brow as an amused smirk crept onto his mouth. "Darcy told me the same thing. Isn't that interesting. Maybe I will," he replied with a wink. "Just don't tell them."

"Porter, just listen to me," Henry stated. "You only have half of the god damned story."

"What? That you are cheating on your wife, my wife's sister, with a man?" Darcy retorted.

"Our marriage is a damned sham, brother. She's been secretly sleeping with Caden. And how stereotypical that he's her secretary, right?"

"That's a blatant bloody lie, Wentworth."

"No. I haven't shared a bed with her for over two years."

"Porter, honey? You have a guest," and Tara appeared, Leo in the perfect spot to catch Henry's eyeline.

"Sawyer," and I saw the chemistry between them.

"No, no, no, you can't be here," Henry exclaimed.

"It's time, Wentworth. Your brother needs to know," Leo replied.

Tara was so elegant as she walked to Darcy. "Porter? What is going on? This young man, well, he says he knows Wentworth?"

"What? No, he doesn't. *Do you*?"

Leo frowned, but his face softened as he gazed at an angry Henry. "Oh, we know each other intimately. We're in love," he stated.

Darcy stilled, his eyes fixed on Henry. "How dare you say that. Wentworth is a married man and father," Tara exclaimed.

"If you loved me at all, you'd let me be who I am, Porter. Don't try to hide me away like some dirty little secret," and Henry marched over to Leo and grabbed his face. "This ends today."

He slammed his lips onto Leo's and kissed the life out of him, Darcy marching over and trying to pull them apart.

"Okay. That's bloody amazing, guys. Let's leave it there till after lunch," I called.

They all grinned and Darcy winked at me. Leo and Henry grabbed Tara's hand as they strode down the steps. Darcy made a slight gesture with his eyes and that meant we had a secret guest hiding out watching the talent on stage, and I wanted to jump up and down with excitement, but not yet. The time would come very soon for my talented actors.

Confrontations

Leo

Henry kissed my temple and smacked my ass. "I need to grab coffee, you two coming?" he asked.

"I need a bit of air, so grab me one, H. Won't be long."

"Be careful, babe. Side door? You want me to get one of our hot bodyguards?" asked my boyfriend.

"No, I'm literally right outside and I won't go far."

I strode to the stage door which was at the far end of the auditorium. I pushed it open and took a breath of the cool, crisp air and took out my phone to send a message to Mia, and I never heard a thing.

A strong hand grabbed my wrist and swung me around, then the fist slammed into my jaw. The pain lanced through my face, phone scattering to the floor. The next hit my stomach and it knocked the air clean out of me.

"I'll knock this dirty crap out of you," and the sound of Dad's voice caused my entire body to seize up. "Then I'll sort out that dirty fucker who touched you."

"No, dad, please," I croaked.

His fist connected to my face again, causing my nose to crack, eyes watering as the blood gushed out, and down my throat, threatening to choke me. Another punch into my stomach then his knee flew up into my ribs, making me drop to my knees, pain crashing through every part of me, making my vision blur.

"I won't have a dirty queer son," he growled.

"Stop, please... dad... please," I rasped, begging for him to stop his attack.

He grabbed my hair, yanked my head up, then punched me again, right over the brow of my right eye, whipping my head to the side, and knocking me to the ground.

The pain was all encompassing, nausea creeping up my throat and the taste of blood erupted in my mouth but I couldn't do anything, as he didn't give me a chance to retaliate. His boot connected with my ribs again, and I wanted to scream for help, but nothing happened. I couldn't breathe as he kicked me again and again.

"No son of mine will ever be a dirty queer," he growled as he continued to kick.

"Get the fuck off of him you homophobic bastard," came a familiar voice, and I literally cried with relief.

There was a scuffle then more footsteps, but I heard his voice. "He needs to be taught a fucking lesson. It needs beating out of him."

All I could do was curl up in agony on the floor, the taste of blood in my mouth, tears rolling down my cheeks. I heard running from more than one person, yells and shouts, but the pain racking my body rang loudly in my ears.

"You dirty son of a bitch. You fucked up my son."

"No, I did no such thing. You did that all by yourself," and more scuffles.

"You're all sick fucking perverts. Get the fuck off me, I haven't finished. That dirty queer ruined my boy."

I tried to move, shuffling onto my ass, sitting up while holding onto my ribs, then I felt warm hands on my shoulder, but the pain continued to pound in my ears. Every inch of me hurt, and a sob fell from me as I spit blood onto the ground.

"Henry?" I whispered.

"Hey, my sexy angel, Yeah, it's me. Let me help you, beautiful."

"Get the fuck off my son, you dirty sick bastard."

Henry's hands came under my arms and he helped me to my feet, but I winced as the pain shot across my chest. I looked up to find his beautiful face, a bust lip and bruising appearing over his eye, and his clothes all dishevelled.

"Get your dirty gay hands off him. He needs it beating out of him," yelled Dad.

I fell into Henry's arms and took a couple of painful breaths. "I've got you, Sin," whispered my man as he helped me into the theatre.

"Oh my god," and Tara was next to me, helping Henry get me into a seat.

"Jesus, what the hell happened?" Asia gasped as the other cast members came striding over.

"Get your filthy queer hands off him. I need to beat it out of him," screamed dad.

"I suggest you shut your hateful mouth Mr Trent," I heard Stefan warn him. "Otherwise I'll shut it for you."

Henry was lifting my face to check my wounds and I heard him curse. "Shit, I think he broke your nose. Call the police, Tara. and an ambulance."

I could hear voices echoing around me, but the searing pain blurred the words, every part of me hurting, tears rolling down my cheeks as I tried to process what had just happened.

"Leo? Can you hear me, baby?" Henry asked, and I lifted my eyes to his. "Hey, we need to try and clean you up, beautiful, okay?"

"You're hurt too," I croaked.

He smiled, kissing my forehead and gently touching my lips. "I'll be fine, Sin. But you need checking over," he whispered.

"Don't you fucking dare touch my boy. Get off him. Stop fucking touching him you sick bastard," yelled my dad.

I stopped for a second, holding onto my ribs. I turned to look at the man who was supposed to love and protect me. "And beating me is an option?" I questioned, angrily. "I've been gay for years, dad."

"Not possible. I won't have a disgusting queer son," he yelled back.

I tried to stand up, Henry cursing as I refused to stay sitting. I turned to face him, and he looked murderous as he glared at my boyfriend.

"And beating me to death is a fucking choice? Look what you've fucking done to me. Does this make you feel good?" I cried, the hurt and rage clear in the broken tone of my voice.

Dad's eyes narrowed as he glared at Henry. "You're not fucking gay. No son of mine will ever be that sick. Never," he growled.

"I fucking hid it, dad. Jesus, you scared us both to fucking death. What the hell happened to you in prison?" I fired at him. "You hated us before, but after?"

Dad visibly flinched and he stopped struggling for a few seconds, then he glared at me and Henry.

"A dirty queer attacked me in the showers. Took what he wanted and left me bleeding on the damned floor. Put me in hospital for fucking weeks. They all want stringing up and beating. Dirty, sick fucking perverts. And you are *not* going to be one," he hissed.

Henry's arms came around me, gently holding me up and I tried to take a couple of breaths, but I gasped as the pain shot through me like a fucking bullet, making Henry hold me closer, dropping a soft kiss at the back of my neck.

"No. Don't fucking touch my boy. Get off him. I need to sort him out, you've poisoned him," he threw at us, struggling in our body guards arms.

I brought my eyes back up to dad and touched my broken nose. "So all gay men are rapists now?" I threw at him.

"All sick fucking perverts," he snapped.

"So, you're calling your own son a god damned rapist and sick pervert?" Henry yelled.

Dad looked as though he wanted to murder my boyfriend as he glared at him. I staggered on my feet, starting to feel dizzy.

"My son will not be gay. He's been fucking brainwashed. Let me fucking go so I can take my son away from here," he demanded.

"Not happening," Ben stated.

I felt my knees buckling and Henry's arms tightened a little around me, Tara suddenly grabbing my arm to stop me from collapsing.

"I hate you, dad," I stammered. "A parent should love their kids no matter what. Unconditionally, not scare them so fucking much that I had to hide who I am since I was sixteen," then I gave in, crumbling into a heap.

His eyes flickered with some sort of regret, but it vanished so quickly I thought I might have imagined it.

"You're the one who's sick," Henry snapped, lowering me back into the chair.

"Don't you *dare* speak to me you dirty, sick fucker. You attacked my son, and I should've smacked you first," he hissed.

"I think you need to shut the fuck up," Stefan warned. "Because I'm tempted to smack you myself, fella."

Ben and Stefan had a tight hold of him as he struggled in their arms. His eyes landed on me and I saw a flicker of emotion, but I turned away as they began hauling him from the auditorium. That was the moment our director and the star strode back in, panic in their eyes as they saw the state of us.

"What the feck?" Darcy exclaimed as he saw the scene they had walked in on.

Chapter 24.

The two security guys were hauling Dad outside towards the lobby. Darcy called out and strode over.

"What are ya doing with him? Have the police been called?" he asked.

"I call them, Darce," called Tara.

They stopped and Dad's eyes came to me and Henry. "What we were ordered to do if he showed up, Mr O'Sullivan. Detain until the police arrive," Stefan replied.

Henry took the seat beside me, holding my hand and turning me away from them.

"Leo. This isn't you. That dirty queer has corrupted you," my Dad's voice rang out.

Henry kissed my forehead and stood up. "Whatever fucking happened to you in prison? It doesn't mean we're all the same, Mr Trent," he yelled back.

I tugged his sleeve and winced as I tried to move in my chair. "Don't bother, H," I croaked, tears escaping again as the reality of what had just happened hit me.

"No. He needs to realise that he's dealing with trauma. And spouting hatred and lies and beating the shit out of his own son isn't the fucking answer," and his hand touched my shoulder.

They hauled him from sight and I held onto my ribs, struggling to take deep breaths. I was sure he'd bruised my ribs, or even worse, cracked some. He'd kicked me with such rage that I'd be surprised if I'd gotten away with any more broken bones.

Sophie was there and she crouched down in front of me, her face awash with worry. "Shit, Leo. This looks bad," she said gently.

"It hurts, but I'll recover," I replied, wincing in pain as I tried to move. "I think he broke my nose."

"I've got you, my beautiful angel," Henry whispered, kissing my temple gently.

Henry helped me into the car after Dad had been hauled off by the police. I'd given them a statement about what had happened in the alley, including all the crazy shit he'd spouted over the years.

They had taken pictures of my injuries and spoken to the paramedics that cleaned me up and reset my nose, which hurt like a fucking bitch, but I refused to wait. They had also taken a picture of Henry's injured face.

"We suggest you go get checked out then go home and rest, Mr Trent. Also, call your Mum and your sister," said the officer.

"He's been in prison before," I replied. "He beat a man for touching Mum when we were eight."

"Thank you for that. Anything else?"

I winced as I staggered onto my feet, Henry wrapping his arm around my waist. "He's always been homophobic. But he was worse after he came out of prison. Told me and my sister that he'd beat it out of us if we ever turned out that way."

"When did he threaten you and your sister?"

"We were thirteen."

The officer frowned as he jotted down that final piece of information. "Okay, Mr Trent, your dad will be detained until he's charged with hate speech as well as assault, as he was very vocal when we arrived. Get looked at by a doctor, and Mr Trent?"

"Yes?"

"I suggest you get a restraining order against him. This will be flagged as a hate crime, Mr Trent. So someone will be in touch with you so you can talk about this. Trust me, it does help, and they will give you information on support groups."

I nodded as Henry took details from another officer. "Thank you," I said.

She gave me a warm smile and touched my shoulder. "You've been through an ordeal, Mr Trent. Take some time out. Rest, okay? We'll be in touch," and she turned to leave.

"You're sure he won't be able to come back?" I asked.

The officer glanced back at me and the fear coursed through me as I waited for her to answer.

"He won't. Take care of yourself, Mr Trent," she finally replied, then they left.

Tara was by my side, Henry gathering our things. Asia joined me along with the rest of the cast.

"Shouldn't you go to the hospital?" she asked.

I shook my head, but Henry crossed his arms, frowning at me. "We are. I want you x-rayed," he stated.

Sophie stood in front of me, hands taking mine. "If you get x-rayed and you have broken ribs it will mean more evidence against him, Leo. And I know it will put my mind at rest. All of our minds."

I let out a painful sigh as I was eased into my jacket. "Come on Sin," said my boyfriend, but Darcy stopped us. He pulled out a card and his phone.

"Take him here," and he handed the card to our new security team.

"What?" I gasped.

"It's me private doctor's surgery. They have everything you'll need to check ya over. I'm going to call them and inform them ya're on ya way," Darcy said. "Now, go."

I couldn't say anything, tears forming in the corners of my eyes. He simply touched my shoulder with a knowing smile, then Henry helped me from the building.

Now, we were being taken home by Stefan. Henry kept a tight hold on my hand as we travelled home after being checked over at Darcy's plush private surgery.

"God, Sin, I'm sorry," he finally said.

"Why? You came to my rescue," I replied.

"I shouldn't have let you go out there alone. Should have insisted on calling one of our sexy bodyguards," he said.

I squeezed his hand and smiled, wincing at the pain across my jaw. "Don't fucking do that, Henry. My bloody dad did this to me."

Henry let out a sigh and leaned closer, so I did the same even though my body screamed in pain. Our lips met and I kissed the man who'd rocked into my life and turned it upside down in the best way.

"Sit back, Sin. You've got badly bruised ribs," and he stroked the line of my jaw, his eyes following his finger.

"Yeah, it's pretty painful," I muttered.

"They said you were lucky they weren't broken," he said.

Henry held onto my hand and shuffled close, his scent soothing me. He was a natural mix of pure man and peppermint. That shower gel he used.

I laid my pounding head against the back of the seat, relaxing, my boyfriend's arm wrapping around my shoulders. I leaned my head into the crook of his arm and closed my eyes.

"I still can't believe your Dad did this to you," he whispered.

"I can," I simply replied.

I pulled my phone out and called Mum. "Leo? Oh God, are you alright? Did Dad do anything?"

"Yeah. The police took him away after he beat the shit out of me."

"Oh god. I'm coming to you and I'll bring your sister."

The rush of relief and joy at her words were immense, and the tears appeared as I allowed the emotion to take over.

"Thanks Mum," I replied, my voice breaking.

"Is your boyfriend with you honey?"

"Yeah," I managed to say.

Henry sat up and touched my face, his expression concerned. "We'll be there tomorrow, honey," Mum said. "Hang in there. Are you in the hospital?"

"No. But, Darcy sent me to his own private doctor. They x-rayed my ribs and I was lucky. Bruised only, mum," I replied.

I heard her suck in a breath and let out a little gasp, and more tears escaped. "I'll be there as soon as possible, honey," she croaked.

"I'm staying with Henry," I replied.

"Send me the address, and we'll see you soon. I love you, my beautiful boy."

"Love you too, Mum."

The car pulled up outside Henry's house and Stefan got out and walked to the passenger side.

"Door to door," he said.

"Cheers, Stefan. Thanks," I said as he helped me out.

"Your Dad did a number on you, and I'm sorry we weren't there for you, Mr Trent."

Henry patted his shoulder and gave him a half smile. "We don't blame you," he said and I nodded. "I should've insisted on getting one of our sexy bodyguards."

I smirked and winced as I did, but Stefan chuckled. "Took a lot of blood sweat and tears to get this body, lads," he drawled.

As we reached the front door, I had to ask, so I looked up at the ruggedly hot guard. "Are you married?"

He arched a brow and grinned. "Yeah. Fourteen years this year."

I had to smile again then cursed at the pain in my jaw and sore nose. "Shit," and Henry dropped a light kiss onto my temple.

"Goodnight you two. We'll be here to pick you up for rehearsals tomorrow?" he asked.

Sophie had literally ordered us to have the following day off. I didn't want to, but she'd insisted.

"No. The day after, Stefan."

He nodded with another smile then waited until we were safely inside before leaving. Now, I just needed to lay down and relax, possibly a whiskey too. I craved a fucking drink after today. Henry took my hand and helped me into bed, undressing me, then laying down beside me.

"I'll get us a drink in a minute. I just want to hold you, Sin," he whispered. "Because that scared the fucking crap out of me, seeing you on the floor while your son of a bitch Dad beat the shit out of you."

I turned and looked at Henry's beautiful face. His dark chocolate eyes and that damned sexy mouth. I gave him a smile and reached out to touch his cheek.

"I'm not religious, but I was praying for you to come and find me," I whispered.

He raked his hand over his face and sighed. "Fucking hell, babe. I'm so bloody sorry. I should have made you take Ben or Stefan."

I tried to sit up and Henry moved like lightning, helping to prop me up with pillows. "Don't do that, H. Don't feel guilty," and I stroked down the line of his jaw.

"I can't help it. I promised you that no-one would lay a fucking finger on you," he replied.

I touched his lips with my finger as his eyes danced with guilt. "No. You saved me, Henry. He could've bloody killed me. Don't you dare think that you failed me."

He let out a sigh and ran his hand over his face as I gazed up at him. "I don't know how, but you seeped into every fucking inch of me, and I love you Henry," I whispered.

He sat up taller and gazed down at me, his finger tracing a line down my face, neck and arm.

"And I love you Leo, my sinful angel," and he leaned in and captured my lips in a tender kiss. "All fucking mine, and now I'll get us both a drink," and he climbed from the bed.

I watched him leave the room then slowly got up as I wanted to get rid of my clothes. They were splattered with my own blood and dirt from the alley. I peeled them from me, flinching with each movement, then caught my reflection in the mirror.

It caused a sharp pain to slam into my heart as I saw the blackening eyes, bruised jaw, cut over my eye and a swollen nose.

"Jesus Dad. Why?" I whispered.

Darcy

The state of Leo made my blood boil. And the fact that his Dad had done that to his own son? I literally couldn't comprehend how someone could do that to their own child. His father was spouting some vicious shite as the police bundled him into the squad car. I picked up Sophie's bag and coat, my own jacket too.

"Come on love. Let me get ya a late lunch, then we'll go and see Leo and Henry," and I took her hand in mine.

"Great. I need to know he's okay," she said.

So did I, but I smiled and led us out to the massive gathering of soul sucking reporters. There were more now after the police had joined the damned party.

"Hold tight, love," I whispered, then the questions and flashes exploded.

"Why were the police here, Darcy?"

And that one voice made my entire body lock up, and Sophie's eyes snapped up to mine in recognition, so I crushed her to my side and picked up the pace.

"You two a couple again?"

"Feck off, Casey," I fired at him.

"You get her pregnant? Is that why you're with her?"

Rage flew into every pore as he spoke and Sophie buried herself into me, and it felt like the car was fucking miles away.

"Keep moving, love," I whispered into her ear.

"Or is it all fake?"

"Ignore him, love. He's trying to get a rise out of us."

"She's not your usual fuck buddy is she? And she was all over the young Mr Trent earlier. You shagging him too Mrs Carter?"

Sophie stopped and I stared down at her, and the fire behind her eyes made my heart go fucking crazy. She stood up taller and whizzed around, her hand moving like lightning, slapping Casey's cheek, hard.

"How fucking dare you," she hissed. Then she shoved him with practically each word that came next. "You are a slimy piece of dog shit. You print anything like that? I'm going to hunt your sorry pathetic ass down, and smack you into the next century," then she took my hand, and dragged me through the rest of them as he stared after her in shock. "Get out of the damned way," she ordered, barging through them.

We both froze as we heard the rumble of claps and cheers, and I turned to see the other reporters applauding my lady.

"Well said, Miss," the familiar face of the reporter from the Savoy called.

She winked at me and then waved at him as Carl opened the car door.

I didn't know what to say as we clambered inside. Sophie shuffled closer and I wrapped my arm around her shoulders.

"Ya just slapped Casey in front of other reporter's lass," I finally said.

"She ripped him a new one if you ask me," Carl piped up as he got the car moving.

"And he deserved it. Let them tell everyone. I'm done letting that prick do that to us again," she stated.

I chuckled and pulled her in for a kiss. "That'll be the new headline tomorrow, love," I said, proudly.

"I hope it is. Now, let's get some food and go and see Leo and Henry," she replied. "I want to pick up a few treats for the guys too."

I cupped her face and kissed her. "I love ya, lass," I whispered. "Ya crazy bare."

After treating my beautiful woman to lunch, I had Christian send me Henry's address. Sophie had a bag full of treats, wine and books for the two of them, and it made me love her all the more as she cared so much for her friends and family.

Carl dropped us at Henry's rather elegant terrace town house, and we climbed out and walked to the dark blue door. I knocked and we were greeted by Henry's bruised but smiling face.

"Shit, get inside before the neighbours see you, Irishman," he stated.

Sophie shook her head as he yanked me inside, and strolled in after us. She handed the bag over and Henry hugged her tightly.

"Shit, Henry, crushing me," she gasped.

"Not sorry. And Darcy? You'll have press crawling all over my fucking street turning up in the middle of the day," and I was smacked on the shoulder.

I smirked at the actor and said, "So, you think turning up in the middle a the night is a better option?"

He chuckled and crossed his arms over his chest. "Very fucking funny, Irishman."

Sophie grabbed his hand and dragged him to the kitchen as I followed. "There's wine in there, some books and your favourite sweet treats," she said.

Henry's entire face lit up and looked inside. "You found cannoli's?" he asked, grinning up at the two of us.

"All Sophie, fella."

Henry gave her another swift hug and kissed her on the forehead. "Grazie, bella," he said with a grateful smile.

Sophie grinned at me then turned to Henry. "Where's Leo? I need to know he's okay."

"In the living room now. I wanted him to stay in bed, but he refused. This way, boss."

I followed them and Leo was laid out on the sofa reading his bloody lines of all things. I had to smile, as I recognised the love for his craft in his eyes.

I sat across from him and inwardly winced at the bruises on his face. His usual sapphire eyes were blossoming into two black eyes, and another huge dark purple one graced his jaw. His nose was swollen and I wanted to punch his piece of shit dad.

"Lines?" Sophie questioned. "Seriously?"

Leo smiled with a slight wince and nodded. "Still have a play to put on, so I'm making the most of being able to go over them,"

I shook my head a little as he reminded me of a young Darcy, constantly carrying around my current script wherever I went, face always stuck in it when I had the opportunity.

"Leo, ya want to run some lines?" I asked.

"Oh yeah. That'd be amazing Darcy. Scene five in act two, you know? Where it's just the three of us?" he said, grinning with a wince.

I had to smile back and Henry rolled his eyes as he came in with their drinks. Sophie sat on my lap and handed me a glass of wine, kissing my lips tenderly.

"Fine, Sin. You just can't shut off," Henry chuckled, kissing Leo.

Leo winked at him and then his eyes went back to the play. I had to do it, so I pulled out my phone and fired off a swift message to my agent, then settled down to an afternoon with two very dedicated young actors, and my sexy woman in my arms, and a great idea forming in my head that would help these two youngsters climb the difficult ladder in our business.

Chapter 25.

Opening Night

The next two weeks had gone without a hitch. Sophie and me? Never bloody better. Leo and Henry were almost fully free of bruises and very happy, and the play was set to be a great hit.

"Hey, handsome," and the love of my life appeared.

"Get over here, love. Ya need to kiss me," I ordered.

She smirked and strolled over, sitting on my lap. "You used to want to be alone before curtain up," she purred.

"Yes. Now? I want me sexy little minx. I need ya in here with me before I go on stage," I replied, and she simply leaned in and kissed me.

I crushed her into my body, hands caressing her curves. My lady forever, and I smiled into her lips.

"What's funny?" she asked.

"Nothing. I'm just deliriously happy, love. All because I've got ya right here," and I winked.

She licked her lips and a wicked sparkle appeared in her eyes.

"Isn't it your birthday soon?" she asked.

I groaned and smacked her ass. I hated my birthday and never celebrated, but this year was different.

"Why are ya asking?" I questioned.

"Because I need to know what you'd like?" she asked.

I ran my hand up her spine and kissed her slowly, lovingly and spoke into her lips. "I've already got what I need right here on me lap, love."

Sophie brought her eyes to mine and rolled them as she smirked. "That doesn't bloody help, O'Sullivan. And I can't wrap myself up in a bow for you," she said.

"Why the feck not?"

"Really?"

"Really, lass."

"Shithead," and she slapped my chest.

"All naked wearing nothing but a red fecking bow," I growled into her ear. "And I'd unwrap ya with me teeth before," but she snorted into giggles.

"You randy fucker, O'Sullivan," she exclaimed.

I just chuckled and tilted my head to one side as I gazed up at her. "I love this smart, filthy mouth a yours, love."

"Very funny," but she smiled and it made my heart swell with love for her.

I stood her up and smirked. "Straddle, love," I ordered.

Her brows arched but her eyes sparkled with that wicked fire I loved. "Before a performance?" she questioned.

"Sit down, cheeky bare."

She paused then swung her leg over my thighs, but remained standing. "We don't have time to fuck, handsome," she purred.

I smirked as my hands flew to her hips, yanking her down. "Come here, sexy minx," and I gripped her face and pulled her down, slamming my lips onto hers.

She moaned as my hands moved around to her sexy ass, pulling her as close as I could get her. Her hands were in my hair, as we devoured each other, and Sophie started to rock over me, making my dick start to harden.

The knock was swift, and a voice rang out. "Five minutes to curtain up. Beginners to stage. Beginners to stage."

"Oh fuck," she gasped into my lips.

"No time, love," I replied, earning me a slap on the arm. "And if this show runs smoothly tonight? Ya gonna have to make out with me before every fecking performance."

Sophie let out that adorable snort again as she sat back and gazed at me. "Actors are fucking weird," she stated.

"We are that, lass. And I want to spend me birthday with ya in bed. That's all I want, lass."

She stood up and touched my face gently. "That sounds fantastic, you randy bugger. So, I'm going to have to think out of the box. Now get down to the stage, handsome," she replied, smacking my own ass as I stood up.

I grinned and turned to the mirror, checking my suit and microphone taped to my forehead. "Alright. Let's get this show on the road," I said, then kissed Sophie on her right cheek and walked to the door. "I love ya, lass."

"Love you too, handsome."

I walked back and crushed her against me for a brief moment, then I left her in my dressing room, striding towards the stage.

Leo

Henry hugged me tightly and started towards the stage, leaving me to pace as I ran lines in my head. Mum and Mia were in the audience tonight and I was shitting myself because this was the first *ever* gay role I'd played.

There was a knock and Sophie appeared, a huge smile on her face. "Max and Teagen are here tonight. You doing okay?" she asked.

I grinned and gestured for her to come in, checking my mike and make-up. "Nervous as hell, Sophie. It's the first gay role for me. And for the first time I finally feel free to be myself."

She strode over and gave me a gentle hug, as my ribs were still a little sore. "You are a very gifted actor, so I have every faith in you. But, how are *you*?" she asked.

"I'm fine now. The police told me he's been officially charged with assault, and it's been recorded as a hate crime, due to his rhetoric," I replied. "And I'm organising a restraining order so he stays away."

"Good news. But seriously, how are you *really* doing?" she asked.

Sophie wasn't just my director anymore. She was my friend and I adored her, along with her brother and Teagen.

"Ribs are still a bit sore, but all in all, I'm good. Mum and Mia have decided to stay at my place as I'm moving in with Henry," I replied.

Sophie stared at me with surprise, then her arms came around me, hugging me again. "Oh god. That's amazing news," she exclaimed.

"Right?" I replied as I chuckled.

She kissed my cheek and leant against the dressing table. "You two are perfect for each other. And I'm really bloody happy for you. Now, remember that cue in scene four, and go out and smash it," and she winked.

I nodded, sat down and leaned back against the chair, eyes closed, as I was left alone. This was a big moment for me. I was about to play a gay character, kiss a man on stage without any fear of dad coming after me, and I couldn't quite believe how happy I finally felt. I opened my eyes and stared at my reflection, the voice on the tannoy telling me that it was about to begin.

This was it. My time to really fucking shine. Show the world what I could do. I smiled to myself and stood up.

"Leo Trent, you've fucking got this," I whispered.

I didn't appear until scene four, so I decided to go down and watch my divine boyfriend in the wings. I left the confines of my dressing room and started toward the door leading down to backstage.

"Hey Leo," and I turned to see Carlton smiling at me.

"Oh hey," and I smacked his shoulder with a grin.

Carlton was tall with salt and pepper hair, and the bluest eyes I'd ever seen. He touched my arm and handed me a card.

"Darcy told me to give you this," and I looked down to see Christian's name embossed on it.

"Oh, why?" I asked.

"You'll find out after the show, lad. This guy's in the audience," and I stared at him for a second, making him chuckle at the look of concern in my eyes. "Go on. Go get ready. Show the world how talented you are. And have a good one," and he winked, then strode off to wait for his own first appearance.

As he disappeared I looked down at the card in my hand, confusion in my expression. I frowned and waltzed back to my dressing room, dropped it onto the table, then cleared my mind, ready to play one of my favourite roles so far.

Sophie

I stood in the wings as the applause erupted through the theatre. The curtain came down on an amazing first night, and Darcy was in front of me in a flash, hugging me to him and kissing me ravenously.

"Get back on stage, O'Sullivan. Curtain call," I gasped.

"I'm going, lass. Just needed to kiss ya," and he smacked my ass before striding back onstage.

They took three lots of bows, then the curtain closed for the final time after the playwright took a bow with the actors. I never usually appeared until closing night. That was my own personal rule, and everyone still ribbed me about it, including Tasha, the playwright. Leo was the first off stage, followed by Henry, and I was squashed from both sides in a gay men sandwich.

"You are a fucking genius," Henry announced.

"Isn't she just," drawled my Irishman as he strolled over.

"Fucking hell, boys. You're crushing me," I gasped, giggling at the same time.

I was dragged onto the stage as Tara, Zane, Asia, Fiona and Carlton laughed loudly. "To our awesome director," yelled Zane.

I couldn't help the grin that appeared on my face as Darcy tugged me into his side. Tasha came and shook my hand, her eyes a little teary.

"That was amazing, Sophie. I can't believe my play is finally out there for the world. And sold out for the entire run," she gushed.

"It was an absolute joy, Tasha."

"No, you all brought the characters to life for me, turned them into real tortured people. And these beautiful souls gave them passion, hatred, love and heartbreak, and I can't thank all of you enough," she said, her voice cracking from emotion, and I was hugged tightly.

I heard their voices before I saw them, and Max, Teagen and Christian came sauntering onto the stage to join the merriment.

"That was bloody amazing," stated my brother. "And not fucking Shakespeare."

I rolled my eyes then I was tugged into his arms and hugged. Teagen grinned and kissed the top of my head.

"That ending was bloody cruel, but awesome all at the same time," Max said.

Tasha smirked and patted his shoulder, making him grin wickedly. "Sorry not sorry, Mr Ashforth," she purred.

Teagen took my brother's hand and winked at me. "It was absolutely bloody fantastic," he added. "Horrible that Wentworth had to go to those lengths to be happy."

I glanced over at Leo as Teagen spoke, thanking the lucky stars that he was finally free of his dad. The character had to fake his death to finally be free to have a life with Sawyer. Tragic.

Tasha took a cheeky bow and threw them a devilish smile. "I'm just thrilled that you enjoyed it," she replied.

I noticed two of the actors waving at Max. Teagen clocked them too and grabbed Max's hand.

"It was amazing, Tasha. We need to go and chat to our friends. Catch you all later," then he tugged my brother towards Henry and Leo. Christian appeared beside Darcy and he winked at me.

"Well done Sophie," he whispered, then turned to look at Leo and Henry. "Now I have to go and give those two some good news," and he strode over to the loved up pair. "Now, Mr Trent. I want to have a few words, so I'll need to extract you from your fans, then it's your turn," drawled the agent, looking at Henry and smacking them on their shoulders as they both arched confused brows at him.

Leo looked a little nervous, so Henry leaned in, kissing his lips lightly. "What's it about?" he asked, and Darcy smirked as I glanced up at him.

And low and behold, there was a very knowing twinkle in his emerald eyes. "You know what's going on don't you, you sly fucker," I fired at him, nudging his shoulder.

"Don't know what ya mean, love," he drawled.

"Oh you bloody do," and I smacked his arm.

"Come, I have some things to discuss with you," said Christian.

We watched as they walked off the stage and disappeared into the wings. Henry raked his hand through his hair and all eyes landed on a smug looking Darcy.

"What?" he questioned.

"What does your agent want with my man and me?" asked Henry.

"He wants to take him on as a client," Darcy simply replied.

Henry's eyes went wide and I stared up at my Irishman in equal surprise. I smacked his arm again and he chuckled, squeezing me into his side.

"Really?" I asked.

"Really, lass. Christian wanted to see what a few of ya were made of," he replied. "So, it's not just Leo he has his eye on."

Darcy looked at Henry then Asia, and they simply stared right back. "Are you shitting me?" fired Henry.

"No. I'm not shitting ya, fella," said Darcy.

Asia was in front of us in a flash as everyone else continued chatting around us with their own family and friends.

"Seriously?" she asked.

Darcy nodded and grinned like a wicked devil. "Seriously, Asia," he said.

I noticed an older lady and a very familiar looking young woman looking a little lost, and I had to go to them. "I'll be right back, handsome," I whispered to Darcy.

"Alright lass. Don't be long, love."

I smiled and he pecked my lips before Asia and Henry started firing questions at him. I strolled over to the lost looking pair and smiled.

"You're Leo's family?" I asked.

"Oh yes. The play was amazing," said the older lady, whom I presumed was Leo's mum.

"Leo was bloody brilliant. I'm such a proud sister right now," said his twin.

I glanced over at Henry who was still grilling Darcy and smirked. "They all were. Just know that your son is very talented. I think he's going to have a glittering acting career," I replied. "You must be Mia?"

She was indeed a female version of Leo, just a little smaller in height, eyes a paler blue, but the warm smile, straight nose, defined jaw and the heart shaped upper lip were identical. Well, Mia didn't have a neatly trimmed beard.

"I think I have to thank you and your man for looking after my son?" Leo's mum said, her eyes warm and sparkling with gratitude.

"Please call me Sophie and that's Darcy. And yes. He fitted right in with us. And he's made great friends with my brother and his fiancè, so he's got a good bunch in his corner now," I replied.

I had to smile as I shook her hand and then Leo's twin. "That makes me so happy. He's been so lonely for a long time."

"And Henry has been a fantastic boyfriend too," I replied.

She nodded, her eyes glazing over a little with emotion. "He seems to have found a very wonderful circle of friends, finally," she whispered.

Leo's sister let out a little cough and I smiled, then she threw her arms around me and hugged me tightly.

"Thank you."

"For?" I asked, chuckling.

"For looking out for my little brother. It's about time he found his happy ever after," she gushed.

"He's a very lovely human. And I'm proud to call him a close friend now," I replied.

I glanced around and caught Henry's eye. I gestured for him to join us and he bound over and swiftly hugged Mrs Trent.

"Hello again, Mrs Trent," he said, grinning at Mia.

"You looked after my baby," she stammered. "You were there for him."

"I already explained, Mrs Trent, don't blame yourself. You were there for him the next day. And I hope you'll come for dinner tomorrow?" Henry asked.

"God, yes. We'll be there with bells on," Mia replied.

Leo's mum hugged Henry again and I had to smile. "Thank you Henry. For making my son happy, finally," she said, her voice cracking a little.

"I love him very much, Mrs Trent, and he makes me very happy too," he replied.

I touched his shoulder lightly, leaving them to chat, then headed back to my Irishman.

The theatre had emptied out, Max, Teagen, Leo and Henry heading back to my brother's place. It was Sunday tomorrow, so no performance.

Darcy took my hand and grabbed my bag. "I need ya home, love," he whispered, kissing my lips gently.

"Oh really?" I purred.

"Yes lass. And naked."

I snorted into giggles and nudged his arm with my shoulder. "And once I'm naked?" I asked.

"Oh, I'm gonna do all manner of naughty things to ya, love," he said, leading us through the quiet theatre.

I smiled smugly as we left the building, the cool night air skirting around us. The car was waiting in its usual spot, and due to our loved up mood we never saw him.

"You know one of the cast has a criminal for a father?"

Darcy gripped me tighter, but didn't turn around. "Keep walking lass. Ignore the fecking parasite."

"I hear his dad beat ten bells out of him for being gay?"

"Go away," I shot at him.

"And Mr Trent had a stalker. She's a piece of work too. Hear she ratted out Mr Trent's discretions to his bully of a dad?"

We reached the car and Carl was there to greet us. He opened the door to let us inside, but the bloody shit stain that was Casey kept going.

"I heard a rumour that she's pregnant and you're not the father, Darcy?"

I paused and turned to glare at him. Darcy's hands were bunched into fists, but he didn't turn around.

"Get in the car, Sophie, Darcy," Carl whispered.

"It's supposed to be Mr Trents kid," Casey drawled. "She's *real* friendly with him. Trying to shag him straight?"

"You want me to smack you again?" I snapped. "Because I bloody will."

The fucker simply smirked and winked at me. "You got me on the front pages of the top dailies. Never had so many people sign up to my newspages. So knock yourself out, love."

That was the moment Darcy whirled around. "Get in the car, love," he ordered.

Chapter 26.

Darcy

I looked down at my beautiful woman and kissed her lips. "Get in the car, love," I whispered.

She frowned at me, her eyes filled with nothing but pure rage too. "Trust me, beautiful."

"Don't smack him, handsome," she whispered, but loud enough for the slimy fucker to hear.

"I promise ya, love."

Sophie hesitated, chewing on her bottom lip, then disappeared into the car.

Carl knew something could possibly escalate, so he stepped beside me as I turned to face the scumbag. My driver wasn't hired just for his skills behind the wheel. He looked a lot like a Gladiator, tall, mousy brown hair cropped short, and he was an ex SEAL. So he had another set of rather lethal fucking talents too.

Casey seemed to look rather smug with himself and that wound me up so much more. The other reporters had now noticed and were edging closer, flashes already capturing every moment. I closed the door after giving my lady a cheeky wink. I moved swiftly and I grabbed a hold of his shirt, my face right in front of his.

"Don't ya ever speak to me woman ever again, ya fecking parasite. I see ya even glance at her? I'll fecking smack ya into the next century. Then again, she might do it herself. Now, listen to me, one more fecking lie that comes out of ya mouth? I'm gonna take ya to the cleaners," I growled at him, then I shoved him backwards and barged past the piece of shite and walked to the other reporters.

"I have a brief statement, for ya. There will be a limited number of places at the closing night's performance as I will have a very important announcement to make. Sophie Carter and myself are a couple, happy and in love. Mr Trent is a good friend only, and he is very happy with his *boyfriend*. So, I look forward to seeing which six of ya will get the exclusive."

I turned and pulled out my phone, calling my agent. "Hello Christian. I want six spots opened up for press on closing night. And Casey is barred from attending. I also want a restraining order drawn up. Sure thing. Cheers fella," and I hung up.

"I'm equally entitled, Darcy," Casey drawled.

"No. Ya not. Ya spout nothing but fecking lies."

"Just giving the public what they want."

My hands landed on his chest and I shoved him. "Ya know, not one other reporter in this crowd would piss on ya if ya were on fire, ya fecking piece of shite, now take ya filthy lies and piss off, ya fecking gobshite," and applause erupted around us.

Casey shrugged his shoulders, looking suddenly very uncomfortable as some of the other reporters started cheering and shouting.

"You tell him, O'Sullivan."

"Couldn't have said it better."

"Feck off Casey," I growled. "Even the other members a the press can't fecking stand the sight a ya," and I turned away from him and climbed into the car to join my lady.

Sophie looked at me with questioning eyes, but I simply winked and took her hand in mine. I leaned in and kissed her cheek.

"Dealt with. That scum prints one fecking word? I'll sue the fecking shite out of him," I said.

"How could Leo be the bloody dad even if I were pregnant? He's gay for fuck's sake," she groaned.

I tapped her bag and said, "Give him a call, love. He needs to be in the loop about that fecker," and she pulled out her phone and fired off a message then sat back with a sigh.

"Just when everything seems to be settling down, drama bloody kicks us again," she muttered.

"Don't worry lass. I'll call Christian tomorrow. Tell him what the gob shite said," and she snuggled into me as we headed home.

Leo

My phone buzzed in my pocket as we sat on the sofa at Max and Teagen's place. Henry had his arm draped over my shoulders as I pulled it out to find out who it was.

"What in the actual fuck?" I groaned as I read her message.

"What's wrong?"

"That bastard, Casey? He collared Sophie and Darcy. Said she was rumoured to be pregnant with *my* fucking baby?" I said.

"What? That can't be right, Sin?"

I rolled my eyes and smacked his shoulder. "Well, obviously, H. I don't sleep with women. That fucker is a parasite. Darcy warned me about him."

My boyfriend nodded and read the message. "He is. He caused drama a few years ago for Sophie. Darcy ended up fighting with her man Jake because of that piece of crap," he said, kissing my forehead and pulling me closer. "Christian had him pull the story."

Max sauntered over and handed us each a glass with whiskey in. "What's up, fuck faces?" he asked.

"Apparently, Leo got Sophie pregnant," Henry stated.

"What?"

"Remember Casey?" I asked.

Teagen dropped down next to his fiancè and kissed him. "What have I missed, baby?" he asked.

"My sister is pregnant with Leo's baby, according to that scumbag Casey," Max announced.

"What?"

Henry pulled me close and kissed me, hands running through my hair. "Reporters are toxic, but Casey is on another level. My man's sperm miraculously floated into Sophie's womb."

I had to get up as the frustration and rage whirling through me made me nauseous. How could this be happening again. First dad and fucking Eve. Now a scum reporter spreading utter crap.

"Sin?"

"I need to, well, I can't," and I grabbed my phone, walking to the spare room.

I wanted to punch something, but I knew that wouldn't change anything. I needed the one person who always knew what to say, so I rang my sister.

"Hey Leo? Are you alright? Are we still fine for Sunday lunch tomorrow?"

"Hey you. No, I'm not okay."

"Shit, what's happened?"

"Fucking reporters. Seems I miraculously got Sophie up the duff," I replied.

"Excuse me?"

"A scumbag of a reporter is spreading rumours. He knows about dad, the beating and Eve. And he collared Darcy and Sophie."

"He said what?"

A frustrated sigh fell from me as I slumped onto the bed. Just as everything was settling down, some other fucking drama crawled out of the woodwork.

"Seems I'm having a bloody affair with Sophie. She's pregnant with my damned baby, and the scumbag knows what dad and Eve did to me," I said.

"Jesus, why would anyone think you are sleeping with Sophie?"

"Exactly. It's bloody ridiculous."

"Leo, listen to me. You aren't alone anymore. You have me and Mum. And you've got the seriously sexy Henry. And your new friends. We will bloody weather this together."

I raked my hand through my hair as I noticed Henry standing in the doorway. "Thanks Mia. Just thought I'd warn you and mum in case something appears tomorrow. Better go. We'll see you tomorrow."

"You will. Good night little brother. I love you."

"Love you too, big sister. Night," and I hung up.

My man sauntered over and pulled me to my feet. He took my face in his hands and kissed me slowly, lovingly, and I instantly relaxed.

"I think we need to do something about this. Call our new agent. See what he says, okay Sin?" he whispered.

I held onto him and sighed. Yes, both me and Henry had been taken on by Christian, along with Asia. And that was fucking amazing, but the constant shit being thrown at us was seriously getting on my god damned last nerve. I rested my head on his shoulder, burying my face into the crook of his neck, my arms wrapped tightly around him.

"I'll call him in the morning, babe," I replied.

His eyes sparkled and he grinned. "I like being your babe, Sin."

I smirked and squeezed his sexy ass. "It just slipped out, but glad you like it," I replied. "Shall we go back to the living room?"

"I love you, and we'll get through this together," he whispered.

"I'm so fucking glad I have you, and the guys out there. I love you too... babe," and I gave him a small smile even though my insides felt as though a hurricane was barrelling through it.

Henry simply kissed me again, took my hand and we joined our friends and tried to forget the possible coming ridiculous shit storm that Casey was about to unleash.

Darcy

The ringing pierced the morning and I cursed as Sophie let out her own swear words and an annoyed moan. I grabbed the phone and looked down to see my agent's name.

"Jesus, fella. It's fecking five thirty in the morning," I complained.

"Let us sleep, Christian," Sophie announced, rolling over and pulling a pillow over her head.

I dropped a gentle kiss on her naked shoulder and spoke into the phone. "Why are ya calling so early?"

"Casey has struck."

"Feck. What shite is he spouting now? I fecking warned him."

There was a tense pause, then he let out a very familiar frustrated sigh. "Sophie has been secretly sleeping with Leo and there is a possibility that he has gotten her pregnant."

"Jesus fecking Christ. I'm going to take him to the fecking cleaners."

"I can look into it. I *do* think someone needs to teach the lying prick a lesson."

"Grand. And I'll happily be the one to do it."

Christian didn't answer immediately, then I heard the sigh. "I had a call from Theo last night."

"So?" and the annoyance was clear in my tone.

"He wants to talk to you."

"I don't want to talk to him."

"It's been far too long, Darcy."

"I don't fecking care. After what he did? No."

I felt Sophie's eyes on me and I wanted to throw the phone across the room. The last thing I wanted was to speak to him after that day.

"He came to see you last night."

"What?"

"He was in the audience, Darcy."

Sophie's hand was on my shoulder as she sat up, hugging me from behind, and I closed my eyes for a few seconds as she trailed kisses across the back of my neck.

"He's in London?"

"Yes. He really wants to talk."

My mind dragged that memory from the depths and it still hurt to this day, but he was my little brother. I needed to talk to my beautiful lady first and ask for her advice.

"I'll call ya back," I said and hung up.

Sophie was gazing up at me, her eyes filled with warmth and love. "Darcy? Who wants to talk to you?"

I sighed and ruffled my hair, rubbed my eyes and pulled her into a tight hug. "I need caffeine," I said. "And I want some advice, love."

She touched my face and I kissed her. I had to talk it through, as I was too close to this. I missed my little brother so damned much, but I didn't know if I could ever forgive him for what he did. Or could I? It had been such a long time ago.

Sophie made the coffee and I sat staring out of the window, my mind replaying that day over and over again.

"Here you go, handsome," Sophie said, passing me my mug. "Now tell me what's going on?"

She sat beside me and I wrapped my arm around her shoulders, tucking her into my side. I sipped my coffee and set it down on the table in front of us then took a deep breath.

"Ya remember the way I used to be, lass?" I started.

"Yep. A cocky arrogant prick," she reminded me.

I grimaced with a mixture of both guilt and shame. "Not mincing ya words, but yes love. There was a reason I acted that way."

Sophie snuggled closer and put down her own mug, bringing her eyes to mine. She stretched up and kissed my lips tenderly. "Tell me," she said quietly.

I kissed her temple and took another deep calming breath. "When I was nineteen I started dating a girl called Isabelle. I fell hard for her and I thought she loved me too. I asked her to marry me, love."

"What did she do?" asked Sophie.

I sighed and stood up, rolling my shoulders. "Ya too smart lass. But, ya right. We got engaged, and she wanted a fecking engagement party. Mam organised one at the local restaurant. Isabelle went to the bathroom, and she was gone for ages, so I went looking for her," and my hand flew through my hair at the memory. "I heard a familiar female moaning when I pushed the ladies bathroom door open to see where she was."

Sophie jumped to her feet and came to stand in front of me. "Who was she having sex with?" she asked.

I had to take a moment, sucking in a deep breath before answering her. "Theo. Me little brother. She was riding him in the cubicle. She looked up as she fecking moaned his name. He was lit, and he fecking grinned at me."

The hurt of his betrayal slammed into me as Sophie wrapped her arms around my waist, and I crushed her closer.

"He did what I did to ya, love. Me own brother, fecking me fianceè at our damned engagement party. I punched him, and told her it was over. After that? I locked away me heart, until ya came waltzing into the bloody theatre, and I was hooked instantly. But it terrified me. I didn't want to feel that pain ever again, so I treated ya so fecking badly," and I stopped.

Sophie looked up at me, reaching for my face, and she pulled me down into a slow, tender kiss.

"And you haven't spoken to him since, right?" she asked.

I nodded, and let out a frustrated groan. "He came to the play last night. He wants to talk, but I don't know if I can, love."

She took my hand and gestured for me to grab my coffee. She then led me out of the kitchen and upstairs to the living room, talking as we walked.

"Family is important, Darcy, regardless of what happens between them. You only get one, and I know you already lost your sister. I also know you would never forgive yourself if something happened to him without clearing the air," she said as gently as she could.

Every word she spoke hit the mark like a bullet and I raked my hand through my hair, a frustrated sigh leaving my lips.

"Do you miss him?"

"If I'm honest, yes love."

"Were the two of you close?"

"We were inseparable when we were wee kids."

"Then I really think you should talk to him. It might be time to build bridges. Let him try and mend what was broken?" she added.

I sighed and ruffled my hair again. The pain of that day fluttered back to life, but the thought of losing Theo without making amends caused a much more vicious feeling to bloom in my chest. We entered the living room and Sophie took us to the sofa, sitting us both down.

Her eyes fixed onto mine and she snuggled into my side, draping my arm around her shoulders. I leaned in and kissed her sexy lips and relaxed back against the cushions.

"Inseparable how?" she asked.

I raised my brows in amusement and she simply gazed back up. "We got into trouble together," I replied.

"What kind of trouble?"

I had to smirk as the memories came flooding back of all the shite we'd caused, and all the times our Mam had smacked us.

"All sorts a shite. Mam knocked sense into us on a regular basis. Once, we were playing football in the garden and the ball got kicked into the window a the kitchen. Glass everywhere. Jesus, Mam went fecking nuts. Had us both doing chores for months."

She snorted and giggled before draining her mug. "Then you need to do this. Talk to him and get your fellow partner in crime, little trouble maker brother back."

"Ya right, lass. Will ya stay with me?" I asked.

"You know I will, if you need me," she replied.

"I need ya, beautiful," I whispered, and my cock started to twitch a little.

She gave me her beautiful smile and I had to kiss her. This would be hard for me, but Sophie was right. I'd never forgive myself if anything happened to him, and I *did* truly miss my little shithead of a brother way more than I admitted. I picked up my phone and fired off a message to my agent.

"Thanks love," I whispered.

"For?" she asked.

"Listening, lass."

She rolled her eyes at me and slapped my arm. "We're in a relationship, Darcy. That's what we do."

"I'm not really used to it, lass," I admitted, and she climbed onto my lap, straddling me, her arms resting around my neck.

Her mouth covered mine and she lazily kissed me before lightly running her hands through my hair, and the way she was gazing at me had my cock standing to attention.

"Well, handsome, get used to it, because I love you and I'm not going anywhere," she whispered. "Oh, hello," and her eyes dropped down to my crotch and the huge fucking tent in my pants. "Someone's very happy to see me."

I smirked and my hands immediately roamed up her spine, my lips slowly making my way down her neck, shoulder and back towards her mouth.

"Mmm," she moaned.

"Feck, lass," and I rocked her over me.

My hands moved downwards, finding a completely fucking naked ass under her t-shirt, so I moved swiftly, lifting her ass and freeing my cock.

"Sit down, love," I ordered, and she smirked at me.

"How did you know?" she asked as I massaged her bare ass.

"I didn't ya cheeky bare," and I smacked her ass. "Now, ya little devil, I need to be inside ya." I growled.

She took me in her hand, eliciting a hiss to fall from me, lined herself up, then dropped in one swift motion.

"Oh my god," she moaned, throwing her head back for a moment.

"Yes, feck. Give me control," I ordered.

Sophie fixed her eyes on me with a naughty smirk. "Aren't you bossy, O'Sullivan," she purred.

She moved her hips in lazy circles as she rocked back and forth, making me groan loudly at the sheer fucking pleasure flying through me. I watched as she moved, her hands on my shoulders, breaths short and shallow as she rode me, my cock sliding in and out of her tight pussy.

"Jesus, love," I croaked.

"Still want control, handsome?" she purred into my ear.

The growl rumbled from deep inside me and she giggled as it escaped my lips. "Ya naughty bare," I replied. "I want to make ya fecking come all over me cock."

Sophie smirked at me, then she kissed me hungrily. "Alright, sexy Irishman. I'll let you fuck me until I come all over you," she purred into my lips, then relaxed into my body.

I gripped her hips tightly, rocking her roughly back and forth. And fucking hell, she felt divine. Tight, wet and I moaned into her neck before I nipped her with my teeth.

"I can't get enough of ya, love."

"Oh god, Darcy, yes," she gasped, her fingers digging into my shoulders.

I smirked as I thrust into her over and over, picking up my pace, our sighs, grunts and moans echoing through the room. Sophie dropped her head onto my shoulder, fingers in my hair, gripping handfuls tightly as I rocked her over me, my cock hitting that sweet spot with each forward thrust, making her let out those sexy fucking gasps that got me even harder .

I panted into her ear as this was bloody heaven. The way she stretched around me was like a fucking drug.

"God, yes, feck," I groaned as I felt her begin to tremble, her climax building.

"Oh fuck, I'm gonna.... I'm gonna....Yes, god, yes," and she arched into me as I watched my Sophie come undone.

Her body went rigid and she moaned out loud, shaking, her pussy clamping down on my cock.

"Yesfuckyes," she cried out, and I groaned as I thrust hard and exploded as my own orgasm slammed into me.

"Feck, yes," I cried out as I ground her over me, head dropping into the crook of her neck as we trembled in each other's arms, and I continued to gently rock her over my semi hard cock.

We stayed that way for a few more moments, bodies pressed together, a fine sheen of sweat covering our skin, short breaths coming from the two of us.

"Fucking hell, handsome. I'm bloody knackered," she muttered breathlessly.

"Me too, love," I admitted, holding her tightly against me. "More coffee, gorgeous?"

"God yes. I need a bloody vat of the stuff," she replied.

I chuckled and lifted my head, gazing into her dark, tempting eyes. "I love ya, Sophie," I whispered.

"I love you right back, O'Sullivan," she replied.

I wrapped my arms around her, cupping her sexy ass, then stood us up, making her grip me with her legs around my waist, arms around my neck.

"You're me forever, love," I whispered into her ear as I carried her back to the kitchen.

Chapter 27.

Sophie

We were showered and dressed, eating Darcy's famous Irish breakfast when the doorbell rang. I touched his arm as he stood, eyes filled with apprehension.

"I'm right here for you, handsome," I said.

"I don't know," he answered.

"You can do this, Darcy. You miss him and you both need this," I said, and he slowly nodded.

"Thanks, love," he whispered.

He kissed me and swiftly walked out, tension clear in his posture. As I cleared away the empty plates I heard muffled voices and started to make more coffee. We were both exhausted as we'd done nothing but fuck each other like rabbits since the film premiere.

Darcy was very dominant in the bedroom, clear about what he wanted, and I loved it. The only thing that was different from Jake? He wasn't into toys. He was so strong that he could pin my arms easily, roll us over without pulling out of me, and rail me so fucking hard from behind it made the bloody bed rattle.

He also enjoyed me taking charge sometimes. A few nights ago I'd shoved him into the wall in the hallway again, ordered him to strip and fuck me hard and fast against said wall. And safe to say, we both had a lot of bloody hot and steamy fun for the rest of the night.

Darcy came striding back in and Christian followed looking rather ruffled. The third person, however, was simply a younger looking version of Darcy. Same dark hair, similar nose and jawline. Lips a very familiar shape, but his eyes were dark brown and he was much leaner than his big brother.

"Hi," I said, holding out my hand.

"Hi lass," and his voice was a little lighter than his brother. "Good to finally meet ya."

My Irish actor was standing by the back window, staring out into the garden. His hands were shoved inside his trouser pockets, tension obvious in his demeanour.

Christian hugged me and leaned into my ear. "Thank you, darling. They need this. I'll see you soon," and then he was gone.

I smiled at Theo Finn O'Sullivan and he threw me a smile. Seemed they shared that trait too, as his face lit up when his lips curled up into that very familiar famous grin.

"Coffee?" I asked.

"Grand lass. Cheers."

His eyes were on the figure by the window, but he looked absolutely terrified. I touched his arm and gestured for him to go to his brother. He bit down on his bottom lip and hesitated, but I gave him a gentle push and winked with a kind smile. He shot me a grateful smile back and looked at his big brother.

"Ya alright Darcy? I've followed ya career. Proud of ya," he said. "Mam has a scrap book full of ya reviews and she brags about ya to everyone who listens."

Darcy didn't move, but his head tilted a little at his brother's words. I handed Theo a mug, sliding over milk and sugar. He smiled and took a sip of the coffee without adding either.

"I'm sorry Darcy," he said.

"That it?"

"Shite, Darce. I can't take back what I did to ya, and I sometimes wish ya'd squeezed harder when ya rammed me against that fecking bathroom wall."

Darcy spun around, his eyes glaring at Theo, but there was a flicker of emotion in his expression. He held out his hand for me and I walked to him.

"Squeezed fecking harder?"

"Yeah. I deserved ya to squeeze the fecking life from me after what I did."

"Ya had ya dick in me fianceè, Theo."

"And ya think I don't regret it every fecking second of every bloody day since then?"

"And so ya fecking should."

Theo looked as though he was about to break down, but he took a deep breath and raked a frustrated hand over his face, then took a sip of his coffee. The silence was immense for a few tense moments, then Theo's eyes went down to his mug.

"Ya know, it was her fecking idea to go into that stall. And I'd practically drank me weight in beer. She asked if I wanted a free ride before she got married, Darce. Did ya know that? *She* propositioned *me*."

"What?"

"She suggested it. Jesus, Darce, I was lit. She didn't deserve ya and I ruined our relationship over that, that selfish, uncaring bitch."

"She what?"

"It was her fecking idea."

"Shite."

They each fell silent, Darcy clearly allowing his brother's words to sink in. Theo took a tentative step closer and said, "Got herself knocked up about a year after ya left. She's married now with three kids. Works at the post office."

"Serves her fecking right."

Theo took another step closer and Darcy's eyes seemed to soften a little. "She never cared, ya know. When ya left? She went back to the party and acted as though nothing had happened."

As I listened, the rage slowly rose to the surface. I wanted to find this lady and slap her into next year. No, I'd punch the fucking slutty bitch into the next bloody century, but I squeezed his hand, reminding him that I was here for him.

"I always wanted to be just like me big brother. I thought I might lose ya to her, ya know, when ya married her. I was a fecking stupid teenager, Darce. But, she didn't fecking care. I think ya were her prize, a trophy so to speak, and she wanted to just show ya off. I don't think she really loved ya."

Darcy froze for a moment as he processed what his little brother had just said, and Theo looked so upset as the silence descended, tears glistening in the corners of his dark eyes.

"Why do ya think that?" Darcy finally questioned.

Theo didn't answer right away, his expression filled with both hatred and sadness. He put down his mug and shoved his hands through his dark hair.

"After ya stormed out, she just shrugged her shoulders, fixed her clothes and face, then she took off her ring, handed it to me, slapped me on the arm and said '*Thanks for the ride*'. Tell Darcy sorry, and I just watched her waltz out while I was bleeding from me nose," he replied.

I couldn't quite believe what I was hearing, but a lot of things began to fall into place. The way my Irishman used to act. The arrogant and cocky attitude. The way he slept with women but never committed to any of them. It also made much more sense what Darcy had told me that Christmas. That he was terrified to get too close and it caused my heart to ache. I squeezed his hand, and his eyes came to mine for a moment.

His hand flew through his hair, the realisation of what his brother was telling him finally registering on his face, and he let out a sigh, seeming to relax a little, sipping his coffee.

"I want me big brother back," Theo said quietly.

Darcy didn't reply immediately and he downed the last of his drink. He gazed down at the empty mug and I felt him squeeze my hand tighter.

"Ya stupid, idiotic, horny fecking shite," he said.

"And I'm so bloody sorry, Darce. I've missed ya. Wanted to explain to ya for years," and I had to smile as Darcy strode over and engulfed his little brother in a hug. "I'm really sorry, Darce. I've hated me self all this time, wanting to clear the air with ya," he said.

"Sounds like ya inadvertently saved me from making a fecking monumental mistake," Darcy whispered.

"Didn't go about it the right way, though," Theo replied.

"No, ya fecking didn't."

I walked to the sofa and sat down, allowing them their moment of reconciliation. But, I couldn't help the smile that appeared on my face as I watched them.

"Mam smacked me after she found out what I did. Then she marched round to Isabelle's house and tore strips off her," Theo said. "Her Mam and Dad were fecking livid too."

Darcy finally smirked and punched his little brother's shoulder. "And ya deserved it. So the feck did that cheating cow," he replied.

My man gestured for his brother to sit at the kitchen island. "Ya want another coffee, shithead?"

"Really? Still?"

"Ya want me to change it to prick?"

"No. And I'd love another coffee, Darce."

Darcy caught my gaze and winked at me. "Come here lass. I need a hug, and a kiss," he ordered.

I rolled my eyes but smiled at him as I got to my feet. I was yanked into him and pressed tightly against his body. He tilted my face up to his and leaned down, kissing me tenderly.

"Thanks for finally letting me talk, Darce," Theo said.

"Welcome. Now, ya staying for lunch?"

Theo's entire face lit up at the offer and he grinned, making my heart warm. "Ya sure?" he asked.

"Wouldn't have asked, shithead."

I smacked Darcy's arm playfully, and he smirked at me. "Please stay, Theo. You two have a lot of catching up to do," I asked.

"I'd love to, Sophie lass. Thanks," he replied. "And I need to show ya something."

He reached into his pocket and flipped through his phone, then he slid it across to us. Darcy's eyes dropped to a picture of a very beautiful woman with long auburn hair and green eyes. Two little girls stood in front of her. One with the same colour hair as the woman, hazel eyes and a cheeky smile. The other had dark hair, green eyes sparkling with a very familiar grin on her face.

"This is me wife and girls. Ya nieces."

Darcy

My eyes glazed over as tears threatened to make an appearance. Sophie's arm was around my waist and I felt her squeeze me a little.

"Shite," I muttered.

"They are all beautiful," Sophie said.

I turned away for a second to try and compose myself, running my hands over my face as I sat beside my lady, taking her hand and gripping it tightly. I looked back down at the little family, heart hammering like a fucking train.

"How long?" I asked.

"Orlaith married me seven years ago. That cheeky imp is Roisin and she's four. And that's Saoirse, and she's almost two," Theo replied.

Jesus Christ, I had two new nieces, and the joy that blossomed in my chest was immense. Sophie patted my ass and kissed my cheek.

"Go talk. I'll bring coffee up," she stated. "Go."

Theo was watching the two of us with curious eyes as I hugged her, kissing her lovingly. As she walked past, my hand shot out and I smacked her sexy ass harder than before, making Theo dive onto his feet and he disappeared out the door.

"What was that?" Sophie whispered. "Did you just spank my ass?"

"Not sure what came over me, lass," I admitted, but I noticed the sparkle in her eyes. "Ya liked it though."

Sophie snorted and giggled, making my dick twitch at that sexy sound. "Yes, O'Sullivan. I did," and she sidled closer, arms roaming around my waist, landing on my own ass.

She smiled with a very naughty glint in her expression. "What are ya doing, love?"

"If I'm a bad girl, will you spank me later?" she purred quietly.

I stared into her eyes, a wicked smirk appearing. "Bad how, bare?" I growled into her ear.

"Oh, I don't know, I'll think of something," she whispered, cupping my face.

I leaned down and started towards her mouth, but I noticed the smirk as she turned her head and kissed the crook of my neck. Then she bit down and nipped me hard, before smacking my ass almost as hard as I had hers.

"Shite, love," I gasped, but grinned at my bad little director.

"Hope that counts as being bad," she purred. "Now get up those stairs, handsome."

I grabbed her hand and slammed her into me, dirty and filthy images flying through my head. "We'll come back to this later, love," I growled, then crushed her lips with mine, plundering her sexy mouth.

I wanted to take her over to the dining table, bend her over and ram my now hard cock into her, but I let her go, slapped her ass again, then winked.

"I like this naughty side, love. Can't wait to see more," and I adjusted myself, making her snort into a giggle again.

She literally walked to the coffee machine, twirled, then blew me a kiss. "I aim to please, O'Sullivan. Go catch up. Your bad girl will join you shortly," and I had to chuckle as I left the most beautiful, perfectly delicious woman I'd ever met.

And she was in love with me. All bloody mine.

Theo was waiting for me on the stairs, gazing at the photographs on the walls. "Did ya take these?" he asked.

"I did. It's home. Ya recognise it?" I questioned.

"Yeah, I do. That hill? We rolled ourselves down it so many times I lost count," he replied.

I had to smile at the memories, but nudged past him, heading upstairs towards the living room. Theo's footsteps echoed behind me as he followed.

"Sophie's a surprise, Darce."

I walked inside and my brother went straight to the jam packed bookshelf. "Still into reading, I see. I'm surprised this thing is still upright."

"It relaxes me. Ya still play the piano?" I asked.

"Yes. Orlaith is wanting to get our little ladies learning. Mam is letting us have the piano from home."

His eyes scanned the shelves, then he turned to look at me, his hands shoved into his jeans pockets.

"Why is she a surprise?" I fired at him.

"Not like the ones ya were photographed with. All glammed up and fake looking. Sophie is all natural and much prettier," he replied. "She seems like a keeper."

That took me by surprise and I arched my brow. I watched his eyes move around the room and they landed on the mantelpiece. There were numerous framed family photographs, and I saw the flicker of surprise mixed with emotion as he noticed the picture of all of us.

"Ya have a picture of us all?" and he picked it up, staring down at our family.

"Why wouldn't I?" I questioned.

He stared at me as though I'd spoken in a different language. "I just thought, well, ya might've, ya know," he stuttered.

"Ya thought I wouldn't have photographs of ya?" I asked.

He looked up at me and the tears were evident at the corner of his eyes. "I guess, yeah. After what I did to ya," he said, his voice breaking as he quickly put the picture back.

I sighed and walked over to him. Theo was the youngest now after we lost our sister, and I'd looked out for him, got into trouble with this guy. And I missed him. I didn't want to see him for so fucking long, but Sophie brought us back together. Now, seeing the guilt and shame in his face had my heart aching.

"Look, Theo. I know I haven't wanted to see ya for fecking years. But, Sophie made a valid bloody point. If anything would've happened to ya without sorting this out? I would never have forgiven me self," I said, and I smacked his shoulder.

I didn't expect it, but he threw himself at me, hugging me tightly. He was shaking a little as he broke down, his emotions taking over.

"Shit, Theo," I gasped as he crushed me with his arms.

"I'm so fecking sorry, Darce," he croaked.

All I could do was hold onto my little brother, feeling really shitty that I'd left it this long before talking to him.

Chapter 28.

Leo

I was skimming the dailies online, hoping and praying that there wasn't any more fucking drama and crap being spouted about me again. Christian paced the living room talking on the phone as Henry made coffee. We were expecting my Mum and sister any time, but we wanted to get ahead of this before that scumbag released anything else.

"Shit, found it," and my eyes landed on a photograph of Dad being led away by police. "For fuck's sake."

There was another lower down and Christian was by my side as he read over my shoulder. Sophie was hugging me by the theatre front door. Her arms were wrapped around me, head resting on my shoulder. My own were holding her tightly against me too, my head nestled in the crook of her neck.

"Two friends hugging," Christian said.

The second one? She was kissing my forehead, her hands still on my waist and mine still around her, eyes locked onto her face.

"Oh this is fucking unbelievable," I groaned.

"Listen, Holly. I need that as soon as possible. Casey is at it again. Thanks," and Christian hung up.

The title of the piece also included a picture of Eve bloody Hemlock.

'The Plot Thickens For Mr Leo Trent, Darcy and His little director. A stalker and a bully

Of A dad being thrown into the mix."

"Does he ever print *anything* true?" I muttered, and my eye's swiftly read the article and it was full of crap. Very Casey. But, there was also some private things in there that I never wanted the whole fucking world to know about.

'The drama is unfolding yet again for Darcy and his little director. They made one hell of a statement at his latest movie premiere 'Lost Love's Revenge'. *That epic kiss and carrying her from the building. But, there seemed to be more to their story hidden beneath the surface. After Mr Leo Trent's bully of a father appeared at the theatre and gave his son a severe beating for being gay, the police arrested him, keeping the famous Irishman occupied while the director made her move on the younger Mr Trent. There are even rumours flying around about the possibility that Ms Sophie Carter is actually having an affair, and may be carrying Mr Trent's baby.'*

"What have I ever done to the guy?" I exclaimed, leaning forward onto my thighs, head in hands, but unable to look away from the article.

"There was clearly an attraction between Ms Carter and Mr Trent. They have been

Seen holding hands and hugging on many occasions. Darcy? Does he know his little

Director is possibly banging the sexy blonde? Is his story about being gay just to cover

Up the fact he is sleeping with her. And what about the flamboyant Mr Henry Rossi?

Is he really the predator that Mr Trent's stalker has been screaming about?"

My head was pounding, heart racing as I stormed into the kitchen. I suddenly felt as though someone were sitting on my chest. I couldn't breathe.

"Sin?"

"I can't... The fucking piece of shit. I...," and my throat constricted.

"Leo, baby. Eyes on me. This is a panic attack, breathe with me."

"Why? I've never done anything wrong to anyone," I croaked.

"I know. We have him though. The things he's saying is against the bloody law. Deep breaths. In then out, Sin."

"Henry, I can't do this," but I tried to do as he asked, dragging the oxygen slowly into my lungs as best as I could.

"That's it, Sin. Keep doing that."

His arms wrapped around me as I sank to the floor, tears escaping from my eyes. I'd had enough of this shit. I wanted that piece of crap to burn in fucking hell.

"Christian is sending our story out today, along with photographs. That's why he's waiting on your Mum and Mia. For a brief statement from them too," and he pulled me closer. "I'm right here for you, my beautiful man."

I relaxed into his body, allowing him to simply hold me. "Christian? We need to let Darcy and Sophie know," my boyfriend stated.

"Already done. But they have a visitor right now," he replied. "We need to get ahead of this. Leo, please don't panic. I have ways and means of dealing with his kind. I also have the best team of lawyers on my payroll," and he winked at me with a warm smile.

The knock rang out and Henry kissed me briefly before helping me from the floor. He walked me to the sofa then went to answer it. I raked my fingers through my hair in frustration, swiping the tears from my eyes. Eve started this fucking chain reaction, and it was her I blamed.

"Leo," and I turned to see my Mum and sister.

"Oh god," and I was engulfed in their arms.

The recent events resurfaced and the tears rolled down my cheeks as my family held me. "It's okay honey. We're right here."

"That son of a bitch did it, Mum."

"We saw it, Leo," Mum whispered. "Your new agent informed us as he read."

I lifted my head and Christian winked at me. "It's my job to protect you as a client, Leo. We come back with your story and how you met Henry. Your lovely mother and sister will add in some history, but know you will be officially outed with this."

"Thank you so much," said Mum. "Look after my boy and his boyfriend."

"Do not worry Mrs Trent. We will make all of this better."

She suddenly hugged my agent and he chuckled. "Thank you for everything. You're making my son's dreams come true."

He smiled at her and patted my twin sister on the shoulder with a wink. "Your son is a gifted actor, Mrs Trent. I look forward to working with him."

Mum took Henry's hand and tugged him to the kitchen, winking at me and Mia took my hand and smiled, nudging my shoulder.

"Congratulations landing a top bloody agent, little brother," she said and pulled me in for another hug.

"Thanks, Mia."

My twin sister was a female version of me, just a few inches shorter. We shared similar personality traits, sense of humour, and tastes in films, books and music. We were practically the same person except for our anatomy. We were the best of friends and we would always look out for each other.

"Great to meet you officially Miss Trent," and Christian held out his manicured hand.

"Hello Mr?" Mia said.

"West. Christian West. And I'd love to chat about your brother. For the story I mentioned?"

She grinned and nudged my shoulder. "Sure. I can share lots of stories," she replied wickedly.

Christian's brow arched and an amused smile crept onto his face. I rolled my eyes and smacked her lightly.

"It's about being gay, you fucking devil," I replied.

She smirked and kissed my cheek. "I know. Just teasing. And don't worry about it. Concentrate on the amazing play you're in. You were awesome by the way," and she left with Christian to have a chat.

I joined my boyfriend and my Mum in the kitchen, and they looked rather cosy whispering over their coffees.

"What the hell are you both whispering about?" I asked.

Henry chuckled and pulled me between his thighs, my back pressed against his chest. "How much I love you, Sin. And how you appeared in the bar like a dream come true," he drawled.

"It sounds like you two were meant for each other, honey," Mum said with her warm smile. "I rather like this charmer."

I had to smile and I covered his hands with mine. "It's true, Mum. I walked into the bar and he was staring right at me. Knew I was in delicious trouble," I replied.

She touched my arm with a wide smile, her eyes sparkling with warmth. "I like this young man."

"Thanks Mum," and she laughed.

She gazed between the two of us and sipped her coffee. "I have to ask, Henry. Why do you call Leo Sin?"

Henry smirked and kissed the spot just beneath my ear. "Because of the way he looks."

"And?" she questioned.

"Mum," I groaned, flushing slightly.

Henry chuckled and fixed his eyes on Mum. "I think he resembles a sinful devil wrapped up in angelic packaging, Mrs Trent."

Mum snorted and choked on the mouthful of coffee. "Well, I've never heard my son described that way before," she exclaimed.

"Was a surprise to me too," I said, grinning down at our hands linked together on my stomach.

"I rather like it. Now, I'd better go and join your sister and you new agent," she replied, standing up and kissing me on my forehead. "Let's get this whole mess straightened out."

And she kissed Henry's forehead too before joining Christian and Mia on the sofa. My man turned me and cupped my cheeks. His mouth covered mine and he kissed me deeply.

"This will get better, Sin. I promise you."

He pressed his forehead on mine as I closed my eyes with a frustrated sigh. But it hit me like a train.

"We're being signed up by a top agent, babe. *Darcy O'Sullivan's* agent."

Henry smirked as he understood what I was getting at. We might land film roles and that meant more publicity, not less.

"Yeah, true. But we'll have each other, Sin. And that's exciting, right?" he replied.

I had to smile at the thought, and he wrapped his arms around me, holding me tightly. At least the threat of Dad showing up was over. Whatever else was in store, however? Who knew?

Sophie

Theo and Darcy were bonding upstairs and I really wanted a sandwich. I grabbed chicken, ketchup, lettuce and... *What in the fuck? Eww... yet yummy?*

I started piling the ingredients into the bread then headed upstairs to join the two brothers. They were sitting on the sofa and looking at pictures on Theo's phone. It was lovely to watch them finally reconnecting. I could tell they had been thick as thieves before the fallout.

"Get in here, love," Darcy announced once he caught sight of me.

I joined him and I was tucked into his other side, but his brows arched as he saw the food in my hand.

"What the feck is in that?" he asked.

"Chicken, lettuce and cucumber with ketchup," I replied.

Theo snorted into laughter as my man crinkled up his nose in disgust, making me smirk. "That's fecking disgusting, lass," he drawled.

I just bit into it and moaned with joy as I chewed. "Mmm, yummy," I purred, eyes locked on his gorgeous emerald ones.

Theo was smiling like a kid in a sweet shop as he watched the two of us. He really was a younger version of Darcy, and I had to return the smile.

"This looks serious," he said.

"It is, shithead," Darcy answered without hesitation. "I love Sophie."

I looked up and smiled at the man who had swept me off my feet all over again, making my entire body go crazy, pulse to race and lady parts to flutter. My cheeks even began to burn at the way he was gazing at me.

"Does Mam know? Because she keeps all ya reviews and articles about ya. She'll be raging if ya don't tell her first," Theo replied.

Darcy groaned and sat up, kissing my forehead as he moved. "I'll tell her," he said and reached for his phone.

"Now?" I asked, panic suddenly rearing its ugly head.

We had been together for just over a month and a half now, and meeting the parents had not even crossed my mind.

Well, holy fucking shitty shit balls.

Darcy winked at me and left the two of us together, my heart racing at a million miles a minute as I watched him stride from the room about to announce to his mum that he was in a fucking relationship with me. I felt Theo's eyes on me and he let out a chuckle.

"Ya have nothing to panic about, lass."

My eyes landed on the younger O'Sullivan and he was smirking at me in amusement. I frowned at him, making him chuckle again.

"What?" I questioned, fidgeting where I sat and stuffing more of the weirdly delicious sandwich into my mouth.

"Mam'll love ya. And ya know why?"

"Why?"

"Ya not an actress, lass. Ya the boss. Of me big brother. She'll love that."

I looked up and his expression was warm as he finished his coffee. I had to smile and polished off the last of my sandwich.

"And I want to thank ya for getting Darcy to finally see me. It means the fecking world to me to have him back."

I put down the plate and brushed the crumbs from my fingers. After swallowing the last of my food I fixed my eyes on Theo.

"I lost my husband just like that," and I clicked my fingers. "I was so thankful that I'd been forced to go home and work it out with him. I couldn't have lived with myself if I hadn't. Darcy would have felt the same. I just pointed that out to him."

Theo's eyes glazed over a little and he stood up, walking to the fireplace. He picked up one of the picture frames and stared at it.

"This picture was taken on Mam and Dad's anniversary. She still celebrates even though he's been gone for years. I was surprised to see it," he said quietly.

I stood up and joined him, gazing down at the picture. They made a very handsome family. Darcy's sister had the same dark hair and green eyes.

"What happened to your sister?" I asked.

Theo sighed and put the frame back in its place. But Darcy answered for him, making us both spin around to see him leaning against the door frame, watching the two of us.

"She was hit by a kid who ran a red light. He did jail time, as the little fecker didn't have a licence," and he walked over and wrapped his arm around my waist, kissing my temple.

Theo's eyes darkened and he shoved his hands into his pockets. "Mam was a mess, and I remember having to go and stay with Uncle Liam and Aunty Caitlin for a few days," he said.

"Ya were the youngest from that point on, Theo. Me and Shay wanted ya out of the shite. We did it to protect ya," Darcy replied.

Theo smiled at his brother and it lit up his whole face as he gazed at Darcy. The love he had for him was clear to see.

"Now, lass. Mam wants to meet ya. She's coming to the show on closing night with Shay and the family. *All* me family," he said, smacking Theo on his shoulder.

And holy shit, the panic slammed me again.... Meeting the fucking family. Crap, crap, fucking hell....

Chapter 29.

Leo

Christian left us after chatting to Mum and Mia, our story of how Henry and I met with a little background covering when and how long I'd known I was gay. He had to be careful about Dad as he was awaiting sentencing due to admitting what he had done.

"Now, what's for lunch, little brother," Mia asked.

"You'd better ask my boyfriend. He's taking the lead today," I replied with a grin.

My twin sister stood up and held out her hand to Henry. "Let me help. And I can interrogate you at the same time," she announced.

I rolled my eyes with a smirk as she tugged my sexy man to the kitchen. "And I can learn lots of Leo's dirty secrets," he drawled, and winked at me.

"Be bloody careful lady," I fired at her.

"Nope. Never, blondie," she threw back.

I threw a cushion at her as Mum settled back into the sofa. I turned to find her staring at me, and I smiled, taking her hand.

"Are you sure you're alright, honey?" she asked. "After what Dad did?"

"I'll never forgive him, Mum."

"Neither will I, honey. I'm so sorry, Leo."

"Why?"

"Because a parent should be there to protect their children. I wasn't there for you."

"You've always been in my corner, Mum. You and Mia. You've got nothing to be sorry for," and I pulled her into a hug.

She sighed and stroked my head, just like she always did when I was a kid. "Still, I wasn't this time."

"You remember the day I'd been out with Alfie? He had a hold of my hand and gave me my first kiss at the side of the house. You saw Dad coming," I whispered.

She squeezed me tighter as she answered. "I distracted him by asking him to help me get the Christmas tree back into the loft," she replied.

"I managed to get Alfie through the back garden gate and bolted through the back door and into the hall and up the stairs. That was one of many times you were in my corner, Mum."

We stayed quiet for a few moments and I knew it was because she thought she'd let me down.

"I can't believe he hurt you."

I sat up and rubbed my ribs where he'd kicked me over and over. I raked my hand through my hair and sighed.

"I can Mum. He threatened to often enough."

Mum sat up and took my hands, squeezing tightly. Her eyes glanced over at my sister and boyfriend laughing and preparing food and she smiled. There was something in her gaze and I had to ask.

"What are you thinking about?"

"I have always loved your dad. Even though he had some radical views. But, well, I can't ever forgive him for hurting you the way he did. I hope you don't hold it against me? That I still love him?"

I groaned and took her hands in mine, squeezing. "Jeez mum. I could never hate you for that. Dad's your husband."

Her eyes had tears glistening in them and I had to give her a hug again.

"I'm still so sorry he hurt you, honey."

"It's all done now, but," and I paused, taking a moment. "I asked Dad the day he attacked me. Asked him what happened. He said a gay man attacked him.... In the shower?"

She sat back and looked at me keeping my hand in hers. Mum glanced at my boyfriend and Mia in the kitchen, laughing and chatting happily then she touched my cheek with a sad smile. "Do you remember the few weeks that I didn't go to visit your dad?"

"Yeah. Why?"

"He *was* attacked in prison, honey. They called to inform me that he'd been hurt, and he didn't want to see me for a while. They said another inmate had raped him in the showers. He was badly hurt"

I stared back and the shift in his behaviour now made complete sense. Dad was different when he came home. His language had become darker, more vicious.

"That makes sense, Mum. He changed after he came home. Yeah, he was homophobic before, but after? He was scary and really bloody cruel."

She sighed and touched my arm. "That's true. His words and rhetoric were terrifying after he was released. But, it does *not* excuse him from hitting you, hurting you and I can't ever forgive him, no matter how much I love him. To attack you alone in an alley? That's cowardly."

"Henry was there for me, Mum. And you know we're going to live together. I think he's my one," I whispered.

Mum glanced over at my sister and Henry, busy preparing lunch, giggling and chatting as though they'd known each other for years.

"He fits in with us. And it's so lovely to see you being your true self, honey. Finally," she whispered.

I smiled and glanced at my hot boyfriend. "I never thought I'd get to have a man I could introduce you to, Mum. I never thought I'd ever get the chance to be happy."

She pulled me back in and hugged me tightly. "Now you don't have to hide away. You should never be ashamed of who you fall in love with."

I sighed as Mum released me, her eyes sparkling like I hadn't seen in a long time. "I found him, Mum. Henry's my forever."

"And I can see that. *And* you two were amazing last night by the way. A fantastic role, a very good agent. My boy is going places. I'm super proud of you," and she kissed my forehead.

"Love you," I whispered.

"Love you too, honey."

Our story hit the following day and the media went nuts. We were escorted to the theatre every day with Ben and Stefan and we were sent really amazing messages over social media. Sophie and Darcy also had a ton of coverage, headlines about their sham of a relationship and how Sophie was possibly using the famous guy for his money. We all had to deal with the fucking fallout sparked by Eve bloody Hemlock and the snake that was Casey.

Christian organised a press conference for the play and the questions were ridiculous. But, they were given the truth from both myself and Sophie. Darcy and Henry joked about the rumours, and we won over the media, following with positive stories about Darcy and Sophie, Henry and me.

Now it was the day before closing and we were all chilling in the dressing rooms after a Matinee. Darcy had ordered in food and we were all chattering amongst ourselves. It was really lovely to be a part of such a great group of people.

"Oh, for fuck's sake," Asia groaned.

"Oh fuck, what now?" I asked.

She grinned and showed us the story. "That Casey dude has had to recant his story about Sophie and Leo. He was threatened with a law suit," she announced.

At that moment, Tasha, the playwright strode into the green room. "Oh my god, ladies and gentlemen," and she threw newspapers at us. "My play has hit the top five of the month by the bloody critics," she exclaimed.

I grabbed one and stared down at the article, and it was true. Tasha was now famous. There were mentions of the movie star Darcy O'Sullivan being poignant and tragic in his lead role, and two gay men taking the acting world by storm.

"Fuck," I gasped.

"Indeed, Leo. They are all gushing about the fact that you and Henry are gay men playing gay roles. They love the two of you," Tasha replied.

I picked up the paper and read through the review. It did indeed say that Henry and I were talent to watch. The grin erupted on my face as Henry read through it too.

"Fucking hell, Sin, we're famous," he drawled, then yanked me in for a delicious kiss.

Closing Night

Sophie

The alarm pierced the room and I groaned, rolling over and snuggling into the warm naked body of my boyfriend. Darcy's arms wrapped around me and pressed me closer, his lips lightly grazing my forehead.

"I want to stay right here, love," he whispered.

I snorted into giggles, burying my face in his chest, the smattering of dark hairs tickling my nose.

"It's the final night, then we get a few weeks off, loverboy," I teased.

"Loverboy? Well that's grand. Haven't been called a lad for fecking years, ya cheeky bare," he replied.

I lifted my face and gazed up into his. He ran his hands through my longer hair and winked.

"Are ya hungry, love?"

"Bloody starving."

"Let me cook for ya after me workout. Stay in bed, beautiful," and he kissed me lovingly, possessively and I sighed into his lips.

He reluctantly headed for the wardrobe and I relaxed into the bed, glancing at the small clock on the bedside table. It read six am.

"How do you manage to get out of bed at this time?" I groaned.

My gorgeous Irishman chuckled as he re-emerged dressed in gym shorts and a very tight fitting vest, showcasing his muscular, seriously hot body.

"For as long as I remember, love. Now go back to sleep," and I watched his fine ass disappear.

I covered my head with the duvet and closed my eyes, snuggling into the comfiest bed I'd ever slept in. *But,* after ten minutes of tossing and turning I let out an annoyed groan.

"Shitty fuck balls," I grumbled and sat up.

I looked at the clock and it was already six thirty, and I groaned, trying to rub the tiredness from my face. I saw Darcy's shirt hanging from the chair and I smirked, a naughty idea forming, so I climbed out of bed and headed for the shower.

Darcy

I finished the warm up, and slowly came to a gentle stop on the rower. All I could think about was how happy I was. My little director had filled my damned heart. She made my life complete, but I had to concentrate.

I walked to the weights rack and considered whether to kill my legs or my upper body. I considered my options, and as I was about to make my decision

I thought about what I was about to do at the end of the show. So, I headed for the dumbbells and started my main workout.

I was about to do something absolutely huge tonight. And I was fucking nervous.

I glanced at the door, praying for my beautiful woman to re-appear in my shirt, but nothing yet. As I worked through an upper body workout my eyes kept glancing at the place where she had shown up last time. No signs, unfortunately, so I finished up and picked up the towel to wipe my face and neck. But, like a sexy miracle, at that moment, she appeared and my body went into overdrive.

She was wearing one of my shirts and nothing else, hair all damp from the shower, face completely natural.

Jesus holy fucking hell.

"Hey you," she said, leaning against the doorframe.

"Hello, ya bad girl," I drawled.

I jumped to my feet and was in front of her in a flash, hoisting her up into the air and striding to the wall. She giggled, her gorgeous legs wrapping around my waist.

"Well hello, sexy man," she said, kissing my neck as I did the same.

"Gods lass. I fecking love ya," and I crushed her against said wall.

"Then show me with your huge cock," she purred into my ear.

I let out a happy groan, hand freeing my now painfully hard dick. My fingers found her entrance and she was deliciously wet.

"Feck, love. All wet for me."

"Always, O'Sullivan. Now fuck me hard and fast, like you hate me," she whispered and I looked into her dark eyes and they were sparkling with wickedness.

"Oh really, ya naughty minx?"

"Just fucking do it, handsome," she ordered.

I had to grin at her as I lined myself up against her slick entrance, then, in one swift thrust forward, I slammed home, and groaned into her neck.

"Yes, fuck, yes," she cried, and I did exactly what she wanted.

I didn't hold back, and I pounded her so hard that there might be a Sophie shaped hole in my gym wall. I put my hand behind her head as I crushed her with my body, violently fucking her beautiful pussy.

"Fucking.... Hell.... Yes, yes, Christ, Darcy, there, don't.... Fuck... ing.... Stop..." she cried.

I grunted as I hit her over and over, then she let out a loud cry, fingers digging painfully into my shoulders.

My Sophie enjoyed it rough sometimes, and I was all for it. She gasped, nails now dragging down my back, and a feral growl came from my lips.

"Lass... yes, Jesus... fecking....Christ," I croaked, lifting her higher as I rammed harder, hitting so much deeper, making her cry out, body locking up, and we fell together for the first time.

Sophie's pussy clamped down on my cock and I exploded inside her, grinding my hips into her as she milked me dry. Our hot skin was slick against each other, breaths coming short and sharp, and I lifted my head and looked at my beautifully stunning girlfriend.

"Happy, my sexy little devil?" I whispered.

"More than, my sexy demon," she gasped with a cheeky smile.

I chuckled as I buried my face into her neck, kissing her as I ground my hips against her. I knew I had to put her down, but I didn't fucking want to. Ever.

"I love ya, Sophie lass," I said.

"And I bloody love you too, O'Sullivan," she replied, then kissed me. "You hungry?"

"Fecking starving love. Let me grab a quick shower, then I'll make us breakfast," I suggested.

After the best day filled with more food and more hot sex, we eventually made our way to the theatre. My nerves were starting to bristle, one hand fiddling with the box in my trouser pocket, the other holding tightly to Sophie's.

"You okay, handsome?" she asked.

I turned and gave her my winning smile, hiding the sheer terror deep inside. "Always when I'm with ya, love," I drawled and winked.

"Charmer," she replied with her own beautiful smile.

"Telling the truth, lass."

She shuffled closer and I saw the spark in her eyes. "Get over here and kiss your woman then, O'Sullivan," she whispered.

I smirked and yanked on her hand, making her yelp and giggle before I silenced her with a very possessive kiss. The car pulled up at the stage door and we noticed the gang of press hovering at the front of the building. We snuck out of the car and into the alley where young Leo had been attacked, then we entered without any issues.

"I need to pee. See you backstage, handsome," she said as we headed towards the stage.

"Sure love."

I jogged up the steps and marched across the stage and into the wings, around the back and up another flight of stairs, and I pulled open the door to the dressing rooms.

Mine was the largest and the first one along the corridor. I opened the door and yanked the small box from my pocket. It was a huge fucking deal for me, and I stared down at the item inside. My hand whirled through my hair, but I didn't hear his footsteps.

"Shit," he gasped, and I whipped my head around to see Leo staring at me in shock. "Is that what I think it is?"

Chapter 30.

"Christ, fella. Ya almost gave me a heart attack," and I shoved the box into the pocket of my costume jacket.

Leo strolled inside and leant against the frame of the door. "You didn't answer the question, Darcy."

I sighed as I tugged off my suit jacket and draped it over the chair. "Yes, fella. It is what ya think. I'm gonna do it after the bows, before the curtain closes."

Leo grinned at me and I had to return it too.

"She's going to smack you for that," Leo drawled.

I smirked as I knew exactly how she'd react, but the thing that terrified me? Would she accept?

"She's going to say yes, Darcy. You know that, right?"

"Feck. I bloody hope so. And don't rush off afterwards. Christian wants to talk to ya both," I replied.

He nodded and grinned at me. "Sure thing. I came to ask if you both wanted to come for lunch tomorrow?"

"That'd be grand, fella. We'd love to."

He walked toward me and smacked my shoulder lightly. "Great. Max and Teagen are coming too, my mum and sister as well."

I smiled and nodded. "If we bring extra food, can I bring me Mam and me two brothers?" I asked.

At that moment, Henry appeared and he stepped inside. "You asked him yet, Sin?"

"Yeah. Can we fit Darcy's family too? Three more?" Leo asked.

Henry chuckled and said, "Why the fuck not. The more the merrier."

"Grand. We'll bring extra alcohol. We might be celebrating," I said with a devilish wink.

Henry arched his brows and crossed his arms over his chest. "And why would that be, Darce?"

I simply said, "I have a very important question to ask me bare tonight."

Henry's eyes narrowed a little and they sparkled with nothing but bloody mischief. He wrapped his arms around Leo, resting his chin on his shoulder and grinned like a devil.

"You are going to pop the question, aren't you?" he asked.

I groaned and raked a hand over my face. He was too fucking smart for his own good. Leo smirked and dropped his eyes from my face.

"Jesus, fella. Nothing gets past ya does it," I muttered.

I turned to deposit my phone onto the dressing table then two strong arms wrapped around me in a crushing hug.

"Feck," fell out of me as Leo's laughter echoed through the room.

"I hope we get invites, Darcy. And Sophie is going to say yes, you know," Henry whispered before releasing me.

I chuckled and turned to look at the talented actors. I ruffled my hair and threw them a grateful smile.

"I fecking hope so, fella."

"She's going to smack you though, you know that? Right?"

"Yeah, fella, I know," but I grinned at them, causing a snort to fall out of Henry.

Sophie

The curtains came down on an extremely successful six week run, and I was a very proud director right now. The applause was deafening as everyone prepared for their first of many sets of bows, but my hand was suddenly grabbed by a very agitated and flustered Irishman.

"Shit, handsome," I gasped.

"Get out here, lass," he drawled, eyes sparkling with energy.

He'd been acting strangely for the last week of the play. Now, I was literally being dragged on stage to take our final bows.

"Darcy, what's the bloody rush?" I gasped as he tucked me into his side.

"Ya taking the last curtain call, love."

"I know, but you've been weird all bloody week, and some."

He didn't get a chance to answer as the curtain lifted and the audience applauded even more enthusiastically. His family were in the audience, along with Max, Teagen and Mum and Benson. Ella, Scott, Cameron and Cora were also here, so this was going to be a very bloody busy night.

We took the first lot of bows, then the curtain dropped again, Darcy yanking me in for a kiss. I was about to stride off stage, but my wrist was gripped tightly, halting my departure.

"Oh no ya don't, love," Darcy drawled, pulling me back to his side as the curtains rose up again.

"What the fuck are you doing?" I hissed then plastered a wide smile onto my face as the audience cheered loudly.

Everyone stepped forward and we all took another bow as a whole cast this time, then Darcy took a solo bow. He stepped back, grabbing my hand tightly and threw me a very mischievous wink, and that set my nerves on edge. Darcy bloody O'Sullivan was up to something.

The Playwright then appeared and she winked at Darcy, stepped forward to take a bow too, then a microphone was handed to her, and she gestured for everyone to quieten down.

"I want to thank every single person that came to see my play. I never believed I'd ever be here. These characters were inspired by real events in my own family life, so thank you for taking time out of your day to see it. But, before you all disappear tonight there's one more surprise for you all," and she grinned at me.

The flashes from the back of the theatre went off as Darcy yanked me forwards. I frowned at him as my heart started to beat faster. He glanced my way and tugged me into his side.

"Before ya all disappear, ladies and gentlemen, members of the press. There is one other announcement that I'd like to share with ya," he stated.

"What are you up to?" I whispered, nerves whirling like a tornado in my stomach.

Darcy turned to face me, taking both of my hands in his, and he looked bloody nervous too.

Shitting bloody hell. What was he about to fucking do?

"Sophie Carter," Darcy started. "I love ya more than any words can describe. I never thought I'd ever get the chance to have ya back in me life."

I stared up at him, confusion clear in my face. He simply squeezed my hand and dropped to one knee.

"Oh shit," I exclaimed, and I heard gasps coming from all around me.

A small box appeared in his hand and he grinned up at me. "Sophie, love.... Will ya marry me?" he asked.

Every part of me was on fire, heart thundering and I stared down at the very beautiful diamond sparkling in the lights.

Darcy fucking O'Sullivan just asked me to bloody marry him. On the fucking stage.

Even though a part of me wanted to murder him for doing this so publicly? I knew exactly what I wanted. And I suddenly didn't care that the entire bloody theatre was packed with strangers and our families.

I looked down at the Irishman who had once broken my heart, then whirled back into my life like a hurricane and literally swept me off my feet, and I grinned as I felt like Cinderella. I'd bagged my Prince Charming, and I was about to get my happy ending.

"Yes," fell out of me as Darcy's emerald eyes glistened with emotion.

"Ya will?"

"Jesus Christ, O'Sullivan. Yes. I will," and he was on his feet, hoisting me into his arms and kissing me like a starving man.

The entire theatre erupted into applause and cheering as Darcy slipped the ring onto my finger. I gazed up at him, and my heart just bloomed with happiness. I glanced around the stage and caught Leo and Henry chuckling. The bloody devils had known. I turned back to my fiancè and smacked his chest, making him let out his divine chuckle too.

"Cheeky, and fucking dangerous, O'Sullivan," I whispered into his ear.

"Took a chance, love," he simply said, and kissed me.

The flashes were going crazy as the curtains closed, then the entire cast went fucking nuts. I was engulfed by my man, then crushed with everyone else, turning it into some sort of weird group hug.

"Where are they?" called out a very loud Irish female voice.

Darcy gazed down at me, his eyes filled with nothing but love. "That's Mam. Come on love. Let us out ya crazy lot."

The cast dispersed and our family and friends appeared and descended on us. Darcy kissed my lips and then squeezed my hand as they practically rugby tackled us in hugs from all sides.

"I'll go see me Mam first," Darcy whispered, then he fought his way out.

Max, Teagen and Ella got to us first and I was crushed between three while Darcy was engulfed in a grey haired woman's arms.

"Fucking hell, bitch. You're marrying a film star," Ella gushed.

"Shit, lady. Congrats fuckface," Max exclaimed.

"Congratulations, sexy little goddess," Teagen said.

"And you're all fucking crushing me, you crazy gorgeous lot," I fired at them through my laughter.

I was released and Max kissed my forehead, Teagen following. Ella slapped my arm and grinned.

"Oh my god. The play was amazing. That blonde? Wow, sexy fucker. Such a shame he's gay," Ella said.

"And you are bloody married, woman," Scott piped up, smirking at her. "Congratulations, Sophie."

"Thanks Scott. And thank you, bloody crazy fuckers," I said, grinning at them all.

I'd missed these guys way more than I had realised, so made a mental note to organise a visit to catch up. I glanced over Ella's shoulder and saw Mum. Benson looked much better, and he was smiling at me.

"Give me a second," I said, and walked across the stage. "Mum. Dad," and they each gave me a hug.

"Congratulations, love," Mum said.

"That was a great play," Benson added.

"Thank you for being here," I replied. "I hope that you're okay with?" and I glanced over at my new fiancè.

"Jake would want you to be happy, love, and congratulations," he said, patting my arm.

I nodded and he took my hand and squeezed. "I know he didn't like Darcy. And I *do* miss Jake every bloody day. Always will."

"I can see that," Benson replied. "And know that you don't have to explain yourself, Sophie. As long as you're both happy, love."

I threw my arms around him and hugged him tightly, making him chuckle as he wrapped me up with his own. His words had settled the nervousness I'd felt seeing them tonight.

"I'm really happy again, dad. Never thought I would be, but I am," I whispered.

He chuckled again and gave me a squeeze. "That's what counts. Now you need to meet the folks, right?"

I groaned and the panic flared in my gut, but Mum and Benson grinned and I was turned and slowly pushed forward.

"Go get em," Mum said.

"You'll be fine, Sophie," Benson added.

It was a fair few moments later and Darcy appeared, eyes dancing with love. He greeted Mum and Benson, said a round of hello's to Max, Teagen, Scott, Cameron and Cora, and a very starstruck Ella, then his focus came back to me.

"Mam wants to meet ya, love."

I sucked in a deep breath and Max and Teagen shot me cheeky winks. Ella and the others shared a look then waltzed towards Tara, Henry and Leo, leaving just the two of us.

"Jesus, handsome. I'm bloody shitting myself," I whispered.

He grinned and kissed my lips gently as we walked to the group of Darcy's family. His Mum, Theo, and another man with similar dark hair and eyes were watching as we approached.

"Mam. This is Sophie. Me fianceè."

"Hello," I said, holding out my hand.

The tall, slender older woman had white hair cut short. She had the same green eyes as Darcy, and almost as tall as him. She studied me for a few moments, then her mouth crept up into a very mischievous smile and grabbed my hand, pulling me into a hug.

"Oh my days. I thought he'd never find someone."

"Cheers for that, Mam," Darcy groaned.

Darcy's Mum raked her eyes over me and I gulped as the nerves went bat shit crazy. "Well now. You are the little lady who's finally tamed me son?"

I had to smirk at my man, squeezing his hand with mine. "I guess I am, Mrs O'Sullivan," I replied.

"Ah, go on with ya. It's Deidre. Ya going to marry me son, and then ya call me Mam," she said, taking my hand in hers, patting it.

The other dark haired man smacked Darcy on the shoulder with a huge, very familiar grin appearing on his face.

"Congratulations, Darce. Ya finally got ya little director," he said, his voice much deeper than his brothers.

"Cheers, Shay. This is me older brother, love," and Darcy winked at me.

Shay smiled and patted my shoulder. "Ya made me brother smile again, Sophie. Welcome to the family," and he winked.

Their Mum took my arm and fixed her darker green eyes onto mine. "I'll let ya go, love," she said, her gaze not wavering.

The men shared a look with each other and Darcy kissed me before they literally walked away, leaving me with their mum.

"How'd ya do it?" she asked once we were alone.

"Erm, do what?" I questioned.

"Ah, go on. Me son had an endless string a airheads for years after that little witch broke his heart. I gave Darcy a good smack for being such an eejit. Theo got a good seeing to as well. Then Darcy practically became a priest. Not one lass after he caused all that drama for ya, and I was told ya wangled a reunion with his little brother?" and her face softened as she spoke.

I glanced over at a very nervous looking actor, his eyes never leaving the two of us, and I smiled to myself.

"He's been quieter, sad and then here ya are, bold as brass, making me boy's eyes alive again."

I bit down on my bottom lip and took a deep breath before answering her.

"I got married, Mrs O' Sullivan. Sorry, Deidre," and she patted my hand again. "We were happy for just over three years, then a drunk driver slammed into their taxi. Jake was killed along with the driver."

"That is awful, love. Go on," and she waited for me to continue.

I sighed and turned to face her. "I moved back to London because I couldn't stay there.... Without him. I was invited to stay with my brother and his boyfriend, and they really helped me to heal. I eventually decided to come back to the theatre as the resident director, and Kate sent me tickets to a show. Turned out that she had organised it for Darcy and me to see each other again."

She simply smiled, not saying anything, so I kept going. "Your son informed me that he loved me that famous year, but I was in love with Jake. But, when we saw each other again? Darcy said he wouldn't let me go this time. I have to admit, we had a fling a fair few years before and, well," but she cut me off.

"He acted like an eejit?" she asked.

I bit down on my lip and sighed. "Yes, he broke my heart if I'm honest. But he apologised and told me about Isabelle."

She paused our steps and turned to face me, hands now on each of my arms. "That girl broke my son. I blame her for all the silly mistakes he walked into time after time with the ladies. Underneath, he's a fecking teddy bear."

I chuckled at her words and nodded. "Yes, he's shown me that side since. And after losing my husband like I did? I decided to live my life to the fullest, so I gave him a second chance, and then your son proposed to me in front of a bloody audience and press, and now we're going to get married."

She let out a lovely light laugh, waving to her son and Darcy rejoined us, taking my hand and tucking me possessively into his side. He also leaned in and kissed his mum on her cheek, smiling warmly.

"Alright, Mam?" he asked.

"Yes, love. Don't mess this up. This bare is grand."

I turned and hid the huge grin, burying my face into his jacket. "Sophie's me forever, Mam. No chance am I gonna mess it up," he said confidently.

We were swiftly joined by Theo and Shay, then I took them over to meet my Mum, Benson, Max and Teagen.

Chapter 31.

Leo

Henry introduced me to the friends he'd made up in the Yorkshire Dales, and they seemed like a pretty tight knit group. But, they accepted me in a flash which made me grin as Henry pressed me against his side.

"Why do you have to be fucking gay?" the blonde asked me.

"And again, married lady," said the man holding her hand.

I had to chuckle as Henry's arm squeezed me tighter against him, and kissed my lips. "This one's my forever, you randy fucker, Ella," he drawled.

"We know. We read that gorgeous article about how you met, and the things you've had to deal with Leo," said the slender darker haired lady holding hands with a tattooed hunk.

The story had done the trick for the two of us, showing the world that I had never been with Eve fucking Hemlock. I had talked a little about how I'd had to hide who I really was due to family issues. Mum and Mia had talked about how they'd supported me, and loved how I had finally found love. It also heightened the awareness of homophobia and brought it back into the news.

I couldn't talk about what had happened to me as it was an ongoing case. I had a restraining order against Dad now, and Ben and Stefan were a familiar sight. Mum had also filed for divorce, unable to forgive him for beating her son.

"I hear you were supposed to be having an affair with Sophie?" the bubbly Ella asked.

"I know, right. I've been gay for bloody years," I replied. "If I'm honest? I've always been gay."

Henry wrapped his arms around my waist and pressed me back against him, kissing my neck lovingly. "Casey is still trying to climb out of the hole he made for himself with Darcy. And he's still trying to suggest that there's something going on between Sophie and Sin, but this sexy angel is all fucking mine," he drawled.

"I noticed. His new one is fucking hilarious. Saying Darcy is *allegedly* being played by Sophie and Leo," Ella replied.

"Sophe couldn't ever do that. She can't lie to save her life," Max said.

Teagen chuckled and nodded. "True. But, you two would make a cute couple," he teased.

"Very fucking funny," I groaned.

Max grinned like a bloody devil and he draped his arm over Teagen's shoulders. "You'd make cute babies, Trent."

I rolled my eyes as they laughed, but I smiled too. For the first time in years I finally felt as though I belonged. I had friends, a gorgeous boyfriend, and I could be myself for the first time in my life. Henry leaned in and whispered into my ear.

"I love you, Sin."

I turned to look at him. His dark hair, those stunning dark eyes, kissable lips and I smiled, heart full of love for him.

"I love you, sexy ass," I whispered back.

He kissed me, slowly, confidently and winked. "And I meant it, baby. You're mine for fucking ever," and I had to grin.

"Forever, Henry," I replied.

That was the moment that a heavy hand landed on my shoulder and we turned to find our new agent smiling at us.

"Evening, gentlemen," he said. "I have some news for the two of you."

Darcy, Sophie and their families joined us and they greeted Christian with hand shakes. Theo gave him a swift hug and I noticed Darcy's eye's light up, as though he knew something.

"Alright, Christian. Ya here to tell them?" he asked.

"I am."

They suddenly had a very intrigued audience as Darcy and our agent turned their eyes onto the two of us.

"Do you both have a valid passport?" asked Christian.

"Yes," said Henry.

"Me too," I replied.

"Then you had better pack for a visit to the States. I believe I have bagged you the lead roles in a new movie," he said.

What the fuck? Did he just say that?

Darcy

The night went perfectly, and Sophie hadn't suspected a thing. The six reporters got their story too, and my beautiful woman had said yes. Now, after meeting my Mam, and charming her socks off, Christian was telling the two gifted actors about the new job. I smirked, as it had been one of my demands as there was a third lead role that had been offered to me.

I would say yes, as long as they took Leo and Henry. I wanted to give them a swift leg up after seeing their work ethic. They reminded me of myself and I wanted to use my own status to help them.

"Wait, what?" Leo exclaimed.

"Yes. What the fuck?" Henry gasped.

"This man here?" and Christian patted my shoulder. "He's the third lead. The three of you are to star in a new movie together."

Sophie's Mam frowned at the language, but Sophie threw herself at them, hugging them to death.

"Oh god, that's amazing," she gushed.

I chuckled at the shocked looks on their faces, but the next part was going to make my little director very happy.

"Wait, does that mean you'll be gone too?" my fianceè questioned.

I tucked her against me again and winked. "I'll be going with them, love. But, ya coming too. Kate's ok'd it. And it's being filmed here. In London," and she stared up at me in shock, so I leaned down and kissed her.

"What?" she whispered.

"It means ya can come and visit me on set while I'm filming, love."

"Really?" she asked.

"Really, love."

I glanced at our friends and family, and said, "We'll be right back. Just need to talk business for a few minutes."

Mam kissed my cheek and hugged Sophie, and the rest dispersed, leaving the five of us to chat.

Leo looked the most shocked and I gestured for them to follow me. I led them backstage and into my dressing room.

"Are you being serious, Darcy?" asked Leo.

"Yes, fella. I saw the way ya both continued to work after ya dad hurt ya. That kind of work ethic is rare."

Henry leaned against the table, arms crossed as Leo dropped into the chair. "We love our job, Darce. You know that, right? A few cuts and bruises wouldn't stop us," and he massaged Leo's shoulder lovingly.

This pair were seriously in love. It was so fucking obvious as they gazed at each other. "And that's why I suggested that Christian come to watch ya both work."

My agent smirked as he fired off emails, messages and he winked at the two actors. "I sneaked in a few times after I met you both. Sophie suggested it too, so that really peaked my interest. And my wife thinks you two are adorable."

I stared at him in surprise."Effie's here?"

"Yes. She's gone to the bar with her parents," he replied.

"And I want ya lovely lady to meet me fianceè, Christian," I exclaimed.

Sophie was frowning at me with confusion, so I took her hand and kissed it. "Alright. The film is about three fellas who have to travel together to a family wedding. It's a comedy with some romance thrown in."

Both Leo and Henry were gawking between me and our agent. "Romance?" asked Leo.

"Yes. Between the two of ya, and I'm Henry's brother who gets a second chance at finding love," and I winked at my sexy fianceè.

"A gay film role?" asked Leo.

I nodded as I saw Henry's eyes light up. Christian touched my arm lightly as he wanted to take over.

My agent placed a hand on each of their shoulders and fixed his eyes on the two actors. I noticed the business-like gaze so I pulled Sophie in for a swift kiss.

"You *will* have to read for the casting director when we get there, but the roles are yours. Darcy secured them for you,"

I smacked the two of them on the back then took my fianceè's hand and winked at her.

"I'll leave ya to sort the details fellas. Now, I'm taking me bare to meet Christian's wife."

Christian smirked and patted my shoulder as I gave his hand a shake. "I'll be down shortly. Just have a few more things to discuss with these two," my agent replied.

"See ya downstairs. And welcome to the big leagues fellas," I said.

Leo was on his feet and I was tugged into a swift hug, taking me by surprise. "Thank you, Darcy. This means so much to me. To us," he said, glancing at his boyfriend.

"I see real talent, Leo. In both of ya. I wanted to help ya, so no thanks needed fein," and I winked at him with a grateful smile.

"Thanks anyway."

"Ya welcome. See ya both in a few days," and I gave Henry and Christian a wave and led my woman out of the room.

"That was an amazing thing you did for them, you know."

"It's what they deserve, love. And I wanted to use me fame for something grand," I replied.

Sophie smiled and I opened the door, leading back to the stage and collecting family and friends along the way.

Sophie

I had a ring on my finger. A very beautiful sparkly diamond which sat on a white gold band. I was going to marry my Irish film star. After everything we'd been through together, the drama of the Christmas that changed everything, the press and then that memorable new year's eve when he had broken down in front of me. Seeing him again in this very building, and the whirlwind romance that had come out of it? I couldn't quite believe it, but I was really engaged to Darcy O'Sullivan.

Now, I was walking into the bar of the theatre that we had met up in a few months ago. DeJa Vu, yet very different. Max and Teagen were engaged, and I had agreed to marry the famous, sexy as hell, Irish actor. And we had also acquired two new additions to our circle of friends. Leo and our fun loving, lovestruck Henry.

"Ya'll love Effie, love. She's precious," Darcy said as he scanned the room, pulling me back into the present.

He grinned suddenly and tugged me towards the bar. We were heading to a beautiful slender and petite brunette with dark brown eyes and a warm smile.

"Darcy," she gushed and gave him a swift hug.

"Effie, lass. Ya look stunning as always. I want to introduce ya to me little director. Sophie, this is Christian's wife, Effie."

She didn't hesitate and flung her arms around me, hugging me as though she'd known me for years. "Oh, I'm so happy to finally meet you, Sophie. This man has been pining for you for so long," she exclaimed.

"Pining?" I asked as she released me.

Darcy groaned and grabbed my hand again. "Effie, lass. Don't tell her that."

"Oh, do tell," I replied.

Effie West giggled as Darcy ordered us a couple of drinks, and this lovely lady took my hand and squeezed.

"He was such a heartbroken, sad guy for so long, Sophie," she whispered. "But you've made him sparkle again. And I have to admit that I've never seen him so happy and alive."

"Really?" I questioned in surprise.

"Really. There was always a sort of emptiness in his eyes ever since I met him. The only time I saw it disappear was when he was playing a character, well, until now," she said quietly.

I looked over at my sexy, talented fiancè and a very smug smile crept onto my lips. "Thank you for telling me," I said as Darcy reappeared.

"Me ears are burning, love," he drawled as he passed me my.... Fizz?

"What's this?"

"What do ya think, love?"

All of a sudden the entire bar of actors and family members began to cheer, glasses raised and all eyes on me and my Irishman.

"Congratulations, you sexy fuckers," announced Ella.

I groaned and smacked a very wicked and smug Darcy, his hand holding mine and tugging me in for a kiss.

"Congratulations," echoed around the bar as everyone toasted our engagement.

"I love ya, Sophie lass. Ya me forever. Me happy ever after," he whispered into my ear.

I gazed up into those emerald eyes that had always hypnotised me, and the love in them made my heart beat faster, a lovely warm feeling blooming in my chest.

"I love you right back O'Sullivan," I replied, and I rose up on my tiptoes and he leaned down to meet me, our lips meeting in a tender and loving kiss.

Chapter 32.

Max

I hadn't seen Sophie as happy as she was right now. Not since her wedding day, and I had to fucking admit that I now actually liked Darcy. Teagen nudged my shoulder as I stared at the loved up couple and I turned to find his gorgeous eyes gazing at me.

The way he did caused my heart to race and flutter with nothing but love. He was *my* happy ever after and I couldn't wait to bloody marry him.

"Earth to Max," he teased. "You okay there baby?"

"Oh yeah," I said, grinning at him. "I'm better than okay. Kiss me," I ordered.

Teagen smirked, then his hands cupped my face and he captured my lips with his, kissing me ravenously.

"How was that, my sexy boyfriend?"

"I really want to leave and fuck my gorgeous man all bloody night long, babe," I growled into his ear.

He snorted into laughter and smacked my ass, making me grin. He raked his fingers through my hair and kissed my lips again.

"I'm on a promise, am I?" he asked.

"Yep," I simply replied with a cheeky wink.

"Max," and I turned to find the famous Irishman smirking at the two of us. "Can I have a word?"

Teagen patted his shoulder and smiled. "Congratulations Darcy. You two look so fucking loved up."

"Cheers, fein."

I pecked Teagen's mouth once more and turned to face my new future brother in law and smiled, shaking his hand.

"Congrats, shithead."

"Thanks Max. I need to ask ya, Will ya be one of me best men?"

I stared at him in utter shock. Did he just ask me that? He smacked my shoulder with an amused smile on his face.

"What?" I finally asked.

"Theo and Shay are me other two, so I want ya to join them. What do ya say?" he asked.

"I, well, sure. Okay."

"Grand. I'll let ya go," he said with a happy grin, then strode back to my sister.

Teagen wrapped his arms around me from behind and pressed me against his chest, dropping a light kiss at the base of my neck and it caused a delicious shiver to run up my spine.

"That's really cool," he whispered.

"Yeah. A bit surprised though," I replied.

We were both suddenly hugged from behind, and a very familiar voice rang out. He chuckled first then said, "Don't you two fuckers look cosy."

"We are, thanks, douche fucker," I replied.

Henry laughed as Leo came into view with a huge grin on his face. "You two on a promise, or do you feel like going to Starlight's to continue our celebrating of your sister's engagement?" Henry asked.

"I am on a promise, H. But, I'm sure we can hold on for a bit longer," Teagen replied.

I arched a brow at him with a filthy smirk. "Can you? Because I'm tempted to drag you backstage right now," I stated.

Leo snorted and laughed as Henry smacked my boyfriend's ass. "There's no-one back there. Go, then we'll meet you at the club," he drawled.

I rolled my eyes and dragged my man and our two friends back to our table where Ella and the rest of the gang were sitting, including Darcy's brothers.

Sophie

I glanced around the room and nudged my man's shoulder as I noticed my mum and his chatting happily.

"That's a really lovely bloody thing to see, handsome," I whispered.

"Yes it is, love. And there," and he pointed to our friends sitting with Darcy's brothers, laughing, joking and getting on like a house on fire.

Darcy handed me a glass of red wine and he tugged me in between his thighs, kissing my neck. "Ya gonna marry me, lass," he whispered.

"I am. Now, this trip to the States?"

"It's for a week, love. Leo, Henry and me? We'll be chatting to the producers, ironing out the details."

"And me?"

"That's where I come in," Effie said, touching my arm. "I'm coming too, so I can show you around while our men talk business."

I turned to see Christian's wife standing behind me, and she touched each of our arms as she smiled at me.

"Really?"

"Yes. It will be so lovely to have some company while Christian does business. Usually, I potter around the hotel, but this time? We can go sightseeing. What do you say?" Effie replied.

This lady was adorable and I couldn't help but grin at her then up at Darcy. "How can I resist? It all sounds fantastic, Effie. I'd love to."

"I feel like we might become firm friends. Have you met Tom's wife?"

"I have."

"Oh, so exciting," and she hugged me again.

Darcy kissed my lips lightly and hugged Christian's wife. "It'll be grand, Effie. Now love, here's to us," and he clinked his glass against mine and Effies.

The smile crept onto my face as I glanced around the room. I had a famous film star as a fiancè, my brother was engaged to Teagen. Leo and Henry were now an official member of our friends group, and about to star in a film with Darcy. He glanced around the room then tugged on my hand.

"Come with me, love," he whispered.

I smiled as he gave Effie a peck on the cheek. She returned the smile and winked.

"Go, Have a few moments alone. Give Sophie my number before we go to the States. And congratulations," then she disappeared into the throng of people.

My man led me from the bar, through the lobby and into the silent auditorium. He suddenly slammed me against the wall and crushed my lips with his own, kissing me like a starving man. I moaned, instantly turned on and my pussy fluttered with excitement. My arms went straight to his soft hair as I shoved my tongue into his mouth, circling his own, tasting the champagne.

"Feck," he gasped as he broke free for air.

"Indeed, handsome."

"I fecking love ya. So much that I can't put it into words," he whispered.

"Life's changed rather a lot, right?" I said.

"It has. All because ya gave me a second chance, love."

I wrapped my arms around my Irishman and pulled him back into me for a kiss. He didn't resist and crushed me against the wall with his divine body, and I held onto him tightly, not wanting to let go.

"Can I say something?" I asked.

"Yes, love."

He was leaving a searing trail of kisses up my neck and I sighed happily and completely turned on. But, I wanted to tell him something that had been floating around in my brain recently.

"When I saw you on stage I kinda felt like fate was stepping in and showing me where I needed to be," I said.

"Fate?" he asked.

"Yeah, well I'm not a Catholic, Darcy."

"God brought us back together, lass. Fate, the fecking moon and stars. All a them brought ya back to me. I don't give a shite which one. Ya made me whole again, love."

I gazed into his beautiful eyes and memories flooded my brain. All the times we had been naked, fighting, not together. And how we were here again in this theatre… together.

Together and engaged.

"True," I replied. "And you've even won over Max," I said.

He held me close, his eyes fixed on mine and I felt so fucking lucky in this moment. "I love you, Darcy O'Sullivan," I whispered.

"And I love ya more than ever, lass. And I can't wait to marry ya."

He pressed me against the wall of the theatre auditorium and kissed the fucking life from me, and I wrapped my arms around him and kissed him just as enthusiastically.

In this moment, I was so happy. Seeing all of our friends and family getting along, and the look of love in my brother's eyes as he gazed at his man. I looked up at Darcy and smiled.

"And I can't wait to marry you too," I whispered.

He winked, grabbed my hand and literally dragged me out of the building towards the car and ordered Carl to take us home.

Chapter 33.

Epilogue

Max

My nerves were pretty much screwed by now. Mum and Benson had left Sophie and Scott with me. Ella, Cora, Henry and Leo were waiting outside as my bridesmaids and men.

"You okay?" asked my sister.

"Shit, Sophe. I'm bloody scared shitless," I admitted.

Scott came to my side and stopped my pacing. "Max. Take a deep breath and you've got no reason to be scared. Teagen's equally fucking nervous."

I groaned and checked my tie, waistcoat and hair for the millionth time. I couldn't wait to marry the love of my life, but holy fucking hell, I was so damned nervous too.

"Max," Sophie said. "Breathe. And you look fantastic."

I smiled down at her. She looked radiant in her dark blue bridesmaid dress, and I kissed her cheek. "Well, cheers, shithead," I whispered.

"It's Mrs O'Sullivan you cheeky shit," she replied with a wink.

I chuckled and pulled her in for a hug. "Love you, Sophe."

"Love you Max. Now let's go get you and Teagen married."

I nodded and she took a hold of my hand. Sophie led me to the door and we were greeted by a very excited Ella.

"Oh fuck, honey, you look gorgeous. Teagen is going to lose his shit when he sees you," and she crushed me in her arms.

"Unhand the groom, woman," Sophie stated, Scott chuckling as he kissed his wife.

I glanced towards the door and my stomach fluttered with nerves again. My soulmate was behind it and I hoped he was as excited as I was.

"Ready?" Sophie asked.

"Shit, Sophe. He *is* in there?" I asked.

Cora and Ella were walking forwards, Henry and Leo in the middle of the two of them. Scott smacked my shoulder and winked.

"Let's get you married."

"He's in there, Max. He can't wait to marry you," my sister whispered.

I took a deep breath in and sighed loudly, hands raking through my hair. "Okay. Do I look okay?"

"You look gorgeous," Sophie said, squeezing me in her arms.

"Thanks, Sophe."

"And it's time," she whispered in my ear.

"Fucking hell, I'm gonna get married," fell out of me.

Sophie took my hand and led me to where Benson was standing and my heart was hammering so hard it echoed into my ears.

"Ready, son?" asked our dad.

Yes, he was in the process of adopting both of us and it felt amazing to have him give me away at my wedding.

"I'm really nervous, dad," I whispered.

"That's totally normal. Teagen is pretty jittery too. Are you ready?" he asked.

I glanced at my entourage and smiled. I took Benson's arm and nodded. "Yeah. Let's get me to my husband."

Sophie, Ella and Cora were in front of us. Henry and Leo behind us, my little niece in Leo's arms. Benson squeezed my arm and the doors were opened, then I was led into the room where my future awaited.

Sophie

Everyone cheered as the registrar announced that they were husband and husband, and they looked so damned happy.

Darcy held me closer and whispered into my ear. "Are ya alright, love?"

"I'm good, O'Sullivan. You?" I asked.

He grinned before kissing me tenderly. "I'm grand, love," and we followed the happy couple from the Bridge Inn's function room. It was a little strange being back here after all this time, but Max and Teagen wanted to get married where they found each other.....

I had been to see Jake when we'd arrived. It was so very strange standing in front of his gravestone, the guilt whirling like a tornado in my gut, as I'd left and never came back to see him.

"Hey you," I whispered.

The wind whipped around my legs and I shivered at the icy feeling, as though Jake had come back to say hello. And probably pretty pissed at me too.

"I'm sorry I haven't been to see you and, well, I'm really sorry that I married Darcy. I know you hated him, but... He changed and he treats me like a princess. I really think you'd like him now. I love him and he loves me. We have a beautiful little girl too.... I know we'd talked about having kids... shit," and tears gathered in the corners of my eyes.

"I miss you every day you're not here. I still have our wedding photograph sat on the bookshelf in the living room at Max and Teagen's place. I just need you to know that I will always love you, Jake. You were my first true love. My first kiss, first everything. Always and forever."

It had been a very hard visit, seeing his grave again. It brought back all the happy memories and I had cried in Darcy's arms. He was amazing and held me, allowing my moment of grief. That was until our little lady had cried for attention....

Now, we were outside in the sunlight, and we had a ton of pictures taken and I eventually tugged on my husband's arm.

"I really need to change our daughter, handsome."

Darcy took our seven month old baby girl and kissed my lips. "I'll change her, love."

"Are you sure?"

"I've done it hundreds a times, sexy Mammy," he whispered with a wink.

I rolled my eyes but threw him a grateful smile. Max and Teagen seemed to notice Darcy walking away with Orla.

"Where are you taking my niece?" called my brother.

"Can't ya smell why?" Darcy drawled.

Orla giggled as her gorgeous daddy lifted her in the air and buried his face into her little belly, blowing a raspberry there.

"Yeah, we can," Henry piped up.

Max grinned and Teagen walked to Darcy. "We'll pause, because this little bundle *has* to be in our wedding photographs."

She reached out and grabbed his hair, yanking with brute strength. "Christ, your daughter is vicious," he gasped and swiftly removed her hand.

Darcy chuckled and winked at him. "I'll be as fast as I can, fella," then strolled out, decked in a sexy navy blue suit, our beautiful dark haired, green eyed little girl, and a changing bag slung over his shoulder.

I giggled quietly as I watched my famous husband disappear and Leo appeared by my side.

"She is the most adorable little girl ever," he said.

I wrapped my arm around his waist and hugged him. "She's a little devil at times, but I bloody love her, and her daddy."

He chuckled and glanced over at Henry who was chatting to the newlyweds. "I'd like to get married one day," he whispered.

I had to smile knowingly as I glanced back at Leo's boyfriend. They were perfect for each other, and I knew a little secret. Darcy swiftly reappeared with our little lady, so the last lot of photographs were taken, then we were finally able to get a well earned bloody drink.

"They look so happy," I said as I watched my brother and Teagen working the room.

"And so they should, love. Are ya alright?" and he shuffled closer, taking my hand.

I looked down at my little baby girl and smiled. I'd found out not long after another much weirder sandwich incident, so we married a few months later and now we were actual parents.

"I'm fine, handsome man. This little one is just sleeping on me," I replied.

He gently eased her from my arms and deposited her into her pushchair, covering her with the blanket from Mum and Dad.

He had taken to being a dad like a duck to water and it made me love him even more than I thought possible.

"Hello mummy and daddy," and we looked up to see Ella, Leo, Henry and Theo grinning at us.

"Me niece asleep?"

"Yes. So be fecking quiet, shithead."

Ella bent down and her entire face softened as she gazed at our little lady. "Fucking hell, you two. You made such a gorgeous human."

"Thank you. It was fun doing it too," I replied.

Darcy smirked and leaned in, kissing my lips. "She's a beauty isn't she Ella?"

That was the moment that my brother and his husband strolled over. I was tugged onto my feet and hugged within an inch of my life.

"Love you Sophe," Max whispered. "Stick around for our first dance?"

"How could I ever miss that, fuck face," I whispered back.

Max

I took Teagen's hand and walked to the patio as our guests danced, laughed and drank copious amounts of alcohol.

"What's up, baby?" he asked.

"I just wanted a few minutes alone with my husband," I replied.

He pulled me into his arms and kissed me, and my heart couldn't get any fuller. I was a married man. I had a husband and the happiness and joy was overwhelming. I wrapped my own arms around Teagen and slipped my tongue into his mouth, savouring the taste of him.

"I fucking love you, baby," he whispered.

"I fucking love you too, babe."

He leaned back and fixed his dark eyes on mine. I had to smile at his dimples and I cupped his face with my hands.

"You married me," he said.

"Yeah. I did. You're my sexy husband, T."

He ran his hands through my hair and kissed me again. "You've made me the happiest man on the bloody planet."

I pulled him back to me and held onto him tightly as I crushed my lips back onto his. I never thought I'd be here, married to a guy, especially Teagen.

But, I'd never been as happy and in love as I was right now. Me and Teagen were forever. He was my soulmate. He was my happy ever after, and I wanted to drag him back to our room and fuck all night long.

"Hey, lovebirds," and we turned to see a smirking Henry and Leo. "Get back in here. You've got the rest of your lives to tongue fuck," Henry drawled.

Teagen snorted and laughed as he pulled me closer. "You have such a fucking way with words, shithead," I replied.

"Try my best, Ashforth-Laurier," he said with a dramatic bow.

And fucking hell, I loved the sound of that. I grinned at my husband and took his hand in mine.

"Mr Ashforth-Laurier, shall we?" I said.

"Fuck, I love that. Yeah, baby. Let's go have our first dance."

Leo

They looked so fucking happy as they slow danced around the floor, and Henry's hand landed in mine.

"Come with me, Sin," he whispered.

He led me from the room and out onto the same patio that we'd found Max and Teagen, but he looked nervous. And that was strange for my usually confident, sexy boyfriend.

He stopped by the edge of the paved area and turned to look at me, his beautiful eyes locked on mine.

"Seeing the two of them getting married was great, right?" he said.

"Yeah it was. They look so bloody happy," I replied.

He smiled, lighting up his entire face, and I had to mirror it. He brought my hand to his lips and left a tender kiss there.

"Leo fucking Trent, I love you so damned much."

"Love you right back, babe."

He reached into his pocket and seemed to be fiddling with something. I reached out and touched his cheek.

"You okay?" I asked him.

He nodded and pulled out his hand, and I saw the small blue box in his hand. "Leo... Sin. You're the love of my fucking life and I want to grow old with you."

I stared into those dark, beautiful eyes and my heart started to beat faster. I had a very strange feeling that I knew what was about to happen.

"I'd love that too, H."

"So," and he held up the box, opening it to reveal a stunning white gold band decorated with small blue gems around the top.

"Shit," I gasped, my eyes flying up to his face.

"Leo, will you marry me?" he asked.

I gawked at him for a couple of seconds, his words rattling around my brain. Then I opened my mouth and it fell out of me.

"Fuck, yes."

"What?"

"Yes, Henry. I'll marry you."

"Fuck."

Then he grinned before slamming his lips on mine, kissing me like a starving man. I held onto him as we ravished each other, stumbling as we got rather carried away. Henry looked at me and slipped the ring onto my finger.

"Fucking hell, Sin. As soon as you walked into that bar? I knew you were mine forever," he whispered.

I had to grin at him and I shoved him a little. "I was terrified. You were standing there like a fucking divine sex god, and I hadn't even come out to anyone."

He pulled me back into his arms and kissed me. "Now we get to spend the rest of our lives together too, my sinful angel," and he grabbed my hand and dragged me down the steps and into the darkened gardens.

Darcy

Sophie sat down with a happy sigh and I smiled at my wife. Not only had she married me, she had made me a father.

"Ya need anything, love?"

"Just you, and a whiskey," she said. "Then sleep, as our little madam will still be waking us up at the crack of dawn."

I grabbed another glass, poured her a shot of whiskey and joined her on the sofa. She snuggled into me as my arm draped over her shoulder. I smiled and left a gentle kiss on her temple, then relaxed back happily.

"Ya want me to whisk ya away for a few days?" I asked. "Orla can stay with ya mam and dad?"

"To where, handsome?" she asked.

I winked at her and she gave me her sexy smile. "Well, Mrs O'Sullivan, the cottage isn't too far away."

Her eyes lit up and she shuffled to get comfortable, turning so she could rest her feet on my lap. I put down my glass and started to massage her feet eliciting a happy moan to fall from my wife.

"That, my gorgeous husband, is the best bloody idea. Can we set off on Monday? Because you start filming in a couple of weeks?"

I nodded and popped her feet down so that I could pull her in for a kiss. "For me beautiful wife? Sure thing.".

Our daughter made a little noise in her cot, so I pulled my wife to her feet and walked her to the bed. I started to undress her and she grinned, allowing me to.

I stood up and swiftly yanked off my own clothes and climbed in with her. I had her sitting in between my legs, her back pressed against my chest. I passed her glass back to her and kissed the delicious skin of her shoulder. I had never been so happy as I was right now. And all because this exquisite, sexy, feisty woman gave me a second chance.

"I love ya, Sophie O'Sullivan."

"And I love you, Darcy O'Sullivan."

I picked up my whiskey and lifted it, Sophie doing the same with her own glass. "To second chances, love."

"Second chances," she repeated.

And to happy ever afters.

The End....

Coming Soon in 2024....

Stolen

Escape

The fear was eating her from the inside out. Could she really pull this off?

She stared at her reflection in the mirror, and the shell of a woman gazed back at her. Dark circles sat under her now dull eyes.

There was once a bright sparkle in them, but it was long gone now. All that stared back was a broken down, thin and tired girl.

Her fingers traced the fresh purple bruise on her defined jaw and winced in pain. The latest gift from her fucking shitty son of a bitch husband.

Sighing, she rinsed her face and took a steadying breath. He would be back soon, demanding sex from her. Almost every night he took what he wanted. He was rough, violent and insatiable. One good thing? He always prepared her first, making sure she was wet, lubed, stretched.

How fucking generous of him.

The timer sang on her secret burner phone and she swiftly silenced it, closing her eyes tightly for a brief moment. She prayed that it wouldn't be positive, but her heart both shattered and soared in equal parts.

She had dreamed of becoming a Mama, but this was the worst fucking environment to raise an innocent child in. A husband that beat his wife? No. Not fucking happening.

This world was dangerous, toxic and she'd never had the choice. She had been born into this life. This little one would have free choices.

Her plan had taken shape as soon as her fucking piece of shit of a husband announced that he wanted her pregnant '*as soon as fucking possible*'.

She had risked her life, sneaking off to shooting practice, hiding clothes, acquiring a burner phone and gun.

The car had been the most dangerous part of her escape plan, but it now sat hidden in shadows waiting for her.

His voice startled her as he returned from a day's work. "Get in here, woman. I need to fuck my wife."

"Si, tesoro," she called, adrenaline coursing through her.

She reached under the sink and retrieved the hidden gun. She swiftly screwed on the silencer and tried to still her trembling hands. Taking one more look in the mirror, her heart hammering at a million miles an hour.

"Ora, Carlotta. I need to be inside you."

She smiled down at the weapon and back up at her reflection. He was about to get something else inside him, the motherfucker. He was about to meet his maker. The fucking devil.

Walking to the door, she opened it and, thankfully, his back was turned, unfastening his shirt.

"On the bed. Hands and knees. I want to go deep tonight after I've gotten your cunt all wet," he ordered.

She lifted her arm, pointing the gun at his back. A smile crept onto her face, waiting for him to turn around. She wanted to watch his expression as she killed the son of a bitch.

"What are you fucking waiting for? Get on the bed," and he spun around, his eyes suddenly widening at the gun in her hand.

It seemed to happen in slow motion as she pulled the trigger, the bullet slamming into his chest, knocking him backwards into the bedside table. Blood oozed out of the hole and his eyes dropped staring at it in shock. "You fucking bitch," he croaked.

She fired a second shot and it knocked him off his feet, his legs crumpling from under him.

He coughed, blood escaping from between his lips, his eyes starting to glaze over. "You.... are... a bitch," he whispered.

She strode over and leaned into his ear. "Pregnant bitch," she whispered.

He blinked with a flash of recognition then a strange gurgle emanated from him as his life swiftly ebbed away, and he fell sideways into a heap.

She nudged him with her foot. Nothing. The fucking son of a bitch was dead. Triumph erupted inside her and she gave him one last kick.

Adrenaline pumping, she raced into the wardrobe and grabbed the duffel bag she'd hidden. The phone and gun were rammed inside and she headed for the window. She shimmied down the trellis and dropped onto the lawn.

Taking one last look up at her prison, she grinned, then she turned and sprinted towards the hidden car. Towards her freedom.

And not just for her, but the innocent life now growing inside her....

Acknowledgements.

Thank you so much for choosing my story to read. I hope you enjoyed Sophie, Jake, Darcy and our two couples, Max and Teagen, and Leo and Henry's stories.

I just wish to thank a few people before you go.

Firstly, I want to thank you, my readers, for choosing my spicy second chance romance. Without you I wouldn't be here. Every single one of you are very much appreciated.

I want to thank my family for their endless patience while I was creating, editing and marketing my books. My daughter, Mia, for telling every person she met that I had a book on Amazon, and informing them to buy it without telling them that it's a spicy book. Oops.

I'd like to thank all the beautiful Arc readers for taking the time out to read my story. Also, Dusty Shirley for my cover design and also Will from Fiverr for his print formatting services on both *Falling All Over Again & Second Chances.*

Finally, for all the other Indie Authors out there doing the same thing as I am. It's a difficult journey, so the support, help and advice I've received from you all has been fantastic. I hope I can do the same one day for other new and upcoming writers too.

Thank you all.

Thank you for making my dream come true.

Shalleen.

Other Titles by S. Werboweckyj.

Falling All Over Again. (Book 1)

Stolen (Coming soon)

Her Lost Alpha (Coming soon)

Printed in Great Britain
by Amazon

37197727R00195